William James Linton

The Masters of Wood-Engraving

William James Linton

The Masters of Wood-Engraving

ISBN/EAN: 9783337386924

Printed in Europe, USA, Canada, Australia, Japan

Cover: Foto ©Andreas Hilbeck / pixelio.de

More available books at **www.hansebooks.com**

THE MASTERS
OF
WOOD-ENGRAVING

By W. J. LINTON

"Me list not of the chaf ne of the stre
Maken so long a tale, as of the corn."

ISSUED TO SUBSCRIBERS ONLY.

AT THE RESIDENCE OF THE AUTHOR, NEW HAVEN, CONNECTICUT, UNITED STATES:

AND LONDON: B. F. STEVENS, 4 TRAFALGAR SQUARE, CHARING CROSS.

CHISWICK PRESS:—C. WHITTINGHAM AND CO., TOOKS COURT,
CHANCERY LANE, LONDON.

PREFACE

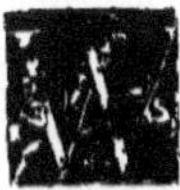

ANT of any treatment of Wood-Engraving in a manner satisfactory to an engraver is the reason and may be sufficient occasion for my book. It is as an engraver, not as a bibliographer, that I write. My purpose is not so much to give account of the books in which engravings in wood have appeared as to collect together the finest examples of the Art and to give its history through the exhibition of its Master-Works. This as yet has not been done or attempted to any good purpose. Chatto, to whom I owe a large indebtedness, for without him my work had been hardly possible, was only a most conscientious and excellent bibliographer, not by any means qualified, even with such help as he had from Jackson, to criticise and judge the works which he chronicled and described. And, as furnishing examples of Wood-Engraving, his *Treatise* only misleads. Jackson was perfectly right in illustrating the history with copies of wood-cuts: but these copies, by his assistants or by himself, *as examples of the original engraver's work*, even when of the same size, are worthless. When copied on a reduced scale, a fourth of the original size, or less, they give no idea of the *engraving*. We need the engravings themselves: the best of counterfeits will not avail us.

Not copies, but reproductions, by one or other process, have been given by Sotheby, Humphreys, and others; nevertheless I am bold to say that in no work on engraving in wood have I yet found any signs of choice or sufficient judgment. Good cuts and bad have been confounded together; and exact reproductions made from foul impressions, the ink over the sides of the lines too often supposed to be a portion of the engraving.

Neither the most careful copies of Holbein's *Dance of Death*, edited by Douce, nor the photo-lithographic reproductions from the originals, issued by the Holbein Society, give any idea of the cutting of Lutzelburger. These two imitations are types of all.

With an engraver's technical knowledge I hope to remedy this; and toward such end I have not only closely examined all the cuts needed for my history, but have compared edition with edition, and chosen for photographic reproduction the purest impressions. For these I have searched through the Library and Print Room of the British Museum, and had also considerable private advantages, especially as to proofs of modern works. Though nearly all reproductions fall short, I think those here executed by Messrs. Dawson, Mr. W. L. Colls, and Messrs. Walker and Boutall, are sufficiently close to satisfy an engraver. Where, in some few cases, they may be unsatisfactory, it is because I have been unable to obtain good impressions of the originals; and any imperfection can only be repeated in the photograph. Sometimes I have been fortunate enough to obtain electrotypes from the original blocks; and with few exceptions (noted in the list) every cut I give is closely to the size of the original.

Farther, in the course of inquiry I have found numerous errors in most writers, based mainly on their want of technical knowledge; such as the attribution of early engravings to painters who were not engravers, undue praise of cuts on account only of the designs, and the mistaking of metal for wood. Indebted as I am glad to acknowledge myself to Dr. Willshire, for his *Introduction to the Study and Collection of Ancient Prints* (to which, with some note also of Modern Prints, my book may, I hope, be deemed a not unworthy supplement), I have still to object to him upon certain occasions, venturing where as an engraver I may be allowed to speak with authority.

So far as regards Engraving in Wood I claim the right of an expert; my title earned by more than fifty years' practice and study of the art. I do not pretend to so much of bibliographical research as would warrant me in criticising work in that department, nor do I assert general authority as an artist; but in my own province I have qualifying knowledge, and on this ground hope to show sufficient reason for my book, and reason for a belief that it will be found of value to the general print-collector, to the professional engraver, and to all real lovers and earnest students of Art.

Briefly, my object is to correct a number of misconceptions, to furnish some data for accurate judgments, and to give samples of the best work in Wood-Engraving: samples hitherto beyond the reach, many beyond the cognisance, of those most interested; so to make my book a trusty guide (there is none yet) to the study and right understanding of Wood-Engraving, the least understood, not the least important, of the Graphic Arts. If successful in this, it will surely be because an engraver best knows what engraving is. If not successful to my full desire, I may fall back on the apologetic words of Michelet: " *Un livre est toujours un moyen de faire un meilleur livre.*"

On disputable points I have tried to fairly state the opposite opinions. And if by too positive assertion or rudeness of language, by seemingly too hard criticism, by what may be thought unjust depreciation, or neglect, I have laid myself open to rebuke,—I plead in advance that I have written always free from personal feeling, with conscience as my prime motor; and that the "tender heart," which should accompany that, has not been altogether an unknown quantity. I have kept in view one single purpose: a fair and a sufficient exposition of Engraving in Wood with honour to the Masters of the Art.

Modern German and French works are but lightly treated. Each is a subject in itself. Any considerable account of either would have too much increased the bulk of my book, and other reasons will appear for the narrower course I have had to adopt. For some omissions else want of space may be excuse enough.

Many literary and artistic friends deserve my thanks for suggestions and corrections. That I do not name them is because I could not always point to the special help, and I would not have them charged with errors possibly my own. Not supposing myself to be a "faultless monster," I prefer to bear the whole responsibility for the work which goes under my name. I may not however omit my most grateful public acknowledgments to Mr. Dond and Mr. Thompson, Principal Librarians of the British Museum, for unstinted facilities granted me for obtaining photographs, and to Dr. Bullen and Dr. Garnett, of the Library, to Mr. Reid and Professor Colvin, of the Print Room, and all authorities or officials of the Museum (without exception), for unvarying courtesy and very valuable and ever ready assistance during many months in which I was preparing for my work. Some special thanks are also due to the Highland Society, to Messrs. George Bell and Sons, Messrs. Seeley, and Messrs. Cassell, for the loan of blocks and electrotypes, and more than thanks to my good friend Mr. B. F. Stevens, of Trafalgar Square, London, without whose generous aid and counsel my book had hardly made its present appearance.

W. J. LINTON.

CONTENTS

PART I — KNIFE-WORK

CHAPTER I—The Beginning of Engraving :—*Page* 1, Wood-Cuts in early times,—2, in Babylon and Egypt,—4, India and Rome,—5, Greece,—metal plates and stamps,—Dr. Willshire's difference of ancient from modern engraving,—6, Prints not engravings,—7, ancient engraving identical with modern,—9, Varro's invention,—stencilling,—Roman books,—10, 11,—monograms, ciphers, coins, notaries' and merchants' marks, signs, and seals,—13, progress from rudest engraving to sculpture,—14, engraving and printing shown to have been practised in old days,—15, and upon various fabrics, unfit material,—16, invention of moveable types and manufacture of linen paper.

CHAPTER II—Saints and Playing-Cards :—*Page* 17, The history of Wood-Engraving in Europe,—the *Helgen*, or Saint-Pictures,—borrowing from China,—18, Papillon's story of the Canton,—Books in the Middle Ages,—19, Illuminators, stencilling and engraving,—20, on Playing-Cards, Singer, Passavant, and, 21, other writers,—cards from the East,—first cards in Europe, in Italy, Germany,—21, Spain, France,—method of production,—23, Chatto's mistake of stencil,—24, the Craftsmen,—25, Paul of Prague, his "Tiripagus,"—26, Prints altogether in stencil, difficulty of knowing stencil,—27, the Helgen, earlier than engraved cards, Dominotiers, what *découpde* implies,—28, the Brussels Virgin of 1418,—30, St. Christopher of 1423,—33, indications of date uncertain, the *frottee*,—34, the Annunciation,—35, St. Bridget,—36, the Virgin of Berlin,—object of these *Helgen*,—37, colours employed on them, supposed technical differences,—38, by whom produced.

CHAPTER III—The Block-Books :—*Page* 39, Pictures with engraved text,—40, the Apocalypsis,—41, the Canticum Canticorum,—44, the Biblia Pauperum,—47, the various editions,—49, Sotheby's mistakes,—50, copies compared,—52, additional cuts,—53, the Ars Moriendi.

CHAPTER IV—Wood on Metal :—*Page* 59, Some later block-books, Fust and Schœffer's Psalter,—60, Pfister's books,—61, the Alphabet of 1464,—the Speculum Humanæ Salvationis, printed from moveable types,—64, its origin, its description,—66, comparison with Biblia Pauperum,—67, Books in Germany, and

Italy,—69, Mediations of John of Turrecremata, Valturius' De Re Militari, works of Caxton, Breydenbach's Travels,—70, the Nürnberg Chronicle,—71, Hypnerotomachia Poliphili,—73, Metal cuts in intaglio and relief, difficulty of distinguishing metal cuts from wood,—74, Weigel's means for deciding,—75, various works instanced,—76, French Books of Hours, *criblé* work.

CHAPTER V—JEROME OF NÜRNBERG :—*Page* 79, Jerome Andreæ,—80, Nürnberg and Germany in the time of Dürer,—81, Dürer's Apocalypse,—83, Dürer not engraving in wood,—84, Engraving no more needing to be coloured,—85, Dürer's other books, the Life of the Virgin, the Greater Passion of Christ, the Lesser Passion,—87, the Triumph or MAXIMILIAN, the Arch, the Procession, the Car,—90, the Engravers of the Procession, Dienecker,—91, Sir Theurdank, the White King,—92, Jerome Andreæ, his work and, 93, character,—94, Dürer's single wood-cuts,—Cranach's St. Jerome.

CHAPTER VI—LÜTZELBURGER :—*Page* 95, Hanns Lützelburger, his life and, 96, work,—97, Holbein's DANCE OF DEATH, several editions,—98, many copies and reproductions,—99, subjects of the fifty-eight designs,—103, delays in using the cuts, who engraved the last,—104, evidence insufficient of Lützelburger's death,—Ottley's probabilities,—105, it is properly the Masque of Death, meaning of Macabre, books repeating the subject, and wall-paintings,—106, Lützelburger's work depreciated by Hamerton, Hamerton contradicted,—107, Holbein's Bible,—108, Initial Letters.

CHAPTER VII—ALTDORFER TO PAPILLON :—*Page* 109, Large wood-cuts—110, Andrea Andreani,—111, Artists wrongly credited with engraving in wood, Boldrini's work in metal, Vico and Altdorfer exceptions,—112, Sebald Beham's Apocalypse, by whom engraved,—113, Beham's larger works, and his New Testament and Bible, Cranmer's Catechism, Jackson's copies,—114, Wood-cuts given by Humphreys, Holtrop, Ames, Dibdin, and Becker,—Artists of the sixteenth century after Holbein and Beham,—Virgil Solis,—115, Bernard Salomon,—116, Jost Amman, Tobias Stimmer,—117, who were the engravers,—Van Sichem, Feig, and Feyerabendi,—initials and monograms unsatisfactory,—118, German and Italian work compared,—two Decamerons and a Dante,—suspicion of metal in Italian cuts,—S. Elizabeth giving alms,—French and English work,—119, Jeghar, a younger Van Sichem, Switzer,—120, Art in a low state at the close of the sixteenth century,—Le Sueur and Papillons,—Jean Michel Papillon, his Almanac, the Recueil des Papillon,—121, Papillon's Treatise of Wood-Engraving,—the two Ungers,—122, Unzelmann,—late knife-work in Germany, France, and England,—Watts, Deacon,—123, Knife-work of three classes, tools used for it, the kinds of wood, laboriousness of the process,—124, its limitation.

PART II—GRAVER-WORK

CHAPTER I—BEFORE BEWICK :—*Page* 125, The graver and the maiive,—engraving on the butt of the wood,—126, Papillon's denial of the possibility,—127, J. B. Jackson, Kirkall,—128, doubt of Kirkall engraving in wood,—129, Jackson again, his title-page to Suetonius,—the Kirkall ticket in metal,—130, Croxall's Fables of Æsop probably metal also, praise and, 131, description of these Fable cuts,—132, unequaled until the time of Bewick.

CHAPTER II—BEWICK :—*Page* 133, General ignorant worship of Bewick, Hugo's Bewick-Collection,—134, Stephens' Notes, Canal Thomson's Life and Works, Dobson's Bewick and his Pupils, Jackson's and Chatto's Treatise, Bewick's youth,—135, apprenticeship,—136, book-work, the "Old Hound,"—137, cuts for Saint and Angus, Hieroglyphick Bible, Fables of 1776, of 1779, Select Fables of 1784,—138, Charnley's edition, Pearson's edition,—139, character of Select Fables of 1784,—140, Bewick's Quadrupeds,—141, Land and

Water Birds,—143, the Tail-pieces, Bewick's limitation as an engraver, the Chillingham Bull,—144, Bewick's large cuts, Waiting for death, work in copper,—145, Parnell's Hermit, Somerville's Chase,—146, Goldsmith's Traveler and Deserted Village, best of engravings in the Quadrupeds and, 147, Birds,—149, tail-pieces done by Pupils, Chatto's list of Bewick's own, the Fables of 1818, current criticisms, 150, disputed,—151, examples given of the best,—153, who drew and engraved them,—154, Bewick's work appraised, his apprentices-list,—155, Indiscriminate Heaps for sale, the Daughters' Collection in the British Museum, Bewick's real claims,—156, printing his original drawings,—157, summing up,—John Bewick,—Robert Bewick,—158, his Fables.

CHAPTER III—CLENNELL AND NESBIT:—Page 159, CLENNELL, his early work,—160, his Tail-pieces to Bewick's Birds, Chatto's list,—161, the Hive, Craig's Scripture Illustrated, History of England,—162, Hermit of Warkworth, Pilgrim's Progress, Vicar of Wakefield, Religious Emblems,—164, the Diploma of the Highland Society, 165, compared with knife-work, Clennell preëminent, Thompson's copy, Rogers' Poems,—166, pure Stothard, Clennell as a painter,—167, cuts falsely called his.

Nesbit, 167, his early work, St. Nicholas' Church, Scripture Illustrated,—168, History of England, Thomson's Seasons, Religious Emblems,—169, Quillinan's Wood-cuts and Verses, Somerville's Rural Sports, Fables of 1818,—170, Savage's Hints on Decorative Printing, Rinaldo and Armida, Chatto's criticism,—171, Puckle's Club, Northcote's Fables, Blind Beggar of Bethnal-Green, Natural History of Selborne, Harvey's influence,—172, Latrobe's Scripture Illustrations,—Hole.

CHAPTER IV—BRANSTON AND THOMPSON:—Page 173, BRANSTON, first work in Bath, Lottery Bills, Scripture Illustrated,—174, History of England, Religious Emblems, Puckle's Club,—175, Chorley's Metrical Index, the Cave of Despair, Savage's Decorative Printing, Chatto's comparison with Nesbit, the Two Schools, the white line of Bewick and the black line of Thurston,—176, Butler's Remains, Hudibras, Walton's Angler, Fables to rival Bewick,—177, Lee Priory books, Northcote's Fables.

THOMPSON, 177, his general work characterised,—178, apprenticed to Branston, day of Thurston, Dibdin's London Theatre,—179, Puckle's Club, Fairfax's Jerusalem Delivered,—180, Hudibras,—best wood-engraving (under Bewick and Thurston) in the first quarter of the nineteenth century,—181, Thompson's cuts for Whittingham, his other important works,—184, engraving in gun-metal and steel.

CHAPTER V—AFTERMATH:—Page 185, Decadence begun, HARVEY great as an engraver, Fables of 1818, Assassination of Dentatus,—186, Henderson's History of Wines,—187, Harvey as designer,—WILLIAM HUGHES, Puckle's Club, Butler's Remains, and other works,—HUGH HUGHES, Beauties of Cambria,—188, SAMUEL WILLIAMS, peculiarity of his work,—189, the Olio, Hone's Political Tracts, London Stage, Thomson's Seasons, Wiffen's Tasso, and other,—190, THOMAS WILLIAMS, Northcote's Fables,—191, Bible Illustrations, Paul and Virginia,—BONNER, Northcote's Fables,—192, title-pages, animals,—JACKSON, Penny Magazine, Arabian Nights, Pictorial Prayer-Book, Shakspere, Northcote's Fables,—193, Fowls, Dance of Death, engravings with Jackson's name,—194, Scripture Illustrations, Martin and Westall's Bible, Gray's Elegy,—SMITH, most excelling in animals,—195, Solace of Song, Arabian Nights, Paul and Virginia, Meadows' Shakspere, Heads of the People, Gilbert's Cowper,—196, Harvey's Milton, Harral,—ANDERSON, his copies from Bewick, two large cuts in white line,—197, ADAMS, his Bible and other works.

CHAPTER VI—IN THE WINTER:—Page 199, Decadence, the law of line, early graver-work incised,—200, the Kirkall ticket, Bewick's line following, and carried out by Nesbit and by Clennell, Clennell's potentiality,—201, the separation of draftsman and engraver, characteristics of different engravers,—202, monotony of

English book-work after 1839, French work,—102, German work,—work of Smith and Linton, and their Assistants,—John Leech,—205, Gilbert,—free-hand drawing and mechanical engraving, wood-engraving as a distinct art,—206, Pannemaker, Hamerton on the new development in America,—207, Hamerton answered,—208, concerning tone, texture, and line, Marsh, difference between the new school and preceding work, promise of better doing,—drawings by the Painters in Water-Colour, — 110, can Wood-Engraving be revived as an art?

CHIAROSCURO

Page 111,—Chiaroscuros of two kinds, with and without lines, many not in wood, —112, the earliest are German, Cranach, Baldung Grun, Burgkmair, Dienecker,—Italian work, Andreani, Da Carpi,—113, Coriolano, Zanetti,—114, Nicolas le Sueur, John Baptist Jackson, Skippe, Savage,—115, little of the merit of Chiaroscuro due to the engraver.

117,— Index to Names: Artists and Engravers.
121,— Index to Subjects.

LIST OF ILLUSTRATIONS

The St. Christopher of 1423
Initial W (*Branston*)
Graver and Pen

PART I — KNIFE-WORK

CHAPTER I — THE BEGINNINGS OF ENGRAVING

Initial P (*reduction from the Alphabet of 1464*)
Brick-Inscription from Babylon
Egyptian Stamp
Roman Brass Stamp
Stamps of Theodoric and Charlemagne
Gothic Monograms, Runic Cipher and Notary's Stamp
Merchants' Marks
Roller-Printing (*Papillon*)

CHAPTER II — SAINTS AND PLAYING-CARDS

Initial O
Early Playing-Cards
The Draftsman and the Engraver, Jost Amman
The Colourer, Amman
The Brussels Virgin, of "1418" (*reduction*)
The St. Christopher of 1423 (*reduction*)
The Annunciation (*reduction*)
St. Bridget (*reduction*)
The Virgin of Berlin (*reduction*)
A Wood-Engraver's Knife

PART I — KNIFE-WORK — *continued*

CHAPTER III — THE BLOCK-BOOKS

Initial O	*page* 39
From the Apocalypse (*reduction*)	. 40
A Page of the Apocalypse	*facing* 40
From the Canticum Canticorum (*reduction*)	. 41
A Page of the Canticum Canticorum	*facing* 41
From the Biblia Pauperum (*reduction*)	. 44
Ornaments and Tiaras	. 48
From the Biblia Pauperum	. 50
A Page of the Biblia Pauperum	*facing* 50
Part of another Page	. 51
From the Ars Moriendi	. 53
A Page of the Ars Moriendi	*facing* 57
Tail-piece from the same	. 58

CHAPTER IV — WOOD OR METAL

Initial P from the Hypnerotomachia Poliphili	59
Letter L, Alphabet of 1464	61
The Rebus	—
From the Speculum Humanæ Salvationis (*reduction*)	—
Part of Page of the Biblia Pauperum	. 65
Two Page-Headings from the Speculum Humanæ Salvationis	*facing* 66
The Flight into Egypt, Meditations of John of Turrecremata	. 68
Frontispiece to Breydenbach's Travels	*facing* 70
From the Hypnerotomachia Poliphili	. 71
From the same	. 72
Initial N, 1551 (*relief work*)	73
From a Dante of 1491	. 75
Title-page of Hours, Simon Vostre	*facing* 76
Initial T	. 78
Feather	—

CHAPTER V — JEROME OF NURNBERG

Initial SO, or part of Durer's Arch of Maximilian	. 79
A Page of the Apocalypse	*facing* 82
A Page of the Life of the Virgin	*facing* 86
A Page of the Greater Passion	. —
A Page of the Lesser Passion	. —
Part of the Arch of Maximilian	*facing* 88
Another Part	—

PART I—KNIFE-WORK—*continued*

THE TRIUMPHAL CAR, Dürer . . . . *in pocket*
FROM THE PROCESSION, Burgkmair . . . . . . *facing page* 90
FROM THE SAME . . . . —
ST. JEROME IN PENITENCE, Cranach . . . . *facing* 94

CHAPTER VI—LUTZELBURGER

INITIAL W, Holbein's Larger Alphabet 95
ADAM AND EVE IN PARADISE, Holbein's Dance of Death, 1538 . 100
ADAM TILLING THE EARTH . . . . . . —
THE JUDGE . . . .
THE BISHOP 101
THE OLD MAN . . . . —
THE DUCHESS . . . . —
BOY BACCHANALS, 1545-7 103
THE YOUNG HUSBAND, 1562 . . . . —
THE TEMPTATION OF EVE, Holbein's Bible . . . 107
INITIALS, Holbein's Smaller Alphabet . . . 108
INITIAL H (*Hanns Lutzelburger*) . . —

CHAPTER VII—ALTDORFER TO PAPILLON

INITIAL T, about 1500 109
DEATH OF THE VIRGIN (*Altdorfer*) . . . —
PART OF CUT (*Æneas Vico*) 110
FROM BEHAM'S APOCALYPSE (*Jerome Andreæ*) . 111
FROM THE SAME . . . . . . —
A PAGE OF CRANMER'S CATECHISM . . . 113
FROM THE SAME . . . . . . —
FROM OVID'S METAMORPHOSES, Virgil Solis . . 114
FROM Æsop's FABLES, Solis . . . . —
FROM QUADRINS HISTORIQUES, Salomon . . 115
FROM OVID'S METAMORPHOSES, Salomon . . —
THE TEMPTATION IN PARADISE, Jost Amman . . 116
TITLE-PAGE TO LIVY, Amman . . . *facing* 116
HAGAR AND SARAH, Stimmer . . . . —
FROM A DECAMERON 118
FROM HOLINSHED'S CHRONICLES . . . —
ST. ELIZABETH GIVING ALMS, Caccia . . *facing* 116
FROM PARADISUS TERRESTRIS (*Switzer*) . . 119
TITLE-PAGE OF PAPILLON'S ALMANAC (*Papillon*) . 119
A PEASANT (*Unger*) 121
ROPE DANCING (*Papillon*) . . 124

PART II — GRAVER-WORK

CHAPTER I — BEFORE BEWICK

MARK OF SHARAPERE (*screw-work*)
INITIAL I (*Brunston*)
GRAVER AND SCRIVE
THE CUT WITH EK
PROOF-READING FROM DRYDEN'S PLAYS
TITLE-PAGE TO SUETONIUS (*J. B. Jackson*)
THE KIRKALL TREAT (*Kirkall?*)
THE LION AND FOUR BULLS, Croxall's *Æsop*, 1788
THE OLD MAN AND DEATH
THE TWO FROGS
THE YOUNG MAN AND THE SWALLOW
PART OF A FRONTISPIECE (*Hodgson*)
THE LION AND FOUR BULLS (*Bewick*)

CHAPTER II — BEWICK

INITIAL M (*Brandon*)
"A BEWICK"
AN EARLIER OLD HOUND
THE MILLER, HIS SON, AND THEIR ASS, — Fables, 1784
THE OLD MAN AND DEATH
THE TWO FROGS
THE YOUNG MAN AND THE SWALLOW
THE SHEEP AND THE BRAMBLE
THE CUR FOX, Quadrupeds, 1790
THE SPANISH POINTER
THE HEATH RAM, 1798
THE PEACOCK, Land Birds, 1797
THE NIGHT-JAR
THE COMMON GULL, Water Birds, 1804
THE SCAUP DUCK
THE TAME DUCK
THE FARM YARD, Land Birds
THE SNOW MAN
THE DOG WITH A KETTLE AT HIS TAIL, Water Birds
COWS AND MAGPIE, Land Birds
OLD MAN BREAKING STONES
WAITING FOR DEATH, Fables, 1818
WAITING FOR DEATH, Bewick's last work

PART II — GRAVER-WORK—*continued*

The Hermit and the Angel, Parnell's Hermit, 1795
Huntsman and dogs, Somerville's Chase, 1796
The Cheviot Ram, Quadrupeds, 1798
Pulling the Colt's Tail, Quadrupeds, 1791
The Yellow Bunting, Land Birds, 1797
Poachers tracking a Hare
Night—Mist and Rain
Sportsman with dogs
Boys flying a kite, Water Birds, 1804
The Lion and Four Bulls, Fables of 1818
The Fighting Cocks
The Two Bitches
The Eagle, the Cat, and the Sow
The Cat and the Fox
The Fox and the Bramble
Sow and Pigs
A Windy Day
The Little Stint
Sandpiper's Feathers
From the Looking Glass for the Mind (*John Bewick*)
The Lumpsucker (*Robert Bewick*)

CHAPTER III—CLENNELL AND NESBIT

Initial E (*Harvey*)
Angler, Water Birds, 1804 (*Clennell*)
River Scene
Stranded Ship
Coast Scene
Rocks and foam
Two Cuts from the Hermit of Warkworth
The Soul encaged, Religious Emblems
Diploma of the Highland Society
From Rogers' Pleasures of Memory
Two Cuts from the same
From the same (*Thompson*)
Cranmer's Martyrdom, History of England (*Nesbit*)
Wounded in the mental eye, Religious Emblems
From Somerville's Rural Sports
Rinaldo and Armida, Savage's Decorative Printing
Zany, Puckle's Club

PART II—GRAVER-WORK—*continued*

The Redbreast and the Sparrow, Northcote's Fables (*Noble*) .   *page* 171
Tail-piece to the Ermine and Polecat .   —
Seed sown, Religious Emblems (*Moir*)   172

CHAPTER IV—BRANSTON AND THOMPSON

Initial J (*Branston*)   173
Rescued from the Flood, Religious Emblems .   174
The Lawyer, Puckle's Club .   175
Title to Chorley's Metrical Index   —
Philosophers and Mouse, Butler's Remains   176
In the Stocks, Hudibras   —
The Cave of Despair, Savage's Decorative Printing   *facing* 176
Pike, Walton's Angler   177
The Fight with the Soldan, Wiffen's Tasso (*Thompson*)   178
Moroso, Puckle's Club   179
Youth, Puckle's Club   —
Sophronia and Olindo, Fairfax's Tasso   —
Title-page to Puckle's Club .   *facing* 180
Title-page to Hudibras .   —
Portrait of Butler, Butler's Remains   181
The Bourdis, Young Lady's Book .   —
Lion and Lioness .   182
Trout, Walton's Angler   —
From Mornings at Bow Street .   —
Diploma of the Highland Society   182-3
A Dinner at Versailles .   183
The Hay-field, Mulready's Vicar of Wakefield   —
The Witches in Macbeth .   184
Griselda, Northcote's Fables   —

CHAPTER V—AFTERMATH

Initial A (*Harvey*) .   185
From the History of Wines   186
The Assassination of Dentatus .   *facing* 186
Gambler, Puckle's Club (*W. Hughes*)   187
Falls of Fair Mawr, Beauties of Cambria (*W. Hughes*) .   188
The Arch of Titus, Solace of Song (*S. Williams*)   189
Fogarty's State Cabin, Three Courses and a Dessert   190
Habakkuk Bullwinkle, Three Courses and a Dessert (*T. Williams*)   —
Prudence and her Advisers, Northcote's Fables   191

PART II — GRAVER-WORK — *continued*

THE PARROT, Northcote's Fables (*Branston*) . . . . *page* 191
JAGUAR, Tower Menagerie . . . . —
THE BEACON AND THE CHANDELIER, Northcote's Fables (*Jackson*) . 192
THE PEACOCK AND THE OWL, Northcote's Fables (*Powis*) . . —
NINEVEH . . . . . *facing* 192
A HOUSE IN CONALAREA . . 193
RHINOCEROS . . . . —
THIBET DOG (*Smith*) . . 194
THE DAY OF PORTUOLI, Solace of Song . 195
WATER FOWL (*Anderson*) . . . *facing* 196
THE MASSACRE OF THE INNOCENTS (*Adams*) . 198

CHAPTER VI — IN THE WINTER

INITIAL I (*Remston*) 199
TITLE-PAGE TO FONTAINE (*Bewick*) . *facing* 202
THE COURT OF THE LION, Reineke Fuchs (*Allgeier and Siegle*) . 203
THE PEACOCK AT HOME (*Linton*) . . . *facing* 204
DEAD BIRDS . . . . —
AN OLD MILL . . . —
LANDSCAPE . . . . . . —
GENERAL ZIETEN, Return of War and Peace (*Kretzschmar*) *facing* 206
LA VIE HUMAINE, Magasin Pittoresque (*Bertrand*) . . —
SATAN RESTING (*Ligny*) . —
PILOT BOAT (*Clennell*) . 210
LUDWIG RICHTER (*Klinkicht*) . *facing* 210
DELACROIX (*Strixhoff*) . . —
NARCISSUS (*Linton*) . . —
BOOTH AS DON CÆSAR DE BAZAN . —
INFANT BACCHUS . . —

CHIAROSCURO

INITIAL O (Design by Holbein) . 211
ADAM AND EVE, H. Baldung Grün . *facing* 212

KNIFE-WORK

KNIFE·WORK

CHAPTER I

THE BEGINNINGS OF ENGRAVING

IRST OF THE ARTS,—of the origin and actual beginning of Engraving-in-wood there is no record attainable. Some antediluvian patriarch, Enoch, or another, who shall say that he might not have cut two simply-linked initials, his own with that of his Chaldean Lady, in the bark of a fair-spreading tree under whose young boughs had been his first and happiest trysting-place? Or one yet elder, as Evelyn will tell us,—Adam himself, taught our art by the angel Razael: or not so taught, may not he have set his mark upon the apple-tree of Paradise, scratching with a sharp stone an earlier name than Eve? Used they not axes, felling timbers for the Ark? Noah "hewed him kipples and hewed him bawks:" were they engraved in single line or cross, axe-cut, to indicate their fitting-place? Who shall answer the presumption, confirming it or contradicting? This at least may be allowed :—In prehistoric time, haply before the days of Tubal, men may have cut notches

The unknown beginnings.

The earliest of Engravers in wood.

Enoch.

Adam.

Noah.

in sticks or on unfelled trees, to guide them through primeval forests or noting something to be remembered ; the first of these Notch-Cutters may be considered, in default of other claimant, Noah, Adam, or the angel Razael, as the Father of our Art, the Inventor (need one be had) of Engraving-in-wood.

Leaving these dark and unprofitable surmises, and approaching the dawn (must we say —the misty twilight?) of History, we do get sight of the practice of Engraving in ancient Babylon and Egypt. And we are upon stable ground amid these ruins of undated or not surely-dated time. Babylonish bricks and Egyptian stamps are to be seen by whoso will in the British Museum. Some bricks there exhibited (brought from the site of Babylon),

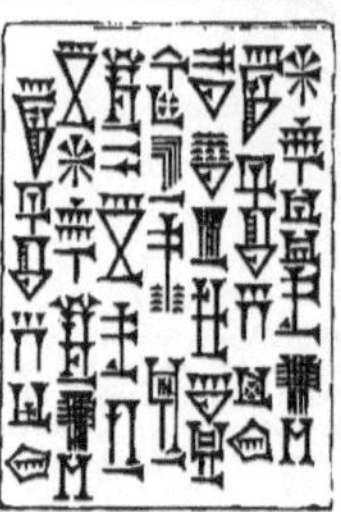

about twelve inches square, and three inches in thickness, have their one broader side indented with cuneiform — arrow-headed — wedge-shaped characters, such as are here represented at about a third of the actual size. On close examination I judge these indentations to have been made by wooden stamps in which the characters were on the surface, in relief, the interstices having been cut away, precisely as would be done in a stamp or rude wood-engraving of to-day. The bricks, stamped before they were hardened by the sun, appear to be of clay, mixed with straw or stubble to hold the clay together : reminding one of the brick-making in Egypt (*Exodus*, chap. v), when the Israelites complained of the taskmasters who aggravated their labour, no more giving straw to them, scattering them abroad through all the land to gather the necessary stubble, yet never diminishing the ordered tale of bricks. The characters upon these Babylonish bricks, I have said, are indented, the stamp having them in relief. A print from one would appear like our engraving. A reversed treatment will be observed in the annexed

representation of the print of an Egyptian stamp, one of several in the British Museum, found by Edward William Lane in a tomb at Thebes. This stamp, cut in intaglio (like a modern butter-stamp) in wood, five inches long, over two in width, and having at the back a handle of the same piece, is a veritable wood-engraving : supposed to be of the time of Moses, the hieroglyph on it deciphered to read " *Amenoph, Beloved of Truth* " (approved of Ammon, according to Champollion), Amenoph the First, second king of the eighteenth dynasty, the Pharaoh of the Israelitish Exodus. Two ancient Egyptian bricks, (also in the British Museum), bear impressions from similar stamps.

So that we have here unmistakable evidence of engraving in wood in the far-off days of Egyptian Thebes,—engraving, it matters not how rude, cut in the white-line (white in black) manner of Bewick; and we have moreover proofs of engraving in relief done at Babylon of the same nature and description as the wood-cuts from Durer's drawings, and other wood-cuts of the fifteenth and sixteenth centuries.

Less satisfactory, but not absolutely to be discarded, is the plea for ancient knowledge of our art in China: certain writers having asserted that it was practised in the reign of We-wung, eleven centuries before Christ. We may pass this as "not proven."

Stamps for bricks may suggest the use of stamps for other purposes. Baldwin, in his *Prehistoric Nations*, accepts the following, from Rawlinson's *Five Great Monarchies of the Ancient World*:—"We are informed by Simplicius, that Callisthenes, who accompanied Alexander to Babylon, sent to Aristotle from that capital a series, which he had found there, of astronomical observations extending back through a period of 1900 years from Alexander's taking the city." These were on tablets of baked clay. Brass stamps (not for bricks), stamps in relief, and reversed so as to be right when printed, are exhibited among the Roman Antiquities in the British Museum; and Lambinet, in his *Recherches sur l'Origine de l'Imprimerie*, gives account of two stone stamps with hollowed reversed letters (a Roman inscription) found in 1818, in France, near the village of Nais, in the department of the Meuse. Whether such stamps are of stone or brass or wood matters not; a single stamp, of whatever material, proves a knowledge of engraving. We need not look for the preservation of many of wood: the perishable wood is lost; the harder material remains. And without one wooden stamp to assure us, it would be impossible to suppose that engraving in wood was not concurrent with engraving in metal.

Metal plates engraved have been found in Egyptian mummy-cases; and we may read in *Exodus* of Aholiab, son of Ahisamach, of the tribe of Dan, an engraver and cunning workman, who "wrought onyx stones inclosed in ouches of gold, graven, as signets are graven, with the names of the Children of Israel," and made the plate of the holy crown (for Aaron) of pure gold, and "wrote on it a writing like to the engraving of a signet." Homer and Æschylus tell of engraving; the shields of the Seven Chiefs against Thebes, as well as the more celebrated shield of Achilles, are described as ornamented with rich engravings, heraldic and historical. A plate of brass, on which was engraved a map of the then known world, is mentioned by Herodotus. Strutt's *Biographical Dictionary* has a representation of an Etruscan *patera*, the workmanship upon it "consisting of carving and engraving." In the same book is figured a sheath (of a sword or dagger) brought from Italy by Sir W. Hamilton, with rude engraving on a flat surface, needing "only to be filled with ink" to yield a fair and perfect impression. And in the Imperial Library

Roman metal plates.

at Vienna is a metal plate, bearing on it some Roman police ordinance, of two hundred years before the Christian era.

Indian plates in copper.

In India, long before our era, transfers of land were recorded upon plates of copper. Our great engraver, John Landseer, in his *Lectures on the Art of Engraving*, speaks of a plate (then, 1806, in the possession of the Earl of Mansfield) on which was engraved a Sanscrit inscription recording a grant of land. It is dated twenty years before the birth of Christ. Another such grant he mentions, of nearly the same age, likewise engraved on copper, and having a seal appendant, which seal is impressed into a ponderous lump of copper attached to the deed by a massy ring of the same metal. "It appears to me," he observes,—"on a careful inspection, that this seal is not cast, but struck as coins are struck; whether cast or struck, the matrix must have been an intaglio engraving, of no mean workmanship. It exhibits a style of art similar and not inferior to the best of the present productions of the art of Hindostan. It is in high relief and, being imbedded in the metal, in good preservation. It is about ten inches in circumference, and contains, besides human figures and animals, a Sanscrit legend —' *The Illustrious Karna Dtoo.*'"

Metal work of the Greek and Romans.

Roman mirrors.

"That the ancient Greeks and Romans were accustomed to engrave metal "— writes Dr. Willshire, in his *Introduction to the Study and Collection of Ancient Prints*, " is proved by a particular ornamentation of certain *pateræ* and like utensils which have come down to us. In the cabinet of Roman Antiquities in the British Museum the case of the Mirrors contains some very beautiful examples of engraving on metal." He notes particularly, among several, a mirror which has the Birth of Minerva engraved upon it; and another, a "rich engraving" of Menelaus seizing Helen. The Roman metal-workers, engravers of these mirrors, engraved vases, chamfers, ornaments, figures, which they afterwards filled in with gold, silver, or enamel. Jansen names two of these workmen, whom Pliny praised; and gives account of several noted works.

Bronze plates for slaves.

By a law of Constantine, Roman slaves instead of being branded (by a stamp) had a metal plate fastened to the collar. Fabreni gives us the following inscription, engraved on one of these plates, of bronze.

TENE ME ꝘUA FVG-ET REBOCA ME VICTORI-
ACOLITO,
    A DOMINICV CLEMENTIS,

Brands used for slaves, captives, and criminals.

Hold me because I am a runaway, and return me to Victor the Acolyte, to the lordship of Clement. His master probably a Christian. Before Constantine it was usual for the ancients to brand slaves, captives, and criminals, as they branded their cattle, with heated stamps, burning in the letters or figures denoting ownership. The Athenians, according to Suidas, marked their Samian captives with the figure of an owl, the bird of Pallas, the guardian deity of Athens; Athenians captured by the Samians were marked with a figure of a galley; and those captured by the Syracusans with the figure of a horse. Here was engraving of a kind. Even the cattle-brands spoken of by Virgil were engraved. I have said such brands, for slaves and criminals, to prevent escape, were in use before the time of Constantine; they were used afterwards, during the Middle Ages; they were used also in England so late as James I, in accordance with a statute passed in whose reign "rogues, vagabonds, and sturdy beggars," convicted at the sessions, and found to be incorrigible, were to be branded on the left shoulder with a hot iron, of the breadth of a shilling, with a great R, for *Rogue*,—such branding to be so thoroughly burned and set upon the skin and flesh that said letter R should be seen and remain, a perpetual mark on such Rogue during the remainder of his life.

Cattle-brands.

Rogues' brands in England, Act of James I.

To go back to ancient times :—Stamps for bricks or branding, or (as also employed by the Romans) for marking cloth,—metal plates used in Egypt and India, used also by the Greeks and Romans, though the graven figures or letters were never so slightly scratched (gravers such as we employ not yet invented),—letters impressed on tiles, lamps, pottery and domestic utensils of many kinds (all of these, again referring to the British Museum, having been found with the lettering in relief—perhaps the potters' names, or indicating only the contents of the vessels), evidently stamped upon the moist unbaked clay from a hollowed or incised mould,—all these things point to a general knowledge in very ancient times of engraving in both methods, that of intaglio and that of relief, the method of the ordinary engraver in copper and the method (in order to print or impress the surface) of engraving in wood.

Proofs of early practice of both methods of engraving.

Singer (*Researches into the History of Playing-Cards*) may persuade us farther: on the track of printing from engraving. The custom of scaling or stamping with coloured inks appears, he says, to be of the highest antiquity in the East. A similar art, writes Heller, was found by captain Cook to exist among the Sandwich Islanders. "Their clothes had printed borders." In one of the Leeward Islands he obtained "a stamp with which they printed their clothes." And again (Singer), the metal stamps, of monograms, marks of goods, etc., in use among the Romans afford examples of a "near approach to the art of printing." Von Murr, in his *Journal*, deems there is distinct proof that the Romans had nearly arrived at both wood-engraving (as afterward practised in Germany) and printing. "Letters cut on wood they certainly had, and very likely grotesques and figures also, the hint of which their artists might readily obtain from the coloured stuffs which frequently were presented by Indian ambassadors to the Emperors." While M. d'Ankerville remarks that the ancients "only wanted the idea of multiplying representations." Commenting on which remark of M. d'Ankerville, Dr. Willshire has the following.

Coloured inks in the East.

Prints made by the South-Sea Islanders.

Roman letters and grotesques in wood.

"But in this lies the point,—here is the *essential difference between what we now term engraving and a process often practised by the ancients.* They made the first step; but there they halted. They were arrested by an obstacle, which was not surmounted until many centuries after their time, and hence *engraving in the present acceptation of the term is not known to have been practised by them.*

"The word engraving" (he goes on) "now very generally implies something beyond its simple denotation. It connotes in addition, in the greater number of cases, that such 'scratching or cutting into tablets,' blocks, or plates, be done for, or be capable of being readily applied to, the purpose of yielding upon a more delicate texture, or upon fabrics like parchment or paper, fac-simile impressions in some ink or colour of the original design worked out on the tablet. It is true that we speak of having our names 'engraved' on silver spoons, door-plates, etc.; of 'engraving' complimentary addresses and dedications on presentation ornaments; and we 'engrave' monumental brasses. These we do without intending or expecting that such engravings will be used for the purpose of producing impressions on any other surfaces. For such purposes, no doubt, they could be employed under certain conditions, but it was not intended that they should be so used when the metal was incised.

"Should it be asked how long engraving has been practised for the purpose of giving off an impression in black or colour to another and a more yielding substance than that which has been engraved, the answer must be guarded. That the ancients engraved in the one sense of the word, we are certain; whether they ever engraved in its other and modern meaning is perhaps scarcely doubtful. They did not, most persons would answer —and they used such of their engraved tablets as were in the guise of either intaglio or relief stamps to produce solely a *change of form* by indentation in another object, and not as charged with ink or colour, for the purpose of stamping parchment, such kind of paper as then existed, and other like substances little or not at all capable of marked and permanent indentation." (*Study of Ancient Prints*, p. 3.)

I of course perceive Dr. Willshire's drift in the distinction he would make. None the less an engraving is an engraving, albeit not intended to be inked. Because we miscall *prints* by the name of engravings, what we yet continue to call *engraving* is not therefore a different process from that practised by the ancients. The different purpose for which an engraving is intended can not make the process other than engraving. An engraved tablet, in whatever guise, is an engraving : the "cutting" and "scratching" is engraving. If not "done for" it may be "capable of being readily applied to the purpose of yielding . . facsimile impressions in some ink," etc. The present acceptation of the mere word, *engravings*, is simply incorrect. A print is not an engraving. The universal use of the term beyond its simple denotation does not destroy the real and precise meaning of the word ; and since, as Dr. Willshire allows, "*we are certain the ancients engraved* in the one sense of the word" (the only sense in which it should be used by an exact writer), is not it merely confusion of speech to talk of essential difference because we are not certain of their having "engraved in its other and modern meaning;" that is to say—not certain of their having printed in ink or colour upon parchment or paper, so producing what is now improperly called "an engraving." It is not impossible that they did this too, taking the second step as well as the first.

Dr. Wilshire's view, previously advanced by Ottley, of some distinction of importance between an engraving, in intaglio or relief, which produces by indentation only a change of form and one (may it not be the same?) which produces a print by ink or colour may be sufficiently answered by Chatto:—" It certainly would be difficult if not impossible to produce a piece of paper, parchment, or cloth, of the age of the Romans, impressed with letters in ink or other colouring matter; but the existence of such stamps as [one given, a brass stamp, in the British Museum, with the word LAR in relief, reversed] renders it very probable that they were used for the purpose of marking cloth, paper, and similar substances, with ink as well as for being impressed in wax or clay."

Engraving as now executed (the term also yet accepted), meaning strictly the process of cutting in metal or wood or any material whatever with or without reference to taking prints from the incisions, the process also by cutting of leaving surfaces for stamping, or printing, is not essentially different from, but is precisely identical with the process often practised by the ancients. Our Egyptian bricks are all-sufficient evidence. Varieties of method in metal ("mezzotint," "aquatint," "stipple," etc.) were, it may be said, unknown to them; but in ordinary engraving they did what we do, and as we do, if they had not the same tools, and though they were not so expert. They may not have bitten in their plates; but a line cut by them in copper or brass was *an engraved line*, whether the tool called graver was used by them or not. Nor does it matter with what sort of scratching instrument their dry-pointing was effected. An engraved plate can not be other than an engraving. There is no essential difference between what is now termed engraving and the process practised by the ancients. And so far as regards engraving in wood, I can see no difference whatever between that Egyptian wood-cut with a handle now shown in our Museum and the wood-cut I have printed at page 2. Each is an engraving in wood of the same hieroglyphs. To be quite exact, I must own that I cut mine with a graver, and probably the Egyptian whittled out his with a knife. Well, the best wood-cuts from drawings by Dürer and Holbein are also knife-work; and had my block been engraved by a German, he too might have used a knife, excellently fine engraving being yet done with knives in Germany. Or, if a block of box-wood fit for use of a graver had not been at hand, I myself had possibly accepted the softer wood, and done my engraving with a knife, precisely in the manner of my Egyptian predecessor.

But although the ancients made the first step, engraving, "they halted, arrested by an obstacle which was not surmounted until many centuries after their time." Could this be the want of the printing-press, without which it is supposed they were not able to print and to multiply prints ? Yet taking an impression is printing, even without a " printing press," and without or ink or colour. And those brick-prints must have been multiplied at Babylon. It is not likely that a separate stamp was cut for every brick. Also, in an extensive empire laws or edicts might require publishing : such as are seen inscribed on some cylinders of baked clay, found by Layard at Babylon, stamped or engraved with characters so minute as to be read only by help of a magnifying glass. Layard indeed, though agreeing that the bricks were stamped, thinks these inscriptions were engraved ; but De Vinne assures us that many of them show the clearest indications of impression. In his *Invention of Printing* he gives a figure of a cylinder, seven inches wide at the ends and somewhat wider in the middle, on which is a ragged and bulging line about a quarter of an inch wide, which seems to have been made by the imperfect joining of the moulds. If the inscription had been cut in the clay, this defect would not be : the vertical lines in which it is arranged would have been connected and the ragged gap not seen.

" We do not know by what considerations Assyrian rulers were governed when about to choose between engraving or writing on clay ; but it is not unreasonable to assume that the inscription was written or cut on the clay when one copy only of a record was wanted,—if numerous copies were wanted a die or an engraving on wood was manufactured, from which these copies were moulded. No surer method of securing exact copies of an original could have been devised by a people that did not use ink or paper. These cylinders are examples of printing in its most elementary form."

Referring again to the characters on these Babylonish bricks, De Vinne confirms my own observation ; " they were not cut on the brick, . they were made on the plastic clay by sudden pressure of a xylographic block." Proof of this is seen " in the nicety of the engraving and its uniform depth ; in the bulging up of the clay on the sides where it was forced outward and upward by the impression."

Of our brass LAR (at page 7) De Vinne writes :—" The letters are cut in relief, with a rough counter or field," proving it could not have been used as a seal. And of another similar brass stamp, Roman also, his words are :—" If this stamp should be impressed in wax, the impression would produce letters sunk below the surface of the wax in a manner unlike the impressions of seals. The raised surface of the wax would be rough where it should be flat and smooth. This peculiarity is significant. As this rough field unfitted it for a neat impression upon any plastic surface, the stamp should have been used for printing with ink."

M. d'Ankerville's remark is just if restricted to " prints" and books. The ancients had there for obstacle the lack of any idea of multiplying impressions of the same engraving : popular editions not thought of because there was no public to create a demand.

Not that the Romans were without books, and some scant multiplying so occasioned. They had even a daily newspaper, the *Acta Diurna*. But there was no call for a larger supply than could be met by the labour of the scribes, educated slaves, whose work also would not be so costly as to call for the competition of mechanical cheapness. Martial says that his first book of *Epigrams* was sold in plain binding for six sesterces, or about one English shilling; and he complained that the thirteenth went for only four. Roman Scribes.

The elder Pliny tells us of an invention by Varro, by which portraits were multiplied, and which Varro used in his book of *Imagines*, containing some seven hundred portraits; but it does not appear that *the book* was multiplied [Enough for an idea if, as not unusual in much later days, one portrait was repeated for several persons], nor have we any sure account of what these portraits were. Firmin Didot admits the possibility of engravings in relief; Delaborde thinks they may have been stenciled. In either case would they be more than such portraits as were cut out with scissors in our grandmothers' days, profiles in one colour? Even this may be giving too much weight to the few uncertain words of Pliny. His words are—"*ut præscriptæ esse ubique et claudi possent.*" May it mean nothing more than that they might be *kept together* in one book, or roll?* Portraits by Varro.

Whether from wood or stencil these Varro portraits, it is certain that stenciling was in use in the time of Pliny: that is, in our first century. On the general subject of stencils I may here borrow sufficient for my purpose from Chatto's *Treatise on Wood-Engraving*, to which I shall have often to refer on historical or bibliographical questions. The book of the ancients.

"From a passage in Quintilian" (Pliny's contemporary), writes Chatto, "we learn that the Romans were acquainted with the method of tracing letters by means of a thin piece of wood, in which the characters were pierced, or cut through, on a principle similar to [identical with] that on which the present art of stenciling is founded.† He is speaking of teaching boys to write, and the passage referred to may be thus translated:—' When the boy shall have entered on joining-hand, it will be useful for him to have a copy-head of wood in which the letters are well cut, so that through the furrows, as it were, he may trace the characters with his style. He will not thus be liable to make slips on the wax [writing on waxed tablets with a style, or point], for he will be confined by the boundary of the letters, and neither will he be able to deviate from his text. By thus more rapidly and frequently following a definite outline, his hand will become set without his requiring any assistance from the master's to guide it.'" Sparing the teacher and learning to swim with corks. Well ordered, master Quintilian! if one could but stencil a joining hand. Stenciling in first century.

---

* The Roman book was a roll, or volume (*volumen*), a succession of pages on a length of papyrus, to be unwound by the hand of the reader as he went on. The period which may be assigned for the general use of the squared form (the *libri quadrati*, a series of pages bound together at the back, and tied with a cord) is, according to Noel Humphreys, probably not an earlier one than that of the fourth century.

† A stencil is a piece of card, or thin metal or wood or any other material, which has been pierced with lines or figures, so that, when it is laid upon paper, parchment, or cloth, or held against a wall, a brush charged with colour passing over it will colour the uncovered lines or figures below. The stencil-plate must of course be one piece, connected everywhere. The process of stenciling can so be easily detected. The nature of a stencil.

Imperial signatures.

"In the sixth century, as appears from Procopius, the Emperor Justin I made use of a tablet of wood pierced or cut in a similar manner, through which he traced in red ink, the imperial colour, his signature, consisting of the first four letters of his name. It is stated also that Theodoric, king of the Ostrogoths, the contemporary of Justin, used in the same

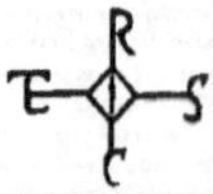

Monogram of Theodoric.

A stencil book.

manner to sign the first four letters of his name through a plate of gold," it being impossible, if we may trust Cochlæus, to teach His Majesty to sign without this assistance. Prosper Marchand, in his *Histoire de l'Imprimerie*, gives the following title of a book wholly produced by the stencil, "*percé au jour*" (pierced through) —*Liber Passionis Domini Nostri Jesu Christi cum figuris et characteribus ex nullâ materiâ compositis.* True stencil-work, figures and characters formed out of nothing. One would like only to inspect the title.

"It has been asserted, by Mabillon, that Charlemagne first introduced the practice of signing documents with a monogram, either traced with a pen by means of a thin tablet [or stencil-plate], of gold, ivory, or wood, or impressed with an inked stamp having the

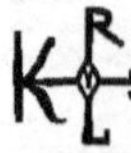

Monogram of Charlemagne.

characters in relief, in a manner similar to that in which letters are stamped at the Post-Office. Ducange however states that this mode of signing documents is of greater antiquity; and he gives a copy of the monogram of Pope Adrian I. who was elected to the see of Rome in 774 and died in 795." *

Stampille.

Continuing from Chatto—The monogram, stencil or stamp, consisted of the letters of a person's name, a fanciful character, or the figure of a cross accompanied with a peculiar kind of flourish called by French writers *parafe* or *ruche* (a simple flourish or one complicated). This mode of signing seems to have been common to most nations of Europe during the ninth, tenth, and eleventh centuries; and was practised by nobles and the higher orders of the clergy as well as by kings. It continued to be used by the kings of France to the time of Philip III (1270-1285), and by the Spanish monarchs to a much later period. We have a recent instance of the *stampilla* [diplomatists so call it] in affixing the royal signature. During the last sickness of George IV, in 1830, a silver stamp, counterfeiting the king's sign-manual, was printed on the documents requiring his signature by commissioners in the royal presence. A similar stamp, it is asserted, served during the last days of Henry VIII to authenticate the iniquitous warrant which sent the poet Surrey to the scaffold.

In Sempère's *History of the Cortes of Spain* several examples may be seen of the use of

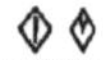

Impossible by stencil.

* The monograms of Theodoric and Charlemagne, if correctly given (here copied from Chatto), must have been done with stamps. The parts figured in the centres could not have been preserved with the stencil, as my readers themselves may easily prove. The whole of the first figure would be solid, owing to the dropping out of the unconnected square, and the second also would be lost for the same reason.

fanciful monograms in that country at an early period, probably introduced by its Gothic
invaders. Two may be sufficient here. No. 1 is the monogram of a certain Gundisalvo
Tellez, affixed to a charter of the date of 840; the same "sign" also used by his widow Gothic stamps.

 Flamula, who granted some property to the abbey of Cardeña,
for the good of her deceased husband's soul. No. 2 was used
by the four children of one Ordono as their mark to a charter
of donation executed in 1018. No. 3 is a Runic cipher, copied
from an ancient Icelandic manuscript, given (by Chatto) not as being from a
stencil or a stamp, but for the sake of comparison with the Gothic monogram Runic cipher.
used in Spain. Mr. Chatto seems not quite sure that the examples here given
are stamps. They unmistakably are. Not one of the three, if the fac-simile
be correct (and there is no reason to doubt that), could by any possibility be produced
by stencil. I continue to borrow, with occasional abridgment, from the *Treatise.*

In their inscriptions, and in the rubrics of their books (says a writer in the *Edinburgh
Review*, No. lxi, p. 108) the Spanish Goths, like the Romans of the Lower Empire, were Monograms on
Spanish shops.
fond of using combined capitals, "monograms," a mode of writing still common in Spain
upon sign-boards and shop-fronts. The Spanish Goth sometimes subscribed his name;
sometimes, like the Roman Emperors, he drew a monogram; sometimes, like the Saxon,
he drew a cross; and not infrequently to deed or charter he affixed fanciful signs having
close resemblance to the Runic or magical knots of which so many have been engraved
by Peringskiold and other northern antiquaries.

To the tenth or the eleventh century are also to be referred certain small silver coins, Silver coins.
between counters and money (as observed by Pinkerton), which are impressed, on one
side only, with a kind of Runic monogram; and which are commonly found in Sweden,
Denmark, and Germany.

The notaries of a later date, on their admission to practice required to use a distinctive
sign in witnessing a deed or instrument, continued occasionally to employ stencil, though
the use of a stamp for that purpose appears to have been more general. The annexed
monogram was the official mark of an Italian notary, Nicolaus Ferenterius,
who lived in the first half of the thirteenth century. It is plainly a stamp. Notary's stamp.

Many of the merchants' marks of our own country, which are to be seen
so often on stained-glass windows, monumental brasses, and tomb-stones,
from the thirteenth to the seventeenth century, bear considerable likeness to the ancient Marks or signs
used by English
merchants.
Runic monograms. The English trader was accustomed to place his mark as his "sign"
on his shop-front, in the same way as the Spaniard did his monogram; the wool-stapler
stamped or stencilled it on his packs; the fish-curer branded it on the ends of his casks.
When the successful merchant built himself a house, his mark would be placed, between
his initials, over the principal doorway or over the fireplace in the hall; if he made a gift

The signs on
windows and
on tombs.

or a bequest to his church, his mark was emblazoned on the windows, by the side of the knight's or nobleman's shield; and at his death his mark was carved in stone or engraved in brass upon his tomb. Of the merchants' marks given below (from Mackerel's *History of King's Lynn*, 1737, where more than thirty such marks are shown) the first is from the tomb of Adam de Walsokne, who died in 1349; the second from the tomb of Edmund Pepyr, who died in 1483: two tombs in the church of St. Margaret, at Lynn.

In *Piers the Plowman's Crede*, written about 1394, merchants' marks are mentioned, in a description of the windows in a Dominican convent:—

Piers Plowman.

> "Wide windows ywrought, ywritten full thick,
> Shining with shapen shields, to shewen about,
> With marks of merchants ymeddled between,
> Mo than twenty and two twice ynumbered."

Stamping coins.

Concerning the first invention of stamping letters and figures upon coins, it is fruitless to inquire, as the origin of the art is lost in the remoteness of antiquity. [Chatto still.] More than eight hundred years before Christ gem-engraving had attained to a perfection which is not yet surpassed, if even it is equalled. The art of coining (and ornamental art generally) declined with the decline of the Roman Empire, but continued to be practised: from the twelfth to the sixteenth century very extensively,—many of the more powerful bishops and nobles assuming the right of coining money, even as the king. In England the archbishops of Canterbury and York, and the bishop of Durham, exercised the right of coinage until the Reformation; and local Mints for coining the king's money were also occasionally fixed at Norwich, Chester, York, St. Edmund's-bury, Newcastle-on-Tyne, or other convenient places. Independently of these royal Mints, almost every abbey struck its own *jettons*, or counters, thin pieces of copper, used in casting up accounts, commonly impressed with some pious legend. Such Mints were at least as numerous in France and Germany as in England. The art of impressing legends upon coins is nothing else than the art of printing. That the art of casting letters in relief, though not separately, was known to the Romans is proved by the names of the Emperors Domitian and Hadrian on some pigs of lead to be seen in the British Museum; and that it was practised during the Middle Ages we have ample testimony in the inscriptions upon church bells.

In the fourteenth century, a hundred years before our earliest dated wood-cuts (1418, -23) the use of seals impressed in wax for the purpose of authenticating documents was general throughout Europe: kings, nobles, bishops, abbots, and all who came of "gentle blood," corporations also, clerical and lay,—all had seals. Most were of brass, with the device or legend sunk, cut or cast in intaglio, in order that the impression might appear raised, in low or often high relief. The workmanship of many of these seals (especially of some of the conventual, in which figures of patron saints or a view of the abbey could be introduced) displays no mean degree of skill. Looking on such specimens of the art of the engraver, we need not be surprised that the cuts of the early "Block-Books" are so well executed.

So far chiefly from Chatto. Farther detail and instances of the practice of engraving in both earlier and later time will be found in his well-considered *Treatise*, in Landseer's *Lectures on Engraving*, and elsewhere; but I have perhaps brought together sufficient to prove the assumption, that, through the ages, among all civilized peoples with whom we have acquaintance, Chaldean and Assyrian, Egyptian, Chinese, and Indian, Greek, and Roman, Gothic, Scandinavian, Italian, Spanish, French, German, and English, the art of engraving, by incision and in relief (figures sunken or hollowed and figures prominent), has been both known and practised. Can we suppose that the sculptors of Athens, or of Persepolis, Nineveh, and Egyptian Thebes, were ignorant of that simpler art which is but the beginning of sculpture? Look again at our Babylonish brick, that rudest print of a relief-engraving! The first step in engraving is the cutting of a single line. When the engraver, following the figure drawn for him, had outlined with his knife the simplest of his hieroglyphs, ▼ ▼◀, he might have stopped, leaving the outlines ▽ ▽◁ to stand in slight relief upon the impressed brick, the print of his engraving. But these would have too faintly shown, and been too soon obliterated from the face of the clay; and the hieroglyphs were wanted to be conspicuous, and to last. For the same reason of preservation they must be indented in the brick. So, dissatisfied with only outlines, he proceeded to cut away the wood between the characters to a sufficient depth to obtain a clear and durable stamp. Were it the first stamp ever cut, what special teaching would be needed to tell this first engraver how to complete his work? He knew all when he had cut out a single piece of wood,—at his first notch. Put a knife in a child's hand, he will not stop to question you, how to use it. Has he not already scraped—scratched— engraved a line with stick or finger, in the soft ground, or in some other softness? The whole process of engraving, in metal or in wood, intaglio or relief, is apparent in this one brick. How could the Sculptor of the Parthenon be ignorant of a process so simple and direct? Has not all sculpture grown out of this? What is a brick-stamp, with its flat-surfaced straight-sided prominent characters, but a bas-relief? The next step from this simplest, easiest form, would be to one less simple. From a figure perfectly flat on the face and straight-sided the next progress is to rounded extremities, readily suggested by the roundness of the object, bird, beast, or man, attempted to be represented. Rounding extremities may lead to caring for inner inequalities of surface. After the bas-relief the statue. By-and-bye we have the grandeur and majestic beauty of the Phidian marbles. It is a mistake to call all this invention. It is evolution. New tools can be invented, to expedite or facilitate our work; the ambition of succeeding generations, each striving to excel those gone before, reaches on to greater and undreamed-of triumphs; but, as from

Differences not essential but of growth, degree, and in kind.

a single minutest plant the many-aisled and myriad-columned banyan forest has had its growth; so from that simple outline, the beginning of a stamp for bricks, or other rudest purpose, has proceeded all the achievement of sculpture, of which engraving is a branch. The difference between the work of Bewick and that of the Babylonian is not essential: it is only a difference of growth, of degree, and in kind.

Printing known and practised in old days.

And concurrently with the art of engraving the process of printing, by whatever rude or imperfect means, must have been known and practised by the ancients. One cylinder from Babylon, a single brick, as already argued, brings proof; and proof, although books were not, of some idea of "multiplying representations of the same engraving." It could not but be so. As the first line, never so accidentally cut, in wood or stone, was lesson enough for the engraver, so the first bare-foot-print in the sand or mud of earliest time revealed to the first man, Adamite or pre-Adamite, the meaning of an impression. The use of the stencil was not printing; yet the piercing of the plate was engraving. When the Babylonian brick-maker stamped his brick, he printed—from an engraving: can we guess how large an edition? When the Egyptian for the same purpose used our handled stamp of the Museum, he printed from an engraving in wood. Engraving and printing, both were in practice in those early Egyptian and Assyrian days; for how long before it is impossible to learn. How general the continual practice since is sufficiently recorded.

Printing from engravings.

Bas-reliefs on Assyrian and Peruvian temples, and Greek gems of yet unrivaled beauty, and the sunken moulds for coins and for later seals authenticating royal charters,—these perhaps we would distinguish as Sculpture;* but in what do the stamps of antique kings and notaries, the marks of tradesmen, or the monumental brasses in our churches, differ from that which we call engraving now? And for printing, need we summon the myriad ghosts of slaves, criminals, captives, to count their scars, those multiplied representations of the same engraving, while to-day we repeat their process, the brand of ownership (not indeed burned in) on the cattle of a thousand hills? Engraving and printing,—in brass, in copper, in silver, in gold, in stone, in clay, and in wood,—our museums are full of the proofs of the early knowledge and perpetual exercise of the cognate processes: nothing indeed wanted by our forefathers of all possessed by us to-day (allowing for growth and improvement from continual endeavour) except our increased and readier power, through the printing-press, for multiplying impressions,—only increased and readier, for prints of

And before the invention of typography.

the Block-Books were multiplied, and possibly by use of some kind of press, before the advent of Gutenberg. Only, comparing modern with ancient times, the Arts "become more varied, growing out of richer bases of civilization, and extend over a wider field."

A great and important step indeed was the printing of books from moveable types;

---

* Sculpture is a generic term, proper to engraving as well as to statuary, "comprehending both: just as the term Art comprehends, in addition to these, painting, poetry, music,—every mode of practically exhibiting refined mental operation, and is therefore applicable to either or all of them." (Landseer.)

(a great step also has been printing by steam-power). That does not alter the process of engraving, nor denote essential difference therein. The advantage of a linen paper,[*] then coming into use, still farther helped the progress of the printer, not occasioning the rapidly increasing demand for his work which marks the close of that fifteenth century, but only meeting the demand. The great occasion seems to have been the need of new exertion by the Church, to counteract the dangerous tendencies of the time: for the days of the first religious prints, to be so soon succeeded by printed books, were of the period between Huss and Luther,—between the martyrdom of Huss, in 1415, and the birth of Luther, in 1483.

"According to Weigel and Passavant there can not be any doubt that engraved blocks were employed toward the close of the twelfth century for giving off impressions in colour on to the smooth surfaces of silks and like fabrics. In Weigel's work [*Die Anfänge der Drucker-Kunst in Bild und Schrift*] is figured a portion of a band of taffetas, of a reddish brown colour, having impressed on it a flowing ornament, the shape of an *S*, with flower buds attached, the blackish contour of which ornament has evidently been printed, and not painted. This is the earliest specimen known to Weigel and Passavant, and they believe it had its origin in Saracenic Sicily, toward the close of the twelfth century, and from its appearance not to have been the first of its kind. . There appears no sufficient reason for doubting either the genuineness, age, or mode of production of the several examples which are given in Weigel's treatise. No less than ten illustrations are afforded of printing from wooden blocks, on coverlets and garment fabrics, from the eleventh to the fifteenth century. Such imprints on analogous textures increased considerably during the thirteenth century, when liturgical vestments and choice draperies were often elaborately adorned. Linen, silk, satin, and in the fourteenth century leather, received such impressions in red or dark blue or black colours, and sometimes in gold. For such work we are indebted, in earlier periods at least, to Italy; though in Weigel's collection were two specimens of German imprints in black on a strong linen ground. They are thought to have belonged to *antependii* of the middle of the fifteenth century. One represented a Crucifixion, with Mary and John, on an ornamental ground, the whole requiring three

---

[*] Typography, writes De Vinne,—"had to wait for the invention of paper, the only material that is mechanically adapted for printing. Paper was known in civilised Europe for at least two centuries before typography was invented; but it was not produced in sufficient quantity, nor of a proper quality, until the beginning of the fifteenth century. The elder Romans had no substitute for paper that could have been devoted to printing or book-making. Papyrus was so brittle that it could not be folded, creased, and sewed, like modern rag paper . The Scribes of later Rome and the book-copyists of the Middle Ages preferred vellum. It was preferred by illuminators after printing had been invented." (*Invention of Printing*.) Vellum was never liked by printers. Dry, it is too harsh; moistened, it is unmanageable. And the cost would be too great. Three hundred sheep-skins, it is said, were used in a single copy of the first Bible. Typography must have failed with only sheep-skins. There were not sheep enough.

blocks for its perfection. The other was the Blessed Virgin holding the infant Jesus in her arms under a rich Gothic tabernacle flanked by two columns, each column supporting a Prophet. Below is the name Maria. All is on a dark ground. Besides referring to these examples brought forward by Weigel, we may direct attention to the fragments of tapestry described by Dr. Keller and belonging to the *convent* Odet of Sion, in the Valais. These tapestries are formed of a raw hempen cloth now become of the colour of leather. They are divided into compartments, with ornamental borders, within which are subjects from the *Odyssey*, the figures being detached light, off a dark ground. Early as some of these imprints may be, they serve to show only that blocks were engraved for the purpose of stamping woven fabrics as early as the tenth or eleventh centuries." (*Introduction to the Study of Ancient Prints*, pp. 16-28.) Is not the "only" showing enough? Dr. Willshire adds :- " The great desideratum is to know when they were first engraved and used for the purpose of giving off their designs to parchment or paper." This does not appear to me to be of so much importance in the history of Engraving. The blocks engraved for woven fabrics could also have been printed on parchment, and on paper so soon as paper was to be had. The exact date at which an engraving was done *for the purpose* of being printed on paper is of little consequence, and surely will never be obtained.

Preceding the printing-press, Weigel considers the probability of "a joiner's press, or screw, and that such could be readily employed for the pressure of books. But we may assume too that where books, particularly those of parchment, were bound as in our still existing form, a book-binder's press could not have been wanting," available for printing also, as indeed any ordinary screw-press would have been. And though there were no press, the use of a hand-roller, such as is shown in the cut below (taken from Papillon) might have been sufficient.

After long-time knowledge of engraving and printing the altogether new requirement of extensive publication for popular needs is answered by the invention of moveable type (the letters made by Gutenberg in brass moulds and matrices) and by the manufacture of linen paper.

CHAPTER II

SAINTS AND PLAYING-CARDS

F the beginnings of Engraving in ancient times I have said perhaps enough. I may now proceed to the consideration of the actual progress of engraving in wood as known and practised in modern days: engraving in wood (or, having regard to the process rather than the mere material, relief engraving) for the purpose of producing upon paper what we now call Prints.

Early in the fifteenth century (we have a certain date of 1423), at least a quarter of a century earlier than what is called the "invention of printing" (more properly to be called the invention of moveable letters), and so before anything like editions of books, we find, first current in Southern Germany, single-leaf rudest wood-cuts, of various sizes, with and without text or legend, known by the name of HELGEN, or Saint-Pictures. Mere outlines for colouring, printed on paper, a manufacture but recently introduced, they were the immediate result of the first opportunity afforded by fit material for multiplying impressions of engraving. They appear to be the earliest of modern "Prints." With them we fairly begin the history of Wood-Engraving.

The history of wood-engraving in Europe, whether it were true or not that the art had been brought from China, introduced into Europe through the commerce of Venice with the East: a view which Ottley takes, but for acceptance of which Chatto sees no reason. Certainly this importation lacks proof, and is not more worthy of implicit belief than the before-noticed attribution of wood-engraving to the reign of We-wung. Engraving and printing may have been practised in China, and in Japan likewise, from time immemorial. In that I find no difficulty; but in the way of farther assertion is the little dependence we can place on Oriental annals. Our best accounts and indications of European borrowing are very indistinct and unsatisfactory. Also, I do not see the need of Chinese teaching.

With this claim for China we may also put away, in this case not only as "not proven" but as outside of serious consideration, the story told by the French engraver, Papillon, in the first volume of his *Traité de la Gravure en Bois*, 1766, of certain engravings by two young Italian nobles, so early as 1284-7, illustrating the "Chivalrous Deeds of the great and magnanimous Macedonian King, the brave and valiant Alexander: imagined, and executed in relief with a little knife upon tablets of wood," by Alexander Alberic Cunio, knight, and Isabella Cunio, twin brother and sister, and printed by them for gifts to their friends, their age being only sixteen years. The story can be read in Chatto's *Treatise*, by him faithfully reported from Papillon, and as carefully shown to be unworthy of belief. Briefer and less particular refutation might have sufficed, depending only on these facts: that no one but Papillon could give evidence of these wonderful prints; that he had for a time lost all recollection of them, having mislaid for thirty-five years his memorandum (as much as eight closely printed octavo pages, written, he tells us, "on three sheets of letter-paper"); that, having recovered this, he could not produce it, after the publication of his book, when called upon by inquiring Heinecken; and that, subject from an early age to hallucinations, he was, a year after he told this story, placed in a mad-house.

Yet Noel Humphreys writes, in his *History of the Art of Printing*,—"I have, since the first issue of this work, seen a letter from a well-known bibliophile of Moscow, in which he states that, on reading in my work the account of the wood-cuts described by Papillon, he referred to a memorandum-book kept during a tour, in 1861, and found that, on the 9th of September in that year, he had seen in Nurnberg, in possession of the antiquary Herdegen, seven pages of the eight described by Papillon, for which Mr. Herdegen asked a very high price. The same letter contains an interesting account of a xylographic block discovered in Spain, and from which some impressions had been recently taken,—the execution of the block being assigned, on pretty sure grounds, to the year 1233." (Noel Humphreys, *History*, etc., 1868, Appendix, pp. 209, 210.)

Evidence in the memorandum-book of an unnamed correspondent: of what worth is such a statement? In Dr. Willshire's words—"The story of the Cunios has received its death-blow at the hands of Mr. Chatto," Mr. Humphreys' correspondent notwithstanding, and independently of M. Firmin Didot's word that paper was not manufactured in Italy at the pretended Cunio date,—something to be weighed in consideration of likelihood, if not proving impossibility.

During the Middle Ages books were expensive luxuries. Their production, down to about 1350, writes W. Bell Scott (*History and Practice of the Fine and Ornamental Arts*), "was the work of those who wanted them. The clergy, lawyers, and public schools, had retainers employed in transcribing: the *scriptorium* in the larger monasteries a principal scene of their labour. But a public trade in books had begun to a small extent, and the calligrapher and the miniature-painter were independent artists and craftsmen long before

1400, when the Middle Ages give place to what are called modern times. In Italy the 'Renaissance' was initiated and ready to develop itself for the delight of the world. The illuminator of the day has left us many portraits of himself. He sits on a chair, or stool, before a solid desk with sloping top, having two receptacles for ink, red and black, sunk into it; the reed pen which the early writers used has given place to the quill; and in his left hand he holds a knife, or bone instrument, wherewith he keeps the page flat under his writing. The space to be filled is circumscribed by a red line, and he leaves room for the vignette or picture: the artist being now quite distinct from the scribe. The labour of this individual was soon to be set aside by printing; and oil-painting introducing small pictures about the same time, both the manuscripts and their splendid illustrations were gradually discontinued, and at last laid by as antiquated curiosities. The illuminator at his work.

. . " In the latest age of manuscript-painting the men thus employed were the greatest artists of that period out of Italy. Their veracity and study of Nature express a perfect freedom and mastery. The *Hours* of Anne of Brittany is a collection of the most lovely pictures of flowers, fruit, and insects; and so true to nature that M. Denis calls the artist, Poyet, the greatest naturalist of the age. The historical subjects too, then executed by the miniaturists, are quite equal to the best works of the Italian contemporary painters. As examples may be mentioned (because some of their pictures have been repeatedly engraved, and the originals themselves may be seen in the British Museum), Froissart's *Chronicles* and the *Romance of the Rose*, both largely and elaborately illustrated. These bring us to the period of the invention of engraving. The beauty of the illuminated books.

" The earliest discovered impression from a wood-cut is dated 1418 ;* early specimens may yet be discovered, for the invention of stamping pictures made no way, nor touched the painter till it was combined with types. The stamps from rude wood blocks which first circulated in Holland and Germany were coarse, and gaudily coloured, and were the people's pictures of the day, bought only to adorn the humble homes of artisan or trader [or freely distributed among them with pious intent]. No one suspected that the farther development of the process would sweep before it the Scriptorium and the Scribe, and revolutionize the whole structure of modern mind and manners." The earliest wood-cuts.

Of these illuminated books, so many as I have had the opportunity of examining (and I have examined many), while some, and perhaps all the earlier, are altogether painted, others, later, appear to have been partly done with the aid of a stencil, and some look as if they had stamped, that is engraved letters. I am inclined to think that many of later works, generally taken for illuminated manuscripts, have been done, not wholly with pen and brush, but with an admixture of stencil and stamp, the printing concealed by colour. " Illuminated books produced with stencilling and print.

---

* 1423: 1418 is doubtful. But Passavant speaks of prints of wood-cuts in the Munich Cabinet, brought from Tegernsee in Bavaria, which he supposes to be of a date perhaps as early as the fourteenth century.

Renouvier (*Des Types et Manières des Maîtres-Graveurs*) notices the use of outlines for after-colouring, the outlines showing through on paper, but not on vellum : the vellum copies so mistaken for illuminated manuscripts. The absence of any hint of the practice by contemporary writers may readily be accounted for by the want of observation of men who were not experts, to whom these works were sold as veritable manuscripts, and who had no doubt in their minds, nor reason for doubt. When good and inquiring critics of our own sceptical time, such as Mr. Chatto, fail after careful examination (as I will have occasion to prove) to distinguish stencilling from the print of a wood-cut, there need be no wonder that such differences escaped the notice of unprepared contemporaries. The illuminator would find use for the stencil when, in a long work, he had many repetitions of the same initial letter. It would not only save much labour, but it would also insure a desirable regularity in his work. And the use of the stencil would naturally lead to the use of the stamp (already known and employed on other occasions) for letters and forms more complicated than those within the scope of stencil. Not that it is at all likely that whole books should be so produced : the supposition of a modern Italian, Sig. Requeno, based on the test of measurement with a fine pair of compasses. A fallible test at best : the same steady and accustomed hand plodding through a whole book might well arrive at sufficient similarity of forms to deceive one looking for likeness and not for difference. However, both stencil and stamps (stamps of wood or metal) were surely used at times, though we can not tell to what extent. Passavant thinks that so early as in the twelfth century stamps were used for initials in manuscripts.

It seems likely that such use, however limited, might have suggested to illuminating monks the availability of wood-engraving for the production of prints on a larger scale, those pictorial religious tracts, the HELOSH ; though whether this was the first extensive employment of wood-engraving, or its earliest employment was in the manufacture of PLAYING-CARDS, is a question yet undecided.

Singer writes :—" Whatever may have been the origin of cards, it seems probable that they were in use in Europe previous to the invention or adoption of the xylographic art. . . At what time the application of xylography to the purpose of multiplying cards took place, it is not now possible to ascertain with certainty; but there can be no doubt that they were among the first objects it produced, and we have every reason to conclude that they were printed from engraved blocks of wood at least as early as the commencement of the fourteenth century, if they were not derived together with this art [here agreeing with Ottley] from the East at an earlier period, a supposition which is not entirely devoid of probability." (Singer, *On Playing Cards.*)

Passavant writes :—" It has been supposed that the first application of wood-engraving in Europe was made in the fabrication of playing-cards. It were better to say that it has been believed that this fabrication gave occasion for the invention of wood-engraving :

since it is to be presumed that the use of cards passed soon from the palace to the hut of the poor man, who instead of cards magnificently painted and ornamented had to content himself with cards cheapened by means of stencilling or engraving in wood or metal." *

Becker thinks the Pictures of Saints preceded Playing-Cards.

Chatto (*Treatise*, 1839) thought it "not unlikely" that wood-engraving was employed first in the manufacture of cards; and that the monkish use was an afterthought. Later, (*Facts and Speculations on the Origin and History of Playing-Cards*, 1848), he oppositely concludes that "wood-engraving was employed in the execution of the Helgen before it was applied to cards," but "there were stencilled cards before engravings of Saints."

Von Muar, again, will tell us that both card-painters and card-makers were in Germany eighty years before the invention of typography, that is to say in the third quarter of the fourteenth century; and that the card-makers were engravers in wood.

Of the earliest actual use of Playing-Cards we have few trustworthy dates. Not to be trusted is Papillon's discovery of an edict of Louis of France (in 1254, on his return from the Holy Land), forbidding games with cards. From a passage in a manuscript copy of the old romance of *Reinart le Contrefait* we might be led to date the time of their use in France so early as 1341; but this passage, Passavant assures us, is an interpolation, as it does not appear in earlier copies of the same manuscript. Bullet claims their invention, or first use, for the French, at about 1376. Passavant, who thinks their first use in Italy sufficiently proved by their Italian name—*Carte*, would have them known there "about 1350, thence spreading in all directions, and passing quickly into Germany, where they became the object of a very considerable commerce," which however "scarcely took place before the end of the fourteenth century." The earliest known German cards he takes to be stencil-work; and would have them belong to the first half of the fifteenth century, before which "we find no playing-cards, neither printed from wood nor done by stencil."

---

* He considers the Helgen to have been preceded by Cards, and wood-engraving a consequence of the introduction of cards, brought from Arabia to Sicily by the Saracens about the middle of the fourteenth century (yet he speaks of stamps, surely likely to be not only of metal, as early as the twelfth); an Arab origin, he thinks, clearly indicated by the very name first had in Italy—*Naibi*, and that they still keep in Spain—*Naipes*. Nevertheless he says:—"There is nowhere mention of the manner in which the Arabs arrived at a knowledge of playing-cards: their cards could not have human figures as in Europe, for the Koran prohibits the reproduction; and yet the first packs we know in Europe represent not only human figures but objects which belonged to the circle of ideas and beliefs of the time, to that of the legends (sagas) above all, and in particular to such as were current in Italy about the fourteenth century." It is plain, he says, that, if they came from the Arabs, they must have received at the onset "a complete modification, not only of their governing rules, but also of outward appearance." (*Le Peintre-Graveur*, pp. 6, 7.) Is the objection met by our borrowing the cards, as Chatto seems inclined, directly from India, where (at the present time) these same anti-Koran figure-cards appear to be used by Mahometans and Hindoos alike? Or may Passavant's mention of the Sagas lead us to suspect some possible interference of Norraena, homeward-bound Varangians leaving Constantinople, at the close of the Eastern Empire?

Heinecken's claim for Germany.

Cards in Spain.

The Cards for Charles VI.

Cards common before 1400.

But not earlier than Helgen.

The methods of production are clearly seen.

But the earliest positive date which Passavant can give for Italy is found in the *Chronicle* of Niccolò di Coveluzzo da Viterbo, who writes:—"In 1379 was brought to Viterbo the game of cards, which came from the Saracens." Heinecken claims, if not their first use, their first manufacture for the Germans. Von Murr, in his *Journal*, refers to a book of Nürnberg bye-laws, between 1380 and 1384, in which cards are included among games allowed to be played for small stakes. They were in such general use in Spain as to be prohibited by John of Castile, in 1387. Passing some probably ante-dated interpolations or mistaken references, we find the first notice to be trusted of their usage, in France, in 1392, in an account-book of Charles Poupart, treasurer to Charles VI., wherein is found an entry of fifty-six *sols Parisis* (about one hundred and fifty francs), a fair sum in those times, "given to Jacquemin Gringonneur, painter, for three packs of cards in gold and diverse colours, ornamented with many devices," for the king's diversion. On this entry, taken by Menètrier to denote the first use of cards, was built the story of their invention for Charles, for the solace of his madness. In the registers of the city of Ulm for 1402 may be seen the earliest record of a German card-painter; and in the books of Augsburg for 1418 we obtain a card-maker's name. All these dates, Italian, Spanish, French, and German, are so close together, 1379 the earliest of certainty, that we can only take them as indications that the use of cards had become very general at the end of the fourteenth century, their manufacture probably beginning in Italy, but soon carried on in Germany to a much larger extent. I see nothing in these dates to warrant us in a conclusion that card-making was antecedent to the production of *Helgen*, or in supposing (with Prosper Marchand, Heinecken, Von Murr, Jansen, Singer, and De Vinne,*) that the introduction of cards may have preceded or could have caused the adoption (as Singer would have it) of the xylographic art.

Neither in the records is there any certain account of the method of production. The mention of Gringonneur as painter (not as card-painter) may lead us to infer the hand-work of the higher artist. No doubt the more extensive cards were painted. It was, as we have seen, an age of miniaturists. But various processes may have been employed: first prints coloured by hand, then prints coloured with a stencil for yet cheaper copies. Artistic hand-work is not likely to have sufficed to meet a demand so universal as must be implied in the necessity for ordinances to regulate or restrict or prohibit too popular a pastime. How much may have been done by stencil and how much by engraving we can not know. Even examination of ancient cards will not inform us. Where the pips —or numerals, or other parts of the cards, are without outline, the forms defined only by

---

* De Vinne argues that cards were the only kind of printed work which promised to pay for the labour of engraving. Surely he over-estimates the cost of that. In those days also were other motives than a trader's profit. I take it that the *Helgen* were done with pious intent rather than for a pecuniary result.

colour, we may be sure of stencil; hardly else. Mr. Chatto's proof of the use of stencil ["from the feebleness and irregularity of the lines, as well as from the numerous breaks in them which in many instances show where a white isolated space was connected with other blank parts of the stencil,"] is of no worth.* Feeble and irregular lines, and breaks, are common enough in wood-cuts: the faults of the engraver, or consequent on damage or from wear. Breaks in *many* instances, never so numerous, are not proof. They need be omnipresent. A single absence of this connecting link overthrows the stencil-proof. Referring my readers back to the monograms and cipher at pages 10, 11, (given also in Chatto's *Treatise*), I repeat that not one of them could have been done by stencil; and the cards I print, here below, from a photograph of the originals in the British Museum

(the very uncoloured cards upon which Mr. Chatto makes the remarks I have just cited, and copies of which he has entitled "Old Stenciled Cards"), are not by stencil, but most surely are prints, from an engraving in relief. I have no doubt whatever, an engraving in wood. They want the breaks to which Mr. Chatto appeals as evidences of stenciling, want them, most remarkably, even in the inexact copies given in his book. There is not a single card of the seven he has printed which has not parts impossible to be stenciled.

* " From a repeated examination of them I am convinced that they have been depicted by means of a stencil, and not printed or rubbed off from wood-blocks." . . . "That these cards were depicted by means of a stencil is evident from the feebleness and irregularity " etc. (*Facts and Speculations*, pp. 88-9.)

A broad white gap, across an upper row of cards on the same sheet, which he supposes
to be occasioned by the slipping or breaking of the stencil-plate, should have made him
pause. Had the plate slipped or been broken, the paper would have been smeared with
colour. It is possible that the paper might have been doubled; but I think the break is
of the plank, from the splitting of the wood or the disjoining of glued pieces.

Engraving used for cards, but first employed in production of the Helgen.

We may accept it then as certain that wood-engraving was very early employed in the
making of cards; and I have no doubt (agreeing with Breitkoph) at a yet earlier date in
the production of the Saint-pictures, the *Helgen*, though never a writer of the fourteenth
century informs us of it. Let us now search the records to learn something of the card-
makers and engravers themselves!

I pass the French painter Gringonneur, 1392, and a certain card-painter (*kartenmaler*,
I suppose,— *peintre de cartes* Passavant calls him,) whose name appears in 1402, in the
Ulm registers. Neither of them perhaps had anything to do with engraving. The first

The Craftsmen: —their names.

mention of a card-maker (*karten-macher*) is in the burgess-book of Augsburg, in 1418;
and the first indubitable *formschneider* (wood-engraver, the term still used in Germany),
is in the town-books of Nurnberg, of 1449.* But at the outset we are embarrassed by a

Wood-engraver.
Card-maker.
Print-colourer.
Card-colourer.

confusion of terms. What distinctly was the profession or practice of the *Formschneider*,
the *Kartenmacher*, the *Briefmaler*, or the *Kartenmaler?* Ottley writes, after Heinecken,
that the *formschneider* was so called as being a "cutter of moulds." Chatto corrects this
to cutter of figures; and thinks the term "more specifically applied" to distinguish him
from the card-engraver: though "till toward the year 1500 the terms *formschneider* and
briefmaler appear to have been frequently used as synonymous." Yet he says that the
word *kartenmaler*, displaced by *briefmaler* by 1473, is frequently found on the same page
as *formschneider*, expressive of some distinction between the professions, or occupations.
Heinecken, and Breitkoph with him, is of opinion that the term *Briefs* (meaning prints)
is older than that of *Karten* (cards); and he makes the *briefmaler* the colourer of prints
of all kinds, not only of cards. Breitkoph also speaks of a separation of the *Bildermaler*
(picture-colourer) from the card-maker so early as 1430. Then, Chatto again, we have
the *briefmaler* who "not only engraved figures occasionally, but who also printed books."
I suppose much of this confusion of times, and of terms proper to several occupations, to

All belonging to one guild.

have arisen from the different artists or craftsmen, belonging to one guild or fellowship,
not being exclusively devoted to a special object, but, perhaps for a long period, aiding
each other as occasion offered. And taking an opposite view to Von Murr, in so much
as I believe that the wood-engraver was employed upon the Saint-Pictures before he was

---

* The first trust-worthy. A Hans Formannschneider is found in the books of Nurnberg so early as 1397; but Von Murr will have that to mean Hans Fortzan. *schneider* (tailor's cutter). Passavant also speaks of an indication of a *formschneider* in 1398, one Ulrich. "It is doubtful that he surnamed blocks for cards."

employed on Cards, I find in that sufficient reason for his designation, at whatever date acquired. He may have been a card-maker also, probably was, though not distinctively so called except when he confined himself to that special branch of his business. The distinguishing terms for engravers, or makers, and colourers, and printers, would follow naturally the separated employments, the first engravers, whether of Saints or of Cards, printing and colouring their own engravings. Of the stencil-cutter I find nothing except this following description in an old Latin manuscript of the date of 1459, said to be preserved at Cracow, written by one Paul of Prague, a doctor of medicine and philosophy. He defines the term *Tiripagus* as "an artificer who cleverly cuts figures and letters, or whatever it pleaseth him to cut, on plates of copper or iron, on solid blocks of wood (*ligneis solidi ligni*), and other materials, that he may print upon paper or a wall, or on a clean board. He cuts everything he likes, and acts in the same manner with pictures. In my time some one at Bamberg cut a whole book on plates" [*integram bibliam super lamellas*,—which is read by Chatto as a whole Bible]. If, as I suppose, the cutting in *ligneis solidi ligni* means engraving in wood, it makes the *formschneider* a stencil-cutter too. Stencil-cutting would have been no difficulty to him. The cuts here annexed [designs by Jost Amman for Hans Sachs' *Self-like Description of all ranks on earth, all Arts and Trades*, etc., 1568,—a first copy in 1564 noted by Heinecken] show the Designer, the Wood-Engraver, and the Colourer, at their different tasks : the engraver with his knife,* the colourer with brush and stencil-plate and saucers of colour. I suppose the methods unaltered from earlier days. We shall find no stencil-cutter among "all the arts" : an indication, it may be, that he and the engraver were the same.

Yet some words before I quit the consideration of stencilling. The following paragraph from Chatto.

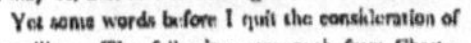

---

* Chatto, translating Sachs' verses under this cut of *The Formschneider*, gives him a graver, and writes also that the wood-engravers of that period used a "tool with a handle rounded at the top, similar to the graver used in the present day." I know not of the handle, but a graver can not be used on a plank.

(*Treatise*, p. 57), may not be passed without comment on the conclusion.   He writes :—

"A great many wood-cuts of devotional subjects, of a period probably anterior to the invention of book-printing by Gutenberg, have been discovered in Germany.   They are all [he is writing of the *Helgen*] executed in a rude style, and many are coloured. . .

The figures are not generally impressions from wood blocks, but are for the most part wholly executed by means of stencils."

And elsewhere he writes :—" Although the earliest of professional card-makers might generally impress the outlines of the figures from engraved blocks, it is certain that they also were accustomed to form them by means of a stencil." (*History of Wood-Engraving*, in the *Illustrated London News*, April 20, 1844.)

Mr. Chatto's meaning is not clear to me. If I take the "wholly executed" literally, I can but say I have seen no such figures ; if he only means *the outlines by stencil*, as he thought was the case with the cards at page 23, I dispute his judgment.   Such work would be very unlikely, and quite incapable of proof. That outlines are not by stencil may be proved ; I do not know by what examination of prints we can be sure that they are not printed by either wood or metal. *Not stencil* is plain whenever the requisite connections of the plate do not exist. Breaks, though showing all needful links, would still leave the question undecided. As said before, there may be breaks in the engraving. In masses of only colour I have found it difficult to determine what was coloured without and what coloured with a stencil-plate, observing excesses of colour, and departures from outlines as if done by a careless or unequal hand, even where I was most confident of the use of a stencil.* Nor do I think the stencil-use can be quite satisfactorily ascertained without comparison of the edges of colour in several copies. This would throw all unique copies out of the possibility of proof. Little more need be said of stencilling.

Useless also is it to pursue further the question of priority between Cards and Saints. Interesting to us here as a part of the history of wood-engraving, it yet matters little, if even we could surely learn, whether a Knave of Hearts (or Acorns) or a St. Christopher was first produced ; whether the Devil-serving trader or the pious conventual craftsman has right of precedence.   Taking into consideration all the materials for judgment I have

---

* I find Dr. Wiltshire remarking that "some of the earliest coloured cuts appear to have been tinted by hand alone, and more or less carefully, while those of somewhat later date have been often very clumsily and coarsely coloured with the aid of stencil." But here again, if there are outlines, why do we assume the stencil?   Even in the days of illuminators some unaided colourer might do coarse or careless work

been able to collect together, I subscribe to Chatto's conclusion, and can not but believe that monastic leisure and ability first found opportunity for employment of wood-cuts, in the service of religion, and that the wage or profit to be had for an article of commerce in growing demand would be the later temptation of the card-maker. Those rude wood cuts of sacred subjects, common in Suabia, known there as *Helgen* or *Helglein* (corrupted from *Heiligen*—Saints or Little Saints), a word which in course of time came to merely signify Prints,* were at least contemporaneous with, if they did not precede the engraved picture-cards. In 1418 we find the first record of a card-maker; and our first sure-dated wood-cut, certainly not the first done, is but five years later.† By 1440 the card-makers of Augsburg, Nürnberg, and Ulm, are exporters of cards and coloured prints to Italy;‡ and 1440 also may be safely assumed as an approximate date for the appearance of the "Block-Books," which mark a considerable advance and very notable improvement in the art of engraving in wood.

Previous to 1844 the undisputed earliest dated print from a wood-cut was known as the St. Christopher of 1423, in the possession of Earl Spenser, a coloured print found by Heinecken in 1769, pasted inside the cover of a manuscript volume, in the Library of the Chartreuse convent at Buxheim, near Memmingen, in Suabia. In 1844 an architect of Malines, M. de Noter, examining an old coffer which had been used to contain some

---

* In France cuts of the same kind had the name of *Dominos*, the affinity of which with the German one is obvious. The term was subsequently applied to coloured or marbled paper; and the makers of such paper, as well as the engravers who were colourers also of wood-cuts, were called *Dominotiers*.

† I take no account of the term *Incisor lignorum*, said by Ducange to have been found in a charter of 1233: agreeing with Dr. Willshire that it has first to be proved to mean an engraver in wood, and not a carver. Or was he haply a cutter of stencil-plates, a *Tiripagus*? Who can tell?

‡ "It was probably [writes Chatto] against these foreign manufacturers that the fellowship of painters at Venice, in 1441, obtained from the magistracy an order, declaring that no foreign manufactured cards or printed coloured figures should be brought into the City, under a penalty of forfeiting such articles and of being fined xxx *lire*, xii *soldi*. This order was made in consequence of a petition presented by Venetian painters, wherein they set forth that 'the art and mystery of card-making and printing figures, which were practised in Venice, had fallen into total decay through the great quantity of foreign playing cards and coloured printed figures (*carte e figure depente stampide*) brought into the City.'"

Cards and coloured prints:—Does that old word *stampide* imply, asks Dr. Willshire, "printed with a press, or merely—printed, stamped, or stenciled?" And he refers to Planché, who thinks that, in 1441, "it might simply mean formed, figured, or shaped by means of the stencil," he having observed that, according to Florio, *stampire* signifies to print, to presse, to stampe, to form, to figure, and *stampe* in like manner, besides a print or impression, is said to be a *marke, a shape, a figure*." I have before me Florio's *Dictionary*, revised by Torriano, edition of 1659; and I find no *stampire*. *Stampare* is given as to stamp, to imprint; *stampato* as stamped, printed; *stampatore*, a printer; and *stampa* (plural *stampe*), a stamp, a print, an impression, a mark, a brand, a pressing,—*by metonym* [only so] the quality, kind, making, or form of any thing. But without need of dictionary, a figure formed by a stencil is certainly not stamped, that is printed. The printing "with a press" is beside the question. *Stampide* is simply *printed*, no matter how. An engraver's proof, taken with a burnisher, without a press, is no less printed.

of the city archives, and which had become the property of a tavern-keeper of Malines,
discovered a "scarcely visible" coarsely coloured print, a wood-cut, pasted within the lid.
He detached the fragments, reunited them, and found thereon, "clearly expressed, the
date of 1418." *

This print, the BRUSSELS VIRGIN, bought at first by M. de Noter, was bought of him

for the Royal Library at Brussels by the
Baron Reiffenberg, on whose authority
the above account of discovery is given
by M. Ruelens. The print is described
as taken in a pale, yellowish distemper,
"unimpeachable evidence of antiquity,"
the paper appearing to have been laid
upon the block and rubbed at the back,
"such proceeding and the depth of the
lines indicating a novice." The print is
fourteen inches and a half high by nine,
taking no note of border lines. Sitting
in a fenced garden, the Virgin-Mother,
draped and crowned, holds in her arms
the naked child Jesus. Over her hover
three angels bearing wreaths; two birds
are in the air, why a third on the fence?
Their labels name the attendant saints:
St. Katerina with the fatal sword, while
her right hand is held up to receive her
Lord's betrothal ring; St. Barbara with
her three-windowed tower; Theoritches

(St. Dorothy) with her heaven-sent fruit and flowers; and St. Margoreta with a Cross
and book. The rabbit outside the garden M. de Reiffenberg deems important. Seeing
that there is a rabbit also in the St. Christopher of 1423 (as indeed there is in many of
these old prints), he thinks it possibly may have some punning allusion to the name of
the unknown engraver of both engravings. And now we may notice, at the entrance
to the garden, a three-barred gate, with a diagonal cross-bar, latch, and hinge. On the
top bar appears conspicuously the date M·CCCC o XVIII. The lowest part of the print,

---

* Il "en détacha les fragments, les réunit ensuite avec
adresse, et comprit, à l'inspection de la date de 1418,
qui y est clairement exprimée, que cette feuille pourrait
intéresser l'histoire de l'art." (LA VIERGE DE 1418.

—Documents Iconographiques et Typographiques de
la Bibliothèque Royale de Belgique : fac-simile photo-
lithographiques, etc., etc. Avec autorisation de M. le
Ministre de l'Intérieur: par M. Ch. Ruelens, 1845.)

all across, has been torn off, so that we can not know what, of inscription or else, may originally have been there.

Of course so early a date is not to be accepted without inquiry. Discussion has been rife, as to evidence of style as well as to veracity of date. M. de Reiffenberg supposes it to be by Van Eyck or of his school; and attaches more value to it as supplying some proof that wood-engraving was of earlier date in the Low Countries than in Germany. M. de Brou contends that the style of drawing is manifestly of a much later period, 1460 to 1480. The style of the engraving also, showing "a very sensible progress," he thinks induces the same conclusion. Agreeing with M. de Brou as to the drawing, I must yet remark of the cutting, that in work so purely mechanical the most apparent superiority (I see none here) would only show some difference of care or hand-deftness, and could give no indication whatever of the date of production.

For the date's veracity the Baron's words, as quoted by M. Ruelens, are as follows:— " Falsification was impossible, since the print came to us directly from the coffer turned out of the archives of Malines. It was only for some days in the possession, first of a tavern-keeper who had no idea of either art or engraving, afterwards of the architect M. de Noter, whose probity precludes all suspicion of fraud and deceit, whose character does not admit the supposition of a pleasantry which, without being incompatible with probity, ought to be banished from good society, particularly from the scientific world, where it could throw trouble and disorder." Pleasant considerations and protestations, (not saying that "the gentleman protests too much"), not quite proving impossibility of falsification! " *Le compte moral de l'acquisition*," rendered by M. Ruelens, gives the print to De Noter for three weeks after the Belgian Minister had been notified of the finding and informed that it was for sale for five hundred francs. But without imputing fraud, we may be allowed to ask for more than the mere words—" Falsification is impossible." M. de Brou, who at first made no question of its genuineness, came, after examination, to the conclusion that it was " no longer in its primitive state, and might very well have been altered." Indeed he thought all the ciphers " had been gone over (*repassés*) with a pencil, the M·CCCC lightly, so as hardly to be distinguished, but in the ciphers XVIII the X and the V marked with such force that it is impossible to say what ciphers they at first were. Only the units are probably as first printed." (*Quelques Mots sur la Gravure de 1418*. Brussels, 1846.) To this the only reply of Baron Reiffenberg is:—" I declare that when I saw the print and bought it there was not on the date a trace of lead-pencil; if, to throw suspicion on this monument, or through imprudence, some one to whom it has been confided, or who has traced it [M. de Reiffenberg had been permitted to have copies taken, for which the print was traced], has allowed himself to apply the pencil, I am ignorant of it. All I maintain is that I have seen the date perfectly intact both with the naked eye and with the glass." This is as inconclusive as impossibility of falsifying.

It must be added that M. Jules Renouvier, who examined the print in 1858, could find no alteration. "At the first inspection I refused to admit what appeared to be indicated by the ciphers. Having seen it again, and very scrupulously examined it, I should say (*je dois dire*) that the place where they are is intact, and I no longer find any reason not to accept them." (*Histoire de l'Origine et des Progrès de la Gravure dans les Pays-Bas.*)

M. Ambroise Firmin-Didot likewise believes that he may place full confidence in the recital of M. de Reiffenberg.

There the discussion rests, so far as I have been able to ascertain. I have not seen the original in the Brussels Library; and I have before me only the two copies (of the same size as the original) which are given in M. Ruelens' authorised work, from which alone I have taken the foregone particulars. My judgment goes against the veracity of the date. I do not therefore agree with M. Passavant who, examining the print in 1850, thought that between the fourth C and the XVIII there had been rubbing out, and an L (of which he believed he could detect the traces) replaced by a circular sign. I believe that circular sign may be the nail fastening the transverse bar, and if the alteration of a cipher be suspected would rather look for it in the V the first stroke of which is nearly upright, as might be if altered from an original L. So, avoiding the nail, we may jump at once to a likely M·CCCC o XLIII. I could almost persuade myself to this, looking at the chromo-lithograph given with M. Ruelens' *Documents*. Nothing is ascertainable from the badly traced and inexact outline also given: it merely shows the design. But my doubt of the date is for no more tampering with a cipher. The style of the design, the insufficiency of evidence as to the actual condition of the print when first found, and the too noticeable prominence of the date,—these things weigh more with me. In the coloured copy with the *Documents*, while the names on the scroll-labels are so faint that they can scarcely be made out (it may be my copy that is in fault), the date is distinct, as if later printed. There is nothing to surely prevent affixing a date at any time after the printing of the wood-cut.

I would maintain, then, that the ST. CHRISTOPHER holds its place of precedence; that we may still consider 1423 as the earliest date we possess for the print of an engraving in wood. Some doubt may also attach to this date: not of authenticity, but based upon the presumption that it was intended to mark some event rather than to fix the time of production. There is reason in the presumption; but, failing the discovery of an event to which it might be assigned, we may fairly deem the date to belong to the engraving. There is nothing in the print to lead us to suspect a later period; and the earliest-dated does not imply the earliest ever done. Indeed there is nothing *in the cutting* of these early prints to stamp priority on any. Minuteness and intricacies of line not attempted, the first wood-cuts are without distinction. The *St. Christopher* is fairly cut. But when Mr. Chatto remarks that "the engraving, though coarse, is executed in a bold and free manner," his words are not applicable to *the engraving*, the actual cutting. How should the engraver make it other than coarse? And what of boldness or freedom is manifest in this quite unintelligent cutting with a knife on each side of a black line drawn on the wood for the cutter's guidance? This sort of inaccurate talk, confounding the drawing with the engraving (common among art-critics, Mr. Chatto not preëminent), has done more than perhaps anything else could do to lead inquiry astray and to prevent a clear understanding or correct appreciation of engraving. In what I shall write of engraving let me be understood as writing always (unless I plainly except) of *engraving only*, kept distinct from the draftsman's part. Mr. Chatto is correct in writing—" If mere rudeness of design and simplicity were to be considered as the sole tests of antiquity, upwards of a hundred engravings positively known to have been executed between 1470 and 1500 might be produced as affording intrinsic evidence of having been executed at a period antecedent to the date of the *St. Christopher*." Quite true! since though the advance of years may be marked by degrees of excellence, the rude and bad are found in all ages. In Art also, the poor shall be always with you!

I am well content however, albeit not concerning the engraver, to give some words of unstinted praise to our *St. Christopher* for the design. I mind not the "disproportionate" space he occupies in the picture. Is not he famous as a giant? and are not all the incidents outside of his personality mere minor adjuncts? The perspective also is good enough for me, as doubtless it was for those in whose interest the print was issued. It is certain that he is crossing a stream: we see a fish beneath the waves. He supports his colossal frame and helps his steady course with a full-grown fruit-bearing palm-tree, fit staff for saintly son of Anak. No heathen he: the nimbus is round his head. As on his shoulders he bears the Lord of the World, can we fail to remark his upturned glance, inquiring why he is so bowed down by a little child? The blessing hand of the Blessed plainly gives reply. Look again, and see on one side of the stream the merely secular life, with its daily bread and poorest daily occupations: is not all expressed by the mill, and miller, and his ass, and far up the steep road [what need for diminishing distance?] the

Description continued.

peasant with his sack of flour, toiling toward his humble home ? while on the other side is the life of the spirit,—the hermit by his windowless hut, the warning bell above, he in front kneeling with the lantern of faith in his hand lifted high, a beacon for whatever wayfarer the ferryman may bring. Rank grasses and the fearless rabbit mark the quiet solitude in which the hermit dwells. I can forgive all short-comings or faults a modern Critic would point out. I have no care for criticism, grateful for a design so expressive, a story so well told. These old artists were in earnest. I could praise the engraver too (only a mechanic) for that he has used his knife with so much of careful fidelity to keep the lines of drawing, although some shapelinesses of finger-joints, and else, be wanting. It does well enough as he has left it for the colourer's completing. The not too subtle, yet not outrageous,—if we call it "gaudy," not undelightful, colouring will gladden the eyes of an uncritical multitude ; and the pious myth of St. Christopher [the ferryman of an unknown river,—how once he carried across it a little child and, much marveling at its weight, was told he carried the Lord of All] will be remembered through the picture often looked on, not without faith in the cheerful if too superstitious words beneath :—

That day thou Christopher's face shalt see
No evil death shall happen thee !

The *St. Christopher*, writes Chatto, "affords a specimen of the combined talents of the *formschneider* and the *briefmaler*. [Truly it is a coloured print.] The engraved portions have been taken off in a dark colouring matter similar to printing-ink ; after which the impression appears to have been coloured with a stencil." Stenciling would occupy not much less time than colouring by hand, beside the labour and cost of cutting the several plates ; and farther, some overrunnings of colour, the undefined and softened edges of the blue, and the various shades of green, should rather point to hand-work. Why this constant insisting on stencil, used certainly, but, I think, less in those days than since ? Surely the illuminator, or any practised colourer, could have had no difficulty in keeping to given outlines, and so need no guidance but the pattern before him.

Only one other wood-print bears a date earlier than 1450: a *St. Sebastian* with a date of 1437, found in 1779 at the monastery of St. Blaise, in the Black Forest : now in the Imperial Library at Vienna. Two others, supposed to be before 1450, may be noticed : one in the *Kalendar* of Johannes de Gamundia, a thirty-years' Almanac begun in 1439 ; and one found by Mr. Ottley in a manuscript of 1445.

In the same book in which the *St. Christopher* was found by Heinecken [a manuscript in praise of the Virgin, a gift from Anna, canoness of Buchaw, to the Buxheim convent] he also found, pasted in the opposite cover, a print of about the same dimensions, of the *Annunciation*, or *Salutation of the Virgin*, printed on the same coarse kind of paper, and with the same dark ink, also coloured : coloured by stencil, Chatto says ; and Willshire agrees with him. It may be stencil, but I find no proof. It has been made a question too (and, I think, undue importance attached to it) whether these particular impressions have been taken by rubbing or with a press. Regarding also the colour of ink, the use of certain (rather uncertain) kinds of ink, perception of this or that water-mark on the paper, questions which have been the ground for considerable debate,—these likewise, though they help to fix the status of a print, may not touch the engraving. Proved the press or rubber, the ink, the water-mark, of this print before me, what does that say of the time at which it was engraved? Though the date upon it be 1423, a print might be taken in 1823, not contradicting the possibility of earlier printing, nor accusing the date of the engraving of the block. The date of the engraving of Durer's *Smaller Passion* is not affected by any number of prints from the yet existing blocks. I give the following passage from Ottley, not for the value of his conclusions, but to show the character of inquiries, no doubt interesting to Dryasdust, the eminent bibliophile, but which seem to me (only an unlearned engraver) of no great comparative importance in the history of engraving. The history of prints, as that of books, is another matter.

Mr. Ottley writes :—" I formerly observed, in speaking of these two wood-cuts [the *St. Christopher* and the *Annunciation*] that they show no signs of having been taken off by friction, but were evidently printed with a press; but now I find in saying this I went farther than I could be justified in doing without examining the backs of them, which, as they are pasted within the covers of the *MS.* above-mentioned, it was impossible for me to do. For I have since met with early wood-engravings of Germany and the Low Countries taken off in a black ink by friction as well as in the brownish tint which was commonly employed in the ancient block-books; others again I have found taken off in black printing ink with a press,—and indeed I am in possession of a specimen of wood-engraving printed in black oil-colour on both sides of the paper by downright pressure, which I consider to have been printed in or before the year 1445." (*Inquiry concerning the Invention of Printing.*) It appears therefore, he concludes, that both methods were used and both kinds of ink. What guide then is there to the date of printing?

A reason for the light ink, if originally light, may be that the prints were intended for colouring. The much vexed question of the methods of printing may be set forth very briefly. Passavant is sure of a *frotton*, or rubber, the printing-press not being invented, Noel Humphreys, press or not, is also satisfied of the *frotton*, so judging from the gloss, caused by rubbing, on the backs of prints. Chatto has the same notion, but sees much difficulty in the operation. Willshire doubts the decisive character of the gloss, and is not sure that the use of a press or roller of some kind was unknown before Gutenberg's appearance. The practical printer, De Vinne, may sum up. "Almost every author who has written on printing has said that [the *Helgen*, and Block-Books later] were printed by friction, with a tool known as the *frotton*, which has been described as a small cushion of cloth stuffed with wool. It is said that when the block had been inked, and the sheet of paper had been laid on the block, the *frotton* was rubbed over the back of the sheet until the ink was transferred to the paper. We are also told, that the paper was not dampened, but was used in its dry state. The shining appearance on the back of the paper is offered as an evidence of friction. This explanation of the method used by the printers of engraved blocks has been accepted, not as conjecture, but as the description of a known fact. I know of no good authority for it. I know no author who professes to have seen the process. I doubt the feasibility of the method." And again :—" It is begging the question to assume they were not printed by a press." (*Invention of Printing.*) The discussion has been whether press or *frotton* was employed; but yet a third method may be worth consideration. In Papillon's comprehensive *Treatise*, published so late as 1766, I find no mention of a *frotton*; but he gives, with cuts, a description of the making and the use of a roller * in his time, and I see no reason to doubt its use in earlier days. It may farther be observed that, while the roller would give a face-impression not to be distinguished from one taken by the press, it might also produce a gloss on the back to seem an effect of rubbing. Surely consideration enough for the backs of prints!

In this ANNUNCIATION print we see the Virgin at her devotions, kneeling in an arched room of curious perspective. She turns toward Gabriel who, kneeling too, appears to be addressing her. Twined round a pillar between them a scroll has these words—' *Hail · full of grace the Lord ther*— The Holy Ghost in the form of a dove descends on a ray of light from God the Father (a corner torn off Lord Spencer's print). Respecting this cut, M. Krismer, the librarian of the convent at Ilmxheim, writes to Von Murr : —" It will not be superfluous to point out a mark by which, in my opinion, old wood-engravings can with certainty be distinguished from those of later date. It is this. In the oldest wood-cuts only we perceive that the engraver has frequently omitted certain

---

* His directions are precise. After inking, a sheet of damp paper is to be laid on the engraved board, or plank (*planche*), taking care to make no crease. Then we pass over it the roller (*rouleau*), lightly at first, afterwards with increasing force. When lines of the engraving appear everywhere on the back of the paper, the proof or stamp will without doubt be well printed. Then it may be lifted from the plank, taking hold of one corner of the paper. According to its appearance, whether too much or not enough charged with ink, it will be a guide for after prints. (*Traité Pratique de la Gravure en Bois*, pp. 358-9.)

parts, leaving them to be afterwards filled up by the colourer. In the *Annunciation* the upper part of the Virgin appears naked except where it is covered by her mantle. Her inner dress had been left to be added by the brush of the colourer." He refers also to another print, a St. Jerome in penance, in which we may see the Saint, the instruments of suffering, and a whole forest besides, hanging in the air, waiting for the ground to be put in with colour. "Nothing of this kind," he says, "is in more recent cuts [so proved more recent?] when greater progress was made in the art. What the early wood-engravers could not readily effect with the graver they performed with the brush, as they were both wood-engravers and colourers." If they coloured with a stencil-plate, the loss of a few lines would have no importance. Against M. Krismer's view, I suspect in the print of the *Annunciation* a possible line of the drawing accidentally or carelessly cut out by the engraver. In the St. Jerome, or others, if the drawing on the wood were from a tracing, what then more likely, whatever the progress of the art, than that a line, or even lines of the tracing should be overlooked? As to "what the early engravers could not readily effect with the graver," it has only to be said that one line was as readily effected as another.*

A third wood-cut of the same *halcyon* period (this print also in the possession of Lord Spencer) is a St. Bridget,—of Sweden, but no less a favourite saint in Germany. She is sitting at a desk, writing. Over her head are the words — *O Bridget, bid God for us!* The emblems around her speak her story: the half-length of the Virgin with the Child intimating that the pious widow is perhaps writing of those visions in which the Virgin was in the habit of appearing to her; the Swedish lion, on the shield, and the crown at her feet signifying that she was of the blood-royal of Sweden; the pilgrim's scrip and hat and staff referring to her pilgrimage to Jerusalem; and the shield with *S P Q R* for Rome, where she died. This cut has been printed in a lighter ink, more like distemper or water-colour, than that used for the *St. Christopher*. It is coarsely coloured : Chatto says—"apparently by the hand unassisted by the stencil." The face and hands are of a flesh colour; her gown and pilgrim's hat and scrip are of a dark grey; her veil, worn

---

* According to Berjeau, the practice of the earlier wood-engravers was as follows:—The plank being prepared, either the drawing was made directly on it, every line exactly as it was to be cut, or else, the drawing first done on paper was glued, with its face downward, on the wood, and rendered transparent, perhaps by oiling. Of course when this mode was adopted the engraver had to cut through the paper.

hood-wise, is in part black, in part white; and the wimple she wears round her throat is also white. The bench and desk, the staff, the letters *S P Q R*, the lion, the crown, and the nimbus surrounding her head and the Virgin's, are yellow; and the ground is green. The whole picture is framed in a border of mulberry or lake colour.

Another of these prints, unknown to Chatto, deserves notice: the VIRGIN OF BERLIN. In the Berlin Cabinet, of apparently the same time as the Brussels Virgin, if the style of drawing may inform us. The print is nine inches and three quarters wide and thirteen and three quarters high, as now measured, a strip seeming to be lost from the bottom. Draped and crowned, and standing on the crescent moon, she holds on her right arm the Holy Child, also draped, and in her left hand is an apple. The flamboyant aureole against which she stands is borne by boys; and, at the corners, four birds have each a scroll, with a rhyming couplet, in Flemish.

Who is this Queen that standeth here?
'Tis She who saves the world from fear.

How shall Her name be named to us?
Mary, mother, maid glorious.

How did She reach that height above?
Humbly, by charity and love.

Who shall be lifted next to Her?
Whoso is most Her follower.

These prints may be taken as samples of a numerous series of pictures popular in the early part of the fifteenth century, perhaps yet earlier: all of the same character, little varying in quality, altogether unvarying so far as the engraving is concerned. At first only pictures of saints and martyrs (illustrations of Bible story came later) they served as pious reminders and, carrying out a precept of St. Gregory, filled the place of tracts, or books, for the illiterate multitude; coloured to attract attention, to please. and also to induce more careful preservation. Though probably at first the work of the Monks, coloured in imitation of monastic illuminations, they were likewise prepared by order of Town-Councils, as is proved from the public registers of Ulm, Nurnberg, Nordlingen, and Augsburg. They have also been attributed, at least in part, to the " Brotherhood of the Common Lot," a pious fraternity which had for object the copying of manuscripts and otherwise helping to spread religious knowledge. From M. Michiels' *Histoire de la Peinture en Flandre*, we learn that the Lazarists and other religious brethren, who were

accustomed to nurse the sick, carried, on fast days, through the streets, large candles of
wax, richly ornamented, and distributed to the children these coloured prints. Whether
so given gratuitously, by religious or secular corporations, or sold for the benefit of the
monasteries, they were widely strown. They were the home-pictures of the poor.

The colours employed on the cuts varied with the schools of different places, as shown
in the following abridgment of Dr. Willshire's account, taken from Weigel.

SUABIA—*Ulm* and *Augsburg*. Bright red, amber, yellow, umber, slate grey, green,
and black. The red "juicy," from bluish carmine to cinnabar, often almost violet. No
blue in drapery, as a rule. Colours frequently overlaid with varnish.

FRANCONIA—*Nuremberg* and *Nördlingen*. Colours not so bright as the Suabian: the
red deeper, more brown than carmine; red lead often employed. The yellow usually a
pale ochre. Blue used occasionally.

BAVARIA—*Friesing, Tegernsee, Kaisersheim*. Colours not lively, mostly pale, except
in certain coats of arms: a deep and pure carmine; yellow ochre, often turbid; ochrish
green, passing into a moss-green. Blue to be met with. The most lively-coloured are
from Tegernsee: cinnabar red and "may-green," yet keeping the Bavarian pure carmine
and ochre. The Bavarian the most artistic of the schools.

LOWER RHINE—*Cologne* and towns of *Burgundy*. Pure but not strong colour; tints
generally pale.

Dr. Willshire considers that "the style of engraving, or 'technic,' varies in goodness
and character," . . . and elsewhere, "the technic evinces care and better drawing." And
Mr. Conway, in his *Woodcutters of the Netherlands*, writes copiously of "the first Louvain
wood-cutter," "the first Gouda wood-cutter," "the second Gouda wood-cutter," and the
"same workman or his School at Antwerp," as if there were grounds for discrimination
in the various styles and treatment of the works assumed to be by the different cutters.
I confess I can find no such distinction in the mass of early wood-cuts, nor any varying
whatever except in the more or less careful attention to a work so entirely mechanical.
I am speaking here of the *Helgen*, but the same judgment holds good for all engravings
in wood up to quite the close of the fifteenth century: three or four books excepted, to
be spoken of farther on. All else is one monotonous level.

How could it be otherwise? Consider what kind of work it was! On a plank, planed
smooth, of pear or other fair-fibred wood, not too hard, unmistakable black lines were
drawn with brush or pen. The only engraving-tool required, or available, was a knife,
such a blade as one might have for a pen-knife, two-edged sometimes, fixed in a handle
for easy holding. So little of difficulty is in the process of cutting, that any boy or girl,
not so aged as those Cunio twins, might be trusted to do it. All distinction would be
owing to the drawing. The sole difference in the cutting would be between the sound
or clean work and the unclean or broken. Distinguishing merit else or character in it

there was not. Papillon tells of his wife succeeding on a first attempt: a perfect work, " *sans avoir jamais manié le point auparavant.*" In a question of dates, of the production of *this* or *that*, by what inspection shall we know that *this* was the decent performance of Yesterday's lad and *that* the master-work of A-century-before? Speculations of critics and bibliographers seem to an engraver sometimes vain, their comments uninstructive.

By whom were these earliest *Heligen* cuts engraved? The supposition of Cards being earlier would make engraving to have been taken up as an independent craft for merely trading purposes with the very smallest incentive of hope for gain. I do not believe it. I am convinced that the knowledge of the use of wood and of metal, for stamps, during a time long anterior to any indication we have of card-making implies a different outset. Who had this knowledge but the old scribes and illuminators, of the monasteries? And what easier employment than engraving should we invent for monastic leisure? If so, what then more likely than the purpose of some artist monk to multiply his drawing by cutting it on a plank? I imagine some such beginning of holy prints as more probable than only speculation on the sale of a cheaper pack of cards.

So, I think, the first designers of wood-prints may have cut their own designs. Once done, the thing known, as any body could do it, the practice, for *Heligen* or cards, might quickly become general. Soon would be no need for the draftsman to waste his labour with the knife; and occasion would be found for the *formschneider*, a mechanic, who had no need to be an artist.

The first professional wood-engraver was but a mechanic. I see no ground of reason for attributing to him anything like style or character; and certainly he had no controul over the treatment of his work. Judgment, or any thought of purpose or effect, was not expected of him; he had to cut whatever was drawn for him. At most there may have been some rare exceptions when artist and wood-cutter were one.

CHAPTER III

THE BLOCK-BOOKS

F later date than the *Helgen* is the first sign of excellence in Wood-Engraving. Quitting these undated Saint-Pictures, [the date of a particular print indeed of small importance, since there is one general sameness of the engravers' work through all, and we know at what period they were done,] we reach the "Block-Books," an advance beyond the Saints in as much as the drawings are more elaborate: there is an approach to shading and no longer any stint of the amount of text, the engravers by this time more expert at least in letter-cutting. These books are not exactly what we ought to term "illustrated books," the prints (mostly coloured as the *Helgen* were), and not the text, being the primary object. By bibliographers they have been called Block-Books, because picture and text are both cut on the same "block." Strictly, as it was on planks, wood sawn lengthwise with the grain, that knife-work was done, and not on blocks, the name is wrong. These block, or plank books immediately preceded the invention of movable types; and were perhaps the directest cause of that invention, wanted as means of escape from the labour of engraving so great an amount of lettering. The noteworthy block-books are the *Apocalypsis*, the *Canticum Canticorum*, the *Biblia Pauperum*, and the *Ars Moriendi*. With them is usually classed the *Speculum Humanæ Salvationis*, in one edition of that some pages having the text engraved. The production of the first three Mr. Chatto would assign to a date between 1430 and 1450; and he takes the *Apocalypsis* to have been the earliest. That the *Speculum* should have been printed before 1460 he deems to be "in the highest degree improbable," on account of the employment of movable types for the earlier editions. For the same reason I will not count it among the genuine Block-Books, but reserve it for later consideration.

The time of the *Ars Moriendi* I would imagine to be close upon that of the *Biblia*; but there is no possibility of any certainty: better cutting, as already said, not surely telling us of date. Of this book, it would seem, Mr. Chatto had not any knowledge; he names it as a block-book, but with neither description nor remark concerning it.

The APOCALYPSE, or *Historia Sancti Johannis Evangelistæ ejusque Visionis Apocalypticæ* (the Story of Saint John the Evangelist and his Apocalyptic Vision), as it is termed by bibliographers, for the book itself is without title, consists of fifty wood-cut pages varying slightly in size, from ten inches and two-eighths to ten inches and five-eighths in height, and from seven and three-eighths to seven and six-eighths in width, printed on stout paper, on one side only, with ink of thin body, distemper or water-colour, and of a greyish brown,—the lines much indented in the paper. The cuts, placed in the book, face each other: two pages probably engraved on the same plank, and printed together. Each page always contains two equal-sized subjects. The following explanation is of the page before us.

The upper subject is from the thirteenth chapter of the book of *Revelation*: "I beheld another Beast, coming up out of the earth; and he had two horns like a lamb; and he spake like a dragon." The legend is from verses 16-18: "And he maketh all, small and great, and rich and poor, and free and bond, to have a mark in their right hand, or on their forehead, that no man may buy or sell save he who has the character and name of the Beast or the number of his name, . . and his number is six hundred, three-score and six." The under subject is from the fourteenth chapter: the Vision of the Lamb. John himself holds the descriptive text: "And I looked, and behold a Lamb stood upon Mount Sion, and with him a hundred and forty-four thousand bearing his name and the name of his Father on their foreheads." As it were in a separate vision to the right, we see the Lord on his throne with the elders and the four beasts (the first like a lion, the second like a calf, the third with the face of a man, and the fourth like a flying eagle); and below the Lamb, as shown by the text in front, are those who follow whithersoever he goeth, who "sang a new song before the throne and the beasts and the elders."

The page here given shows the general treatment of the book, the archaic character of the designs, and the rude simplicity of the cutting. The drawings perhaps were rude, but I should judge them to have had more expression and to have been better than the cuts. Some differential touch there surely was, if only in the heads, which the unartistic knife has pared away. The copy in the British Museum (Case 9. d. 1), from which my photograph was taken, is the copy described by Chatto, who also has reductions of two pages, sufficient to show the nature of the designs, but not to represent the engraving.

Heinecken calls this the fifth of six editions enumerated by him : judging however, as it seems to me, from very unimportant particulars. I take it to be the first ; or certainly earlier than his "second," a coloured copy, also in the British Museum. I take it to be so from its great superiority : copies are not usually better than their originals, nor does the abler artist copy the inferior. This coloured copy, coarsely and vilely coloured, has lost the Blake-like character to be seen in the earlier designs, in those of my first edition — Heinecken's fifth. I should think it has been traced and redrawn by a poorer artist, who could not sufficiently appreciate the original to care for correct rendering ; or it has been engraved from prints set off upon the wood, with farther loss of expression in the second cutting. For the sake of the cutting, of even the original edition, I had hardly cared to give a page of it ; but I could not leave unnoticed the perhaps earliest printed book of which we have any knowledge.

The place of its production is unknown. Germany, Holland, and Flanders, have been supposed. Passavant says Upper Germany, supported by Willshire, who observes that the colouring (purple violet and bright green) is of the Suabian character, and that the short proportions of the figures are not agreeing with the Van Eyck school, but in close likeness to the schools of Upper Germany. Chatto conjectures that, wherever engraved, the designs might be by a Greek, one of many artists fleeing from the Turkish invasion before the final overthrow of the Byzantine Empire by the taking of Constantinople in 1453. He sees reason for this conjecture in the presence of the Crescent (the badge of Constantinople) and the Cross of the Knights of St. Constantine on some shields in the fight of Michael and his Angels against the Dragon ; finding too in the drawing of some of the figures an accordance with the style of Greek art in the early part of the fifteenth century. His opinion that a Greek would be most likely to choose the Apocalypse for a subject might have more weight were we unmindful of Durer and Schald Beham.

Our second block-book, CANTICUM CANTICORUM — *Historia seu Providentia Virginis Mariæ ex Cantico Canticorum* (History or Prefiguration of the Virgin Mary from the *Book of Canticles*, or *Song of Songs*), deserves more notice, though it is but a small folio, of only sixteen leaves, printed on one side. the ink used seeming of very poor consistency, as it varies in an uncoloured copy in the British Museum from pale brown to almost black. Each page, or folio, contains two distinct pictures of equal size filling the upper and lower halves of the page ; figure-subjects with scrolls above or between the figures. Some brief account of the whole series may be worth giving, if only for the sake of the curiously quaint and daring adaptation of Solomon's Love-Song, as prefiguring Christ's love for his Church.

The title—*Providentia Virginis Mariæ*, prefixed to the first cut in a copy belonging to the city of Haarlem, accepted by Heinecken and repeated everywhere without thought, is a misnomer. The queenly Bride can be considered as typifying the Church; but the story surely is not that of the Mother of Jesus. The book is indeed nothing else but the *Song of Solomon* in pictures: Christ instead of Solomon as the Bridegroom.

Page 1—The upper subject represents the Bridegroom standing by the Bride, who is attended by two handmaidens. In front of them (to our right in the picture) in a field are distant figures of monks binding sheaves and threshing out the corn. In the picture beneath, the Bride stands in the centre, with a glory around her; three maidens on her right, on her left a fourth with her hands clasped as in prayer.

2—Four standing figures: the Bride and Bridegroom, conversing, and two maidens. Underneath, she is seated, two maidens sitting beside her; he stands in front.

3—A medieval dude, holding a lily; the Bride facing him, followed by her maidens. Underneath, a chamber: she kneels, her head in his lap; her maidens look away.

4—She offers him apples over a fence. Underneath is a dual picture: on one side she is sick in bed; on the other, she stands before a tower on which are an archer and a swordsman; four angels with a Christ enthroned fill the corner.

5—The Bride with three maidens; a windmill in the distance. Underneath, at the porch of a house, the Bridegroom is seated, the Bride fallen before him, her head in his lap; three maidens, their hands clasped, kneeling. Deer in the distance.

6—The Bride and Bridegroom eating grapes in a vineyard, three maidens waiting, all seated. Underneath, he stands outside a garden wall, over which she is watching him. An angel is going in at the gate; others with drawn swords are on the wall. "A garden enclosed is my sister, my spouse."

7—Bridegroom and Bride and two maidens walking in a fenced garden. Underneath we have again a dual picture: he stands outside her chamber-door; she inside, kneeling on her bed (having just arisen, with her crown on), lifts the latch for him. Her maids beside the bed look as in wonderment.

8—The Bridegroom as a shepherd, talking with the Bride; two maidens waiting at a respectful distance. Underneath, the Bride on a raised seat, or throne; on either side a maiden with clasped hands, attentive to her.

9—Bridegroom and Bride stand in an attitude of affectionate reserve; to their right a castle, or pinnacled house. Underneath is an interior: they are sitting together; they hold between them a cup with a dove at the top; an angel is drawing wine from a cask; the maidens wear their usual expression of admiration, approval or surprise.

10—A chamber, with cupboard and plates; a fire on the hearth. The Bride stands as in meditation; before her, of smaller stature, her two maidens, now like young girls. One carries a jug, holding it so that the liquor runs out; one has a lamp. Kneeling on

the floor, so far behind the Bride that she could not possibly see them, but the turn of her head indicating that she does, are two very small figures, a man and a woman: the *St. Christopher* lack of perspective. Underneath, an eagle carries the Bride to heaven; two angels on the ground and her kneeling maidens looking on.

11—She is standing with two maidens among some trees much less than themselves. [Like the "Noah's Ark" trees of children's toys: such as are seen in our print from the *Biblia Pauperum*.] The Bridegroom comes from a door behind them. Underneath, we see, among more of these diminutive trees, a figure of Christ on the Cross. The Bride points to it as she comes, two maidens following her, from a castle, or turreted house, on the wall of which stands an angel holding up his hands admiringly. 

12—Outside a gabled house Bridegroom and Bride are conversing; the three maids posed as usual. Underneath, an interior: the Bride holding an image of the Crucified. Only one maiden is in attendance.

13—The upper half of the page is divided. One picture has the Bride sitting up in bed, her maidens waiting. Over the bed, separated by a scroll, are battlements, above which rise four half-figures, a pope, two cardinals, and a bishop, all armed. The other picture shows a street. Two horsemen, with drawn swords, threaten the Bride and her maids; one has torn off her mantle. Underneath is a chamber: Bride and Bridegroom sitting at table, the maidens waiting.

14—Again the upper design is divided. The Two are standing outside a bed-room. Inside is a bed with wreaths upon it; the maidens waiting by the door. Underneath is only the bed-room. The Bride is leading in the Bridegroom, who seems to be uttering a preliminary discourse, and in no hurry. The maidens in retiring attitudes are waiting for the order to leave.

15—The Bride is sitting in front of a castle, an angel standing on either side of her. Underneath, the Bridegroom and Bride are in bed: he faint or asleep, with his head in her lap. She is clothed and wears her crown; he naked so far as the coverlet is turned down. Armed men stand beside the bed. On a scroll we read—*In lectulum Salomonis sexaginta fortes ambiunt, omnes tenentes gladios*, in our English version —" Behold his bed, which is Solomon's, threescore valiant men are about it, . . they all wear swords."

16—He sitting, she presents him with a picture of a kneeling figure holding a Cross. Her two maidens attend her. Underneath, he is handing to her a crown; she has also one on her head. Her maidens are behind. In the distance a Queen is seen sitting on a rock—the Church founded on a rock.

The style of the designs, Mr. Chatto thinks, gives evidence of a more advanced state of art than is seen in the *Apocalypse*. "The field of each cut," he writes, "is altogether better filled, and the subjects contain more of what an engraver would call 'work'; and shadowing, represented by a course of single lines, is introduced. The backgrounds are better put in, and throughout the whole book may be observed several indications of a perception of natural beauty, such as the occasional introduction of trees, flowers, and animals. A vine-stock with its trellis is happily and tastefully introduced at folio 4 [6]; and at folio 12 [9] a goat and two sheep, drawn and engraved with considerable ability, are perceived in the background." From their delicacy Dr. Dibdin was led to conjecture that these cuts were "productions of some metallic substance, and not struck off from wooden blocks." They are delicate, if not so delicate as such a mistake would imply. Pages 15 and 16 the best in copy at the British Museum [Case 17. b. 23] are printed with so little ink that some of the lines are discernible only by the indentations in the paper. The grey, nigh ink-less, print betrays a refinement not suspected from a full impression, and shows how thin and cleanly cut are draperies and lands. The faces also are finely cut, though with little expression. All however are not equally good : in some the lines are infirm instead of delicate. But evidently they have been very daintily drawn on the wood, in the lightness of touch resembling the Italian *Hypnerotomachia* of half a century later. The draperies are simple, but well falling ; the attitudes of the figures expressive, and graceful, if affected. I note that with but two exceptions the feet are always hidden by the dress. The exceptions are in two figures of Christ on the Cross, where the feet are better drawn than in either the *Biblia Pauperum* or the *Speculum.* The costume is that of the Court of Burgundy of the early part of the fifteenth century. The production of the book is credited to the Netherlands.

There is another copy of this *Song of Songs* in the British Museum [Case 17. c. 4]: in part coloured by hand, mounted, and the pages not arranged as in the uncoloured copy, to which it is altogether inferior, the cuts not the same, poor copies, badly engraved.

Very excellently engraved is the best copy (that in the Print Room) at the British Museum of the BIBLIA PAUPERUM (the Book or Bible of the Poor), perhaps more correctly entitled *Biblia Pauperum Predicatorum* (the Poor Preachers' Bible), since, though the pictures might be shown to the people too poor to buy and unable to read, it was the showman himself, the poor unready preacher, whom the accompanying text was to remind and help. The subject matter affirms its purpose. It is a series of skeleton sermons in cramped or abbreviated Latin, a warehouse of texts and sermon-suggesting pictures, scenes illustrative of the Bible History, and embellished with "portraits" of the patriarchs and prophets, David and Isaiah being allowed to stand for many.

The Book, Netherlandish work, according to Passavant, is

a small folio of forty leaves, printed in distemper or water-colour and, as the *Apocalypse* and *Song of Songs*, on one side only,—a necessary course with no means of registering to make the second impression exactly back the first. On each page are four portraits, two at the top and two at the bottom, above and below a central picture taken from the New Testament. On either side of this picture is another, out of the Old Testament, elucidating or in some way related to the teaching of the New; for instance, at page 10 we have in the middle Christ tempted, the Devil bidding him make bread of stones, and at the sides the Temptation in Paradise and Esau selling his birthright. The principal portions of the text, probably to be enlarged and expounded at the preacher's discretion, are at the top of the page on each side of the upper portraits. Below each side-picture is a Leonine or rhyming Latin verse, and a third verse is at the foot of the page; while Scripture texts and moral sentences, having regard to the three pictorial compartments, appear on scrolls proceeding from under each of the four portraits. This arrangement holds throughout. The reproduction of page 32 [given farther on] may stand in place of a longer description. In the following account of the subjects in the book [for some of which not easily recognisable I am indebted to Mr. Ottley] I may be allowed, to avoid repetition, to note that the compartment on our left, as we look at the picture, will be always first named, then the centre, and the right hand subject last.

Page 1—The Temptation of Eve; the Annunciation; Gideon's Fleece.

2—Moses and the Burning Bush; The Nativity; Aaron's Rod budding (two Priests before the Altar, one swinging a censer).

3—Abner with David; Adoration of the Magi; The Queen of Sheba and Solomon.

4—Presentation of a First-born in the Temple; the Presentation of Jesus by Mary; the Dedication of Samuel.

5—Rebekah sending Jacob to Laban; the Flight into Egypt; Michal helping David to escape from Saul.

6—Worship of the Golden Calf; the Sojourn in Egypt (Idols falling at the presence of the Holy Child); Dagon fallen before the Ark.

7—Saul slaying Ahimelech and the priests; Massacre of the Innocents; Prediction of the death of Eli's Sons.

8—David consulting God, respecting his return after the death of Saul; the Return from Egypt; Jacob's Return from Laban.

9—The Passage of the Red Sea; Jesus baptised by John; Joshua's Spies returning, laden with grapes.

10—Esau selling his birthright; the Temptation of Christ; the Temptation of Eve.

11—The Widow's Dead Child is brought to Elijah; the Raising of Lazarus; Elisha restoring the Widow's Child.

12—Three Angels appear to Abraham; the Transfiguration; the Three Children in the fiery furnace (three small children, the flame bursting out and evidently scorching a man with a fork who has thrown them in,—Nebuchadnezzar and his Queen looking on from the top of a wall, or terrace).

13—Nathan reproving David; the Magdalen washing the feet of Jesus; Aaron and Miriam before Moses.

14—David with the head of Goliath; Christ's Entry into Jerusalem; the Sons of the Prophets coming to Elisha.

15—Esdras petitioning Darius for the restoration of the Temple; Christ driving out the traders; Judas Maccabæus ordering the Temple's purification.

16—Joseph sent to his brethren; Judas offering to betray Christ; Absalom seducing the people.

17—Joseph sold by his brethren; Judas receiving his pay; Joseph sold to Potiphar.

18—The meeting of Abram and Melchizedek; the Last Supper; the Israelites have manna given to them.

19—Micaiah prophesies the death of Ahab; Christ rebukes his Disciples and washes their feet; King Joram's Gate-keeper crushed at the gate.

20—The five Foolish Virgins,—descending steps into the mouth of Hell, devils with hooks ready to hale them in; Christ in the Garden, the soldiers falling back; the fall of the Rebel Angels.

21—Joab treacherously stabs Abner; Judas betrays Christ; during a parley Tryphon takes Jonathan Maccabæus captive.

22—Jezebel compasses the death of Elijah; Pilate washes his hands; Daniel accused by the Babylonians.

23—Ham disgracing Noah; the Crown of thorns squeezed on; Elisha mocked by the little children.

24—Abraham with Isaac going to the place of sacrifice, Isaac carrying the faggots; Christ bearing his Cross; Elijah and the Widow of Sarephath, with her "two sticks" in the form of a cross (1 *Kings*, xvii, 12).

25—Abraham's sacrifice; the Crucifixion; the Brazen Serpent in the Wilderness.

26—The Creation of Eve; Christ on the Cross (beside him the Centurion, and the soldier with the spear that pierced him) Moses striking the rock.

27—Joseph let down into the well; Christ laid in the tomb; Jonah flung to the whale.

28—David slaying Goliath; Christ harrowing Hell; Samson killing the lion.

29—Samson carrying off the gates of Gaza; the Resurrection; Jonah is vomited up.

30—Reuben seeking for Joseph; the Maries at the Sepulchre; the Daughter of Sion seeking her Spouse.

31—Daniel released from prison by Nebuchadnezzar; Christ discovering himself to Mary; the Daughter of Sion beholding her Spouse.

32—Joseph discovering himself to his Brethren; Christ's appearing to the Disciples after his resurrection; the Return of the Prodigal. On the page are these verses :—

Quæ vex[ar]li pridem Flens amplexatur :
Blanditur fratribus idem. Natum pater ac terrentur.
His iterus apparet : surgentis gloria claret.

The which rough Latin, freely rendered into English, may be read as here following :—

Whom he so lately vex'd The wept one is embraced :
He charms as brothers meet. And as a son replaced.
To them doth Christ appear : in rising glory clear.

33—An Angel exhorts Gideon; Thomas touching Christ's wounds; Jacob wrestling with the Angel.

34—Translation of Enoch; the Ascension; the Translation of Elijah.

35—The Law given to Moses on Mount Sinai; the Holy Ghost descending on the Apostles; Elijah's Sacrifice accepted.

36—Solomon placing his Mother beside him; Coronation of the Mother of Christ; Esther triumphing over Haman.

37—The Judgment of Solomon; the Last Judgment (the Dead coming out of their graves); David slaying the Amalekite who slew Saul.

38—The Destruction of Korah, Dathan, and Abiram; Hell (a crowd of souls haled thither by devils); the Doom of Sodom and Gomorrah.

39—Job's Sons feasting; Christ carrying souls in his mantle; Jacob's Dream.

40—The Crowning of the Daughter of Sion; Christ crowning his Church (a virgin kneeling); the Angel of the Apocalypse talking with John.

Chatto tells us of a manuscript, in the National Library at Paris, of which this block book is little more than an abstract, which "appears to have been known in France and Germany long before block-printing;" a manuscript containing four hundred and twenty two pages, with eight designs upon a page.

Of the *Biblia Pauperum* he says [*Treatise,* p. 84] there are, according to Heinecken, five editions with the text in Latin. Four, containing each forty leaves, differ so slightly that it is not unlikely that three of them are from the same blocks. The other edition described by Heinecken has fifty leaves, with the figures apparently designed by another artist. Beside the above there are two editions, also from wood blocks, with the text in German; one with date of 1470 and the other 1471, 5. And there are two editions, one German, one Latin, with text from movable types, by Pfister, of Bamberg.

"Without pretending to decide on the priority of the first five editions, as I have not been able to perceive any sufficient marks * from which the order they were published in

---

* Which should imply that he had examined them : but, except for this uncertain remark, I would have no hesitation in saying that he had seen but a single copy   the uncoloured copy in the King's Library.

might be ascertained, I shall here give a brief account of the copy of that edition which Heinecken ranks as the third. It is in the King's Library at the British Museum, and was formerly in the collection of M. Gaignat, at whose sale it was bought for George III.

"It is a small folio of forty leaves, impressed on one side only, in order that the blank pages might be pasted together, so that two of the printed sides would thus form only one leaf. The order of the first twenty pages is indicated by the letters of the alphabet —a to u, and of the second twenty by the same letters having as a distinguishing mark a point before and after them, thus . a . In that which Heinecken considers as the first edition the letters n o r s of the second alphabet, marking pages 33 34 37 38, want the two distinguishing points which, according to him, are to be found in each of the other three Latin editions of forty pages each. Mr. Otley has however observed that Earl Spencer's copy wants the points on each side of the letters n o r s of the second alphabet, thus agreeing with that which Heinecken calls the first edition, while in other respects it answers the description which that writer gives of the presumed second. Otley says that Heinecken errs in asserting that the want of the points on each side of said letters is a distinction exclusively belonging to the first edition, since the edition called by him the second is likewise without them. In fact the variations noted by Heinecken are not only insufficient to enable a person to judge of the priority of the editions, but they are such as might with the greatest ease be introduced into a block after a number of copies had been taken off. Those which he considers as distinguishing marks might easily be broken away by the burnisher or rubber, and replaced by the insertion of other pieces differing in a slight degree. . . . Each of the triangular ornaments in which he has

observed a difference might easily be re-inserted in the event of its having been injured in taking an impression. The tiara of Moses in page 35 [another of Heinecken's signs] would be peculiarly liable to accident in taking an impression by friction : I am disposed to think that part of it has been broken off, and that in repairing it a trifling alteration has been made in the ornament on its top.[*] Heinecken, noticing the alteration, took it as a criterion of two different editions, whereas in all probability it only marks a trifling variety in copies taken from the same blocks." (*Treatise*, pp. 84, 85.)

Heinecken, as Chatto sees, discovers his editions in minute unimportant variations ; and I would add, so far as I dare trust my own examining, is not always correct in his statements. He says that the tiara of Moses has two horns in what he calls the second edition, and a little round button at top in the third. There is no button in the edition I take to be his third. He knows the first edition as having no points to certain letters :

---

[*] "In some of the earliest wood-blocks which remain undestroyed by the rough handling of Time there are evident traces of letters broken away and of the injury having been remedied by the introduction of a new piece of wood." (*Treatise*.) For the damage, that might happen whatever the mode of printing, Chatto is right in pointing out the little reliance to be placed on such accidents in judging of editions.

those letters are without points in two copies in the British Museum (the coloured copy and that in the King's Library), neither of which I could believe to be the first edition. Again, he would fix the second edition by a triangular ornament between the two upper portrait niches: the same ornament is on the same page in three editions in the British Museum. I could get at no order of editions from his distinctions.

Sotheby's opinions are "totally at variance" with Heinecken's. He gives a list, in the *Principia Typographica*, of twelve copies, of six editions; and concludes that, of the four copies in the British Museum, the copy in the King's Library (Heinecken's third) and the coloured copy are both of the second edition, a copy in the Grenville Library of the third, and a copy in the Print Room of the fifth. The Grenville copy, however, "might have been issued after that in the Print Room."

While Heinecken depends upon the presence or absence of some unimportant details as proofs of priority, Sotheby compares a few sets of trees (the little " Noah's Ark " toy trees which I have elsewhere noticed) to find indications of artistic precedence. I may not agree with him on even so small a point. For the rest, the value of his judgment is shown in the following notable remarks on examining the " Lucca " copy—the coloured copy of the British Museum. "Our first idea," he writes, " was that it was executed in Italy (from the peculiar appearance of the colouring and extreme delicacy or thinness of the lines); examining more minutely we discover the impressions to have been taken off from the same series of blocks that were used for the Spencer and Renouard copies, when in an almost worn-out state. The wood-blocks were no doubt well cleaned prior to the impressions in the Lucca copy being taken off; but in consequence of their having been previously so much used and worn the impressions then taken off become weaker, and in many instances the more delicate lines become scarcely visible."* Did he suppose

---

* That I may not be thought misjudging only a slip of the pen, I quote farther :—

"The effect produced on the surface of an engraved wood-block in the taking off impressions by friction and working it off by a common printing-press is, in our opinion, diametrically opposite. By friction the paper is somewhat forced into the hollows or cut out parts of the block ; and by the constant rubbing and pressure of the paper against the originally squarely cut lines _⌒⌒⌒_ left by the engraver, aided by the constant wetting, the surfaces become rounded _⌒⌒⌒_ and ultimately perfectly sharp _⌒⌒⌒_ so as almost to induce us to question the probability of the lines having been cut in some soft metal. . . . By the use of the common printing-press the square-cut lines become broader, owing to the hard vertical pressure, as here shown ▬▬▬.

"We would observe also that, when an engraved wood-block is first used, the surfaces of the lines, being square, receive with ease and retain sufficient quantity of the distemper composition, or ink, so as to require a very slight *friction* either with the hand or the *frotton* to take off an impression, consequently little or no indentation or gloss is made at the back of the engraving, as is verified by the first editions or impressions of the work. Progressively, in the constant use of the blocks, the lines, by the operation of the friction, become narrower and less capable of retaining on their surfaces a sufficient quantity of liquid, so that greater pressure is necessary to make a perfect impression, by which the indentation and gloss become more apparent, so much that in many instances the sharp lines have pierced the paper." (S. L. Sotheby, *Principia Typographica*, pp. 157-8.)

that heaviness of impression was proof of the newness of a cut; or could he be ignorant
of laws of weight and wear? Strangely equipped are some of our writers on engraving!

The copies of the *Biblia Pauperum* which I have examined for myself are four copies
in the British Museum, and a copy in the Bodleian Library at Oxford. Two of those in
the Museum Library I was able (through the courtesy of Mr. Bullen, the Keeper of the
Books and Mr. Colvin, the Keeper of the Prints,) to compare with the copy in the Print
Room. I find the Print Room copy, mounted, uncoloured, and unbound, from the style
of the engravings, to be unmistakably from the original blocks, if not the first printing.
The question of edition is of less importance, since these impressions show the cutting
in perfect condition. I judge the coloured copy of the Library (Case 17. c. 13) to be a
copy of this, engraved from tracings or transfers. The King's Library copy (C. 9. d. 2),
uncoloured, seems to be copied from the coloured one. How inferior both these are to
those I would call the originals in the Print Room I can best prove by comparison of a
page (folio 32) from the Print Room with a part of the same folio, hereunder, from the

uncoloured copy in the King's Library. In the Print Room cut we see that the engraver
(mechanical as his work undoubtedly was) perceived and felt the value of the drawing,

and so has not only preserved something of character in the faces, but also, throughout the engraving has kept the touch of the draftsman. The work speaks for itself as very faithful cutting of an original and spirited drawing. The later copy as plainly confesses either weakness of imitation, were the subject traced and redrawn, or loss of drawing in cutting a poor transfer supposing it, as I think most likely, to have been so rendered on the wood. One thing is certain : from transfers of the King's Library cuts those of the Print Room could not have been produced. Beside and beyond all other evidence, the unmistakable superiority is proof of originality. As an almost universal rule, the better work, and not the poorer, is the first. I can believe in no series earlier than this in the British Museum Print Room ; and I leave bibliographers to determine when and where it was printed and to dispute as to the number of editions and which may be second, or third, or fourth. I have already said in what order of *engraving*, as regards them alone, I would place the three copies in our Museum. The Museum fourth copy, that in the Grenville Library (12.090), I take to be of still later engraving. It is very inferior to the three, very rudely cut, and much of the drawing is lost. The coloured copy in the Bodleian Library, not having been able to place it in juxtaposition for comparison, I can not identify with nor distinguish from the copies of the British Museum. I incline to think it is not identical with any. Decidedly the cuts are not of the original series.

For those who may not be content with only an engraver's judgment I have further evidence, in the part of folio 24 here reproduced from the King's Library copy. There is a gable roof over the right shoulder of the woman with the sticks. On this roof we count *seven* lines. On the same roof in the Museum's coloured copy are *ten* lines. The Print Room copy has *nine*. And in the less careful Grenville copy there are *six*. Plainly for folio 24 a different block has been used in every copy. Now look at the square tower beside our gable ! In the King's copy two windows above the archway are solid — ▮▮. In the other three copies they are open — ▢▢. Which should say that the Grenville cut was not a transfer from the King's. Other differences are observable in the same building. I also note that in the Grenville cut of the Temptation in Paradise (in that only)

52   THE BLOCK-BOOKS

The Bible Pauperum.

Eve has no apple in her hand: was it lost in the transfer, or cut away by the engraver? These are but proofs of the Heinecken sort: not without value if correctly stated.

Comparison of copies.

Another question will bid us pause before deciding as to earlier or later editions, and earlier or later engraving. Has every cut been printed at one time? Is each a perfect set; or have some sets been made up from others? Two in the Museum best copy are from another set. And, referring again to the uncoloured copy in the King's Library, which I have supposed was taken from the coloured one, I observe that not all the cuts will warrant me so far. Folios 1 2 9 10 11 12 15 16 24 are, I think, new cuts; in folios 3 4 7 8 13 14 17 I have not detected difference. Some cuts in the coloured copy are too much covered with colour for the lines to be well seen; some may appear to be from different blocks merely on account of different printing (lines in the heavier impression overrun by the thin ink, in the lighter impression scarcely visible, even to alteration of the expression of features). Folio 22 looks like the same cut in both copies, only more heavily printed in the uncoloured. Folios 25 26 30 33 34 might be from the same cuts in both; folios 38 39 40, I would say, are decidedly new. Folio 37 seems identical with the same folio coloured; yet it is an eighth of an inch longer and nearly as much wider. Folio 38 has the same increase. Others also differ. Might it be owing to stretching of the paper damped for the transfers, from which, noticing the closeness of the drawing, I am led to think the new blocks have been cut?

Another edition with more cuts.

Yet another Latin edition (which I have not seen), according to Ottley, differs from them all: "not only in the number of the prints, which is increased to fifty, but also in the composition of the subjects, which, judging from a fac-simile given by Heinecken of the last print, were designed by an artist of a very different and inferior school. . . . Heinecken knew but of one copy of it, in the Library of the Convent of Wolfenbuttel." (*Inquiry into the History of Engraving.*) I borrow from Ottley his list of the added and interjected subjects.

Subjects and order of the added pages.

Page 1 — Christ's Genealogy; the Birth of the Virgin; the Angel meeting Balaam.

2 — The Marriage of Tobias with Sara; the Marriage of the Virgin; the Marriage of Isaac and Rebekah.

3 has the subjects of 1 in the original.

4 — Moses visited by Jethro; the Visit of Elisabeth to Mary; the Levite visiting his Father-in-law.

5 has the subjects of 2 in the original.

6 — Circumcision of Abraham; Circumcision of Christ; Circumcision of Isaac.

7 to 17 (inclusive) — the original subjects of 3 to 13.

18 — Isaiah's Woe to Jerusalem; Christ pitying Jerusalem; Jeremiah's Lamentation.

19 to 26 (inclusive) — the original subjects of 14 to 21.

27 has those of 23 in the original.

28— Lamech tormented by his two Wives ; Christ scourged ; Job afflicted by Satan.

29—A Concubine taking a King's crown off his head ; Christ mocked, and crowned with thorns ; Shimei insulting David.

30 and 31 are the same as 22 and 24 in the original.

31--Tubal Cain forging nails; Christ nailed to the Cross ; Isaiah sawn in two.

33 and 34 are the same as 25 and 26 in the original.

35 — The body of the King of Ai (hanged by Joshua) taken down; Christ taken from the Cross; the bodies of Saul's Sons taken down (II *Samuel*, 21. 13).

36—Adam and Eve mourning for Abel; Christ's dead body in the lap of his Mother; Naomi lamenting for her Sons.

37 to 50 (inclusive) have the subjects of 27 to 40 in the same order as the original.

Of the two editions with the text in German, each containing only forty pages, that of 1470 is reported by Ottley as "more modern" in style and executed in a slight manner. The other, with the date of 1471, or 1475, is in the British Museum : a weak imitation of the earlier book, only the designs used, and ill-used.

A fourth Block-Book worthy of our consideration, probably of later production, and certainly the best of the four, is the Ars Moriendi (the Art of Dying)—thus described by the Librarian of the British Museum.

(C. 48. i)—" A block-book consisting of twelve separate sheets of two leaves each printed on the inner side only, so that the *recto* of fol. 1 3 5 etc. and the *verso* of fol. 2 4 6 etc. are left blank, and fol. 2 and 3, and 4 and 5, etc. could be pasted together to form respectively a single leaf. The impression was taken in pale brown ink by rubbing [the old supposal]. There are eleven illustrations, each occupying a whole page, on the *verso* of fol. 3 5 7 etc.: the explanatory letter-press being given on the *recto* of fol. 4 6 8 etc. Fol. 1 *verso* and 2 *recto* contain an introduction in thirty and twenty nine lines respectively. Each leaf is surrounded by a border of three lines. . Without title-page or pagination. Fol. 13 *verso* has in the corner the sign V, which is the only signature in the book. This edition is believed to be the first edition of this often-repeated work," by reason of the beauty and originality of the designs and the sharpness of outline."

The whole book, with introductory notice from Mr. Bullen, the Keeper of the Printed

Ars Moriendi.

Books in the British Museum, has been reproduced in "fac-simile with the pen," for the Holbein Society, by Mr. F. C. Price. Admirably close indeed is the imitation; yet it is not fac-simile. Something of the touch of the draftsman, preserved in the cutting, and of value to an engraver or a print-lover, could not be rendered by the pen. The work, excellent as a translation, is not a fac-simile. Not even the more exact reproduction by photography here given (facing p. 57) is perfect, on account of some hollowness of the lines, seemingly occasioned by their having been traced.

A "fac-simile" with the pen.

This Museum copy is, I believe, the only perfect copy known. It was bought at the sale of the Weigel collection, at Leipsic, in 1872, for £1,072, 10s. The excellence of the engraving suggests, Mr. Bullen thinks, that it is of later date than the block-books we have been considering. "The manufacture of block-books," he remarks, "begun in Holland and afterward practised in Belgium, appears to have travelled, about the middle of the fifteenth century, into Germany and fixed itself at Cologne, where this edition was in all probability executed. Herr Weigel's copy [this in our Museum] was acquired by him, he informs us, from a private person in that city." The designs, Mr. Bullen adds, are "of the Lower Rhenish School of Art, practised at Cologne up to about the second quarter of the fifteenth century, when, according to Weigel and Zestermann, the native German art is shown to have been influenced by the school of Roger Van der Weyde."

Probable place of production.

The subject of the *Ars Moriendi* is of the five Temptations of a man during a mortal sickness,— Abandonment of Faith, Despair, Impatience, Vain-Glory, and Avarice: the Devil, by agency of his demons, at his work in five designs; in five alternate confronted by the man's Good Angel. The eleventh picture is of the sick man's death. I take in great measure from Mr. Bullen, not following him *verbatim*, a concise description of the eleven designs.

The subject of the book.

The first of the dying man's temptations is UNBELIEF. He is represented lying in bed naked (night-dresses not then in use) except for the bed-clothes, which cover him from the breast downward. He is emaciated in appearance, and his thin right arm lies upon the coverlet. In all the designs except the last the head of the bed is on our right hand as we look at the picture. At the bed-head, reckoning from right to left, three figures are seen; the Almighty Father, Christ, and the Virgin Mother. Next to the Virgin, in the centre of the picture, is a hairy demon attempting to pull the coverlet off the dying man. From the left upper corner descends another demon, with a scroll and the words —*Infernus* (for which Mr. Bullen would read *Infirmus*) *factus est*. Below this scroll are three doctors in consultation, one apparently "with good capon lined," a fine contrast to his patient. Elbowing the fat doctor, a third demon presents the sick man with a scroll and the legend—*Fac sicut Pagani!* and points to a king and a queen, at the foot of the bed, kneeling before an image on a pillar. A fourth demon, touching his left shoulder, suggests—*Interficias te ipse (ipsum)!* In front, below this scroll, are two figures smaller

Description of the designs.

He is now weak.

Do as the heathen do?

You may kill yourself!

than the rest, a woman, naked except at the loins, carrying a bunch of rods in one hand and a scourge in the other, and a man who seems to be cutting his throat with a knife. This first temptation is explained, in a page of text facing the picture, as the temptation of the devil against faith—*Temtacio dyaboli de fide.*

"With all this variety of figures," writes Mr. Bullen, and, I may add, notwithstanding some ignorance or neglect of perspective, "the composition of the subject is harmonious and impressive; the figures of the demons are at once grotesque and hideous; while the kneeling queen, in flowing drapery, adoring the Pagan image, is exceedingly graceful. The picture of the dying man thus exposed to the assaults of his ghostly enemies is well calculated to call forth the sympathy even of a generation like ours; how much more so when contemplated by men and women actually believing, as taught by their spiritual advisers, in the personality of Satan and the malignant demons that worked under his direction."

In the second picture the man's good angel comes to his rescue, standing in front of him with wings outspread, a full-length figure in graceful drapery, bearing a scroll with the words—*Sis firmus iside (in fide)!* Below, three discomfited beastly demons hurry off; two like dogs, one with a half-human head; the third a kind of composite maggot, with human face, a hand and a hoof. On the scrolls we see—*Fugiamus; Victi fuimus; Frustra laboravimus*. On the farther side of the bed, beginning from the foot, are Mary, Christ, God the Father, Moses (foolishly supposed by Mr. Sotheby, says Mr. Bullen, to be Judas Iscariot), and glorified saints. The opposite explanatory text has for heading—*Bona inspiracio angeli de fide* (the angel's good inspiration for faith).

The second temptation is to DESPAIR. The demons reappear; six of them now, with increase of hideousness. *Ecce peta (peccata) tua!* is on the scroll of one, holding up also a broad-sheet of accusations; *Periurus es!* is the indictment of a second, pointing back to a young man, against whom the dying may have sworn falsely; a third, close by his head, with the words—*Fornicatus es!* points to a woman who is standing by the young man; in front, at the bed's foot, a fourth demon, with a bag of money in one hand, has just stripped off the shirt from a now quite naked wretch sitting on the ground (had the dying sinner robbed him?]; while a fifth, who brandishes a sword, directs attention to a dying man over whom hangs the legend—*Occidisti!* Another man, meanly clad, sits in the right hand corner, and over him the sixth devil holds the words—*Avare vixisti!* YOUR SINS!—Perjuror! Lecher! Thief! Murderer! Usurer! Well may it be called a temptation to despair: *Temptacio dyaboli de despacione.*

Again at the bed-side is the sorely needed guardian angel. He points behind him to Saul of Tarsus, on the way to Damascus, horseman and horse flung to the ground at the bed's foot, while at the right corner opposite a dog-like demon slinks off, confessing—*Victoria michi nulla!* and another would hide under the bed. On the head-board of the

See friends.

bed perches the cock that warned Peter, who stands by the dying man's pillow, holding his key. At Peter's side is Mary Magdalen with her box of spikenard; and in the rear, at the upper corner of the picture, the Penitent Thief on his Cross. All these pardoned

Never despair!

sinners are shown for his behoof. *Nequaquam desperes!* says the angel.

The fifth design and third temptation is of IMPATIENCE: *Temptacio dyabole de ipaciéria.* The dying man's arms are out of bed; his right foot also, vigorously applied against his nurse or doctor, who looks back in astonishment and anger. A woman behind, higher up in the picture, probably the wife of the impatient, compassionately extends her hand toward him as if to calm his irritation, with the words (always on a scroll)—*Ecce quam*

See how much he suffers!

(quantam) penit patitr! In the front of the picture is a younger woman, who may be the daughter, carrying away in one hand a full cup, in the other a plate with what looks like the leg of a fowl. At her feet is a table which the angry man has overthrown; and cup and spoon and knife are scattered on the floor: he has been too fretful to take his meal.

How well I've deceived him!

A single devil graces the scene, with the legend—*Us bene decepi eum!*

Bona inspiracio angeli de paciencia. The hands of the calmed are folded as in prayer; with penitential hair-pillow under his head he listens to the angel, who has resumed his sway and stands beside him with an expression of satisfaction. At the bed-head stands Christ crowned with thorn and holding the rod and scourge; beside him God the Father with an arrow in one hand and a scourge in the other. Nearer the foot of the bed are St. Barbara with her tower, St. Catherine with her wheel, and (above them, the three forming a pyramidal group) St. Lawrence with his gridiron. St. Stephen, his cloak full of stones, is at the bed's foot. Between Stephen and the angel we see a devil escaping

I am caught!
Lost labours!

under the bed, with *Sum captivatus;* and *Labores amisi!* is on the scroll that overhangs another turning heels over head, as though about to dive into a square hole at a corner of the picture.*

The temptation to VAIN-GLORY is the subject of the seventh picture: horrible in the exceeding ugliness of the fiends. Five of them surround the bed. They offer crowns.

You're firm in faith!

One urges him to boast—*gloriare;* another subtily flatters him,—*Tu es firmus in fide!*

You've earned the crown!

Coronam meruisti! hints a third; *Exalta te-ipsum!* says a fourth; and the fifth chimes in

Exalt yourself!
You patiently persevered?

with—*In paciencia perseverasti! Temptacio dyaboli de vana gloria.* In the background are God the Saviour, and the interceding Mother, saints behind, and a group of children (redeemed souls?) between the dying man and God.

Three angels now (in our eighth design) may well be needed to reclaim him: one on either side of the bed, one at the foot. The angel by his pillow on the farther side has

---

* Which, however, is only a mark for the binder, denoting the beginning of a second half of the book, a dragon tail-piece at the bottom of the text showing the end of the first half. Each half of the book has twelve pages, unbacked. The dragon will be seen at the end of our chapter.

nuncio
nolite marie
Quid faciam

on his scroll—*Sis humilis!* The second, the principal figure, occupying the centre of the picture, with steadfast gaze upon him, points to a hideous Satan-mouth, the flaming mouth of Hell devouring three naked figures. Above is written—*Superbos punio.* At the angelic feet sprawls a demon with the legend—*Victus sum;* another demon creeps under the bed. The third angel is at the bed-foot, about half the height of the picture; and directly above him, reaching nearly to the top, is St. Anthony with bell and crozier. God the Father, the Son, and the Virgin Mother, in the clouds, and the Holy Ghost in front as a dove with outspread wings and a halo round its head, fill a small space above the angels and to the right of St. Anthony. The design is full, and grandly treated.

The fifth and last temptation, AVARICE, *Temptacio dyaboli de avaricia,* the ninth of the designs, differs from the rest of the set. The lower half of the picture is taken up by a two-storied warehouse and a stable. A servant is leading a horse into the stable; and in the lower floor of the warehouse we see a diminutive figure (near but made small to seem distant) drawing wine from one of a row of casks. Regardless of perspective, the upper part of the bed with the sick man is shown above the stable-roof. A devil, taller than the stable, points to the warehouse, toward which floats a scroll with the words—*Intende thesauro!* Two demons on the far side of the bed direct attention to a group, a man, three women, and a child, doubtless the dying man's relations or friends, with the words—*Provideas amicis!*

Again appears the angel with good counsel: *Non sis avarus!* [For the *sis* a plug has been inserted—*es* perhaps first cut by mistake.] The crouching fiend for reply has but —*Quid faciam?* A second angel holds a curtain, screening from the dying two figures quitting the place, a woman and a man, disappointed expectants of his wealth, perhaps only his wife and the physician. This angel's legend is—*Ne intendas amicis!* A figure standing among sheep surely means the Good Shepherd, who will provide for those left behind. Saints or holy women are there also to console and cheer him. The figures of the Crucified and the Mother of Sorrows may have a similar intent, telling the sufferer of suffering overgone.

The remainder I may give almost in Mr. Bullen's words.

The final picture in the series (No. 11) represents the sick man in his supreme agony. In this design his position is different from that in the others: the bed's head being now turned to the left (our left), instead of on the right as heretofore. In his right hand is a lighted candle, which a monk supports with his left while using the right to emphasize his words. And now the last breath is yielded up, and with it the soul, of the size of a child (born again), escapes from the body and is received by an angel, the foremost of four high up in the left-hand corner of the picture. To the right of this group, and just above the monk, are three figures, Peter with the sword, the Magdalen with her box of spikenard, and the Blessed Virgin. Behind are the nimbi of eight saints, the heads of

two of them partly given. To their right is a full-length figure of the Saviour extended
on the Cross. On the right of this again is St. John, almost full-length, his hands in an
attitude of prayer; while above him are seen the heads of two other male figures, each
with a nimbus, and only the nimbi of two others just above. In the lowest part of the
picture are six ugly demons, raging with disappointment at not getting possession of the
man's soul after all their so cunningly devised temptations.

In the last page, of the Latin text, directions are given for prayers to be used by the
dying. First he is to implore Almighty God, of His ineffable mercy and by the virtue
of His passion, to receive him to Himself. Next he is directed to intreat the mediation
of the glorious Virgin Mary. Next to invoke help of all angels, especially his guardian
angel; and then of the apostles, martyrs, confessors, and virgins,—addressing himself
chiefly to any among them whom he has formerly held in particular veneration. Special
prayers and sentences are then mentioned which the dying is exhorted to repeat. If he
can not do this himself, the bystanders are to do it for him. And a recommendation is
given that every one, when expecting the approach of death, should secure the presence
of some faithful friend, to assist him in his last hours with his prayers and exhortations.
" But, alas!" says the writer, (in his abbreviated Latin), "how few are there who in the
hour of death faithfully aid their neighbours with questionings, admonition, and prayer!
Hence it happens that, as the dying persons themselves do not (in general) wish to die
just yet, their salvation is often miserably imperiled." So the *Ars Moriendi* concludes.

Of our four " Block" Books only three, as already said, show any beauty of engraving;
and of one of them I can give no fair presentment. The best cuts of the *Canticum* are
printed too lightly to be well photographed. But these cuts, though very delicate, want
the varied and expressive line of the cuts in the *Biblia Pauperum* and the *Ars Moriendi*.
In all three the drawings must have been very lovely, so much of beauty yet remaining.
Again I speak only of the Print Room edition of the *Biblia*. The other copies of that
are at an immense distance: cut from either transfers or tracings by very inferior hands.
Clean and firm work, mechanically true but tasteless, I find in the *Apocalypsis*, as also in
some of the *Helgen*; but only in the three books can I recognize the work of an artist-
engraver, some enthusiast monk perhaps, with time and care to cut his own designs.

CHAPTER IV

WOOD OR METAL

RESS-WORK with movable types was now, in this latter half of the fifteenth century [dating Gutenberg's invention at 1436 and his first great work, the printing of the Bible, at about 1450], able to assist and in one respect supersede the engraver: that is, the whole book no longer had to be cut in wood; and the Block-Book gave place to the Book of modern use. Still block-books were executed, perhaps the work of engravers who were printers also, who might have presses without having type. Such books seem to have been of a sorry character. *Die Kunst Cyromantia*, a work on Palmistry, bearing the date of 1448, which may be the date of writing, is a book of this inferior description : a block-book, but printed at press on both sides of the paper. A few others may be named, though of no more worth :— *Planetenbuch* (Book of Planets) with their influence on human life, printed about 1470 ; *Defensorium inviolata virginitatis beatæ Virginis Mariæ* (Defence of the inviolate virginity of the blessed Virgin Mary), of the same date ; the 1471 German edition of the *Biblia Pauperum ; Der Entkrist* (Antichrist), with thirty-nine cuts, 1472,— the first edition on only one side of the paper ; and sundry almanacs of Nurnberg, Mentz, and Leipsic, with outline cuts for colouring, between 1474 and 1490. Of import in the history of books, yet without interest as specimens of engraving, they may be left out of our consideration here. Nor need I enter into any detailed account of the great beginning of typography through the invention of type-founding. All that is required here is to note the arrival of the new era in which the printer has become the book-maker, the engraver's business henceforth confined to the province of illustration.

The first printer's book with a printer's name and date, and with supposed wood-cuts, is a PSALTER, issuing, in 1457, from the press of Fust and Schoeffer. Fournier, a type-founder and sometime engraver, speaks of it as having been printed from wood letters :

but De Vinne denies this, positively asserting that "no book was ever printed in Europe with small types of wood." Chiefly notable for us in this *Psalter* are some initial letters, in two colours, red and blue, which have been much admired as marvelous specimens of both wood-cutting and printing. The largest letter, a B, at the beginning of the book, three inches and a half square, has a figure of a hound chasing a bird, showing white on blue in the upright stroke of the letter, and flower-ornamentation in the same manner in the curved portion: with a ground of abundant scroll-work in thin red line and an over-running thin red scroll extending through the whole length of the page. In some copies we find the colours reversed, the letter being red and the scroll blue. This B [of which fair copies are given in the first volume of Dibdin's *Bibliotheca Spenceriana* and Savage's *Hints on Decorative Printing*,—it is given also by De Vinne], this and other large letters in the book Chatto takes without doubt to be engraved in wood, though he is of opinion that they "can not be considered an extraordinary instance of skill even at that period." For myself, I am convinced that this letter B, and some others in the *Psalter*, were cut with a graver in copper or other metal, since I find the delicacy and purity of line in the outline parts superior to any wood-work done with a knife. I am not aware of anything so beautifully regular throughout as the scroll-work of these large letters until we come to the French *Heures*, some of which, we now know, were engraved in relief on copper. I speak only of the large initials. Some small letters, scattered through the book, may be from wood or metal; many appear to be by hand, painted so dexterously as to have deceived the printer Savage when he first examined them. Afterlooking, he discovered that in the small letters "the beautiful red was not printed," and "the delicate blue was painted." (*Hints on Decorative Printing*, p. 50.) In De Vinne's opinion, the work clearly is "an imitation not only of the copyist's but of the illuminator's work on a manuscript:" a scarcely fair advertisement of the new art of printing. The book only here concerns us because so long admired for its "engravings in wood."

A Fable-book—*Liber Similitudinis*, printed by Albert Pfister at Bamberg in 1461, is considered to be the first book printed with movable types which is illustrated by wood cuts of figure subjects: one hundred of them, rudely drawn and of the roughest possible cutting. According to Wace, they were cut on metal; Passavant thinks them on wood. They have a look of metal; but, whether wood or metal cut after the manner of wood (that is in relief), they are devoid of either artistic or mechanical merit. In 1462 Pfister printed his *Four Histories*—of Joseph, Daniel, Judith, and Esther. He is also credited with a *Poor Preachers' Bible* (perhaps the *Biblia* referred to by Paul of Prague); *Plaints against Death*: and other works, worthy only of disesteem. He appears to have been a wood-cutter and colourer, and at one time employed by Gutenberg, from whom he may have obtained types with which to set up in business at Bamberg.

Very superior to the Pfister cuts, and these, I doubt not, in wood, are the Letters of an ALPHABET in the Print Room of the British Museum, to which Passavant assigns an uncertain but acceptable date of 1464. The letters of the *Alphabet* are formed of figures, human or brute, grotesque but not ungraceful, good in drawing, fairly cut; printed in yellowish brown ink and unbacked. The Museum copy consists of nineteen letters: B C D E F G H I K L M N O P Q R X Y Z, part of a torn A, and a page of flower-scroll, perhaps to make up with the missing S T and U, or V, the full set or form of twenty-four. Ottley thinks they are of Dutch or Flemish designing and, because of two words, *London* and *Bethensted* on the L, and other writing by the sometime English owner, imagines "they were engraved in England." Chatto deems them French, by the costume, and from a French rebus in the K, a letter of four figures: a lover kneeling at his lady's feet for the upright line; the other portions

formed by two rejected suitors, an old man going sky-ward and a loutish young fellow flung disdainfully to the ground. The successful fine gentleman offers the lady a ring, and holds forth a scroll with the motto—*Mon Ⓒ aues;*—You have my heart!

The first press-printed book really important for its wood-engraving is the *Speculum Humanæ Salvationis* (or Mirror of Human Salvation), a small folio with neither date nor printer's name. It has been placed wrongly among block-books, since three of the four known editions (which we may call primary, to keep them clear from later issues) and part of the fourth have been printed from movable types. Of these four editions two are in Latin and two are in Dutch. In the Latin copies the book consists of sixty-three leaves, five of an introduction (the Dutch sixty-two, the introduction taking only four) and fifty-eight of wood-cuts and text, the cuts to the width of the page, occupying its upper half, two subjects in each framed in architectural borders, and the text of Latin verse in two columns beneath. The purport of the book is apparent in the first lines under the first subject—*Casus Luciferi* (Lucifer's fall from heaven). I may freely English them thus :—

> The Mirror of Man's Salvation maketh plain
> His fall and how he may return again.

The cuts are in brown ink, printed only on one side of the leaf, and in three editions separately from the text, of which the ink is black. In the fourth edition twenty pages have both text and pictures engraved. The separate printing seems to be shown in the Grenville Library copy by the two not being in register. Differences in impression and colour give the same indication : though these might arise from the blocks not standing so high as the type. Even the out-of-register might be occasioned by bad locking up of a block not properly squared. De Vinne states positively that the brown ink is water colour and can be partially defaced by a moist sponge, while the black ink is permanent oil-colour which has stained the paper with the greenish tinge of oil badly prepared. He says also that the types were printed after the cuts, proved by their overlapping them. He continues :—" The provision of black ink for the types and brown for the cuts seems unnecessary, but Van der Linde's explanation is plausible : that the oily black ink used on the types may have been rejected for the cuts because its greasy surface interfered with the brush of the colourist." Or may it have been (as before suggested) that brown ink was considered more suitable to the after colouring ? De Vinne however thinks the brown ink was once black ; "the variability of colour, so frequently remarked in all block books, is the certain indication of a faded black writing ink," too fluid to be used on the metal types which required an oily ink.

His farther words will be readily appreciated by printer and engraver. " The unequal indentation of the letters indicates that the types were not of an uniform height. Nor is it probable that the engravings, at the head of every page, were always truly flat and of precisely the same height as the type. They were pieces of flat board, which must have warped with every change from heat to cold, or from dampness to dryness. We find in these irregularities the probable reason for the employment of two distinct methods of impression. The types required strong, and the wood-cuts weak impression. If it had been graduated to suit the wood-cuts, the print of the types would not have been visible ; if enough impression had been given to face the types, the wood-cuts in the same form would have been crushed." He adds :—" The neglect of engraving in wood by the early typographers has frequently been noticed as a strange fact. It was, no doubt, induced by the difficulties encountered in trying to print wood-cuts with type. The wood would warp and crack in spite of all precautions. The evil would be but partially checked by diminishing the size of the blocks. To evade the annoyance produced by warped blocks some printers engraved large illustrations on separate pieces of wood, which were fitted roughly to each other, but not conjoined. Other printers printed the wood-cuts of their books by a separate impression. As these illustrations were printed in the same black ink which was used for the text the double impression is rarely ever noticed even by the practical printer."

The *Speculum* appears to be of Dutch or Flemish origin; and according to Passavant, who considers the designs are of the school of Van Eyck, not earlier than 1460. Chatto thinks it was no earlier than 1472. "As the first edition was printed subsequently to the discovery of the art of printing with movable types, and as it was probably printed in the Low Countries, where the typographical art was first introduced about 1472, I can discover no reason for believing the work was executed before that period. Santander, who was so well acquainted with the progress of typography in Belgium and Holland, is of opinion that it is not of an earlier date than 1480. In 1483 John Veldener printed at Cologne a quarto edition in which are the same cuts as in the earlier folio. In order to adapt the cuts to this smaller edition he had each block sawn in two through the centre pillar forming the separation between the two compartments. Veldener's quarto, which has the text printed upon both sides of the paper, from movable types, contains twelve more cuts than the older editions, designed and executed in the same style." (*Treatise*, pp. 106-7.) Veldener also printed in the same year another quarto edition, without the additional cuts.

This *Speculum*, sometimes ascribed to Laurence Coster of Haarlem, who is credited also with the invention of typography,* has, writes Chatto, "been more frequently the subject of discussion among bibliographers, and writers who have treated of the origin of printing, than any other work. A great proportion however of what has been written on the subject consists of groundless speculation; and the facts elicited, compared with the conjectures propounded, are as 'two grains of wheat to a bushel of chaff.' It would be a waste of time to recite at length the various opinions which have been entertained with respect to the date of this book, the manner in which the text was printed, and the printer's name." Here, I think, we may be content with knowing it to be of later date, not much later, than our most important block-books; and value it as one of the earliest and certainly the most considerable of the beginnings of what we call illustrated books.

---

* Coster, we are told by Junius, discovered the art of printing through having accidentally cut upon a piece of beech-bark some letters for the amusement of his grandchildren. Scriverius has a full account of the discovery:—how Coster, walking in a wood, "his custom of an afternoon," idly picked up the bit of beech or oak lying at his feet and, after pleasing himself by carving some letters upon it, wrapped it in paper and laid him down to sleep. The while he slept there was a shower of rain. Awaking, he saw that the paper, moistened by the rain, had taken an impression from his letters. Considering this, etc.

This *Speculum* appears to have originated in an old manuscript, judged by Heinecken to be of the twelfth century. The manuscript consisted of forty-five chapters in Latin rhyme, with an introduction. Each of the first forty-two chapters had four subjects, a principal one and three illustrative of it. For each of these chapters were two designs, divided into two compartments, as in our printed version. The last three chapters had each eight subjects. The whole number of pictorial compartments therefore amounted to one hundred and ninety-two. The printed *Speculum* contains only one hundred and sixteen, two pictures on each of the fifty-eight leaves. All but five are either from the Bible, including the Apocryphal Books, or illustrative of some tradition or dogma of the Church. Even the five from profane story are so employed. The following is a list of the subjects engraved.

1 — The Fall of Lucifer; the Creation of Eve.

2 — Adam and Eve forbidden to eat the fruit of the Tree of Knowledge; Eve seduced by the Serpent.

3 — Eve eating the Forbidden Fruit; the Expulsion from Paradise.

4 — Adam digging and Eve spinning; Noah's Ark.

5 — The Birth of Mary foretold; King Astyages' Dream of a Vineyard.

6 — A Garden and a Fountain (emblematic of the Virgin); the Prophecy of Balaam.

7 — The Nativity of the glorious Virgin Mary; Christ's Genealogical Tree.

8 — "A Closed Gate signifies the blessed Virgin Mary"; Solomon's Temple signifies the same.

9 — Mary dedicated to the Temple; A golden table offered in the Temple of the Sun.

10 — Jephthah sacrificing his Daughter; Queen Semiramis in the Hanging Garden.

11 — Marriage of the Virgin; Marriage of Tobias and Sara.

12 — A Tower, called *Baris (the Egyptians' Boat of the Dead)*, signifies Mary; Shields hung by David on the wall (II *Samuel*, VII, 8).

13 — The Annunciation; Moses and the Burning Bush.

14 — Gideon's Fleece; Rebekah giving drink to Abraham's Servant.

15 — Nativity of Christ; the Dream of Pharaoh's Cup-bearer.

16 — Aaron's Rod flourishes; the Sybil prophesies of the Virgin and the Child.

17 — Adoration of the Magi; the Magi seeing the new Star in the East.

18 — The Three Warriors bringing water to David; the Throne of Solomon.

19 — The Presentation of the child Jesus in the Temple; the Ark, signifying Mary.

20 — The Temple Candlestick; the child Samuel dedicated to the Lord.

21 — The Flight into Egypt, the Idols falling; the Egyptians make an Image of the Virgin and the Child.

22 — Moses breaking up Pharaoh's crown; Nebuchadnezzar's Dream of the Statue.

23 — Jesus baptised by John in Jordan; the Sea of Brass before the Temple.

24—Naaman cured of his leprosy; Jordan dried up for the passage of the sons of God.
25—Christ tempted by the Devil; Daniel destroying Bel and the Dragon.
26—David killing Goliath; David killing the bear and the lion.
27—Mary Magdalen in the house of Simon; King Manasseh's penitence in captivity.
28—The Return of the Prodigal Son; Nathan reproving David for his adultery.
29—Christ weepeth for Jerusalem; Jeremiah's Lamentation over Jerusalem.
30—David's Triumph; Heliodorus beaten with rods.
31—The Last Supper; Manna given to the Israelites in the Desert.
32—Jews eating the Paschal Lamb; Melchizedek bringing bread and wine to Abram.
33—The Soldiers, sent to take Christ, fall before him; Samson slaying the Philistines.
34—Sanger kills six hundred men with a ploughshare; David kills eight hundred.
35—Christ betrayed by Judas; Joab treacherously killeth Amasa.
36—Saul returneth David evil for good; Cain killing Abel.
37—Christ spit upon and buffeted; Hur "suffocated with the spittle of the Jews."
38—Ham deriding his father Noah; the Philistines mocking blind Samson.
39—Christ bound and scourged; Achior bound to a tree by the servants of Holofernes.
40—Lamech plagued by his bad wives; Job troubled by his Wife and Satan.
41—Christ crowned with thorn; A Concubine places a King's crown on her own head.
42—Shimei cursing David; the King of Ammon shaming David's Messengers.
43—Christ bearing his Cross; Isaac carrying the wood for his own sacrifice.
44—The Heir thrown out of the Vineyard and slain; Joshua's Spies bringing grapes.
45—Christ nailed to the Cross; Tubal-Cain superintending the iron-forgers.
46—Isaiah sawn in two; the King of Moab sacrificing his son on the wall.
47—Christ on the Cross; Nebuchadnezzar's Dream of the Tree.
48—Codrus gives his life for his people; Eleazar kills the Elephant. (1 *Maccab.*, vi, 46.)
49—The Descent from the Cross ("Mary's grief"); Jacob mourning for Joseph.
50—Adam and Eve lamenting the death of Abel; Naomi weeping for her sons.
51—Christ buried; David's grief at the death of Abner.
52—Joseph let down into the well; Jonah swallowed by the whale.
53—Christ's Descent into Hell; the Israelites freed from Pharaoh.
54—Abraham quitteth Ur; Lot going out from Sodom.
55—The Resurrection; Samson carrying off the gates of Gaza.
56—Jonah thrown up by the whale; the Corner Stone which the builders had rejected.
57—The Last Judgment; the Parable of the Unforgiving Creditor.
58—The Parable of the Ten Virgins; the Handwriting on the Wall.

It will be seen from this Table of Contents how closely the *Speculum* resembles the *Biblia Pauperum* in both scope and treatment. Some writers judge it to be earlier than that, ignoring the fact that the first printing was with types. The designs themselves,

The *Speculum Humanae Salvationis.*

I think, testify to a later production, though it is possible that in both works the designs were borrowed from the same source, the manuscript before noticed. Still, some seem to me to be copies of the *Biblia*. In the two renderings of *Moses and the Burning Bush* the design is almost identical: only the drawing of the *Speculum* has not been reversed. There is just a slight difference in the action of taking off the shoes. What alteration else is in the *Speculum* cut seems only done to suit the squarer shape; and it is neither so largely treated nor so vigorous as the other. Again, in the cut of *Gideon's Fleece* the weaker and, I think, the later artist is manifest. The composition is not quite so close: Gideon's attitude is a little altered; the angel comes down from the cloud; the dew-drops are added. The whole arrangement may be pleasanter and more learned; but strength and a sense of originality have been lost. *Ham deriding Noah* has also a borrowed look, with some weak "improvement." The design of the *Biblia* is more to the purpose. *Jesus baptized by John* I take to be another copy. It is scarcely altered at all, except in some lines of the water and a bare leg given to the Baptist, and is in every respect inferior to the *Biblia* cut. I agree with Ottley in thinking some of the later designs of the *Speculum* series are by a different artist. The engraving also, though it has little character, is most likely by several hands.

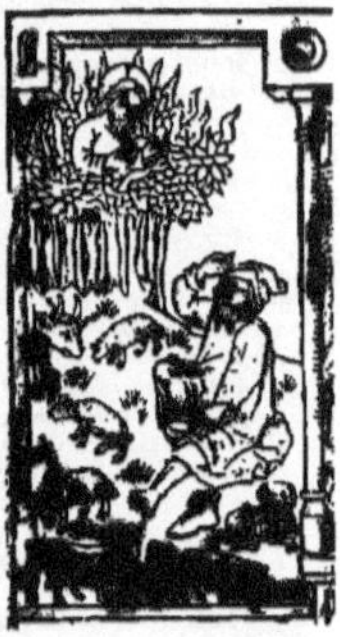

Moses and the Burning Bush: from the *Biblia Pauperum.*

Observations by Ottley.

And here I can not but take notice of certain misleading observations of Mr. Ottley. He says (—*History of Wood-Engraving*, p. 155), "I have observed in a former page that there is reason to believe that the *Biblia Pauperum*, the *Canticles*, and the cuts of the *Speculum Salvationis* were in great part engraved by the same wood-engraver, although from the designs of different artists. This remark, however, must be understood with limitations. There is little doubt that the principal wood-engravers of those times had pupils who assisted them in executing the extensive works confided to their care. That part of a cut which required little skill, or that entire design which least captivated the taste of the master, was often entrusted to the scholar, and hence those occasional dissimilarities of execution which a careful observer will discover in different parts of the same block-book (especially in the accessorial parts) although their general style be the same, and though they bear every

hir annunciatur ihs p angelu virgini marie
Dns apparuit moysi in rubo ardenti

Delph gedeois impletu e dra siccu manente
Rebeca villico abrahe potu tribuebat

evidence of their having proceeded from the workshop of one master artist. Several of the cuts in the *Speculum* bear so striking a resemblance to some of those in the *Biblia Pauperum* as to leave little doubt that they were engraved by the same hand; others in their mode of execution exactly correspond with some of those in the *Book of Canticles.* Upon the whole, therefore, I am of opinion that the same engraver who was employed to execute the blocks of the *Biblia Pauperum* was also, but at a later period, entrusted with those of the *Book of Canticles*, and lastly, or about the same time, with those of the *Speculum*, which work it is probable he did not live to complete."

Farther on (p. 230,) he reiterates his notion of the "resemblance as to the executive part of the work, or what we may term the handling of the graver,* although the artist who made the designs appears to have been a different person"; with later observations by which he finds himself "justified in the conclusion that the three works in question were executed in the work-shop of the same master wood-engraver."

It is hard to have to deal seriously with the plausibility of such errant ignorance, this babble of master-engravers and pupils and occasions of dissimilarity. As an engraver I aver that there is not the slightest ground for Mr. Ottley's conclusion. The observer is credited with too keen perception of unlikeness; and his likenesses (as of a "peculiarity of touch in the mode of executing foliage"—a mere form for colour) amount to nought. It would be clear to an artist that the engraver of the copy I mark as the best could not have descended to the level of the *Speculum*. For other copies, I would only remark that the similarity of the work of poor mechanics is insufficient basis for proof of personality. Better or worse work may indicate a different workman; but that two things of general and most easy practice have been done with equal inexpertness is scarcely an argument that they were done by the same person. This is all the pith of Ottley's opinion.

The practice of introducing cuts into printed books seems to have been first adopted at Augsburg, at which city, in 1471, Gunther Zainer printed a translation in German of the *Legenda Sanctorum*, with figures of the Saints "coarsely engraved in wood." Chatto believes this to be the first book after Pfister's tracts printed in Germany having wood cuts and a date. Italy followed closely with Valturius' *De Re Militari*, printed at Verona in 1472. In this year also Zainer brought out a second volume of the *Legends* with cuts; and other illustrated books were issued by him in the next three years. His example was followed by his fellow-printers, John Bamler and John Schlusser; and by them and Anthony Sorg, who began to print at Augsburg about 1475, more books with cuts were printed there than at any place before 1480. In 1477 Sorg printed the first Bible with

The Speculum Humanæ Salvationis.

Ottley's fancied similarities.

His conclusion unwarrantable.

The peculiar foliage.

Early book-cuts in Germany and Italy.

---

* No graver, but the knife only, being used by the wood-engraver of that day. See cut, at page 38, of a knife in its handle bound round with cord, as fitted for use: the length of the whole about six inches.

wood-cuts, and in 1483 on account of the Council of Constance, with a thousand cuts.
The use of cuts in books became in a few years general throughout Germany. Before
1500 in Augsburg alone there were twenty master-printers; and their use of wood-cuts
was so considerable as to provoke the jealousy of the block-book engravers, and to call
forth a law compelling the printers to procure their cuts of the older practitioners. From
this it would seem that the printer had begun to engrave for himself; which may partly
account for the poorness of the cuts in the early printed books. Of these books I may
briefly chronicle a few more, though scarcely deserving any notice for their illustrations,
be they in wood or metal. "Coarsely executed" is Didot's just judgment of the lot.

Wood or metal: in either case relief-engraving to be printed from the surface. Since
the discovery at Basle of metal blocks of the sixteenth century, says Passavant, there is
no doubt of the use at that date of copper for engraving in relief. Older engravings of
the same nature were, he adds, executed in pewter, a metal softer and more easily cut,
which "came into use in Germany during the twelfth century." That many of the cuts
we have been accustomed to call wood-cuts have been engraved in metal, of some kind,
is very manifest: manifest to an engraver, if not to a connoisseur who is not an expert.
Certain appearances indicating the use of a graver instead of a knife (and metal-work is

THE FLIGHT INTO EGYPT — FROM THE MEDITATIONS OF JOHN OF TURRECREMATA.

all graver-work) enable the practised eyes of the engraver to detect differences hardly to be observed by even an artist-examiner. But these, whether in rough work or work more finished or minute, are not always so clear as to be positively distinguished.

The *Meditationes Johannis de Turrecremata*, printed at Rome, in 1467, by a German, Ulrich Hahn of Ingolstadt, has been generally considered to be the first book with wood cuts printed in Italy. But I have no hesitation in deciding that Passavant was right in believing them to be in metal: some soft metal, pewter or other, as will be plain to any engraver from the graver-indentations seen in the bridle of the ass and elsewhere. The cut I have given is from the edition of 1473; but this also was issued by Hahn, and the cuts are the same as those in the edition of 1467.

The first book with wood-cuts printed in Italy is probably the Treatise by Valturius *De Re Militari*, 1472: containing a number of rude cuts, some large, chiefly diagrams, representing engines of war. The only reason for noticing them here is that they are surely cut in wood. I am doubtful of the cuts in Caxton's books, printed between 1474 and 1491: the *Game and Playe of the Chesse*, the *Mirrour of the World*, the *Golden Legend*, the *Fables of Æsop*, Chaucer's *Canterbury Tales*, etc. If they are wood, whether executed by foreign hands or, as judged by Chatto, "the first-fruits of English wood-engraving," they mark about the lowest scale of xylographic accomplishment. We need only note that the second edition of the *Game and Playe of the Chesse* is the first English book with cuts in wood or after the manner of wood; and that some of the cuts, in that, or in the later books, may be of English workmanship. Supposing the designs to be English, it could hardly have been necessary to send abroad for the cutting.

After the *Block-Books* and the *Speculum* the first undoubted wood-engraving important enough to arrest our attention is a frontispiece to *Breydenbach's Travels*, the first edition (in Latin) printed at Mentz by Erhard Reuwich in 1486. Bernhard von Breydenbach was a canon of the cathedral of Mentz; and his book is an account of his pilgrimage to the Holy Land. He illustrates it with views of the places he passed through or visited, Venice, Corfu, Jerusalem, etc., large wood-cuts, so large as to require folding, the view of Venice over five feet long. Some smaller cuts are printed in the text. None of the illustrations are remarkable for the cutting. The main importance of the frontispiece is that we observe in it a new difficulty for the engraver. The drawing, more minute and elaborate than the usual designs of the period, has been enriched in two or three places with crossed lines. It is the first instance of a deliberate use of this enriching; and the little there is of it, in the shields and parts of the drapery, must have tried the patience if not much exercising the skill of the engraver. In speaking of the engraving I again have to differ from Mr. Chatto's judgment. He judges that the views "with respect to the manner of their execution are superior to every thing of the kind which previously had appeared;" and enthusiastically lauds the frontispiece as "the finest wood-engraving up to that date," the engraver as "one of the best wood-engravers of the period." The views may be praised for a certain regularity and thinness of line; but even in the frontispiece the *engraving* is not equal to that of our best block-books.

Durer's master, Michael Wohlgemuth, producer of the *Nurnberg Chronicle*, a fair folio printed at Nurnberg by Anthony Koburger in 1493, has been sometimes credited with being the initiator or the inventor of this cross-line improvement. Ottley writes:—" It appears anciently to have been the practice of those masters who furnished designs for the engravers to work from, carefully to avoid all cross-hatchings, which, it is probable, were considered beyond the Xylographist's power to represent. Wohlgemuth perceived that, though difficult, this was not impossible, and in the cuts of the *Nurnberg Chronicle*, the execution of which (besides furnishing the designs) he doubtless superintended, a successful attempt was first made to imitate the bold hatchings of pen-drawing, crossing each other, as occasion prompted the designer, in various directions. To him belongs the praise of having been the first who duly appreciated the powers of this art; and it is more than probable that he proved with his own hand, to the subordinate artists under him, the practicability of the style of workmanship which he required." (*Inquiry*, p. 755.) He is incorrect in both suppositions: it is not probable that Wohlgemuth so engraved in wood; and the cross-hatching of the Breydenbach frontispiece anticipates Wohlgemuth's perception of cross-line value. The rest of Mr. Ottley's paragraph (the careful avoiding, the successful attempt, the first due appreciation of the powers of this art, and the praise thereto belonging) is mere verbiage. His exaggeration of the importance of his difficult but not impossible procedure invents a picture which for its exactness may be likened to Breydenbach's Unicorn, "depicted as we saw him in the Holy Land."

The *Nurnberg World-Chronicle*, not engraved by Wohlgemuth, but the designs, with supervision of the engravings, by him and Wilhelm Pleydenwurff, "mathematical men skilled in the art of painting," is a very notable book if we only consider the number of its illustrations: over two thousand: views of cities, subjects from the Bible and profane history, and portraits, of kings and saints and other great folk (from Adam), scattered profusely through the text, sometimes ranged from top to bottom of a page, sometimes across it, or a page filled with them. But "two thousand illustrations" will not mean so many cuts, some being used eight or ten times: the portraits serving generally, Thales, Paris, Dante, having the same head; and places being depicted with a like impartiality. Little need be said of the cuts. They are rude and coarse; and, though they charmed Dr. Dibdin, are not incorrectly described by Chatto, Dr. Willshire agreeing, as rubbish, —"executed for the most part very negligently," says Passavant. Even a page-cut, the Glorification of the Son, which Dr. Willshire excepts as "perhaps the best specimen of Wohlgemuth's power as an engraver," is but a poor affair. The book shows no advance beyond earlier knife-work, and has but little interest for us as a specimen of engraving.

Called the founder of the Nurnberg School of wood-engraving, meaning that to him we owe the addition of cross-lines, some understanding of the value of colour and solid blacks, the extra colour perhaps in some measure due to haste in drawing, partly also to boldness of hand, for Wohlgemuth was an accomplished artist, evidence nowhere appears of his having engraved in wood. Certainly he may in idle hours have tried his hand on a block, or he may have cut some ill-drawn or doubtful part not easy for a *formschneider* to amend or understand (I have seen the poet Hood do so much to his wood-drawing), but such amateur-work would not warrant us in calling him a wood-engraver. Neither Wohlgemuth nor Durer could have found time to do any quantity of wood-cutting; and there is a yet stronger reason against their doing it,—the practised hand of an ordinary cutter would be surer than the draftsman's own. A large proportion of the Durer wood work is far too well done to have been executed by him. There is nothing in the cuts of the *Chronicle* to lead us to suspect even the unaccustomed hand of an artist.[*]

Good work we shall yet find in one book before we begin a new century with Durer. That one book is the *Hypnerotomachia Poliphili*, Francesco Colonna's romance of the

"Strife of Love, in a dream," printed at Venice, by Aldus, in 1499, designs attributed by some to Mantegna, by others to Botticelli or Bellini. Their graceful character has been well rendered by the unknown engraver, if an Italian, a worthy rival of the worthiest of

[*] The notion of a writer in the (London) *Academy* of Feb. 21, 1885, that there was "a great advance in German wood-engraving at the beginning of the last twenty years of the fifteenth century," owing to the newly interested painters not merely providing the designs but their "actually learning the art of wood engraving," scarcely needs serious refuting. There was nothing to learn. Also, it should be added, the great "advance" or "leap" never occurred. Taking account of the exceptions I have noted, and of such greater elaboration as was occasioned by difference of drawing, there was just so much general progress as might be expected in a purely mechanical work: the slow improvement arising from steady practice,

German workmen to that date. Here are engravings which may fairly be called good, albeit not quite deserving Professor Colvin's praise of being "without their like in the history of wood-engraving."   Here, as in our three Block-Books before-signalized, we have not only all the lines of the draftsman (so much we may have in the *St. Christopher* or even in the Pfister and the Caxton cuts) but something like to the lines themselves, the varying touch of the draftsman preserved. Only this could give distinction to the old-time wood-cutter. Artistic originality was unneeded in his mechanical employment; but the perception of an artist would be of service. "The eye sees that which it brings the means of seeing;" and "there are who have eyes, yet see not."

The cuts of the *Hypnerotomachia* are not all equally good, and faces and hands might be better; but the most of these outline drawings, which have a look of pen and ink, are cut with rare delicacy and taste and, as already noticed, with evident close adherence to the drawing. Some parts, of scroll and drapery, could hardly be bettered. The average excellence of one hundred and ninety-two cuts (mythological, emblematic, architectural, and ornamental) is but unsatisfactorily represented by the reproductions here printed. It may, I think, be questioned whether these famous cuts were done in wood or metal.

NOT easy is it to determine, writes Dr. Willshire, "whether wood-blocks or metal plates were first used by the engraver: view them in any aspect we see them had recourse to apparently contemporaneously. If wood was early employed for imprinting textile fabrics, so were engraved *interrasile* [*opus interrasile*— hollowed work] metal plates, decorating book-covers, altar-tabernacles, reliquaries, etc., made to yield impressions, and at the same period,— *i. e.* from the latter third of the fourteenth century to the end of the first quarter of the fifteenth. It is considered by some good authorities that not a few prints exist, of which it is not easy to say whether they have been printed from wooden blocks or from metal plates." Dr. Willshire also notices that "both in the infancy of the art and in recent times metal plates have been cut in relief; and the forms drawn on wooden blocks have been engraved in *intaglio*. In the former case the portions of metal in relief are inked as in the wood block; but in the latter the parts in *intaglio* are not inked as they are in an engraved metal plate" [that is by the ink being rubbed into the lines]. Wood-cuts are always printed from the surface; but cuts in metal can be printed either from incised lines (*intaglio*) or from the surface, as wood. There is difficulty sometimes in distinguishing metal-work even when a print of intaglio lines. Failing some perception of ink above the face of the paper, or of an indentation (caused by a relief-stamp) at the back, we may be deceived. How much greater must be the difficulty when the prints compared are both from surface-printing. Nothing can help us there but some indication left of the engraver's tool.

The wood-cut of those early days was always done with a knife [see figure, page 38]. No other tool was available for engraving on the plank, or "block," the piece of planed pear-tree, or other wood, sawn out lengthwise, with the grain: engraving on the end of the grain (on a section) not yet having been tried. The metal cut, the lines incised or in relief, no matter what metal, was always done with a graver. Sometimes the general angularity of knife-work may be sufficiently apparent; sometimes marks of the graver, graver-shaped indentations in the lines in relief, may give betrayal; sometimes the thin unvarying line, or a line varying as a graver-line would and a knife-line would not, may provoke inquiry and lead to discovery: sometimes breaks or bendings in lines may help to inform us;—but there are times when it is impossible for the experienced engraver, used to both knife and graver work, to distinguish so that he may say with certainty— This print is from metal, that is from wood. It is only after closest examination of the differences noted above that we can now and then form an opinion as to what may have been the material of our engraving: and I would say that not only "not a few," but very many early prints exist of which it is not easy to decide whether they are from metal or from wood. Differences dependent upon ink, such as are referred to by Dr. Willshire, after Weigel, may be set aside as doubtful and deceptive; but there is one consequence of ink which may well be noted, as adding very much to our difficulty of distinguishing. In an over-inked impression it is not the actual lines we see, but lines thickened by ink and with a fur on either side. How in that case may we know what the lines really are? This is one reason why in so many reproductions we are so far away from anything like the work which is supposed to be shown to us.

To Weigel, writes Dr. Willshire, "we are indebted for some valuable information on this matter. He states that, on examination of the oldest prints hitherto considered as produced from wood-blocks, it may be observed that certain of them present peculiarities as regards the states of the impressions, and partly also in respect to the engraved lines. It may be seen that frequently the coloured material used to work off the impression is very unequally distributed, or but faintly given off generally over the print. Upon long lines the colour at particular places is narrow or slight in amount, whilst elsewhere it is dense and broad. Other lines, although of equable breadth, are so imperfectly charged with colour that a number of small uncoloured spots may be seen, even with the naked eye. With other lines the colour has so little connection throughout that the impression may be termed gravelly, or grumous. In some places, where several lines approximate, as in the representations of the eyes, mouth, fingers, toes, and hair, the colour from the different lines may be noticed to have run together, and have given rise to a heaviness or bluntness of impression. In prints where such things are to be found there is also a general deficiency of sharpness, equality, and clearness. The cutting of the acute angles and corners, and also of the more delicate lines, appears to have been 'shirked'; and in obtaining the impression the effects of the *frotton* are scarcely visible, the backs of such prints not being marked through forcible indentation from the front. Such engravings as these, which have usually been regarded as bad impressions from wood-blocks caused by careless or imperfect cutting of the latter, or the insufficient damping of the paper, are denied by Weigel, Zestermann, and Passavant, to be impressions from wood at all. They assert that the material which has furnished such impressions must have been of metal." (*Introduction to the Study of Prints*, pp. 76-7.)

A printer beside me smiles. "Not quite conclusive!" he remarks; "an access of thin ink not fairly distributed, with light impressions, might have the same effect with wood." He smiles again when he reads the following :—

"The peculiarities before mentioned are to be explained by the fact of the material of the plate having something of the property of a fatty or greasy body, which prevents the coloured material becoming readily fixed and allows it to run into greater or less-sized blots or masses. Wood, on the other hand, acts differently, as it seizes and holds the colour equally throughout. A very small amount of curvature of the plate—whether concave or convex, some slight bruise, or easily occurring oxidation of it, will prevent a perfect transcript, and give rise to uncoloured spots, or to the 'grumous' impression.

On some of the metal plates in relief book-printers' ink may have been used, which from the fatty acids it contains is liable, if great cleanliness be not adopted, to react upon the metal and give rise to unequal distribution of the material employed. If these facts be kept in view, Weigel and Zestermann are of opinion that no difficulty need arise as to deciding whether an early engraving be an impression taken from wood or from metal in relief." (*Introduction*, pp. 79, 80.)

An oil-ink, which is requisite for metal, will not run into blots; and metal will take it more readily than it will be taken by wood. Who shall tell us with what ink our early engraving was printed? Curvature and bruises will have the same effect on wood as on metal, in preventing an even impression. The uncoloured spots, the grumousness, the oxidation, the fatty acids reacting on the metal, may be put away among proscriptions to be only labeled as fallacious.

Referring again to the Caxton cuts, I repeat and emphasize my doubt of their being wood. I think I detect graver marks, which would prove them to be metal; but I may not be sure. Of the cuts in the *Meditations* of John of Turrecremata I have no doubt. There I clearly perceive the indubitable graver-marks by which I know that the work was done on metal: on metal after the manner of wood, since there can be no suspicion of it being other than relief. The cuts of the *Hypnerotomachia* I would like to believe to be wood-engravings: there is more expression in the line than I would expect in a poor too-yielding material like pewter (*potin*, an amalgam then in use for engraving). Brass or copper would be too hard for subjects with so few lines and so much of vacant space to be cleared away. The smaller cuts to a *Dante*, 1491, may, I think, be on soft metal: chiefly because of the metallic poorness of the line. I may be wrong. Of both these works I speak undecidedly, not convinced. For the *Psalter* Initials, I make no pause. These I supposed Fust or Schoeffer, both metal-workers, might have chosen to cut in copper so as to obtain a long-continued thin line equally delicate throughout; and my supposition is borne out by the absence of knife-angularity, and by detection, in a second edition, of bent lines, a still surer indication. For, granting that relief-lines could be cut in wood as delicately as in the hardest metal, yet a damaged line would almost always show differently: *broken* in the wood, only *bent* in the metal,—that is, in a metal so tenacious as copper. This test was suggested to me by my friend Mr. Reid,

while Keeper of the Prints at the British Museum. Though of little avail with cuts so rude as those in the Caxton books, it is all-sufficient when the only question is between soft wood and copper.

Our test applies directly to a large mass of French engraving, which is to be found in the Books of Devotion called *Heures* (Hours), for a time in fashion throughout France and, though not to the same extent, in England also: no fewer than sixty editions, says Noel Humphreys, appearing between 1484 and 1494. I may borrow a clear description of them from Dr. Willshire.

"Toward the end of the fifteenth and beginning of the sixteenth centuries, some well known French printers, Pigouchet, Jean Dupré (1488), Anthoine Vérard (1480), and Simon Vostre (1480-1520), published some beautiful 'Books of Hours' ornamented with engravings having some peculiar characters. The chief of these were: first, that the ground, and often other dark portion of the print, was finely *criblé*, or dotted white, serving as means of 'killing black,' a practice then prevalent among French engravers; secondly, each page of text was surrounded by a border of little subjects, engraved in the same manner, and often repeated at every third page. From the addition to some books of separate prints, having rich broad borders of figure subjects in floriated frame work, these *Livres d'Heures* had a fine and ornamental effect. Not unfrequently they were printed in brilliant ink, from picked type, on fine vellum, that they might compete with the sumptuously illuminated MS. 'Books of Hours' then in fashion. The works by Vostre are particularly rich in effect: he being, according to some authorities, designer and engraver as well as publisher of his illustrations. The prints decorating the 'Books of Hours' have been generally considered to be impressions from wood; and Chatto has two examples from an edition of *Heures à l'usage de Chartres*, printed at Paris by Simon Vostre, about 1502, illustrative of this mode of *engraving in wood*, by which are lessened the effects of a ground which otherwise would be entirely black.* Mr. Noel Humphreys too (*History of the Art of Printing*, p. 130) contends that 'most of the works produced by Pigouchet, printed on purest vellum, are in fact the finest possible specimens of early *wood-engraving*.'" Renouvier also, so late as 1862, expressed a like opinion.†

The Hours.

---

* He speaks also of the cuts in "Q. *Elizabeth's Prayer-Book*" as wood. They are metal.

† On rather curious grounds. Vérard, he says, was "according to all appearance the ordinary designer and engraver of his planks (*planches*). I thought at first, I confess, to have found a direct proof of this in the passage of a prayer in the *Heures* of 1488 in which he invokes the aid of the Virgin—*pour faire sa planche*, a figure of a king having a tree cut down, in the dedicatory vignette, seeming a confirmation. But, the example of an artist making such a direct allusion to his work is so singular, that it is more prudent to take this expression in a figurative sense and to believe that the author was rather thinking *of the plank of his salvation.* This concession made, I could not for all that keep myself from suspecting that, in the manner of his time, by one of the plays upon words familiar to gothic authors, he referred also to the plank of wood on which he was at work." (*Des Graveurs sur bois dans les Heures d'A. Vérard.*)

SIMON : VOSTRE
Ces presentes heures a lusaige de Chartres
sont au long sans riens reqnerir: auec ses mira
cles nostre dame: et ses figures de lapocalipse: & de
la bible: z des triumphes de Cesar.

The *crible* (or dotted) work would of itself be generally sufficient to convince me of the employment of metal. The dots give evidence of being punched; and the edges of soft wood might not stand that process without splitting,—to say nothing of the equal size throughout of the dots, which I doubt the ability of any one to produce with such unvarying regularity on a plank or side of wood. I do not say that no such work can be on wood; but that metal, clearly more suitable for the purpose, would be more likely to be employed, especially for small subjects requiring more than ordinary finish. For the above reasons, as well as from the graver-like feeling of the line, I have no doubt, for example, of the initial N on page 73 being on metal: the lines and dots in intaglio, the cut printed as a wood-cut, from the surface. The initial T on page 78 is also, as I take it, metal, relief-work done with a graver. The feather on the same page is wood, work of the graver: the drawing of the feather-blade an incised line (white line), the butt of the feather like the usual black fac-simile work. *(Dotted work in metal. Initials N and T in metal.)*

The famous cut of *St. Bernardin of Sienne* (preaching against card-playing), in the National Library at Paris, a copy of which as an undoubted wood-cut is given by Chatto in his shorter *History of Wood-Engraving*, in the *Illustrated London News*, 1844, is most certainly metal. So also is the page here given from Simon Vostre's *Heures à l'usaige de Chartres*, a volume full of lovely design and excellent graver-work: wanting nothing, as the title informs us, since it contains "the miracles of Our Lady, with the figures of the Apocalypse and Bible and the triumphs of Cæsar." Independently of the regularity of the white dots and any difficulty of producing them, I remark the fineness of the lines of shade and the delicate and even thinness of the outlines as indications of metal; and see besides the unmistakable evidence of bent lines (impossible in wood) in the exposed edges of every one of the eight plates or blocks brought together to compose the page, —so made in pieces in order that they may be repeated in different combinations. But we need no farther inquiry here. The question is set at rest by M. Jehan Dupré, who gives account of his own book, a Book of Hours printed by him at Paris in 1488, an only copy of which is in the British Museum. On the second leaf of this, page 4, we find, in plain print,—" *Les vignettes de ces presentes heures imprimées en cuyvre*" (The vignettes of these present Hours printed in copper). Possibly they are the work of Jollat, credited by Papillon with the engravings of many of the *Hours*, and also with engravings in wood (*grossièrement gravées*) for a French *Herbal*, which I have not seen. Passavant writes (*Le Peintre-Graveur*, vol. 1, p. 100) of copper plates (or blocks, *planches* meaning both) of borders cut in the manner of wood, found in a printing-office at Basle, signed I F, and apparently of the first half of the sixteenth century; and of another, of the same period, preserved in the archives of the Rotenhan family at Rentweisdorf. *(St. Bernardin of Sienne. Vostre's Book of Hours. Dupré's vignettes of copper. Relief copper plates found at Basle.)*

I have looked through very many of these *Hours*, by Dupré, Vérard, Vostre, Eustace, Pigouchet, Kerver, Hardouyn, Regnault, Gillet, Vivian, Tory, and others; I find them

all of the same character; not one among those of the better sort which I could believe to be engraved in wood. One reason for the adoption of the white dotted background is obvious: it saved the engraver's time, as it relieved him from the long tedious task of clearing away the metal in the larger spaces, a task much more laborious in copper than in wood. He could have left the solid black, but the broken ground was richer, and *far* more beautiful. Variety wanted, he could return to outline, as shown in the figures at the two corners of Vostre's page.

Some of these *Hours* were coloured to imitate the older illuminations, coloured richly enough to hide the engraving; of some, I suppose, the simple black-and-white might be deemed sufficient, needing no colour. A most exquisite example of one in pure outline, by Geoffroy Tory (whom Passavant speaks of as engraver as well as printer), too pure and perfect to submit to adornment, may be seen in the British Museum. In a copy of *Hours for the diocese of Salisbury*, in the reign of Henry VIII, we read the following :— " Our holy fader Sixt' the IIII pope hath granted to all thē that devoutly say this prayer before the Ymage of our lady the some of XI. M. Yers of pdõ." (the sum of eleven thousand years of pardon.) Another prayer gets a hundred days from Pope Boniface.

THE question may be asked: why bring these metal cuts among engravings in wood and class them, graver-done, with knife-work? I answer :— Because, in the first place, to use an Irishism, I may fairly call them wood-engravings in metal, the specific distinction of wood-engraving being that it is a stamp in relief; and I place these graver-doings with knife-work because, intending the same result, they were only executed with the graver as the fit tool for metal, the knife fit but for plank-wise wood. They are the equivalents and verisimilitudes of wood-cuts done with a knife, so closely identical that, as we have seen, they are often indistinguishable. They could not have been left out of any history of wood-engraving, though they need not be farther or more fully noticed here.

CHAPTER V

JEROME OF NURNBERG

SPARING is History of exact information, and careless withal of accuracy in questions of most concern, while greedy for fables and old wives' tales, that only under a mask with two names we can identify one Jerome of Nurnberg, who in the years between 1512 and 1522 engraved the best of Durer's great designs in honour of the Emperor Maximilian. Neudorfer names him Hieronymus (Jerome) Resch, or Rösch; Dr. Thausing, latest authority for Durer, calls him Andreæ, ignoring any Resch, except one Wolfgang, an engraver of less account. It is perhaps too late to learn how he chanced to be misnamed; nor is it of paramount importance. *Rripitur persona, manet res.* The worker may be forgotten or little known, his work is here.

Twenty-five years' engraving, following the printing of Zainer's *Legends of the Saints* in 1471, would be a fair apprenticeship for our wood-engravers. Continual practice, not always in that ruder fashion of Wohlgemuth, must have induced some mechanical dexterity. Breydenbach's *Frontispiece* and the cuts of the *Hypnerotomachia* stand in evidence of this. There could have been no lack of well qualified engravers when in 1496 Albrecht Durer began to draw upon wood his designs for the *Apocalypse.* He had drawn on wood for single prints on his return from Venice in 1494. This, his first series, was published in 1498.

By the end of the fifteenth century the free city of Nurnberg (writes W. Bell Scott, in his *Life and Works of Albert Durer*,) "had reached a state of commercial prosperity

NURNBERG in
the early days
of engraving.

second only to that of the great Italian ports, and the architectural splendours of private
mansions and public works kept pace with the wealth. It was a free town, with ancient
guilds governed by a Council tenacious of rights and privileges, the magistrates themselves belonging almost exclusively to old families, or personally distinguished in some
way that gave them the distinction of an aristocracy. It had also an ancient residence,
and entertained the Kaiser, its leading citizens having to turn out in time of war at their
own charges, the city furnishing a contingent to the Imperial army. Nurnberg was,
moreover, a centre of learning and science." Add to this that "the advanced study of
classic authors and a tendency to independence in religion were features in this part of
Germany." Great Masters in Art were then at work in Nurnberg: Peter Vischer, the
smith; Adam Kraft, the sculptor; Veit Stoss, wood-carver; the "red smith," Sebastian
Lindenast, worker in copper; the painter Wohlgemuth; Jacob Walsch, "the Master of
the Caduceus." Inventors and mechanicians, and eminent men of letters, most notably
Hans Sachs, shoemaker and master-singer, were there also. It was the day of Vasco di
Gama and of Copernicus, the eve of the Reformation. Durer, the greatest of German
painters, designer for wood-engraving, and engraver in copper, stood among such men,
an equal in character and genius. In later years the friend of Luther and Melancthon,
his sympathies were early with the Reformers; and his religious feelings as well as his
artistic aspiration and ambition doubtless found expression in his first important work in
wood — the APOCALYPSE.

The condition
of Germany.

The work was fairly born of the time. "At the close of the fifteenth century (writes
Dr. Thausing) men's minds in Germany were profoundly agitated. The national feeling,
so often crushed, reasserted itself with unexpected force against the hierarchical system
which culminated in the Papacy and the Roman Empire. Just at this time in the heads
of these two centres of the principles of the Middle Ages a change took place which was
well calculated on the one hand to awaken new hopes in the slumbering opposition and
on the other to move it to despair. In the year 1492 the profligate Alexander VI, of the
Spanish family of the Borgias, ascended the Papal throne; and in the following year a
youthful, high-minded, chivalrous, and cultivated sovereign, Maximilian I, became the
representative of Germany, at the head of the Roman Empire. The Papacy had justly
recognised in German literature, especially in its eager determination to gain publicity,
the motive power of the opposition to its own supremacy; but it endeavoured in vain to
obstruct the source or stem the flow of the deep reform-current. The new life streamed
through a thousand channels, soon seizing on a fresh field, which even the enlightened
Popes of those days had failed to observe, much less to view with distrust,—the field of
German art. While the Papacy adorned the seat of power with the choicest treasures
of the Renaissance, and the rich maturity of Italian art, formed upon an antique ideal,
was subservient to its commands, the unsightly wood-cuts and the copper-engravings of

Germany attacked and undermined its exalted position: appealing as it did everywhere, even in the public streets, to the hearts of hundreds of thousands, and especially to the poor ignorant minds to which writings and books were as yet sealed treasures [turning the art of the Heilgen-makers to opposite purpose]. . . A preference for Apocalyptic subjects had already manifested itself in early Christian art: as exampled in the works of the old Prague Masters (during the troublous period which preceded the outbreak of the Hussite movement), of which some remarkable remains have been preserved in the castle of Karlstein. The fact that perhaps the oldest German block-book ever printed was of the *Revelation* of St. John, and the special attention given to the illustrations of this subject in the Cologne and Koburger *Bibles*, are farther examples of this preference. And now, as the fifteenth century, which had witnessed strength wasted and endeavours thrown away in vain struggles to improve the condition of public affairs, drew toward its close, and the oppressive air that betokens the coming storm gathered anew over men's minds, the *Apocalypse* once more occupied a front rank in the artist's choice of subjects." (*Albert Durer, his Life and Works*, by Moriz Thausing.)*

Durer's book, printed by himself at Nurnberg in 1498, consists of fifteen large designs (the title of later date). Great as are the drawings, the cuts, as cuts, though good, do not indicate the "sudden and miraculous improvement" imagined by Ottley. The book however may not be left unnoticed; well worthy of description if only as first in a series of great works, in which as they proceed the engraver will not be without some share of honour. The first of these designs represents the martyrdom of John in the presence of the Roman Emperor Domitian and a motley group of spectators. The second is the beginning of the Vision: one like to the Son of Man among the seven candlesticks, and John bowed down before him. The third design is in heaven: One seated on a throne, with the four beasts and the twenty-four elders around him: a scene above the clouds, John kneeling on the cloud-edge in front, a German landscape below. The opening of the first four seals comes next, a wonderfully grand design of the four horsemen going forth conquering and to conquer: Death on the pale horse in the front; king, burgher, peasant, and priest, fallen before him. The fifth and sixth seals are the subject of the fifth picture: the white-robed martyrs in the clouds above; below, the darkening of the sun and moon and stars, and a crowd hiding from the wrath "in the dens and the rocks of the mountains," an emperor, an empress, a wailing pope, a cardinal, a bishop, a monk, and a woman, with a child in her arms, cursing them, as with the curse of the People.

---

* Also, "The adhesion of Nurnberg throughout the Middle Ages to the Emperor in the struggle against the Papacy had tended to make the citizens, while remaining sincerely pious, more liberal in religious matters. The tenets of the Waldenses had already made their way to Nurnberg; the Hussite doctrines quickly found a hearing in the City. . . In no place did the Reformation find the ground so well prepared for its reception as it was in Nurnberg." Time and place were waiting for the artist's work.

In the sixth cut the foremost and main portion is occupied by the four angels "holding the winds;" as a sign of their power, a fruit-laden apple-tree near them stands unhurt; behind, on the right, an angel marks God's servants on their foreheads.* The opening of the seventh seal follows: the seven angels which stand before God, to whom were given seven trumpets; hail and fire poured upon the earth, as a great mountain is cast into the sea, and the star Wormwood falls from heaven. The sounding of the sixth trumpet is the next design: from beneath the altar issue forth the horsemen on their lion-headed horses, and in the foreground the four angels loosed from the great river Euphrates are seen at their task of slaughter, a pope and a king again foremost among the overthrown. The ninth subject is John eating the book, with a literal picturing of the angel "clothed with a cloud, his face as it were the sun, and his feet [and legs] as pillars of fire." The tenth shows the Woman crowned with stars standing before the seven-headed Dragon; two angels carry her child to the throne of God. The eleventh is the "war in heaven," a combat in the air: Michael with three angels against the Dragon and his dragons, the usual grotesques; below is a bird's-eye view of a pleasant German village, with lake and mountains. The twelfth design is of the two Beasts, the Seven-headed and the Beast with horns like a lamb, coming up from the sea and out of the earth; a group of figures kneeling to them; while above the clouds sits the Son of Man with a sickle in his hand, on his right the Woman with her child, on his left an angel with a sickle, and one with a sword. The centre of the thirteenth subject is crowded with the Elect, bearing palm branches; around are the elders, and above is the Lamb, on a rainbow, and radiant as the sun. The four beasts stand next; one of the elders leans forward, holding a cup to catch a stream of blood gushing from the breast of the Lamb; in the front John kneels on the top of Mount Sion, and an elder stoops from the cloud to encourage him. In the fourteenth picture we see the Babylonish Woman, mother of harlots and abominations, sitting on the seven-headed monster (papal Rome). A monk prostrates himself before her; king, peasant, soldier, and artist, look less reverently. "It is easy to understand," says Dr. Thausing, "that the Apocalyptic text would have all the ring of a revolutionary hymn applicable to Rome, and that Dürer's illustrations would at that moment flash like lightning upon the minds of men:" emphasizing the prophetic text—"For her sins have reached unto heaven and God hath remembered her iniquities. Reward her even as she rewarded you, and double unto her according to her works!" The last of the series has the avenging angel about to shut up the Dragon, another angel showing to the Seer the New Jerusalem,—in Dürer's own later words, "the new and beautiful Jerusalem, that is to say, the holy, pure Gospel which can not be obscured by the doctrines of men."

---

* In the reproduction here given justice has hardly been done to the work of the engraver—the print from which the photograph was taken having been too heavy: the lines, in consequence, are blurred.

HOLDING THE WINDS   (Dürer's Apocalypse)

There is no knowing who engraved these designs. Certainly Durer himself did not.
I can not do better here than quote from Dr. Thausing. Durer was not the engraver

"There is no ground for the assumption that Durer handled the knife or prepared the
blocks for printing. It has, no doubt, long been a disputed question whether or not the
old German painters themselves cut their designs in wood; and the partisans of either
opinion have derived their arguments chiefly from Durer's work. They who maintained
that he did cut his own blocks, or at any rate some of them, adduced in support of their
argument the cuts which had succeeded the best, and which appeared most faithfully to
render the original drawing. But this clearly is a most mistaken view: for the technical
work of wood-cutting depends so much on constant practice, that even the most expert
draftsman who only occasionally handled the knife (a very different tool from a graver)
could never have equalled, much less surpassed, the professional wood-engraver. It is
therefore rather among the less successful wood-cuts that specimens of the painter's own
hand-work are likely to be found. For the present, however, the question may be taken
as settled that the practised professional wood-engravers, then numerous in every town,
did all the cutting: that the painter drew the design, with pen, brush, or pencil, on the
block, leaving the engraver to execute the, so to speak, negative task of freeing the lines
from all extraneous material, so making ready for printing. The more carefully and the Professional wood-carvers did the work.
more skilfully he did this, the less he departed from the master's own lines, the better
would the printed wood-cut preserve the character of the original drawing. His knife
could certainly more or less spoil it, but could not improve it. The exercise of his craft
lay quite outside of the province of the creative artist. Their work the best.

"That this was the rule in Durer's case may be looked upon as certain. . . At the
same time, it is not to be denied that Durer [may have] occasionally tried his hand at
wood-engraving. Indeed, he appears to look upon it as quite natural that the creative
artist should lay aside the pencil for the knife of the wood-engraver, so as to be able to
finish off at once *some small work;* and he even declares that 'an intelligent expert artist
can show perhaps more power and skill in the rendering of common unimportant objects
than others are able to display in their more serious efforts : thence it happens,' he goes
on to say, 'that one traces upon a half-sheet of paper, or engraves upon a little piece of
wood in a single day something better than another man's work, the result perhaps of a
whole year's most diligent labour.'*. . . No trustworthy evidence exists however of

----

* Which remark, however, is beside the question at
issue, in so much as, though it asserts the advantage
of artistic labour in every thing, and that the better
artist would even in slight and off-hand work excel
the more laborious endeavour of an inferior, it does
not constitute any comparison between the efficient
mechanism of a practised mechanic and the artist's
unpractised mechanical inefficiency. Blake, artist,
and like Durer a much practised engraver in copper,
failed lamentably in his attempts in wood. In even
so poor an art as the art of cutting a few mere lines
in wood some practice is necessary for perfection.

Durer having worked at wood-engraving; and that most important question whether he engraved or even helped to engrave the *Apocalypse* can but be answered in the negative, and for the following reason. As the well-known monogram, which appears on all the cuts, was first adopted, we know, in 1497, and the book was published in 1498, the cuts could not have taken more than a year, far too short a time for Durer, with all his other occupations, to have accomplished so laborious a task. Once admit, however, that the blocks were handed over to professional engravers, and all possibility of distinguishing Durer's work from that of others is at an end. His share can not, in fact, be subjected to any critical investigation." *

Thausing continues, on the farther question of Durer's influence on wood-engraving.

"It is as a painter and draftsman, and not as himself an engraver, that Durer must be considered a reformer of the old style of wood-engraving. The changes in the technical method hitherto pursued,† and their rapid development, were occasioned by the fresh demands he made upon the art, and the clearness and precision with which he set forth those demands. Until Durer's time wood-engraving was based on the principle of flat outline and polychrome. Deriving its origin from miniature, and acting as a substitute for it, the printed picture with its strong outlines was, in fact, nothing but a framework to be filled in with varied colours by means of the brush or the stencil. So it remained even after drawing had very greatly improved; witness the fact that the copies sold of Wohlgemuth's *Casket* and *World-Chronicle* were chiefly coloured ones. But the advent of Durer's first set of wood-cuts changed all this. No aid from illumination was needed by his *Apocalypse;* indeed none could have been tolerated. A single tint took the place of the immemorial polychrome, one colour that of many.

"Durer's sense of harmony in colour, cultivated as it was especially by the study of landscape, first taught him to combine form and colour, and to distinguish objects from each other, not by different colours, but by gradations of colour. Applied to wood-cuts, this simple method put an end altogether to the use of polychromy, for more effect and picturesqueness were obtained by the mere alternation of light and shade than could be ever produced by the varied colouring hitherto in vogue. Of course, to carry out this new style Durer needed a wood-engraver who would entirely enter into his views [that is to say, one sufficiently docile, patient, and conscientious, such engraver having only,

---

* Dr. Willshire assumes that some of the cuts "are so fine in invention of line and rich in effect that we can not suppose Nurnberg possessed before 1498 a *formschneider* capable of rendering Durer's compositions in so perfect a manner." Invention of line and richness of effect were outside of the engraver's province. He cut what Durer drew; and found no difficulty in the invention or effectiveness of lines.

† We are not warranted in supposing there was any change of technical method except in the drawing. No change took place in the engraving. There can be but one method of executing a wood-cut with a knife; exactly the same technical method for finest and best work as for the coarsest and most careless. This exception understood, Dr. Thausing's remarks on Durer's influence are correct and well expressed.

as heretofore, to cut away the superfluous wood between the lines drawn]; and no one was better fitted than he to train and develope such a craftsman [truly for the following reason] as probably no hand ever expressed its owner's mind so exactly, so firmly, and so unhesitatingly. It is this, I believe, which explains the profound influence exercised by Durer upon the art of wood-engraving. He knew exactly what, and how much, he might expect from the mere mechanical process, and that, and no more, he drew either with the pen, or with the brush, touch by touch, in those clear, regular lines which the eye so readily follows, and which every expert hand if it would could also follow without stumbling. He required more from the block than any one before his time; . . but he told the engraver what he wanted." (*Life and Works*, vol. 1, pp. 259-263.)

Three other books following the *Apocalypse* upbuild the fame of the artist, and must have been excellent practice for the unknown engravers. Unknown to us, and probably unconsidered then, for all crediting of Durer with intention to found a school. It may have been so, but it is reasonable to suppose that the improvement of engraving under him was without such purpose, a natural consequence of his firm and decided handling. There could be no mistaking a line drawn by him, and firmness of drawing afforded no excuse for infirm cutting. Increasing fullness and elaboration would be in consequence of his own increased facility, encouraged, it might be, by the growing expertness of his engravers. Well for the engraver to be so educated into excellence !

The three books of which I have now to speak are the *Life of the Virgin*, the *Greater Passion* of Christ, and the *Lesser Passion*. These three, together with a second edition of his *Apocalypse*, Durer published in 1511, so completing the series : a series, taken in chronological order, the most complete of all pictorial schemes of the Christian religion. This date of 1511 marks only the collective publication of the four works ; their time of production must be differently noted. The *Apocalypse* of 1498 has in 1511 a title design added ; seven of the *Greater Passion* cuts Dr. Thausing refers to somewhere near 1500 ; four others are dated 1510, the title probably of the same date ; the *Life of the Virgin*, most of it done in 1504-5, is augmented by two page designs (two last but one) and the title; and the *Lesser Passion* is placed by Thausing in the two or three years before 1511. The four books published in 1511 bear the same imprint : *Impressum Nurnbergæ per Albertum Durer pictorem* (printed at Nurnberg by Albert Durer painter). He never calls himself engraver. In those days the printer was also publisher.

The LIFE OF THE VIRGIN is comprised in twenty designs :—1, the Title (the Mother with the Child, seated on the crescent moon); 2, Joachim's offering rejected;* 3, the Angel promising a child to Joachim; 4, Anna meeting Joachim on his returning home;

---

* This and other subjects are from the Apocryphal Gospels (the *Gospel of Mary, Gospel of the Infancy of Jesus*, etc.), a fertile and very favourite ground of inspiration for many of the early biblical artists.

5, the Birth of Mary ; 6, the child Mary miraculously climbing the steps of the Temple ; 7, the Marriage of Joseph to Mary ; 8, the Annunciation ; 9, Mary's Visit to Elizabeth ; 10, the Nativity ; 11, the Circumcision ; 12, the Adoration of the Three Kings ; 13, the Purification of the Virgin ; 14, the Flight into Egypt ; 15, Repose in Egypt ; 16, the boy Jesus among the doctors in the Temple ; 17, Jesus taking leave of Mary ; 18, the Death of Mary ; 19, her Assumption,—received by the Trinity into heaven ; 20, a Celebration of the Virgin Mother. " These twenty noble and beautiful works," writes W. Bell Scott (*Life and Works of Durer*), "form the most excellent votive offering ever made to the Mother of our Lord's body. To commend, or describe them one by one is unnecessary ; and now to do so in fitting terms of reverence and love is difficult, so much has passed away, and the rest has got congealed into a dogma by Piux IX."

Of the subjects of the *Greater* and *Lesser Passions* (the passion or suffering of Christ) even a list is hardly necessary, but may be given for sake of completeness* The larger work consists of twelve designs, and the smaller one has thirty-seven. The subjects of THE GREATER PASSION are :—1, the Title-page (Christ mocked) ; 2, the Last Supper ; 3, Jesus on the Mount of Olives ; 4, the Betrayal ; 5, the Scourging ; 6, " *Ecce Homo!*" 7, Jesus bearing his Cross ; 8, the Crucifixion ; 9, the Women mourning over the Dead ; 10, the Entombment ; 11, Descent into Hell ; † 12, the Resurrection. The designs of THE LESSER PASSION are : the Title-page (Christ mourning over Man's Fall), the Fall, the Expulsion from Paradise, the Annunciation, the Nativity, Jesus taking leave of his Mother, the Entry into Jerusalem, Driving out the Money-changers, the Last Supper, Washing the Disciples' feet, the Agony in the Garden, the Betrayal, Jesus before the High Priest, Blindfolded and buffeted, Brought before Pilate, Before Herod, Brought back to Pilate, Scourged, Crowned with thorns, Shown to the Jews, Pilate washing his hands, Jesus bearing his Cross, St. Veronica holding the *Sudarium*, Jesus nailed to the Cross, the Crucifixion, the Descent into Hell, Jesus taken from the Cross, the Women lamenting, the Entombment, the Resurrection, Appearing to his Mother, Appearing to Mary Magdalen, the Supper at Emmaus, Thomas doubting, the Ascension, Descent of the Holy Ghost, the Last Judgment.

The subjects of the *Greater Passion* which bear the date of 1510 are the Last Supper, the Betrayal, the Descent into Hell, and the Resurrection. Excellent engraving is in these, in the *Ecce Homo* also, a noble work, firm, honest, and intelligent. There seems not a faulty line. I can hardly think this is to be counted among the early cuts, though undated, unless indeed the others were by a different hand. Most likely they were not

---

* A third series by Durer, never engraved, twelve drawings on green paper, in chiaroscuro, is known as the *Green Passion*. Their production was of the same period, and they are like in character to the cuts.

† The "Harrowing of Hell" of old writers : another subject from a rejected Gospel, that of *Nicodemus*.

ECCE HOMO [Die große Passion]

DÜRER'S SMALLER PASSION

all the work of one engraver; and we must not expect to track a regular and continuous improvement. In the best cuts of the *Greater Passion* and the *Life of the Virgin* I find the best of knife-work to the date of 1511, a noticeable advance beyond former doings. The *Ecce Homo*, the *Flight into Egypt*, and the *Assumption*, represent the highest mark to that date; and Durer, to whose exactest drawing it owed itself, would be well-satisfied with work so faithful and good. The cuts of the *Lesser* or (as Durer himself called it) *Little Passion* are not so well engraved. Examination of the blocks (thirty-three of the thirty-seven are in the British Museum) proves distinctly that they were cut by several engravers; and I would think that the drawing had not been so precise as was Durer's wont, but that something of shade, of only colour, may have been left to their unequal judgment. Like indication may be observed also in parts of the larger cuts.

And now we reach the Triumph of the *Formschneider*. May not we call it so, though famous as the "Triumph of Maximilian"—Maximilian the first, Emperor of Germany and Magnificent Patron of Engraving in Wood, the orderer of a wood-cut nine feet by ten feet and a half and of a singular series of wood-cuts stretching to a length of nearly two hundred feet. Due credit and well-earned praise be given to Durer, whose use and teaching abled his engravers for their work; to Maximilian also our acknowledgments, who gave the opportunity for performance! We may not grudge him thanks, for all he sought in the first place his own enduring honour. In that were others lifted.

The whole "TRIUMPH OF MAXIMILIAN" consists of a *Triumphal Arch* (*Ehren-Pforte*—the Gate of Honour), a *Triumphal Procession*, and a *Triumphal Car*. The *Arch*, when all the prints, from ninety-two planks of wood composing it, are put together, occupies a space ten feet and a half in height, and rather more than nine feet in width. A copy in the British Museum is in vertical portions on five strips. The *Procession*, incomplete, one hundred and thirty-five designs of several figures or groups on jointed wood, about sixteen inches in height, extends to the length of one hundred and sixty or seventy feet. The *Car*, with its twelve horses, occupies nearly seven feet and a half, the car eighteen inches high. The *Arch* ("the grandest thing ever produced by wood-engraving," says Thausing,—and, considering only its colossal size, I may call it the grandest engraving of any kind) was wholly drawn by Durer; as also was the *Car*. According to Thausing, he was likewise concerned in part of the *Procession*. Scott, however, would ascribe that rather to Burgkmair, who certainly designed and probably also drew on the wood a very large proportion of it, aided to some small extent by Schaufelin. The "projector of the design" (Chatto's expressive term) was the imperial historiographer and poet-laureate, Johannes Stabius, who also supplied such descriptive text as might be required for full understanding of the whole Triumph. The cutting of so many drawings was, as might be supposed, the work of years. The *Arch*, the drawing begun in 1512 and finished in

1515, was not all engraved when the Emperor died, in 1519. The *Procession* also was incomplete. The *Car* was not engraved until 1522. Of the engravers of these I shall speak farther on. I have first to describe the works.

Of the *Arch* I can not better the description by Thausing. "It was to be arranged, Stabius informs us, in the same form as the triumphal arches formerly erected in honour of the Roman Emperors. That this was the intention of both scholar and artist is worth noting, since Dürer's finished work hardly would suggest the idea of a Roman triumphal arch. The whole has more of the look of the lofty buildings, with steep-pitched gables, belonging to the period of German Renaissance. The two circular towers at each end, round which are inscriptions on scrolls, recall the spiral lanterns at the angles of French and German castles; but the cupolas and lunettes which crown the pyramidal erections are unmistakably of Venetian origin. In unison with the generally elevated appearance of the whole building are the three gateways, which are rather narrow, and between and above which is plenty of space for the exuberant caprices of the scholar and the artist. The largest and principal entrance, in the middle, is the 'Gate of Honour and Power,' at the top of which is perched a charming figure of Fortune holding the imperial crown. The wall above is adorned with the genealogy of the House of Austria, the upper part occupied by the Emperor himself enthroned and surrounded by floating genii of victory, while below are his successors, each carrying a pomegranate, Maximilian's emblem, the symbol of plenty. In two lines on raised panels at either side appear a hundred and two escutcheons of subject countries and provinces. Over the two smaller side entrances— the 'Gate of Praise' and the 'Gate of Nobility'—are scenes from Maximilian's history, in twenty-four compartments, and above each of these is a scroll with explanatory verses by Stabius. These scenes represent chiefly military or political events; and are full of picturesque details, and excellently cut. The rich variety of these compositions and of the ornamental accessories defies description. Regarding the work as a whole, its unity and the harmony of proportions necessarily suffer from the profusion of learned material and artistic conceits with which it is overloaded. Most remarkable are the reminiscences of Venetian architecture. The column-clusters, that bulge or taper in arbitrary fashion, have a strange and uncouth appearance. From the size of the work, it is true, there is little opportunity for viewing it as a whole: all the more pleasing therefore is it to note the delicate and ingenious treatment of the details." The whole subject is, says Chatto (who also has a fair description of it), "a kind of pictorial epitome of the history of the German Empire." The engraving, excellent throughout, is worthy of the design: the central Fortune and inscription beneath have the purity of copper-plate.

The *Procession* is altogether well engraved: the cutting is all clean and sharp. But I can not join the editor of the reductions issued by the Holbein Society in lauding them as especially "precious specimens of the art of wood-engraving, for the care and skill of

Eduard prinng
zu portigall gc.
fipt im Vierbē
grab
Albrecht 2. der
glucthafftig.

their cutting;" nor agree with Chatto that they are "the best of all the works" done for Maximilian. They are firmly and carefully cut; but, except perhaps two or three, they do not attain the excellence of the finest portions of the *Arch*. Most remarkable is the generally even quality of the work, with certainly eleven engravers employed on them. It is hardly necessary here to give a full and detailed account of the designs. All usual components of a triumphal procession are there, with such amplification as poet or artist could supply. There are heralds; huntsmen and their quarries, goats, stags (marching five abreast), wild boars, and bears; the various officers of an imperial court; musicians, jesters, mummers; masters of fencing and tourney, tilters (all in full array); soldiers of all arms; richly emblazoned standards borne by horsemen; cars with trophies; statues; chariots with emblematical devices of the wars of Maximilian; baggage-waggons; camp followers; captives; "Savages of Calicut;" etc. In the midst was to be the Triumphal Car of the Emperor; and then a "horseman, in magnificent costume and decorated with the crown of honour, carrying a tablet on which is written — 'The Elected Princes;' the Princes mounted, in ranks of five, carrying their banners with their names," and followed by ranks of Counts, Knights, Soldiers of Merit, etc. A splendid subject for the artist: but how to be made use of? "Imagine," writes Scott, "this immense façade [the Arch] erected, the Triumphal Car placed so as to enter it, and the one hundred and thirty-five sheets of the Procession in a long line advancing! There is a barbaric magnificence in the scheme: it is such a work as could only be inspired by the undefined capabilities of a new art."

Maximilian's Procession.

In the *Triumphal Car*, which is of curious form and elaborately ornamented, sits the Emperor, under a canopy over which is a mask to represent the sun, with the words, in Latin, "What the Sun is in heaven Cæsar is on earth." Female figures, the Virtues,— Justice, Truth, Clemency, Liberality, Fortitude, etc., some perched on pedestals on the Car, some running beside it, present wreaths of laurel to this "Image of a true Prince." Six pairs of horses, richly caparisoned, each led by a female figure, draw the Car. The foremost leaders' names are Experience and Quick-Wit; the others, in their order, are Audacity and Magnanimity, Vehemence and Manly Strength, Swiftness and Firmness, Alacrity and Opportunity, with Foresight and Moderation next the Car, in the front of which sits Reason, holding the reins of Nobility and Power. Guido's " Hours " resemble these Durer figures, and might have been suggested by them.[*]

The engraving of the *Car* was twice printed (perhaps only a few copies) at Nurnberg, in 1522, with descriptions partly in Latin and part German; reprinted, the descriptions

The Triumphal Car.

The Car of Victory.

---

[*] This, *the* Triumphal Car, is not to be mistaken for it a smaller and less important design known as "the Car with the team of Victory," a car drawn by four horses abreast driven by a winged figure. This Car is seen in the *Procession*, though it may be out of the right order. A very much reduced copy of the driver and horses, omitting the car, is given by Chatto. He attributes the design to Burgkmair.

in Latin, at Nurnberg in 1523, at Venice in 1589: all from the original blocks. Copies appeared also: one by Hans Guldenmund (wood-engraver, card-maker, and printer), at Numberg in 1529, immediately after Durer's death; and another, printed by the widow of Cornelius Liefrink (one of the engravers of the *Procession*), at Antwerp, in 1545. It may have been the same copy that reappeared at Amsterdam in 1609. Of the *Procession* a few were printed by order of King Ferdinand, in 1526; no more until 1775, the cuts so long lost. The whole series (except two) only appeared in 1796. Lately a reprint, showing for the first time what the engraving really is, has been taken at Vienna, the cuts with those of the *Arch* remaining in the Imperial Library. Of the *Arch* the whole was first printed in 1559; again in 1799; and again but now.

And now I have to speak of the Engravers, with whom by this time we begin to get some acquaintance. Names and initials and one monogram are found cut or written on the backs of many portions of the *Procession*. Bartsch, who was keeper of the Imperial Library at Vienna in 1796, some of the cuts having then to be planed down to equalise their height before printing, drew up the following list of seventeen engravers: " *Jerome André* (Resch or Rösch), *Jean de Bonn*, Cornelius (de Bonn or Liefrink), *Hans Frank*, Saint German, Guillaume (is perhaps Liefrink), *Corneille Liefrink, Guillaume Liefrink, Alexis Lindt, Josse de Negher*, Vincent Pfarkecher, *Jaques Rupp*, Hans Schaufelein, *Jean Tabrith*, F P, HF (perhaps Hans Frank), W R." Mr. Aspland, editor of the reduced copy of the "Triumph" (Procession) published for the Holbein Society, in 1873, gives on the authority of Herr Anton Von Perger, then Librarian at Vienna, a list of sixteen, of which only ten names (the German spelling of course different), the initial W R, and the monogram HF, agree with Bartsch. Von Perger omits Saint German and Vincent Pfarkecher, giving instead Schriftler, Hans Liefrink, and an initial N. And Cornelius (so only in Bartsch) he gives as Cornelis May.

Sifting these two lists and referring to our latest authority, Herr Franz Schestag, in the *Year-book* of the Imperial Art-Collection at Vienna (*Jahrbuch der Kunst-historischen Sammlungen des Allerhöchsten Kaiser-hauses*, 1883), we find that Cornelius is evidently Corneille Liefrink, and "Cornelis May" is only "Cornelis . . may 1517;" Guillaume also is Liefrink, another duplicate; and there is no Hans Liefrink. Vincent Pfarkecher may be struck out, the name only written, while HF (which is certainly Hans Frank) is cut in the wood on the same plank; Schaufelin was not engraver, but only draftsman; W R is *Wolfgang Resch, or Rösch*; Saint German should be *Claus Seman*, Bartsch misreading the name; the initial N is preceded by *josi*, denoting Josi de Negher, or Dienecker; and "Schriftler," which appears on the Aspland-Perger list as the name of the engraver of sixteen cuts, is not discoverable either upon the cuts or in Bartsch's list or his remarks yet preserved at Vienna, examined and quoted by Schestag. The two lists of seventeen and sixteen may therefore be reduced to eleven [the names in *Italic* here above]. Seven

FROM THE BURGKMAIR PROCESSION.

FROM THE PROCESSION. (Burgkmair—"Savages of Calicut.")

of those [Hans Frank, Alexis Lindt, Jost de Negher, Wolfgang Resch, Hans Taberith, Cornelius Liefrink, and Nicolas Seeman] appear again, engravers of Burgkmair's *Saints*. Hans Frank may possibly be Hans Lutzelburger of later fame. The rest of the eleven, two excepted, are but shadow-names, names of men without mark. The two exceptions are Jost de Negher and Jerome Andre.

Burgkmair's Saints.

Jost (or Jost or Josse) Danneck or Dieneker or, as he sometimes signs his name, De Negher, originally of Antwerp, seems to have established himself as wood-engraver at Augsburg in 1510. We find him in 1512 writing to the Emperor:—"I am informed that your Majesty desires and wills that the works of engraving which I am charged to prepare should advance more quickly than they have hereto, . and that your Majesty has written to Dr. Bewtinger [Peutinger] to join with me two or three other engravers, which is a great satisfaction to me. Now I am acquainted with two engravers [Wilhelm and Cornelius Liefrink, it may be; Liefrinks will be found at Augsburg so late as 1568: or was Hans Frank one of the two to be preferred?] who already know something, and would willingly work in the service of your Majesty." He goes on to ask that they may each receive a hundred florins a year, that so provided they may remain in his employ; and adds that he will prepare the wood for them, and finish and clean (*rein machen*) the work with his own hand, in such manner that the engraving shall appear to be his own, and no one know that others have worked on it.* Then he promises to complete in all perfection six or seven cuts a month [probably those for Schaufelin's *Teurdannckh*, cuts of about six inches square]: so that the printer may not have to wait for them. And he asks his Majesty to command that he and his assistants may have a chamber where they may be undisturbed, "for this kind of work requires that we should be alone."

Danneck.

His letter to Maximilian.

Besides Schaufelin's *Teurdannckh* (or "The Adventures and part of the Story of the praise-worthy, valiant, high-renowned hero-knight, Sir Theurdank"—a poetic name for Maximilian, here shown as Adventure-welcoming), for which it appears that Dieneker and his men (certainly more than two) cut the hundred and eighteen drawings, he also engraved some for Burgkmair's *Saints*; a considerable number of the two hundred and forty-five cuts (cuts eight inches by seven) in Burgkmair's *Weiss Kunig*—the "Wise" or White King, between 1512 and 1519; and during the same period was engaged on the *Triumph Procession*. Of ninety-three cuts there but eleven, not the best, bear his name.†

Schaufelin's Sir Theurdank.

Burgkmair's Saints, White King, and the Triumph.

---

* The preparing may have been only the fixing on the wood the transparent tracing through which, it is said, the engraver had sometimes to cut; or may mean that Dieneker was draftsman enough to copy on the wood the artist's design. "Finish and polish it with my own hand" is the untechnical translation of the Holbein Society's editor (of the reproduction of the "Triumph"), who farther explains, that "the wood-blocks, when the engraving is completed, are polished by being rubbed with the hand;" surely an ingenious device for concealment of bad engraving.

† On some, both his and others, we find *ftelerel*, for *prameterel* (delivered), which by Ottley and Chatto was taken to be *polerit* (poured, or as an engraver would say, touched, refined, the cleaning foul lines). But according to Schestag the word has *fd*, not *fr*.

—prameterel

Dieneeker.

Among all these works, by his hand or under his direction, I find nothing to justify the reputation for exceptional ability implied by the extent of his employment. Neither the cuts for *Teuerdannkh* (the sumptuous types of which were specially cut for the Kaiser) nor those for *Der Weiss Kunig* are of exceptional excellence. In the latter, however, I observe a novel fineness of line in masses of grey tint, as if in such parts colour only had been expressed by the draftsman (as in Durer's *Smaller Passion*) and the ordering of the lines left to the engraver,—cross-hatching generally avoided. But the line in these two books lacks the purity and decision of the best cutting for Durer; in both of them it is poor, meagre and without feeling. Not that colour is wanting; and Burgkmair's crowds of small figures are cleanly cut, very marvels of patience : yet the line is dry, has neither taste nor expression,— Burgkmair's fault perhaps.

That he was a good man of business, a master-engraver in full employ, and also a fair workman, something too of an artist, as shown in two chiaroscuro prints of his doing, a *Flying Woman* and a *Portrait*, each in three cuts : all this there seems reason to allow to Dieneeker ; but I have found no engraving, which I can be sure is his, entitling him to rank above his fellows. One man so entitled is Hieronymus (Jerome) of Nurnberg.

Jerome of Nurnberg.

JEROME OF NURNBERG, whether his surname was Resch or Andreæ (Andrea, Andreas, Andres, Andre, all variations of our English Andrew), stands out as chief of the Durer engravers : the engraver of the *Triumphal Arch* and both *Triumphal Cars*. Neudorfer of Nurnberg, "in his notices of the principal artists of his native city," writes Passavant, "speaking of Jerome (Resch), says—'When Stabius had the Triumphal Arch executed for the Emperor Maximilian Jerome was of all the engravers in wood the first and most skilful. . No one like him could cut so neatly and precisely. . It is he who engraved most of Durer's designs.'" Neudorfer wrote this in 1546, Jerome yet alive, and could hardly have been without knowledge of the name or the doings and repute of his fellow townsman. He goes on to tell of the Emperor's frequent visits to Jerome at Nurnberg while he was at work upon the *Arch ;* which Passavant immediately follows with—"The Arch was then (*fui donc*) engraved in great part by the artists of Augsburg :" a curious *non sequitur*. Everywhere I find confusion, seemingly because of "The Triumph" being used loosely as the title of either *Arch* or *Procession*, or of both. However much of the *Procession* may have been engraved at Augsburg, in Dieneeker's workroom (not all, for we have *Jerome Andre* on seven pieces, and nothing showing that the other engravers were of Augsburg), it seems more likely that the *Arch*, altogether Durer's own drawing, would not have been removed from his supervision, and there is some slight sign of this in an equality and oneness of the work not so sure to have been obtained had part been cut at Augsburg and part at Nurnberg. Even of the *Procession* cuts Dr. Thausing holds that those drawn by Durer were "nearly all engraved by Nurnberg artists, Hans Frank,

Wolfgang Resch; and Hieronymus Andreæ, to whom belongs the Small Triumphal Car with the magnificent team of Victory." The magnificence of which, however, whether as engraving or design, bears no comparison with the larger *Triumphal Car*, also "without doubt cut by Hieronymus," says Thausing. And of the *Arch* he writes:—"With that unexampled precision peculiar to him alone, Durer drew the design, with pen or brush, upon the wood; and Hieronymus, who had trained himself to Durer's hand, engraved each stroke with the same accuracy." It is not too high praise for those principal parts of the great work which I take to be Jerome's own. It is hardly possible he could have cut the whole. The Gate of Honour and Power, of the beautiful centre of which I have already spoken, is expressly ascribed to him by Baader.

"At the Emperor's death, in 1519, certain of the blocks belonging to the Triumph [it is still Thausing speaking] remained in the engraver's hands, unfinished or not paid for. Hieronymus Andreæ, the skilled artist whom Durer generally employed, had several of these for the Triumphal Arch, which he refused to give up unless he was paid for them. Among them, without doubt, were the historical subjects intended for the twenty-four compartments over the two side gateways: from which Andreæ took some impressions, and sold them at Nurnberg to satisfy his wants and indemnify himself for his outlay,"—journeymen's wages, I suppose. Thereupon King Ferdinand, Maximilian's successor in Hungary, applied to the Council of Nurnberg, requesting that the engraver should be made to deliver them. The Council, after examining Hieronymus replied that it was quite true he had such blocks, but that he had often complained of delays in payment; and they rather took his part, esteeming him "a particularly clever artist and the most celebrated in the Empire at the kind of work upon which he had been employed by the Emperor;" farthermore hinting that the work could not be properly finished except by him, and advising that his arrears should be settled, after which he would be willing to deliver the blocks. It appears they thus brought King Ferdinand to a right conclusion and without too much offence, as it was after this, between 1519 and 1522, that Jerome engraved the *Triumphal Car*.

From Baader's *Contributions* to Zahn's *Year-Book* (*Jahrbucher für Kunstwissenschaft*), for 1868, we learn that he was "a restless man, constantly in opposition to the Council [not accommodating, it would seem, even to kings], and considerably mixed up with the religious and political troubles of the time;" associated too with the rebellious peasants, for which, in 1525, he suffered imprisonment. Later, in 1542, he was in exile, banished from the City for "sinful words" against one of the elders of the Council, only at the intercession of Count Otto Heinrich allowed, yet not without penalty and restriction, to abide again in Nurnberg. For all which he may have been only deserving of honour.

"Jerome André, called also Jerome Resch or Rösch," writes Chatto; and he properly so called himself (*s'appelait proprement*), says Bartsch, repeating what had been said by

Neudorfer, who was personally acquainted with Jerome. Had he the name of Resch in addition to that of Andreæ, which is given by Thausing as his family name? He styled himself "simply Hieronymus Formschneider, and was rarely otherwise designated."

In the town archives of Nurnberg is a document, by which we are informed that "the wood-engraver Hieronymus Endres (spelling curiously *ad-libitum* in those days) and his wife Veronica sold in 1555 to the cutler Sebastian Schmid, for the sum of 100 Rhenish florins, their house forming part of the Wälschhof (Italian Court) in the Breite Gasse." It is in the Breitengasse Neudorfer says that Jerome lived when visited by Maximilian. The wife Veronica is probably to be found among Durer's portraits, a masterly charcoal drawing on yellow paper, in the British Museum, of a young woman with a flat cap; at the top of the drawing the inscription—"Fronica, 1525, Formschneiderin." Was it an especial mark of respect, or regard, from Durer in that year of Jerome's imprisonment? And did the *Formschneiderin* sit at work beside her husband, helping on his Triumph?

On a tomb in the cemetery of St. John at Nurnberg was engraved :—

A. D. 1556, jar den 7 tag May verschid der Erbar
Jeronymus Andre Formschneider, dem got gnad. R.

(A. D. 1556, on the 7th of May, died the worshipful Jerome Andre, Wood-Engraver, to whom God be gracious! Amen!) This is all I have obtained concerning him.

Who engraved nearly a hundred drawings by Durer, single prints such as the *Helgen*, some rather large, (a list of which will be found in Scott's *Life and Works*), there is no possibility of knowing: nor would the knowledge be of importance, so few overpass the usual mechanical accomplishment. Yet two, exceptionally good, must be signalised : a *Trinity*,—God the Father, with a triple crown, supporting the Dead Christ amidst the angels, the Holy Ghost given as a dove; and the *Mass of St. Gregory*, picturing the tale of Christ's appearance to that Pope while officiating at the Mass. Both are dated 1511. The first is of the size of the *Larger Passion*, the second of the size of the *Virgin* series. Equal to the best work there or in the *Arch*, faces and hands and drapery engraved with fidelity and feeling, the lines of a most remarkable delicacy, I can attribute them lovely cuts only to Jerome of Nurnberg. To him also, I conclude, we must be indebted for a *St. Jerome* by the elder Cranach; and there is ground for a belief that some surpassing work after Sebald Beham (to be spoken of later) may be likewise from his hand.

ST. JEROME IN PENITENCE. (Cranach.)

 HERE IS the record of him who engraved the Holbein *Dance of Death?* Death took it when taking him. We have raked up a few loose word-scraps telling us of the Master Wood-Engraver of Nurnberg; but for any account of Him of Basle we sift the ashes of Time in vain. There is positively nothing to be found. His name—HANNS LUTZELBURGER, *formschnider, genant Franck,* (for which see p. 108) printed beneath a Holbein Alphabet; "*H. L. F.* 1522" appended to another Alphabet (twenty-three initial letters with ornament); "*Hans Leuczelberger Furmschnider* 1522," printed beneath a remarkable cut, a fight in a forest; "*H. L. Fur.*" to an engraved title-page in a German New Testament of 1523; and the monogram H. on a single cut in the *Dance of Death:* this is all we have by which to identify him. Yet his work in that wonderful series of the *Dance* surpasses all we know of Jerome's, going beyond it in subtle delicacy and refinement. Nothing indeed, by knife or by graver, is of higher quality than this man's doing.

HANNS LUTZELBURGER, FORMSCHNEIDER. Nagler, from the Low German *furmschnider,* on the print of 1522, and from his name, supposes him to have been born at Lutzenburg (Luxemburg). "*Genant Franck*"—called Frank: was it his real name, or was he only called so? Was he the Hans Frank, engraver of Burgkmair's *Images of Saints,* whose name appears on two cuts of the Maximilian *Procession,* to whom also must belong other seven with the monogram H°? So Passavant seems disposed to think, finding at Basle a Hans Frank, painter, whom he supposes to be an engraver also, born about 1495, and whom he sends after his apprenticeship on the usual travel, to work with Dienecker at Augsburg. Dr. Woltmann will not accept the identity; and Dr. E. His considers this painter Frank (the name by no means uncommon) as only a house-painter, who died in 1512. The engraver of very much work done for Froben [the great printer at Basle, of European fame, by whom Holbein was employed and at whose house he met Erasmus]

who is supposed to have been an artist in metal : he, signing his work I F, can hardly be our Hans, though I for Iohannes or for Iehan coupled with F, for Frank, might raise a question. It is all mere conjecture.

Wohnann (*Holbein und seine Zeit*, 1874) speaks of him as "only lately emerged from the darkness which enveloped his personality." Scarcely emergent! Dr. His has found the records, dated 1526 and '27, of certain transactions between the Trechsels of Lyons (the publishers of the *Danse of Death*) and the widow of one Hans Formschneider, of Basle, whom he would identify as Lutzelburger.* It should be conclusive : and yet the identification is not complete. There is no Hans Lutzelburger in the church-registers of Basle,—only a Jacob and a Michel, about 1530 ; but at Colmar, some forty miles from Strasburg, the church-book tells of Margaret Lutzelburgerin in 1495, and John (Hans) Lutzelburger *after* 1536. These are all the records.

The first positive information concerning our Master is the date of 1522 with "*Hans Leuzelburger Furmschnider*," printed with movable types, on the Forest-Fight, a fight of naked men and peasants. Some verses, upon the copy at Dresden, are in the dialect of Augsburg, an indication, whether he and the Burgkmair Frank are the same or not, that he did work at Augsburg with Dienecker If so, his name may have been added to this cut as an advertisement, recommending him to the printers of Basle, against his arrival there. We have not quite done with guessing.

In 1523 he was certainly at Basle : for in that year his *H. L. Fur.* claims the Holbein title-page to a German *New Testament* printed at Basle by Thomas Wolff. Other cuts for the *Old Testament, Alphabets* (initials for printers), and the *Dance of Death*, would be done there also, mainly during the four years 1523 '4 '5 '6. All these are of Holbein's drawing, whose book-illustrations, titles etc., to the number, according to Passavant, of one hundred and sixty designs and series of designs, Wornum (*Life and Works of Hans Holbein*) concludes to have been all done by the great painter between 1521 and 1526, at which latter date he first left Basle for England. Wornum's opinion is confirmed by Wohnann, who speaks of pen-copies of twenty-three of the *Dance* cuts, certainly copies from the cuts, in the Berlin Museum, one of which, the Emperor, is dated 1527.

Besides the works already noticed, Passavant attributes to Lutzelburger a portrait of Erasmus by Holbein, borders to titles, a print of the Traffic in Indulgences, two dagger sheaths, a print of Christ and the Pope, a portrait of Nicolas Bourbon, and a few other engravings : judging all by what he thinks to be internal evidence. Especially he notes

---

* The records found by Dr. His show that, June 23, 1526, Melchior Trechsel has given Hans Lux Iselin as surety for forms (blocks) received of the widow of "the late Master . *formschneider*." The name, here omitted, appears in another part of the record, where Trechsel claims 17 guilders and 15 shillings, advanced to "the late *Hans, formschneider*." Next year, the affairs being wound up, Trechsel's name is not seen as a creditor, his claim probably arranged. Are we sure this Hans can be no other than *the one*?

a small cut at the end of a poem by Leland upon the birth of Edward, Prince of Wales, printed by Reyner Wolff, son of the Thomas Wolff of Basle,— a cut "so well engraved that the execution can only be attributed to Lutzelburger:" which leads him to imagine a visit of the engraver to England. (*Le Peintre-Graveur*, vol. 3, Art. Holbein.) To him Woltmann likewise assigns twenty-one wood-cuts in Wolff's *New Testament*.

Lutzelburger's great work, enough for fame, is the *Dance of Death:* twenty-three cuts engraved before 1527, forty assumed to have been printed at Basle about the same date. The series of forty-one did not appear in book form until 1538; then printed at Lyons by Melchior and Gaspar Trechsel, and issued without name of designer or engraver,— nor signature nor monogram in the book except that one easily overlooked H. before mentioned. Reason for the delay, and for the silence also, may be found in the satirical character of the designs, which, even had there been no objection to Holbein because of his anti-papal patron, Henry VIII, could not but have been likely to give offence to the high dignitaries, from the Pope downward, represented not as simply claimed by Death, but claimed amidst circumstances and in a manner by no means complimentary. Some fear of this kind is betrayed in the artifice, that looks like a purposeful mystification, of a lament in the preface for the death of the unnamed designer of the cuts, and in placing the work under the safeguard of a piously respectful dedication to some unascertainable identity, called the Abbess Jehanne de Toussele, whom Chatto looks upon as a fictitious personage. Leaving this bibliographical speculation, let us look at the book!

This earliest edition known as a book is a small quarto with the following title —" *Les Simulachres & Historiées Faces de la Mort, autant elegamment pourtraictes que artificiellement imaginées: A Lyon, soubs l'escu de Coloigne, M.D.XXXVIII:*" or —The Likenesses and Storied Aspects of Death, as elegantly pourtrayed as artistically imagined:[*] At Lyons, under the shield of Cologne—at the sign of the Cologne Arms. The title-page has an emblematic device, in which, on an open book, we read the Greek adage, Know thyself! Next to the dedicatory preface is an introduction, entitled—Various Pictures of Death, not painted, but extracted from the Holy Scripture, coloured by Ecclesiastical Doctors, and shaded by Philosophers. Then come the Cuts: over each a Bible text in Latin, and under each four lines of French doggrel, "severely rhymed" in French fashion. Eight chapters follow, Figures of Death morally described and depicted according to authority of Scripture and the Fathers (*Saincts Peres*); then a collection of brief sentences of the diverse deaths of the Good and of the Bad of the Old and New Testament; followed by

---

[*] *Images* — *skilfully rendered* is the usual rendering. M. Paul Mantz however tells us that in the language of the sixteenth century *imaginées* would refer to the work of the engraver, and *pourtraictes* to the part of the designer. M. Firmin Didot takes the same view, referring to Du Cange's *Glossary;* but the Preface speaks distinctly of the painter "*qui a ici imaginé.*" Didot would have *imaginer*, to mean *sculptor, graver*.

memorable authorities and citations of Philosophers and Pagan Orators to confirm the living in not fearing death. A chapter of the Necessity of Death, which lets nothing be durable, completes the make-up of a volume of discursive meditations on death, enough to serve as apology for any levity of the designs. On the last page we find, on a scroll, the imprint of the Trechsels: *Excudebant Lugduni Melchior et Gaspar Trechsel fratres.*

A second edition, published by John and Francis Frellon* in 1542, has Latin instead of French verses. Wornum finds a French copy of the same year, perhaps to be called a separate edition. So counting, we have a fourth (else only a third) in 1545, with the title *Imagines Mortis* (some copies have *Icones*), Latin verse, and a new cut, the Beggar, used as tail-piece to a sermon on mortality. Two editions, one French, one Latin, appear in 1547, with eleven additional cuts, raising the number to fifty-three (Wornum assigns these eleven to 1545); and an Italian edition, only the texts in Latin, is brought out in 1549 by John Frellon, whose name alone is seen in and after 1547. Yet another edition, without printer's name, is published at Basle in 1554, probably printed at Lyons, as the blocks are still in Frellon's hands for a last issue, in 1562, with the title—*Les Images de la Mort:* "to which are added (*adjoustées*) seventeen figures," or five besides the twelve already noted, the last a tail-piece to the preface of a devotional tract—the Medicine of the Soul. All these authentic editions, but that of Basle, were published at Lyons.

Very many are the copies of the cuts. Most notable are these: one at Venice, 1545; a set engraved by Jobst Dienecker,† 1554; thirty etchings by Hollar, 1651, and forty-six by Deuchar, 1788; Schlotthauer's *Todtentanz*, the first fifty-three designs in lithography, 1832; the wood-cut edition of Douce and Pickering with forty-nine cuts, 1833; and two photo-lithographic renderings, forty-one cuts edited by Noel Humphreys, in 1868, and fifty-three in the Holbein Society's "Reprint" in 1879. Hollar's cuts in copper, it need hardly be said, had they been faithful to Holbein, could give us nothing of Lutzelburger the wood-engraver. Deuchar's work is in like manner disqualified. Dienecker's cuts, though knife work, are very much larger than the originals, and not comparable. The lithographs in Schlotthauer Douce praises as so beautiful and accurate as easily to be

---

* Chatto is inclined to think the Trechsel brothers were only printers, and the Frellons the proprietors and real publishers of the first edition also. It seems certain, he writes, that John and Francis Frellon at the first issue of the *Dance* "were wishful to withhold their names; and it is likely the designer of the cuts might have equally good reasons for concealment. Had the Roman Catholic party [powerful in Lyons] considered the cuts of the Pope, the Nun, and some others, as the covert satire of a reformed painter, the publishers and designer would have been as likely to incur danger as to reap profit or fame." "When there seems no longer reason for apprehending the censures of the Church of Rome we find the names of John and Francis Frellon on the title-page under 'the shield of Cologne.'"

† A small folio printed by him at Augsburg, which perhaps called forth the authentic work at Basle of the same date. It was reissued at Augsburg in 1561 by David Dienecker, probably a son of John; and may, again, have occasioned Frellon's last edition of the original, in 1562. Dienecker has an Adulteress, not seen elsewhere. Was it by Holbein, omitted to avoid hurting the polygamous Majesty of England?

mistaken for the originals : very close they are, but lithography does not exactly give the wood knife-line. The photo-lithographs given by Humphreys and those of the Holbein Society have but little resemblance, no *vrai-semblance*, to the wood-cuts. Nor is the original knife-work discoverable in " fac-similes " by engravers in wood. Of such the copies in Chatto, 1839, may rank among the worst, the attempts of Jackson's apprentice put forth as samples of Lutzelburger. The best wood-cut imitations are in the edition of Douce and Pickering, by Bonner and John Byfield. Two of these, actually engraved by Powis (then a pupil of Bonner), the Old Man and the Arms of Death, may be seen (added by Bohn) in the later editions of Chatto. These two Powis cuts are as close as copies with a graver can be to knife-cutting ; but none of these can truly inform us of Lutzelburger. We must see and study the originals if we would fully appreciate his skill, if we would know anything of the engraving, not caring only for the design. Something perhaps is lost even in the six (of the forty-one) death-subjects in the following pages, though photographed from the Basle impressions, of " 1527," believed to be Lutzelburger's own proofs, and which show him at his best, carrying on their front sufficient evidence of having been printed before the first edition of the book. These earliest unbacked proofs (a set in the Print Room of the British Museum) are forty of the forty-one in the book-edition of 1538, the Astrologer omitted. They appear to have been printed on four sheets, ten on a sheet ; they have German titles above them, and are without verses underneath.

The following are the subjects of the fifty-eight designs in the several editions.

1 — The Creation of all things. Eve taken from the side of Adam.

2 — Adam and Eve in Paradise. The Temptation.

3 — The Expulsion. Adam and Eve driven out by the Angel ; Death, the skeleton, skips before them, playing on a hurdygurdy.

4 — Adam tills the earth. He is uprooting a tree, with the help of Death who works beside him ; while Eve sits near them, suckling Cain.

5 — Skeletons of All Folk. Crowded in a grave-yard : with horns and trumpets ; one with kettle-drums, one with a hurdygurdy.

6 — The Pope. He crowns an emperor who is kissing the papal foot ; Death's hand is on the Pontiff ; a cardinal and a second Death wearing a cardinal's hat, and a bishop, stand behind ; two grotesque devils hover above.

7 — The Emperor. On his throne, surrounded by his Court, a disregarded suppliant bowed before him. Death is discrowning him.

8 — The King. Seated at table : Death, among those serving, pours out wine.

9 — The Cardinal. Perhaps receiving a gift, or selling an indulgence : it is possibly a portrait of Cardinal Cajetan, who was especially opposed to Luther. Death appears to be taking off the Cardinal's hat.

10 — The Empress. With her ladies. Death leads to a grave in front of a palace.

The *Dance of Death*.

Subjects of the Designs.

Adam and Eve in Paradise.

Adam tills the earth.

The Bishop.

11—The Queen. Death, in the garb of the Court-Fool, shows her an hour-glass, and will drag her away in despite of the vigorous opposition of her attendants.

12—The Bishop. An aged man, in full episcopal robes, led by Death; sheep scattered, and shepherds lamenting.

13—The Duke, or Prince-Elector. He is turning from a beggar-woman and child; Death's hand is on the ermine.

14—The Abbot. Death, dragging him along, wears his mitre, and carries the crozier over his shoulder.

15—The Abbess. Dragged by Death from the convent gate, a young novice bewailing her in the gateway.

16—The Noble, or Gentleman. Brandishing his sword, he would fight against the Inevitable. Behind him we see his bier, an hour-glass on it. A poor cut for Lutzelburger.

17—The Canon. Richly attired, his falconer following, he is about to enter the cathedral. Death stops him.

18—The Judge. Before him are two suitors; the rich one offers a bribe. Death, behind, takes the staff of office at the same moment from his hand.

19—The Advocate. In the street; a rich man is giving him money; Death steps between them. Behind the rich man stands a wretched creature wringing his hands.

20—The Town-Councillor, or Alderman, (*Raths-herr*). Busy with a wealthy burgher, he pays no heed to a ragged beggar who follows him beseechingly. Death, flung to the ground at his feet, holding a spade, would claim his notice. On the magistrate's shoulder is perched a grotesque devil, blowing from a pair of bellows into his ear.

21—The Preacher. In the pulpit. Death in the pulpit too, holding up a jaw-bone, mocking the serious listeners.

22—The Parish Priest. He bears the viaticum, Death preceding him with bell and lantern.

23—The Begging Friar. Before his convent, his wallet in one hand, his relic-box in the other. Death grasps him. Over the cut is the text: " Sitting in darkness and death's shadow, bound in beggary (*mendicitate*)."

24—The Nun. She is in her cell, kneeling and telling her rosary before an altar; but listens to the lute-playing of a lover seated on the edge of her bed. Death is extinguishing the candles on the altar.

25—The Old Wife.   Two Deaths are here, one leading her, one playing on a psalter.

26—The Physician.   Death brings to him a decrepit old man in derision of his skill.

27—The Astrologer.   He sits at a table, contemplating a sphere hung over it; Death holds out to him a skull.

28 -The Rich Man.   Seated, counting his gold; Death there in the strong room, seated too, clutches at the coins. " Fool! this night thy soul is required of thee."

29—The Merchant.   Seized amid his just-landed bales.

30—The Seaman.   A ship in a storm; Death, on board among the frightened crew, is busied in breaking the mast.

31—The Knight.   In complete armour, vainly fighting against Death, who has driven a spear through his body.

32—The Count.   He would flee from a rugged peasant, Death, who threatens to crush him with a piece of his own armour.   At their feet is the peasant's flail.

33—The Old Man.   Death, playing on a dulcimer, leads him gently into a grave, open at his feet.

34--The Countess, or Bride (?).   Her maid is attiring her; Death hangs on her neck a necklace of little bones.

35—The Lovers.   New-married perhaps; of high rank by their dress.   " Thee and me only death shall separate!" Death dances before them, beating a drum.

36—The Duchess, or Princess (*Fürstin*).   Death drags her off a canopied couch or bed, while a second skeleton at the bed's foot plays the fiddle.   The monogram HL here.

37---The Pedlar.   With heavy pack, detained by Death.

38—The Husbandman.   Ploughing; Death driving the horses.   The furrows seem complete, and the sun is setting behind a charming bit of rural landscape: village and fields and trees and church and far off hills.

39--The Young Child.   A woman kneels at a low fire, cooking; the smoke rising in a shroud-like form, as Death leads away the younger of two children vainly looking and straining back toward its mother.

40—The Last Judgment.   Christ seated on a rainbow, over a globe, the glorified on either side; below are groups of naked figures, looking toward their Judge.   Wolmaan has the Skeletons of All Folk next preceding this, as surely the last of the Death series.

41 — Death's Armorial Bearings. On a broken shield a skull with a worm between its jaws; for crest, upon a helmet, an hour-glass between two skeleton arms which hold as in act of hurling a large unhewn stone. For supporters a knight and a lady. "There is nothing more finished," writes appreciative Papillon, "than the engraving of this Print. The head of the Gentleman is of a delicacy passing imagination; his crisped locks, and the plumes of his hat, are engraved with a precision which has required of the engraver an infinite patience; the mantle is not less artistically engraved. . . I have yet seen nothing equal to the engraving of this Print; the more I examine it, the more the art and the boldness of the work cause my admiration."

The foregoing are the forty-one cuts of the edition of 1538. Seventeen added after are these here following.

42 — The Soldier. Death, with a shield and with a thigh-bone for club, striding over the dead on a battle-field, opposes him. A skeleton drummer leads on some soldiers in the distance. This is the mere mercenary, War's hireling.

43 — The Gamester. Three gamesters at a table; Death has one by the throat, and the Devil seizes him by the hair. One of his companions seems interested for him; the other quietly rakes in the money on the table.

44 — The Drunkard. Men with women at supper in a brothel; one man is vomiting; Death empties a pitcher into the mouth of another.

45 — The Fool. An Idiot: stepping jauntily with Death, who plays on the bagpipes.

46 — The Robber. Dismounted from his horse, he attacks a market-woman passing through a wood; Death arrests him. Her face admirable in expression! says Wornum. We may say the same of the faces throughout the series. They are Holbein's.

47 — The Blind Man. Death holds the end of his staff and draws him stumbling on.

48 — The Waggoner. He stands, wringing his hands, by the side of his overturned waggon, a front wheel of which is carried away by Death. One of two horses is down between the shafts; a second Death unfastens the hindermost of three barrels.

49 — The Young Wife. Death invites her to dance, her husband playing the guitar.

50 — The Young Husband. Death blowing a horn; a ruined wall in the background.

51 — The Beggar. A Cripple, his crutches beside him, sitting on the ground near the door of a hospital which other persons are entering; one at a window is looking at him. There is no figure of Death here; nor in these following designs of Children.

52 — A Boy. Naked, bearing an arrow and a shield.

53 — Boys. One striding an arrow as a hobby-horse, one with a bow, a third carrying a hare hanging from a pole across his shoulder.

54 — Boy-Bacchanals. Three carry a fourth crowned with vine-leaves; a fifth walks before with grapes on a pole. The text above: "Whose God is their belly."

55 — Boys with trophy and spoil of war. "He shall divide the spoil with the strong."

56 — Boys with trophies again ; one wearing a wreath borne upon the others' shoulders.

57 — Boys. A group as part of a procession ; one boy on horseback, carrying a flag.

58 — Boy-Musicians. A drum-major and band with horns, again as if designed to form part of a procession. These last three groups are crowded more than the preceding, less simple in composition, and not so good in drawing.

The eleven cuts added in 1545, or 1547, are those here numbered from 42 to 48,—the Soldier, the Gamester, the Drunkard, the Fool, the Robber, the Blind Man, and the Waggoner ; and the four designs of Children, Nos. 52 53 54 55. The five cuts added in 1562 I have numbered 49 50 56 57 58,—the Young Wife, the Young Husband, and three designs of Children. These last five are not in the Holbein Society's Reprint ; and Douce has only forty-nine cuts, Nos. 1 to 48 and No. 51. The veritable masque of Death of the 1538 book is comprised in thirty-seven cuts, the first two, the Creation and the Fall, being preliminary and the Last Judgment and Arms of Death supplementary to the subject. The nine death-cuts appearing later have the look of an afterthought. The Beggar, unless perhaps as a Death-in-Life, bears no necessary relation to the rest. And the Children-cuts seem out of place, mere *addenda* to swell the list : notwithstanding the texts above and verse beneath, which strive to inform us of some possibility of connection.

I have noticed the tardy publication of the first edition, the engraved blocks, it would seem, forty of them at least, lying unused during eleven years. Noticeable also are the several additions of new cuts to the later issues : eleven of them not given until nine years after the first book-edition and five not until fifteen years yet later. Or, if we consider that Lutzelburger's proofs of forty were printed so early as 1527, a period of eighteen or twenty years had elapsed before Frellon made use of the new eleven (twelve with the Beggar) ; and the last five only appeared in 1562, thirty-five years after our date of the first set of proofs. Was it that Holbein, having completed to his own satisfaction the series of forty-one subjects, afterwards made the additional designs, either at his own instance, or at the instigation of the publisher ? If so, as he died in 1543, how happened it that the last five subjects did not appear with the twelve in 1545 or '47 ? And who engraved all these seventeen ? The assumption of Lutzelburger's death has been based, I think, on insufficient ground.

The *Dance of Death.*

56 57 58 only in the edition of 1562.

Boy-Bacchanals 1547

The Young Husband 1562.

Delays in using the cuts

The one really important evidence for any date of death depends upon his identification
with the Hans *Formschneider* of the archives of Basle. Without this finding I should
not regard the preface to the edition of 1538. The writer of that laments the death of
this "*excellent painttre*" who has here imagined for us (*celluy qui nous en a icy imaginé*)
such elegant figures: words known to be untrue of the painter, hardly only therefore to
be accepted as surely applicable to the engraver.* The whole passage looks as if written
with some prudential motive, as a sort of lightning-rod to divert attention from Holbein.
The Waggoner (not used until 1545 or '47) is indeed spoken of as unfinished, but it is
so inaccurately described that it is manifest the writer had not seen it; and though the
words "*ja par lui trasséa*" might be thought to imply the engraver, on the very unlikely
supposition that Holbein would trust him to trace the design on the block, yet even so
taken they may not be less with intention to mislead. On the loose ground of this quite
incorrect statement of the death of the painter was founded the surmise of the death of
the engraver. Curiously however, the recent discovery of the death in 1526 of a Basle
wood-engraver connected with the Trechsels fits in with it: leaving us then to assume
an unknown engraver able to continue Lutzelburger's work with no apparent inferiority.
The twelve later cuts (here agreeing with Ottley), and the last of 1562 also, regarded

---

* As sample of conjectural history it may not be out
of place to cite the following, from Ottley's *Inquiry
into the . History of Engraving*. After remarking
that the words of the preface would, were nothing
opposing them, constitute very strong evidence that
Holbein was not the author of the designs, he goes
on to say, as follows. "But I am firmly persuaded
that it refers in reality, not to the designer, but to
the Artist employed under his direction to engrave
the designs, Hans Lutzelburger. Hollada, I am of
opinion, had shortly before 1538 sold the forty-one
blocks executed sometime previously [say 11 years]
to the bookseller of Lyons, and had at the same time
given him a promise of others, which he had lately
designed as a continuation of the series, and were
then in the hands of the wood-engraver. The wood
engraver, I suppose, died before he had completed
his task, and the correspondent of the bookseller,
who had probably deferred his publication expecting
the new blocks, wrote from Basle to Lyons to inform
his friend of the disappointment occasioned by the
artist's death. It is probable that this information
was not given very circumstantially, . . and that
the person who wrote the dedication might believe
the designer and engraver to be the same: it is still
more probable he thought the distinction of little
consequence. . . The additional cuts (eight of
the Dance of Death and four of Boys) were afterwards finished, doubtless by another engraver who
had been brought up under the eye of Holbein, and
are not apparently inferior, whether in respect of
design or execution, to the others." (*Inquiry*, etc.,
pp. 159, 760.)
  Truly a "complication of probabilities!" Yet it
may be noted that there is, 1—no evidence of the
engraver's employment under direction of Holbein;
2—no evidence of Holbein having sold (or having
property in) the forty-one blocks; 3—no evidence
of his promising others; nor, 4—of having at that
time designed a continuation; 5—no evidence but
the doubtful preface of others being in the hands of
the engraver; 6—no evidence, except the preface,
of the death of the engraver; 7—no evidence that
any correspondent wrote to the bookseller to inform
him of such death. This correspondent being only
of Mr. Ottley's invention, we need not inquire into
his supposed conduct or probable motive or belief.
And finally, if the twelve later cuts are not inferior,
apparently, to the rest, what ground is there for the
assertion that they were done "doubtless by another
engraver, who had been brought up under the eye
of Holbein,"—he not resident at Basle after 1526?

only as engravings, are of the same excellence as the first. And looking to the cutting alone, I can believe that the latest cuts, as well as the earliest, might be Lutzelburger's work, though the 1562 five may not be of Holbein's designing.

Death's Dance, *Todtentanz, Danse Macabre, Danse de Machabées, Machabæorum Chorea* (*chorea* rather *masque* or *procession* than what we now call *dance*): all these are names of the same thing. It is THE MASQUE OF DEATH, or Procession of the Death-claimed. That word *Macabre*, or *Machabd*, has been a stumbling-stone for the book men. Chatto takes it for the name of an obscure French or German poet; while Douce proclaims the poet a "non-entity," and supposes the word is a "slight and obvious corruption of Macarius (Fr. Macaire), a saint who lived as a hermit in Egypt." Fournier thought the word to be derived from the Arabic; others have looked to the Hebrew: either way with some reference to the graveyard. The Abbé Dufour (*Recherches sur la Danse Macabre*, 1873) finds *Machabd* still in use in French *argot*, signifying a corpse, "*un cadavre de la Morgue.*" He adds:—"Its congener *Macabre* is out of use." The two words, he believes, have a common origin, the first somehow confounded with the name of the Jewish heroes, the Maccabees. May they have been so named from their death-dealing activity?

No new or scarce-used subject was the Masque when taken up by Holbein. A small folio, German, supposed to have been printed between 1480 and 1500, had similar wood cuts, of all sorts and conditions of men Death-attended. Paris in 1485 had likewise its *Danse.* And later the same subject, in various forms and variety of treatment, was seen in both France and Germany. We find the Masque of Death repeated frequently in the ornamental borders to the *Hours* of Vérard and other French printers. The characters differ and they are more or less numerous. One, *La Grande Danse de Macabre*, printed at Troyes, contains as many as seventy-five; and in the borders of a Dutch prayer-book of 1520—30 there are yet more. The dismal theme suited the more than serious temper of the time. It was of earlier usage also. In an old building at Basle, once a nunnery, were but lately the remains of a Death-Masque painted on the walls, of the date of 1312. Another, some time attributed to Holbein, but the work of Hans Kluber or Klauber, in or about 1450, was a series of paintings,* forty compositions of life-size figures upon the walls of the cemetery of the Preficanm' Convent, also at Basle. It is said that the work commemorated a visitation of the plague, which in 1439 carried off five thousand of the inhabitants of that city. But no particular occurrence seems needed to account for such a painting in those days. Dufour speaks of the same subject painted in the cemetery of the Innocents at Paris in 1425, and of a manuscript of the same nature so early as 1407.

---

* Painted, or at least repaired, in oil: the repairing with sundry alterations and additions executed by a younger Kluber, about a century later. After other reparations, the paintings were finally destroyed in 1805, in consequence of the wall having to be taken down for some improvements. (*Woltmann's Holbein.*)

The subject indeed had been accepted long before for one demanding men's attention; was old, if not as Christianity itself, yet as the monkish interpretation of that, a natural concomitant of the faith of those who, professing to worship One who overcame Death, despised and trampled on and denied the pagan joyousness of Life. Like the skull in the monk's cell, an object for pious contemplation, the image of Death was ever present to the mind which renounced this world, caring only for another. And when, in a later seething of thought, rebellious or reforming, over the newly kindled dissatisfaction with both Pontiff and Kaiser, the bonds of authority fell off, Death had farther recognition as the Great Equaliser, the Master of the Greatest as the Least. The favourite subject of the preacher was taken hold of by the painter and became popular also. Masques of Death, various in design, were painted in the cloisters of Old St. Paul's, at London; at Salisbury, Hexham, Roslyn, Fescamp in Normandy, Dijon, Lubeck, Minden, Leipsie, Dresden, and elsewhere; such wall-paintings preceding the designs for books.

Mr. Hamerton, in his eloquent *Treatise on the Graphic Arts*, remarks that "it is a great mistake to suppose that fac-simile wood-engraving, like that which bears the name of Holbein, represents the art at its best or even represents it fairly. After all, the Holbein cuts are only drawings in grey and white and they do not make the most of a wood block with its possibilities of fine blacks and other resources." (*Treatise*, p. 320.) I must own to thinking this very unintelligent and not quite intelligible criticism. Are drawings, or engravings, in grey and white less artistic than drawings, or engravings, that make the most of "fine blacks" or other resources? Mr. Hamerton's "only" would imply no less. What sign of inferiority is there in Holbein's choice of grey and white in preference to more or darker shadow, and the finest French black? Many as may be the possibilities of wood-engraving in the wide scope between the simple black line of a St. Christopher and the opposite use of white lines upon a black ground, there is no reason here for the distinction—"at its best." Lutzelburger's cuts, the very best of fac-simile, represent one process of wood-engraving, and the Bewick white-upon-black represents the other. And farther, though positive black in a wood-cut may be of advantage, it may also only be the disadvantage of cheaper or lazier performance. It may be a valuable resource; or it may be worthless. Of fac-simile work, work done with a knife (the wood-cutter's one tool in Holbein's day), Lutzelburger's cuts, I repeat, are the utmost possible of the art. That he did not make the most of other not-wanted possibilities is all the residuum I detect in the objecting criticism. The question, whether Holbein himself knew what was best for his purpose—only grey and white or fine blacks, I may not care to discuss. I am disposed to think he did.

I have been called the "Apostle of white line." I dare accept the implied praise, for with both graver and pen, in season and, perhaps, out of season, I have been earnest in insisting upon white line as the proper office of engraving in wood. But that must be understood of work with the graver, the tool now employed,—a tool with which we can draw. No such work is possible with the knife. I have not been remiss in dispraise of mere mechanical work: much of that yet done with the graver, most (not quite all) of that done with the tool of a mechanic--the knife. Nevertheless, as the draftsman, and now and then even a painter, may be only a mechanic, so *the mechanic* (we must so call him for classification) may be almost an artist. Perhaps quite. Like Lutzelburger, he sometimes comes too near to be fairly called anything less. To show what of art there is in wood-engraving, not to expose its mechanism, I have cared to write. For this, not following the track of the bibliographer, nor only observing the values of design, I have pointed to the artistic cutting (knife-work as it is) of the *Biblia Pauperum* and the *Ars Moriendi*, for this I have exalted Jerome of Nurnberg and now extol our chief of artists in the Mechanics' Walk—Hans Lutzelburger. The mechanical wood-cutter may have a drawing clear as Durer's, as large and firm; as unmistakable—if he could see it. But the mere mechanic does not see. Very deft his hand, from long practice, as he cuts so conscienciously what he seems to see (he can be as blind with a graver as with a knife). To the perceiving artist-eyes of a Lutzelburger is revealed the inner spirit as well as the outer body of Holbein's intelligently formed lines: and so, with perhaps only the same hand-ability, he produces an intelligent and artistic result. This is fac-simile: this only should be so called. Most delicate and full of subtle meaning was each considered touch of the accomplished draftsman, and this engraver has preserved it all: neither leaving extraneous wood to the loss of delicacy, so vulgarising the lines, nor cutting away those nice gradations and inequalities which assist expression. For all our resources, of "fine blacks" or other, we have no Lutzelburger to-day: wanting perhaps the Holbein.

In the same year as the *Dance of Death*, 1538, the Trechsels printed at Lyons a series of wood-cut Figures of Stories of the Bible (*Historiarum Veteris Testamenti Icones*), eighty-six of wider form, nearly twice the size of those in the *Dance*, of which four are used, preceding the set. The *Figures* were also printed by the Trechsels in a *Bible* issued at Lyons in the same year. Wornum supposes them to have been first used in Froschover's *Bible* of 1531: but the cuts in that, despite the earlier publishing, are  plainly copies. The cutting of the *Icones* is unequal, not a few, however, bearing comparison with the *Dance* cuts and well worthy of Lutzelburger. The *Temptation of Eve* is surely his. I find this only in the *Bible*. Three other cuts (Lamentations, Jonah, and Habakkuk) in the *Bible* do not appear in the British Museum copy of the *Icones* issued by the Treschels, in 1539. Five later editions, from 1543 to 1549, have the names of the Frellons as publishers. The Frellons also reproduced the *Bible* in 1543, and later.

I find nothing likely by Lutzelburger, nor anything I would attribute to Holbein, in the cuts of the Coverdale *Bible* (the first complete translation into English printed, says Henry Stevens, by Jacob Van Meteren at Antwerp, in 1534-5) except the title-page and six small cuts of the six days' creation. Nearly all the cuts in Bibles of the period are of a very poor and primitive character, cuts of one frequently used for another, the printer perhaps supplying the illustrations, carelessly using any he might have in stock, and borrowing where he could. In a second edition of Archbishop Parker's Bible, 1572, an initial G of Jove's amour with Leda is prefixed to the first chapter of the Epistle to the Hebrews. Artists' designs too seem to have been looked upon as common property and so by engravers repeatedly copied or transferred.

We have yet to take note of certain ALPHABETS with which Holbein and Lutzelburger are credited. Four of these, done as Initial Letters for printers, have been ascribed to the painter: two very small, a *Dance of Peasants* and *Sports of Infants*; another Alphabet of *Ornaments*; and the " *Little Dance of Death*." I can not assert that any of these are done in wood. If in metal, they are graver-work in relief. A sheet of the *Ornaments*, in the Berlin Cabinet of Prints, is signed — *H. L. F.* 1522. Of the *Little Dance of Death* fair copies are given by Douce; and the same appear in the later editions of Chatto.

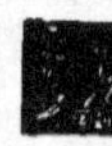

Under the originals of these last, in the British Museum, is the name of the engraver:

THOUGH engravings in copper, the beautiful works of Durer and the " Little Masters," had come in to rival and surpass the best of engraving in wood, and though metal was much employed for cuts in relief (for the commoner cuts in inferior printers' books as well as for those of the finished minuteness of the *Hours*) yet we must not think the *formschneider's* occupation gone. Still for him was left a fairly ample range of use, from a *View of Venice,* nine feet long, drawn on the wood by Jacopo di Barbarj (called also Jacob Walsch), to Altdorfer's series of *The Fall and Redemption of Man* and the inch-square initial letters of Lutzelburger. I set the names of Altdorfer and Papillon at the head of this chapter because in Altdorfer's wood-cuts I find the first attempt to imitate the effective fineness of copper and in Papillon's the same imitation carried to its extreme.

Before considering a class of work to be distinguished as work for books we may look at a few cuts chiefly noticeable for their size. They ask not many words, for after Jerome the best of them appear but rude. The intelligent admirer of good wood-engraving will not care for them except only as works to be catalogued in a history of the art. Enough here to note some of the most important which can be seen in the Print Room of the British Museum. They are these.

A View of Venice, nine feet long and four feet high, dated 1500, on six planks; drawn, but not engraved, by Barbarj. It is very full of detail, every house being faithfully given; and the whole is fairly cut.

Pharaoh and his host in the Red Sea. After Titian, by Domenico dalle Greche, 1549. About seven feet by four. It was vigorously drawn, and is consequently firm in cutting.

Only I can not call the cutting remarkable   It may be by an Italian engraver, but there is nothing to show it.   Indeed, and setting aside the probability of German engravers in Italy, there is nothing to distinguish the Southern from the Northern workman.   Even as a chapter-heading the "Southern Schools of Wood-Engraving" (Dr. Willshire must forgive me) has no meaning, except as the words may be applied to the draughtsmen.   The more cutting is characterless.

Abraham's Sacrifice : from Beccafumi's design upon the pavement of Siena Cathedral. Six feet by two and a half ; with two tints, as a chiaroscuro (to be spoken of later), by Andrea Andreani ; drawn and engraved by him, says Passavant.   The lines of drawing are firm and strong, cleanly cut, but of no remarkable excellence.

Moses breaking the Tables of the Law.   Also from the Siena Cathedral, and by the same artists.   Six feet in length and four feet in height.   As well cut.

Several *Processions.*   One, the *Entry of Charles V into Bologna* in 1529, thirteen sheets (part lost), is twenty-eight feet long and fifteen inches high.   Another, after Titian, of the *Doge and Officers of State*, is fifteen feet long and fifteen inches high.

A Genealogical Tree.   A most elaborate design, crowded with armorial bearings upon shields supported by half-length figures ; with medallion portraits of German Emperors.

French Kings, Bavarian Dukes, etc. ; and framed with a white-on-black scroll border : two feet, four inches, wide, and nearly fourteen feet in upright length.   Well cut.

I may notice one more—a *Christ taken from the Cross* : three feet and a quarter by a little over two feet : bold, and well cut for a poster.   Probably all these big cuts were to be hung on walls ; and perhaps, as in elder time, intended for colouring.   They are cut well enough for such a purpose ; but have no claim to especial admiration.

Jacopo di Barbarj and Domenico dalle Greche, like Durer and many other artists, are said to have engraved their own drawings on wood.   From Papillon till to-day this view has been almost universal.   There is a lack of evidence in support of such an ascription. In these large works the size alone would seem to contradict it.   And of the smaller, I think, all we can say with confidence is that a few painters may have occasionally used the knife, as well as worked in metal.   When on a print, *Venus and Cupid*, after Titian, I read—" *Nicolaus Boldrinus Vincentinus incidebat* " I have no right to doubt that it was cut by Boldrini.   But I am not sure that cut was not done on soft metal with a graver; and I incline to think that where we find *incidit*, or other trust-worthy intimation of the draftsman and cutter as one, we may suspect the easier material.   For whatever weight it can have against my own conclusion, I give, on the opposite page, part of a relief-cut " designed and engraved by Æneas Vico," a copper-engraver of Parma, in 1550.   It is part of a border to a portrait of the Emperor Charles V.   The elaboration of the cross lining is very remarkable, more so as Italian work, if it is by Vico's own hand ; but that elaboration does not tell against it having been cut in wood.   We shall see far minuter knife-work in coming days, by Papillon.

Minuter work is seen in the example I have given of Altdorfer's doing.   An engraver in wood as well as copper Passavant believes him to have been, and the forty cuts of the *Fall and Redemption of Man*, designed by him, to be of his own cutting.   W. Bell Scott, copper-engraver and wood-draftsman as well as painter, agrees with Passavant, judging (I think rightly), from the fineness of the close-serried lines peculiar to Altdorfer, that they could not have been drawn line for line in the usual manner of Durer and of other draftsmen.   (*The Little Masters*, pp. 38, 39.)   The more precise drawing was not needed for the artist's own cutting.   Scott also notices, as unusual in wood-prints of the period, a peculiar and purposed faintness of certain lines as if they had been kept from pressure by the overlaying of heavier parts in the printing.   The faintness, however, would more likely be caused by the lowering of the lighter portions in the wood, another indication of the engraving being by Altdorfer himself.

Nevertheless, the correct attribution of the engraving to the designer can be but very exceptional.   Besides the Vico and Altdorfer cuts, the only exceptions I am disposed to credit, for any considerable amount of work, are our four Block Books : those because I suppose them to have been done by artist-monks.   If writers on early wood-engraving could fully realise the slow laboriousness of knife cutting, they might avoid many errors of judgment in ascription of work, and might escape that most unhappy of the fallacies besetting them—the crediting or discrediting the engraver with beauties or defects for which he is not responsible. The mechanical facility of knife-work, on the other hand, (it is easy, however tedious), may account for much of vile cutting seen in early books, and in later editions of our best block books. What would be easier, for the poorest of knife-users, with his glued transparent print of the *Biblia Pauperum* or other book upon the wood, than to hack it out in some clumsy fashion and, himself printer and publisher, bring out an edition, for the bewilderment of innocent critics in days to come? We need not wonder at the wretched cuts which disfigured early books and, despite the masterly examples of Nurnberg and Basle, were but too prevalent through later times.

Much of a better kind was also done : during that sixteenth century certainly was no lack of princely printer publishers caring for works of worth, nor of able designers and draftsmen, if wanting Durer's vigour or Holbein's delicacy of line. One man indeed stands exceptionally, Hans Sebald Beham, first of "Little Masters." Twenty six cuts of the *Apocalypse*, designed by him, and probably by him drawn on the wood, are of supremest excellence.

Very beautiful the drawing must have been, and the cutting is manifestly close to it. But we need to see impressions without the furred margin of ink from dirty printing which hides the real sharpness of line, to justly appreciate the intelligent perfectness of the work. Here again the wood cutter was an artist. We have no hint of who he was, unless it be in the fact that Beham was of Nurnberg (the *Apocalypse* was printed at Frankfort, where he lived later) and that in 1528 Jerome Andreæ was engaged with him on an unimportant book, *Proportions of the Horse*, the sale of which was stopped by the Nurnberg Town Council on a supposition that it was pirated from Durer, just dead. Were these Beham designs cut by Andreæ, we should have to name him the equal of the man of Basle, even on Lutzelburger's own ground. Or might Lutzelburger have done them? Or was there yet a third, unnamed?

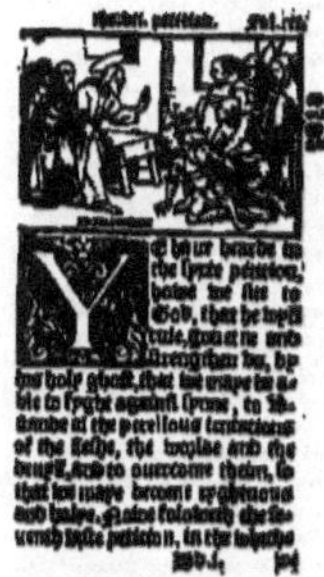

All which is if they are wood-cuts. If on copper they would be altogether by the hand of Beham. Besides this series, Beham made many drawings on wood, some, as remarked by Scott, of "prodigious dimensions." One of these is the *Fountain of Youth*, nearly four feet long; another is a *Procession* of the length of five feet. Of smaller works by him on wood *Des Babstum* ('The Papacy) contains seventy-four prints, of the costumes used by all the orders of the Romish Church. Forty-one small cuts for the *New Testament* and eighty-one to a *Bible* are of his designing also. All of them are very fairly engraved, but none are equal to the *Apocalypse*.

Cranmer's Catechism, 1548, may be briefly noticed here. I had spoken of it before with Holbein's work, but that it has none of Lützelburger's cutting, and two designs only which can be ascribed to the painter. One of them I give here in its place on the page, as a specimen of a book of the period. I take the initial Y to be metal; and the heading may be so too. I am not sure. I do not escape the same suspicion of the cut below, from the same book, one of twenty-five not by Holbein, perhaps (so Woltmann thinks) by Bernard Salomon. Chatto writes of these as "the best executed in [England] up to that time: though none have the slightest pretension to delicacy or excellence of engraving." It is unlikely that these cuts, or any so good, could be engraved in England; but without doubt Jackson's copies of them warrant the depreciating judgment of Chatto. In truth, I can only say that the copies throughout the *Treatise*, even when not by reduction rendered useless as examples of engraving, seldom give much idea of the originals. The subjects also are badly chosen for illustrations of history, instances of wood-engraving "intended to preserve the characteristics of each individual." Is Jackson or is Chatto to be blamed for this? Jackson in his *Preface* seems to claim the responsibility for himself, a number of cuts apparently having been engraved before Chatto had any concern with the work.

In fairness to them both it must be owned that nearly all copies and "reproductions" are of a like naughtiness. The wood-cuts in Noel Humphreys' *Master-pieces of the early Printers and Engravers*, 1868-70, are not often master-pieces of engraving: and, where they are, the engraver's work is lost in the reproduction, either because they have been taken from badly printed originals or because they are badly printed in his book. They are caricature rather than characteristic. His page of the *Biblia Pauperum* is from the spurious edition without the apple, and a poor copy of that; his reproductions of pages of the *Canticum* and *Speculum* are disgraceful; and in a specimen from one of the *Hours*, given as "wood or metal" and "slightly reduced," the beauty of the original has entirely gone. The same fault of unlikeness damnifies the "fac-similes" of Holtrop and Ames and Dibdin. From the best of them I learn nothing of the engravings.

Of the prints in Becker's *Gravures au bois des Anciens Maîtres Allemands*, "taken from the original blocks" collected by Joan Albert de Derschau, I quote this from my Notes made lately in the British Museum Library:—Among the many cuts (some hundreds) here given I do not find one, except Durer's *Christ on the Cross*, that is worth giving for the engraving: a few small cuts may be too badly printed to show what they are; but plainly the mass are worn, and also originally worthless as specimens of *engraving*.

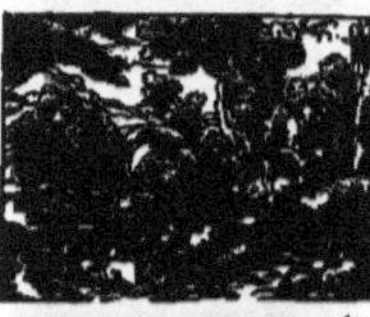

After Durer, Holbein, and Beham, the men of the sixteenth century most notable for us will be Virgilius (or Virgil) Solis, Bernard Salomon (called the "Little Bernard" from the small size of his works), Jost Amman, and Tobias Stimmer. The designs by them are very numerous, and in general are well, that is carefully engraved; but the unnamed engravers show little of artistic feeling and, speaking generally, their best doings after Lutzelburger's *Death-Dance* and the Beham *Apocalypse* are as the thin piping of Marsyas to the music of Apollo.

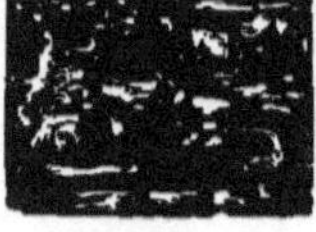

Of drawings on wood by VIRGIL SOLIS the list in Bartsch is very long: the most important are one hundred and forty-seven *Bible Figures*, with sixty nine additional for a later edition, then printed in borders; a hundred and seventy-eight for Ovid's *Metamorphoses*; and a hundred and ninety-four for Æsop's *Fables*. Fair samples of the work of Solis, and of the better book-work, are the two cuts on this page: taken from the *Fables*, 1560, and the *Metamorphoses*, 1564 : these the dates of the Frankfort editions from which my reproductions have been taken. Many of the cuts in the Æsop and the Ovid are used again with Reusner's *Emblems*, Frankfort, 1581. There is no learning anything about the engravers.

The work of BERNARD SALOMON can be easily known by the slenderness and length of his figures. A corresponding thinness of line leads me to doubt that the cuts were done in wood. *Quadrius Historiques de la Bible*, subjects of Bible story and French quatrains underneath, was first printed at Lyons, about 1550. A later edition, 1555, has two hundred and twenty eight cuts, designs from the Old Testament, (one here given), and ninety-six, half the size, from the New. Though with Chatto and other writers these have always passed as wood-cuts, I can not lose a suspicion, increased by their production at Lyons, that they all are on some metal. The borders to the hundred and seventy-eight cuts in Ovid are metal, some scroll-ornament surely so; and I believe the small cuts within the borders are metal too. So far as I have had opportunity for examination, I have found nothing by Bernard which seemed to me distinctly wood. Indeed French book-work of the period bears almost always that thin metallic look. Whether metal or wood, all these cuts are after the fashion of wood, in relief.

Rachel venant autrefois à l'abreuvoir
Secourut Jacob qui descouvrit le puits,
Et la baisa, puis fit il bon devoir
Qu' elle & Laban il espousa depuis. *

* *Rachel her sheep was leading to the well,*
Came to her Jacob and the well unclosed,
And kiss'd her; and his duty did so well
That her & Laban thereafter he espoused.

Solis and Salomon, the one in Germany and the other in France, employed by the competing publishers of Nürnberg and Lyons, would seem to have worked in rivalry or imitation of each other. Bolder work than that of either will be found in cuts from the drawings of JOST AMMAN, a yet more prolific artist, between 1560 and 1590. Besides a hundred and thirty-two figures in his Book of *All Ranks, Arts, and Trades*, 1564, (from which I have taken the cuts on pages 25 and 26), we have from his hand several works of costume, Bible illustrations, mythological subjects, a pack of playing cards, etc. The following list is given by Bartsch:—for Livy's *Roman History* seventy-five cuts; for the *Gospels* seventy-eight; *Works* of Josephus twenty-four; *Saints* two hundred and eighty-nine; *Costumes of Clergy* a hundred and three; *Cavaliers* ninety-two; *Women's Dresses* a hundred and twenty-two; *Beasts of Chase* forty. In the *Künstbüchlein* (Little Art-book), published in 1599, a year before his death, we have a fair selection of his book-designs, most of them well drawn and carefully and intelligently engraved, with fine cross-lining in some. The cutting is generally firm and clean, as seen in this *Temptation in Paradise*

from his *New Bible Figures*, Frankfort, 1564. The supremest piece from his drawing is a *Title-page to Livy*, printed at Frankfort by John and Sigismund Feyerabend, in 1578.

Of wood-drawings by TOBIAS STIMMER (he and Amman both Swiss) some sixty-five subjects and series of subjects, biblical and other, are enumerated by Bartsch; one set of sixty-four accompanying other designs by Jost Amman for the *Works* of Josephus.

TITI LIVII PA-
TAVINI, ROMA-
NÆ HISTORIÆ PRINCI-
PIS, LIBRI OMNES, QVOTQVOT
ad nostram ætatem perue-
nerunt:
VNA CVM DOCTISSIMORVM VIRORVM
in eos lucubrationibus, post omnes aliorum editiones, summa
fide ac diligentia, & veterum & recentiorum exemplarium
collatione nunc denuo recogniti, plurimisq; in locis castigati, &
artificiosis picturis, præcipuas historias apté repræsentan-
tibus, exornati, inq; duos Tomos distributi, qui-
bus quæ contineantur, post præfatio-
nem patebit.

Cum INDICE copiosissimo.

Cum gratia & priuilegio Cæs. Maiest.
FRANCOFORTI AD MOENVM, APVD
haeredes & Iustissima impressoris
M. D. LXXVIII.

Genes. XVI. Cap
Das bild bauer Testament.

Als Agar sich sah Schwanger sein/
Wolt sie kain Straffred nemmen ein
Von jrer Frauen/ floh davon
Da Engel spro sie hinein zu gohn.
Diß schutz vnd low/ sei in der thon.
B iij

Again, who were the engravers? Passavant gives names: Christopher Van Sichem, of Basle, as an engraver of Stimmer's *Bible* drawings; and Ludwig Frig, of Zurich, for designs by Amman: good work, for which they should be remembered. We may imply discover yet another worth recording. In the cut of *Hagar and Sarah*, from Stimmer's *Neue Kunstliche Figuren Biblischen*, Basle, 1576, we observe the monogram MF^2. On one at least of Amman's *Bible* cuts we find S F; and in his *Kunstbüchlein* MF is seen again, and D F and I F. Of these three I get nothing from Passavant. With other separate letters F may sometimes mean only *Formschneider*; but the monogram implies a name. If we can at all trust to too credulous and not over-accurate Papillon, who prints a list of more than four hundred supposed engravers in wood, we may perhaps find some one. He writes particularly of the family of Feyerabendt, at Frankfort, celebrated as artists, engravers, and poets: seven of them,—Jean, Sigismund, S. H., M., L., V., and Jerome. Jean (Iohannes) he recognizes as a wood-engraver by the initials I F. He was father or grandfather (so Papillon) of Sigismund Feyerabendt, "painter, wood-engraver, and learned bookseller of Frankfort, producer of many works." The bookseller, who signed his wood-cuts S F, and sometimes F only, was the printer of one of Amman's costume books—*Gynaceum*, the *Theatre of Women*, brought out in 1586, at the printer's expense (*impensis Sigismundi Feyrabendij*); and he printed most of Amman's works. His name, with that of Johannes (or Hans) is on the title-page to Livy. Is it Hans, or Hierome, who has the monogram IF? Carl Sigismund, a son of Sigismund, was the publisher, in 1590, of Amman's *Kunstbüchlein*, most of the prints in which, continues Papillon, "have been engraved by MFeyerabendt, others by L. and V. Feyerabendt, all of the family of the bookseller." Too much reliance must not be placed on Papillon, who finds two Jost Ammans [generally known as one, but "*telle est l'erreur des Auteurs Copistes*"], proved so to his satisfaction by difference of style and excellence: yet surely it is not unreasonable after all this story to think that some of the undoubted bookseller's family may not only have been employed upon but may have excelled in engraving, so that we may accept a conclusion that the *Title-page to Livy* was cut by a Feyerabendt (MF, HF, or another), and dare to snatch one more name from the abyss of the world's forgetfulness.

But little satisfaction can be gained from any attempt to apply initials or monograms. The attempt scarcely reaches beyond guess-work. St. and C S may convince Papillon of Christopher Stimmer, admirable engraver of his brother's designs: I discover nothing by C S of exceptional or differential quality. We may with Passavant call this one John of Frankfort, and that one Jaques de Strasbourg; we find families of Dieneckers and of Liefrinks, all wood-engravers, at Augsburg; we may identify certain unimportant cuts as work of a certain engraver: that is all. Numerous as might have been the engravers' muster-roll in that sixteenth century, we are able to attach importance to only four or five: the two of Nurnberg and Basle, Dieneeker. Altdorfer, and, perhaps, Feyerabendt.

Here I may close my review of the one especial century of Knife-Engraving in wood.
Nearly all of much worth is of German doing.   I have found no Italian cuts to compete

with the better German. none
I would place beside the cuts
of Nurnberg and of Basle.   If I
had so to place any, it should
be the *Hypnerotomachia* and a
Decameron, Venice, 1550, ten
figure headings and initials to
the Ten Days, very delicately
rendered.   Another of the same
time has smaller cuts, beautifully
engraved.   I might add likewise
a *Dante*, Venice, 1544, the cuts of which are marvelously clean and sweet in line.   But
for all these a suspicion of metal, despite all preconceptions, will creep in.   Metal also, I
scarcely dare to doubt, is the cut of *Elizabeth of Hungary giving alms*, after G. Caccia
(called Montalvo), 1610, which, if Italian knife-work, would deserve to rank with the best
of Germany.   I recall nothing of importance by the knife in France during the sixteenth
century: French best relief-cuts metal, graver-done.   English knife-work makes no mark.
Rastell's *Pastyme of People*, with coarse portraits of kings of England, 1529.   Cuningham's
Cosmographical Glasse, 1559,— Fox's *Acts and Monuments*, 1576,— Hollinshed's *Chronicles*,
1577,—show not even able mechanism.   This from Hollinshed, *Macbeth meeting the Weird
Sisters*, I think metal, fairly represents the English book print of the sixteenth century.

ST. ELIZABETH GIVING ALMS.

Two names of wood-engravers in the seventeenth century may have a passing notice: Christopher Jegher of Antwerp, and a younger Van Sichem (Cornelius or Christopher). Of JEGHER, "one of the best engravers of his time," Passavant (followed by Willshire) writes extravagantly. "Following the example of Durer, Holbein, Lucas Van Leyden, and Titian, this great master [Rubens] not only contributed by his designs to carry the art of wood-engraving to a very high perfection, but he impressed on these engravings a reflection of his own genius. He was powerfully seconded by an excellent engraver in wood, Christopher Jegher, who knew perfectly how to enter into the master's spirit, and who executed, after his establishment at Antwerp in 1620, the greater part of those cuts so sought after in our days." (*Le Peintre-Graveur*, vol. i. p. 134.) Mere words! the usual jargon of the inexpert critic, not knowing how to distinguish the cutting from the drawing. Rubens' designs did not contribute to any improvement *in engraving*. Very boldly drawn by the painter and roughly if firmly cut by the engraver are Jegher's most admired works: cut cleanly, says Chatto,— I would say, carelessly, especially in the cross lines. Neither in these nor in other large cuts by Van Sichem do I find any great merit. The subjects of these Jegher cuts are attractive (they are by Rubens), the drawing is large and vigorous and effective: for nothing of which have we to praise the engraver. The cutting bears no comparison with the work of a century earlier. Chatto has given reductions of two cuts by Jegher: a *Repose in Egypt* and a group of *Two Boys and a Lamb*. His reductions, three inches and a quarter by two inches and a half, show the designs of Rubens, but can not give the least idea of the work of Jegher: the size of the originals being,—of the *Repose in Egypt* rather less than two feet by eighteen inches, and of the group of *Boys* eighteen inches by thirteen and a half.

"Honourable mention" may be awarded to C (or A) SWITZER, an English engraver, but perhaps not English-born, whom Speed styles "the most exquisite and curious hand of that age." For all Speed, he is not a very notable engraver, though the specimen here shown of his cuts for Parkinson's *Paradisus Terrestris* ("A Garden of all sorts of pleasant flowers which our English ayre will permit to be nursed up"), 1629, will not justify Chatto in calling them "the most worthless to be found in any work of the kind." Switzer seems also to have done the cuts for Speed's *History of Britain*, 1611, and (he or a son) for Topsel's *Four-footed Beasts and Serpents*, 1658: these last with clean, firm cutting, notably of a magnificently cross-lined bear, and of some butterflies, caterpillars, spiders, etc., in an added *Theater of Insects*.

JEGHER.
Van Sichem

SWITZER.

Dating his words somewhat later, the close of the century is fairly estimated by Chatto : "Wood-engraving, as a means of multiplying the designs of artists, either as illustrations of books or as separate cuts, may be considered as having reached its lowest ebb. A few tolerably well executed cuts of ornaments are occasionally to be found in Italian, French, and Dutch books of the period; but, though they sufficiently attest the race of *workmen* not wholly extinct, they also afford ample proof that *artists* like those of former time had ceased to furnish designs for the wood-engraver. The art of design was then, however, in a languishing condition throughout Europe."

As the seventeenth century passes we light upon the names of Le Sueur and Papillon representing, like those of Dienecker and Liefrink, whole families of engravers : Peter le Sueur (born in 1636, dying in 1716), his sons, Peter and Vincent, and his grandson, Nicholas; John Papillon (who died in 1710), two sons, and two grandsons : all French. Fair knife-users we may account these, in a poor small style : their fine cuts ornamental letters, flower-vignettes, and tail-pieces, for booksellers; their staple productions blocks for card-makers and paper-stainers, patterns for embroiderers, lace-workers, and ribbon manufacturers. Not much room was there for emulating the work of elder time. Only two of these men require our notice : Nicholas le Sueur, of whom here it has merely to be said that his important work is in *chiaroscuro;* and a Papillon of the third generation, the author of the *Traité historique et pratique de la Gravure en Bois.*

JEAN MICHEL PAPILLON, born in 1698 and living until 1776, was at least an enthusiast in his art, a consciencious worker, a diligent student, and not without artistic feeling and some knowledge of design. His early work had been on cuts for paper-hangings; but this did not satisfy his ambition; so on the death of his father, whose principal business was of that sort, he devoted himself to drawing and engraving on wood for books, labouring earnestly to perfect himself in the kind of engraving then in request. The general character of his cuts is well described by Chatto as, though small, yet having considerable merit, as " not only designed with more feeling than the generality of those executed by French engravers of the period, but also much more effective, displaying a variety of tint and a contrast of light and shade not to be found in the works of his contemporaries." The first appearance, in 1727, of his Almanac, *Le Petit Almanach de Paris,* attracted the attention of critics and the public, and the engraver knew himself to be famous. From that date his work was unremitting : his *Recueil des Papillon,* a collection of the cuts of all the Papillons, which he presented to the Royal Library of Paris, containing more than five thousand by his own hand. Chatto (or Jackson), noticing this collection, and with the *Treatise* full of cuts before him, yet gives as specimen of Papillon's work only a single cut which shows nothing of either his ability or his manner.

As an artist, Papillon is but of the butterfly kind : in his engraving, however, he can cut a firm line when needed, and his minuter productions, even when vilely printed, are marvelously clear and delicate. Yet one can but ask—Of what worth this minuteness, this vain endeavour to rival copper ? and own that talent so employed is misapplied and wasted. It was the fashion of the time, and the artist was not above his age. Papillon claims the merit of not having needed every line to be drawn for him. Indeed he could hardly have drawn in lines the shading or tint of his microscopic work. Our specimens of his doing, at pages 16, 120, and 124, though but reproductions of badly printed cuts, so not rendering him fairly, still give the character of his work.

His *Treatise*, beside a somewhat apocryphal history of the art, contains a most exact and complete account of engraving with the knife, the method of execution and all that could be wanted for instruction in it. It would seem that he considered wood-engraving as the highest of the graphic arts and, though he admired the early work of the men of Nurnberg and Basle, he thought Jean Michel Papillon the chief among engravers.

In Germany during the latter half of the century two Ungers stand out as capable engravers. JOHANN GEORG UNGER, born in 1715, a type-setter to 1757, began then to make his mark as an engraver in wood. His best work, of about the same quality and character as the cuts of Amman and Stimmer, is seen in five designs by Miel, dated 1779. He died in 1788. His son, JOHANN FRIEDRICH GOTTLIEB UNGER, at first also a printer, born at Berlin in 1750, was like Papillon an enthusiast in his art. He not only engraved, but also wrote of engraving, ambitious of raising it to more artistic eminence. Our Illustration, after Miel, speaks well of his talent, in its fine perception of the touch of the draftsman recalling the artist work of Lutzelburger. In 1800 he was well appointed Professor of Wood-Engraving in the Academy of Fine Arts, at Berlin. He died in 1804.

Worthy successors of the men of the sixteenth century were these two Ungers: the son greatly the superior. To a much later period knife-work prevailed in Germany. I am told that UNZELMANN used the knife until his death, in 1855. His cuts in this manner in the *Works of Frederic the Great*, executed for the Royal House of Prussia, maintain the traditions of German faithfulness and patience. I am not certain that in Germany the knife is altogether discarded even yet.

In France, after Papillon, the knife was used for book-work until Charles Thompson, the younger brother of the great English wood-engraver, took his gravers to Paris and introduced the new method, in 1816.

In England the knife was employed for broadsides, house-prints to be hung on walls. Some few of these, very rude, may be found in the Print Room of the British Museum; among them two fairly cut and effective, from Hogarth's *Progress of Cruelty*, designed in 1751, apparently drawn on the wood by him. For ballad-headings also and products of such sort knife-work still sufficed; engraving in copper superseding it for better books. Yet not always. In Bate's *Mysteries of Nature and Art*, 1754, are a few cuts; and in a folio volume, *A Collection of Prints in imitation of Drawings*, edited by Charles Rogers, 1778, beside many small portraits, very clean and firm (some with a look of the graver), I find a number of large cuts, drawn with a pen, and admirably rendered with the knife by SIM. WATTS and JAS. DEACON. Among them I may note an *Assumption of the Virgin* by Watts, and a *Combat with Lions* (eight inches high and three feet long) by Deacon: both subjects dated 1763, and both after Luca Cambiaso. All I have been able to learn of the two engravers is in Redgrave's *Dictionary of Artists*. Of Simon Watts it merely amounts to his having engraved "two or three large cuts in 1736 [plainly a misprint for 1763] and some small circular portraits of painters" [in the same book]; and portraits of Queen Elizabeth and Dudley, Earl of Leicester, in 1773-5; with "some other works." Deacon is spoken of by Redgrave only as a miniature-painter.

Knife-work with the softer woods continued in practice to my own time. During my apprenticeship, 1828-34, I occasionally worked with the knife upon posters for Astley's Amphitheatre, then under the management of Ducrow. Bold designs, too large for box wood, were drawn by the scene-painter, or other draftsman, upon jointed planks of pine or maple; and such work, coming in with other, was not to be refused. But in general at this time knife-work was a separate business. For such cuts there was only the knife until a clever American found that a carver's tool called a *scrive* was fitter for the need.

I have sought out the best of knife-work, to make its excellences understood. Three different classes may be noted, summing up the criticisms already recorded: the simply firm and faithful rendering by Jerome of Nurnberg of the masterful firmness of Durer; the more subtle expression by Lutzelburger of Holbein's delicacy; and the microscopic minuteness of Papillon. Nothing is to be looked for more perfect in the manner of each, nothing more of variety is to be accomplished with the knife. But the two, Jerome and Lutzelburger, stand far above Papillon. Had his drawings been made by an Altdorfer, or a Beham, we might perhaps have admired his cuts as much for artistic beauty as now for mechanical excellence. His wonderful minuteness is only a mechanical excellence after all. So is he inferior to the men of Nurnberg and Basle, inferior as a *petit-maître* to a gentleman, as the artisan to the artist. When I place him among the Masters of the Knife, fitly last of them, it is because his work is characteristic (and good in its way) and also because it helps to make clear two things: that mere fineness (not refinement, but only minuteness) is of little worth in art; and that lines in relief, only to be printed by pressure on the surface, can not rival the fineness of lines incised. Papillon's mistake was in the hope to do what can only be well done by incised lines. Even by his failure he affirms the true province of wood-engraving, dependence on a firm line, not therefore unvarying or inexpressive. Jerome's and Lutzelburger's lines are always firm. I am writing now especially of knife-work.

Yet, after all disparagement, to be just to the old-time wood-engraver we must keep in mind the limit of his means: his tools,—only the knife for his finest or boldest work, and gouge and mallet to clear away broad spaces. His "blocks" were pear-tree planks, or planks of apple, service, or other wood tolerably straight in grain, not knotty or too hard. Papillon seems to have been the first to use box-wood, still cut only plank-wise. Look again at the *Petit Almanach* cut (worn and battered as it is), or at the cross-lining of the *Title to Livy*, or the bolder yet still elaborate lines of Durer, to enable yourself to estimate the merit of such work! Where large and simple, there is no difficulty, if only a line is to be left standing wherever a line is drawn: which is all we find in the *Helgen*, in Jegher, and in the mass of knife-cuts from first to last. That, as I have said, any boy or girl may do; and it is only ignorant affectation that would see merit there. Ruskin well remarks—"Once got into practice, it is as easy as lying." And very little practice may qualify so far. For complicated cross-lines nicer handling is required, more nicely the minuter the work: this too mere result of regular labour, automatic all, "in its finest accomplishment not really difficult, only tedious." Yet let us not deem too lightly of it! Some praise is due to patience and persistence. In a moment the draftsman has drawn half a score of crossing lines. There are sixteen lozenge-shaped pieces to be taken out *within the crossings*, only within them. Four cuts with the knife for each piece will give us sixty-four cuts for this result; and the outer lines remain uncut, the work half done. And think of the care to keep exactly the line drawn, to leave no wood to thicken it, to cut nothing away, and *not* to break the thinnest line left standing!

So much is involved in the most mechanical rendering. Thereafter is the crowning achievement of well-practised skill directed by an artist's intelligence, and we have work

Three classes
of knife-work.

More fineness
of little worth

Relief lines not
so fine as line
incised.

The tools for
knife-work.

The amount
of labour.

so close to the designer's every touch that, from the cut itself, it is impossible to be sure whether the draftsman himself engraved it or not. "I should imagine," writes Ruskin in his *Ariadne Florentina*, "from the character and subtlety of the touch that every line of the *Dance of Death* had been engraved by Holbein; we know it was not, and that there can be no certainty of anything more than most perfect harmony between the designer and the workman."

This is the highest praise we can give to knife-work: its limitation being to efficient rendering, that is perfect preservation, of lines drawn on the wood. When Mr. Ruskin farther would have his wood-engraver, "instead of taking pride in cutting the interstices smooth and alike, resolutely cut them rough and irregular, taking care at the same time never to leave any more than are wanted. this being only part of the general system of intelligent manipulation," (*Ariadne Florentina*, p. 75), he ignores this absolute limitation. In knife-work no such discursive resolution was allowed or possible. The sole business of the cutter (except so far as permitted by the draftsman to choose a certain closeness or wideness of line for a regular series representing merely colour) was to strictly follow the lines before him : enough if like Andrea and Lutzelburger he could see what those lines were and, having seen, preserve them so that his lines might be, not mistaken for, but really the lines of Durer and Holbein.   His utmost was perception and fidelity.

GRAVER·WORK

GRAVER·WORK

CHAPTER I

BEFORE BEWICK

HAVE not been able to discover when graver-work was first done on wood. Such work can only be done upon the end of the wood, the log for that purpose being sawn into rounds instead of planks. The solid graver can not be used with the plank, on account of its tearing up the fibre of the wood and the consequent impossibility of cutting a clean line across the grain. A hollow tool shaped like two knives placed together, called a *scrive*, is at this present time employed for posters, and for any cuts so large that they must be done on joined planks. I give, as specimen of scrive-work, part of a *Mask of Shakspere* cut in pine-wood, from a charcoal drawing by my friend William Page, the American painter. This shows how the scrive, ploughing a clean furrow, acts precisely as the solid graver does upon the end of the wood; and at the same time may serve to explain what is meaned by "*white-line work*" in wood, – of which, as a method distinct from work with the knife, I have now to treat.

I find no evidence for any use of the scrive by the elder wood-engravers; nor of their working with a graver on the end of the wood. And yet, since from old days the graver was employed for metal cuts in relief (in the manner of wood), it is hard to believe that an end (or section) of the wood was never made available. The first words concerning it I obtain from Papillon's *Treatise*. He writes as follows. "There are people who would meddle with wood-engraving without so much as a smattering of it, and who do this in a

On the end of
the wood.

very singular manner: they employ the graver on the wood as if they were engraving in metal, and make their cross-lines in the same manner as in copper,—which produces in the print white cross-lines enclosing little squares of black, a very disagreeable thing. I have in mind the frontispiece of a little work, printed in Holland in 1709, representing a lion rampant, badly drawn, which has been engraved in this manner. However I dare not be sure that this engraving is on a plank of wood, perhaps it is brass in relief; but in that case it ought at least to be engraved as if it had been on wood. It is to be supposed that they who engraved in this bad manner on wood are accustomed to do the same on brass; and I am strongly led to believe they are brass-engravers who make the plates in relief for gilding arms or ornaments on the covers of books. What confirms me in this idea is that I have proofs taken with black printing-ink of several arms engraved in this manner, the lines not held together by the ends and the cross-lines white and enclosing little square blacks,—the natural effect that one and the other should produce engraved in relief for stamping book-covers. From which I infer two things: that the engravers meddled with engraving in wood, understanding nothing of it; and that printers for the sake of economy make use of relief-engravings in brass which were intended only for the covers and backs of books." (*Traité*, vol. ii, pp. 124-5, 1766-8.)

In a note he adds:—"It must be that there are no true wood-engravers in Holland, but only engravers with the graver (*graveurs au burin*) who meddle with engraving in wood, since I have found in the new edition of Richelet's *Dictionary*, Amsterdam, 1732, with the word ENGRAVING these other words—*Art of engraving on wood with the graver*, so confounding it with engraving on metal and on copper, which proves that this art, and the manner of practising it as it should be, is almost unknown in that country. . . The author has not spoken of our engraving-point [*pointe à graver* — wood-engraver's knife], but has given us a *graver*, which we have not. . . Trevoux' *Dictionary* has the same error, speaking nowhere of the instruments of *our* engraving." [*]

He continues (p. 126):—"Some years ago there appeared in Paris a Foreigner who engraved with the graver on the end of the wood, and pretended to much advancement by this artifice: but this man reasoned without principles and without art; he knew not the impossibility of engraving properly with such a tool, since the graver can only lift the wood, and can not cut the lines sharply and cleanly as they ought to be; and, what is more, it renders them all ragged [*barbelées* — bearded or tooth-edged], whence it follows that they always look bruised in the printing; beside which the cross-lines appear white, which is inadmissible; and on the other hand the graver-point can not easily cut and lift

---

[*] The omission from the Dictionaries of the *knife*, and the appearance instead of the *graver*, may have been from technical ignorance of the lexicographer.

Chatto falls into the same error, making Hans Sachs speak of the graver, so mistranslating his lines under Jost Amman's plainly knife-using *Formschneider*.

out the wood at the end, because the strength of the fibre always drags it beneath the lines, despite all sorts of precautions : so that, in whatever fashion it may be pretended to be executed, this method can not be thought well of, and only refutes itself."

Yet Papillon tells of work done with the knife on the end of pear and service woods; and of his own use of the roots of box for delicate work, to avoid the difficulty of fibre. It would seem that he never handled a graver, not valuing or not having occasion for a tool to the use of which he had not been brought up.

Who was the foreigner (Papillon's *stranger*) whom he passes with such contempt, not even condescending to name him, who pretended to this manifest impossibility of using a graver on the end of the wood? Could he have been one JOHN BAPTIST JACKSON, an Englishman, by whom we have certain graver-work in relief, wood or metal, with a date of 1738? He was in Paris and known to Papillon, for whom he worked, and by whose help "he might have perfected himself, had he cared for advice" instead of ungratefully underworking him and behaving in other respects dishonestly. Redgrave writes of this Jackson as born in 1701, apprenticed to a copper-engraver named Kirkall, from want of employment at home going to Paris in 1726, leaving there for Rome in 1731, and living afterward till 1741 at Venice, where he produced a number of large cuts in chiaroscuro. In 1754 we find him returned to England and engaged in printing in colours, papers for paper-hangings on walls; after which the only record of him is a statement by Bewick, that he was an old man in Newcastle-on-Tyne and died in an asylum near the Teviot or on Tweedside (Bewick *Memoir*). He "was employed upon vignettes and ornamental cuts for books; produced a fine *Descent from the Cross*, after Rembrandt [in chiaroscuro, its date 1738], and six landscapes in colours by a process of which he claimed to be the inventor." (Redgrave's *Dictionary of Artists*. See also Chatto's *Treatise*, pp. 453-7.)

ELISHA KIRKALL (not Edward, as in Chatto and Redgrave) appears to have been a general engraver. Born in Sheffield, "about 1695," there instructed in drawing, he came to London as "engraver of arms, stamps, and ornaments for books." He is "supposed by the initials," says Redgrave, to have engraved the large and admirable copper-plates for an edition of Terence (*Opera et Fragmenta Veterum Poetarum Latinorum*) published in 1713; and in 1722 twelve prints, a combination of "etching and mezzotint with wood blocks," a method of his invention,—the outlines and darker parts by copper, the lighter sepia tints as washes by wood. In 1718 he engraved the plates to Rowe's translation of Lucan's *Pharsalia*, and in 1725 those to Inigo Jones' *Stonehenge*. He also did seventeen views of shipping after Van der Velde; and the cartoons of Raffaele.

In *Vertue's MSS.* (in the British Museum) most of the above particulars are given, with mention also of his death, at Whitefriars, London, in December, 1742.

The first English book of this period which requires notice, writes Chatto, is Howel's *Medulla Historiæ Anglicanæ*, London, 1712, the sixty or more cuts in which he ascribes

F. Kirkall.

to Kirkall, whose name appears as engraver of the copper-plate frontispiece. From this, as Chatto observes, the date of birth, 1695, is probably incorrect. He attributes also to Kirkall the cuts in Maittaire's "*Latin Classics*" (a small edition of Sallust from the *Works and Fragments*), 1713, on the strength of the initials E K on a poor little tail-piece at the end of the volume; going on to say that "the cuts in Croxall's edition of Æsop's *Fables*, first published by R. Tonson and J. Watts, in 1722, were probably done by the same person. He refers also to other cuts, in six volumes of Dryden's *Plays*, published by Tonson and Watts in 1717, but without expressing an opinion as to the engraver.

The E K cut.

Chatto's surmise of Kirkall's engraving in wood I believe to be a too hasty assumption. For Howel's *Medulla* the copper frontispiece is so well engraved that it does not seem probable the same man could have done the very wretched cuts, said by the publisher to be on wood, which are given with it. Kirkall's own hand at least is not in them, though they may have been done by his apprentice: he, like the earlier general engravers, and like Beilby & Bewick in later days, probably undertaking all sorts of work, wood or metal, incised or in relief. Head and tail pieces and ornaments in the *Sallust* I take to be on metal; and I think the same conclusion must be accepted for the better headings to the *Dryden* (one shown below).

Uncertainty as to his engraving on wood.

Some of these last may be by Kirkall, if we can suppose that a man of his ability, much employed upon copper, would give his time to the less important, probably worse paid, and unattractive occupation of engraving on metal in relief. Against a likelihood of his

having engraved the tail-pieces in the *Pharsalia*, I note the difference of style between them and the bold plates by him in the same book. And for the *Fables* his work seems yet more unlikely. In the same year he brings out twelve experimental prints of copper and wood combined, the wood only used for solid masses of tint; and there is somewhat of over-occupation implied in the simultaneous production of these and the two hundred not careless cuts of the *Fables*. Had he been employed to execute these cuts, would not the copper-plate frontispiece have been also given to him?* The book was published by

* The first edition, 1711, has a copper frontispiece, with G. Vdr Gucht *in. et sc.* A third edition, 1731, has the same design engraved in relief, metal most likely. In the ninth edition, 1770, is a new copper plate; which, perhaps worn out or lost, in 1798, in a sixteenth issue, is replaced by a poor wood-cut.

GAJO
SUETONIO
TRANQUILLO
LE
VITE DE' DODICI
CESARI.

Mr. ELISHA
AND   KIRKALL.
Mrs. ELIZABETH
August the 31th 1707.
Printed at His Majesties Printing-Office in Black-Fryers.

Tonson, for whom he had already engraved in copper: admirable page-plates in a folio edition, 1717, of Ovid's *Metamorphoses*. Yet though apparently too busy on other work, and though he would hardly leave the greater for the less, he may have done some few of the earlier cuts, in particular the headings for Dryden; perhaps a *Hercules killing the hydra* and two or three other fair cuts among much rubbish by P.H. seen in Concanen's *Miscellaneous Poems*, 1724; and some of the *Fables*.* But if we conclude that Jackson was his pupil, I would be disposed by that and the correspondence of dates to credit Jackson with a considerable share in the work.

Born in 1701, Jackson would be of age, and just completing his apprenticeship, when Croxall's book appeared. Four years later he was in Paris; his character, as more than hinted at by Papillon, perhaps accounting for want of success in England. Certainly he had talent. And if E K has to be taken as evidence of Kirkall's work in 1713, we may also take note of an apparent J. B. J. on one of the Dryden cuts in 1717. Little however is proved by this in either case. Nor can much dependence be placed on dates, except only dates of publications. More important is it that Jackson is known as an engraver in wood, ordinary book-work and the like, before his attention was given to chiaroscuro and colour-printing. The *Title-page* to Suetonius' *Lives of the Twelve Cæsars*, graver-cut, whether in wood or metal, shows sufficient ability, though it be but common, to entitle him to at least a place in our speculations. I may however remark that the frontispiece to the 1731 Croxall is not likely to have been done by him, as he was just then quitting Paris for Rome. Unnoticed in those days may have been engravers in wood, or in the manner of wood, to whom, if we knew their names, we might look as likely producers of the works concerning which we are now hesitating between Jackson and Kirkall.

Works in relief all these are certainly; and I think all I have noticed are graver-cut, but whether wood or metal it is difficult to positively say. Most of them appear to be metal, hard or soft. Undoubtedly metal is the earliest piece of really good graver-work in relief of the eighteenth century which has come under my inspection: a cut with the names of *Mr. Elisha and Mrs. Elizabeth Kirkall* and the date of 1707, a ticket, it may be for some public or private entertainment, and "printed at His Majesties Printing-Office in Black-Fryers." I found it unnoted in a lot of old wood-cuts in the Print Room of the British Museum; and have been unable to obtain anything whatever of its history. If this was engraved by Elisha Kirkall, 1795 as the date of his birth must be far out. Grandly cut, a genuine piece of bold white-line work, the white-line work that has made the name of Bewick famous, it is the first of its kind. I wish I could think it was done on wood, this practical commentary on Papillon's authoritative words against engravers

---

* With his combined prints in the British Museum is a small cut, a naked reclining woman, one older, clothed, standing at her feet, engraved not unlike to the *Fables*, but bolder, with a tint printed over it.

of disagreeable little squares of black, who offended him by venturing upon white lines, an inadmissible opposition to the established black line of knife-work. Notwithstanding that it is the first cut of such importance that I know of in white line, the disadvantage of the soft metal in which, I have no doubt, it was engraved* (a material inferior to the box-wood now used), for all careless heaviness of the print from which my reproduction has been taken, it stands out as *the* relief-cut of the century, not without a certain sense of delicacy and finish, and with a mastery of line which we shall not see surpassed until the hand of Clennell again inform us of the bolder possibilities of white line engraving. Jackson's *Title-page* to Suetonius is poor beside it; and no such graver-handling is seen elsewhere. Much of corresponding character, smaller yet quite as free, in the Croxall *Fables* suggests the same hand for both. The question of the *Fables* seems to rest between Kirkall and Jackson, unless some *Sculptor ignotus* is to be credited with that most notable book of graver-work in relief preceding the work of Bewick. It is nearly all guessing, as with so many of the men of the centuries before.

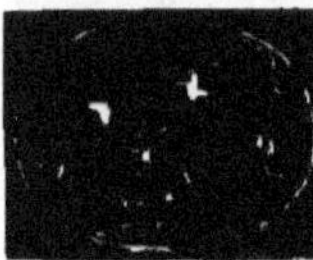

"*The Fables of Æsop and others*: newly done into English; with an application to each Fable:—Illustrated with Cuts:—London, printed for J. Tonson at Shakspear's Head in the Strand, and by J. Watts at the Printing Office in Wild-Court near Lincoln's-Inn Fields." This is Dr. Samuel Croxall's book: most notable in the History of Wood-Engraving: our first English book with cuts of noticeable worth, a book in after time to revolutionize the whole method and process of engraving in wood. Chatto is very far from being just to it. He selects a cut which he acknowledges to be "by no means one of the best" (it is indeed one of the worst, much worsened in the copy); and he gives it chiefly to instance the closeness of the unknown draftsman's borrowing from a French artist, Le Clerc. Bibliographically he has a little to say, but critically, of the cuts, merely that, "If on metal, they are as a series the most extraordinary specimens of relief-engraving ever executed," and that they "are not much inferior, except as regards the animals, to the cuts of fables" by the Bewicks "previous to 1780." Few of these cuts but are superior to anything by Bewick before that date.† The animals and human figures are vigorously drawn; the composition of the designs is good; the landscape, especially when English, is characteristic. It has also to be noted that this book is the fountain-head of the Bewick river and overflow. Of this we do not

---

* The Royal Arms, let into the larger design, is cut in brass or other hard metal. This same cut, or a close copy, will be seen in Maittaire's *Sallust*, 1713.

† Bewick's *Select Fables* did not appear until 1784.

need any proof of comparison : Bewick's own notes, pencilled in his copy of the seventh edition, 1760, mark the cuts he copied. Chatto notices this copying to remark that " in several of the cuts in Bewick's *Fables* the arrangement and composition appear to have been suggested by Croxall ; but in every instance of the kind the modern artist has made the subject his own by the superior manner in which it is treated ;" and he gives a really close copy to show how little has been borrowed. (*Treatise*, p. 451.) He notices the Croxall cuts as copies from plates of 1694 by Le Clerc ; but he should rather have referred to engravings by Barlow,* in 1665, or gone yet farther back to an " Æsop paraphras'd in Verse," by John Ogilby, in 1651. But Barlow's work is the storehouse from which the Croxall series has mainly been supplied : "Æsop's Fables, in English, French, and Latin, illustrated with one hundred and ten sculptures," copper-plates a little more than six inches by five, figures, landscape, and animals, well drawn and excellently engraved. Croxall's artist copies frequently from Barlow, not caring always for variation, careless sometimes of close following. In the same way Bewick continually borrows from Croxall. The *Lion and Mouse*, the *Lion and four Bulls*, the *Belly and Limbs*, among others, have their trinal appearance ; the *Viper and File* reaches all through from Ogilby. The celebrated *Old Hound* has first essay in Barlow. And Bewick's landscape backgrounds have their exemplars in Croxall's scenes. But our business is with the engraving, rather than the designs. What that is may be seen in the cuts here given from the 1722 book. Many more are quite equal to these : the *Frogs desiring a King*, frogs not good, but Jupiter, the Stork, and the landscape, good and delicately engraved ; the *Mountain in labour*, more delicate and surer in line than any thing in the *Select Fables* ; the *Lark and her Young*, the *Shepherd's Boy*, and the *Falconer*

---

* Francis Barlow, "English painter and engraver, born in 1616, excelled in animals." (Bryan's *Dictionary*.)

and Partridge, work which might be mistaken for the best of Bewick's; the *Young Man and Lion*, the *Horse and loaded Ass*, the *Hen and Swallow, Jupiter and the Herdsman*,— all better cuts than anything by John Bewick or much that obtains admiration because ascribed to his incomparably greater brother. Of the rest nothing is bad; a fairly even quality is maintained throughout, if not as work of one hand, yet as under one directing supervision. And, still speaking of them as engravings, it is only in a few of Bewick's *Fables* of 1784 that I find any advance beyond these cuts of 1722. With them the new method of relief-engraving, the drawing with the graver, depending upon the white lines rather than the black, had its fair beginning; only not its origin, because that is seen in metal-work of various kind, for several purposes, even in those disesteemed engravings for stamping covers and backs of books. Metal work most probably are these *Fables*. So Bewick said; and my American friend Anthony and other competent engravers so agree. I confess to a lingering shadow of doubt, my wish that they were wood the father of the doubt. Chatto might have learned of Nesbit, who had the cuts to touch. He has left

us on the very edge of knowledge, and we have but speculation.

Sixty years saw the *Fables* unrivaled. Book-cuts between 1722 and 1784 are of rudest and most unartistic character. Lee, Hodgson, and other graver-users in London at the time Bewick was an apprentice, had little of engraving skill. Lee is very poor; the best I have seen by Hodgson is here above, part of a frontispiece to some Child's Book, which was placed among Bewick's proofs. It is not so good as good knife-work, but it has the distinction of the graver: the lines are the engraver's own.

CHAPTER II

BEWICK

ISUNDERSTOOD and ignorantly worshiped, I doubt that in the history of Art any great name has been so idolatrously misused as this of THOMAS BEWICK. There is indeed no pause in the hymns to his honour, but the words are incorrect or vague, loud-sounding and unappreciative. The restorer of a lost art (could we trust the tablet in the chancel of Ovingham church), and greatest engraver in wood, whose poorest production is to be preserved as a relic: this is the tenour of the continuous applause. As an artist the man was great, a second Hogarth, to be ranked beside our best; but as an engraver he was not so great, not the restorer of the art, nor unequalled. Widely praised by a crowd of unknowing connoisseurs and indiscriminate collectors, we have yet, half a century after his death, to point out how much of what is attributed to him is really by his hand. Little with this object has been even attempted, though one would suppose such an inquiry should have been of preliminary importance. But the method of admiring madness has been simple enough: everything that went by his name, though the ascription were only by some dishonest bookseller or needy printer with worn-out blocks to sell, was accepted as his; anything so warranted must be good. So moved, the Rev. Thomas Hugo, high-priest of this most curious "Bewick" worship, in perfectly good faith and genuine adoration of his fetich, rakes together (selected, he tells us, from upwards of fifty thousand examined by him) *two thousand and nine specimens* of the works of Thomas (and John) Bewick,* among which on careful inspection I find

---

* Mr. Hugo was, I believe, thoroughly honest and in earnest, wanting only judgment: as sufficiently proved by this one specimen, No. 1935 of his "Bewick Wood-cuts," refuse, for the most part, of North-Country printing-offices. Yet he himself denounces the "disgraceful traffic" in the name of Bewick; and tells of "hundreds of volumes which nothing but the most profound ignorance, or the most shameful indifference to honest dealing, can ever attempt to identify with either of the great Newcastle Masters." (*Bewick Collector*) And he went on collecting:

Hogg's Bewick

just *sixty-three* which may have some claim to preservation; among which also I observe cuts by Hodgson, Lee, Clennell, Bonner, Orrin Smith, Green, Welsh, Austin, Peckham, and others, their names in some cuts apparent. Thirty-two "Illustrations from original

Stephens' Notes.

wood-blocks" given with Mr. F. G. Stephens' *Notes* to the exhibition of Bewick's work in 1880, at the Rooms of the Society of Arts, London, without order, worn, and worthless, are a disgraceful presentment of the engraver. Mr. Croal Thomson's very careful and

Thomson's Life and Works.

biographically comprehensive volume of the *Life and Works of Thomas Bewick*, "being an account of his career and achievements in Art," shows, I grieve to say, little engraving doing justice to the engraver: in part because of the unsatisfactory reproduction of the few good cuts there given, in part because of the unhappy selection of cuts, not only not representative of his work but absolutely unworthy of him. Of better cuts in the book, three (at pp. 92, 219, 220,) are not Bewick's, though his name had been printed to them. And the briefer bright book by Mr. Austin Dobson, *Bewick and his Pupils*, though both

Dobson's Bewick and his Pupils.

selection and reproduction are better, is not free from the same reproach. Going back to the *Treatise* of Chatto and Jackson, we have there, except Jackson's attribution of a few cuts to Clennell and others, little besides biography and bibliography; scant means of learning Bewick's work from copies; and, most strangely, little of critical judgment to inform us of the engraver's appreciation of his sometime master's powers. This part of the *Treatise*, in which we would expect some gain from Jackson's personal acquaintance as well as from his experience as an engraver, is the most unsatisfactory portion of the book. Such comments as " he faithfully represents Nature and at the same time conveys a moral,"—"though the subject be simple, the sentiment is the genuine offspring of true genius,"—"this cut is an excellent satire,"—are no clue to the capability of the engraver. Nevertheless, outside of Bewick's own writing, it is to Chatto and to Messrs. Thomson and Dobson that I am indebted for what needs here be said of the man. Of the artist, designer and engraver, and his works, I must depend on my own examination.

Bewick's youth.

THOMAS BEWICK was born at Cherryburn by Eltringham (in the parish of Ovingham) on the south side of the Tyne, about twelve miles from Newcastle, in 1753. His father was a small farmer, also renting a colliery near home. Thomas was the eldest of eight, three sons (the second, John, born in 1760). We hear of him in school-days as neither an apt scholar nor studious, but rejoicing in the out-door life most suitable to a healthy country lad: angling, setting night-lines, riding barebacked horses across the sykes and burns, driving oxen into the river to enjoy the "delightful dash," and other escapades of a like boyish character. So came the love and observation of Nature, the soil in which his genius took root and grew. Drawing-masters he had not, but, in and out of school, incited to some extent by the large wood-cut pictures which adorned the country homes of those days, he amused himself with attempts at drawing, on the margins of his books, on the floor of the church-porch, the gravestones, and the hearthstone at home. At last some one gave him paper, and then colours, and he began to decorate the walls of the neighbours' rooms with his productions,—he tells us "at a very cheap rate." "These chiefly consisted of particular hunting scenes, in which the portraits of the hunters, the horses, and of every dog in the pack, were in their opinion, as well as my own, faithfully delineated. But while I was proceeding in this way, I was at the same time engaged in matters nearly allied to this propensity for drawing: for I early became acquainted, not only with the history and character of the domestic animals, but also with those which roamed at large."

This propensity for drawing was the cause in due time, in October 1767, he then over fourteen years of age, of his being apprenticed to Mr. Ralph Beilby, a general engraver, in Newcastle. We learn from his *Memoir* what sort of work occupied his 'prentice years and the nature of an engraver's business in those days.

" The first jobs I was put to were blocking out the wood about the lines on diagrams (which my master finished), for the *Ladies' Diary*, and etching sword-blades for sword manufacturers. It was not long till the diagrams were wholly put in my hands to finish. After these I was kept closely employed upon a variety of other jobs: for such was the industry of my master that he refused nothing, coarse or fine: he undertook everything, which he did in the best way he could. He fitted up and tempered his own tools, and adapted them to every purpose; and taught me to do the same. This readiness brought him in an overflow of work; and the work-place was filled with the coarsest kind of steel stamps, pipe-moulds, bottle-moulds, brass clock-faces, door-plates, coffin-plates, bookbinders' letters and stamps, steel, silver, and gold seals, mourning rings, etc. He also undertook the engraving of arms, crests, and ciphers, on silver, and every kind of job from the silversmiths; also engraving bills of exchange, bank-notes, invoices, accountheads, and cards. These last he executed as well as did most of the engravers of the time; but what he excelled in was ornamental silver-engraving. In this, as far as I am able to judge, he was one of the best in the kingdom; and I think, upon the whole, he might be called an ingenious self-taught artist. The higher department of engraving, as landscape and historical plates, I dare say was hardly ever thought of by my master; at least not till I was nearly out of my apprenticeship, when he took it into his head to leave me in charge of the business at home, and go to London for the purpose of taking lessons in etching and engraving large copper-plates. There was, however, little or no employment in Newcastle and he had no opportunity of becoming clever at it; so he kept labouring on with such work as before named, in which I aided him with all my might. I think he was the best master in the world for teaching boys, for he obliged them to put their hands to every variety of work. Every job, coarse or fine, cutting or engraving, I did cheerfully; but the business of polishing copper-plates and hardening and polishing steel seals was always irksome to me. I had wrought at such as this a long time, and at

Bewick.

the coarser kind of engraving, till my hands had become as hard and enlarged as those of a blacksmith. I however, in due time, had a greater share of nicer work given me to execute : such as the outside and inside mottoes on rings, and sometimes arms and crests on silver, and seals of various kinds, for which I made the new steel punches and letters. We had a great deal of seal-cutting, in which my master was accounted clever, and in this I did my utmost to surpass him.

" While we were going on in this way, we were occasionally applied to by printers, to execute wood-cuts for them. In this branch my master was very defective. What he did was wretched. He did not like such jobs, on which account they were given to me ; and the opportunity afforded of drawing the designs on the wood was highly gratifying to me. It happened that one of them, a cut of the 'George and Dragon' for a bar-bill, attracted so much notice, and had so many praises bestowed upon it, that this kind of work greatly increased, and orders were received for cuts for children's books,—chiefly for Thomas Saint, printer, Newcastle, and successor of John White who had rendered himself famous for his numerous publications of histories and old ballads. . .

Book-cuts.

" My time now became greatly taken up with designing and cutting wood blocks : for the *Story-Teller*, Gay's *Fables*, and *Select Fables*.* together with cuts of a similar kind for printers. Some of the Fable cuts were thought so well of by my master, that he in my name sent a few to be laid before the Society for the encouragement of Arts, etc. : and I obtained a premium." (*Memoir of Thomas Bewick, written by himself.*)

A premium.

One of the cuts sent is said by Chatto to have been the *Old Hound* (the Hound and the Huntsman), first printed in Gay's *Fables*, Saint's edition of 1779. The premium was in 1775, and Chatto supposes that the cut was engraved after Bewick's apprenticeship. So taken, it may mark his best to that date. It gives little promise of future greatness, however creditable to a beginner ; and the premium says more for the liberality than for the judgment of the encouraging Society. But the work was fine, and the Society may, like George III on a later occasion, have marveled how such work could be done on wood.

An earlier Old Hound

Yet is it sure that Chatto knew for which cut the premium was given ? Was it indeed the cut copied in the *Treatise* (the ruined original also, added by Bohn in the 1861 edition), or may it have been a smaller *Old Hound* of the earlier *Fables* of Saint's publishing, therefore done during apprenticeship, when Beilby's action for Bewick would be more likely ? The Society's praise may better befit the younger man and hardly inferior cut, a pretty close copy from one in Croxall

---

* The firm with that misleading title : *Select Fables* appearing in 1771, 1776, and 1784. Those of 1771 were issued by Saint as a part of Appendix to *Moral Instructions of a Father to his Son*. Miss Bewick is reported as saying they were her father's first year's work ; his own words in the *Memoir* set them later.

His earlier 'prentice-work in wood, the diagrams for Hutton's *Treatise on Mensuration*, only need referring to because they are said to have suggested to the lad the invention of "a graver with a fine groove at the point which enabled him to cut the outlines by a single operation." I do not see the use of such a tool; but it might have been occasion for another premium.

In the cuts for Saint and Angus and whatever else was done in those early days I can not find anything noticeable for its own sake. The *Old Hound* on the opposite page is a fair sample of the lot. The *Moral Instructions*, the *Youth's Instructive and Entertaining Story-Teller*, the *Lottery-Book of Birds and Beasts*, the *New-Invented Hornbook*, the *Child's Tutor*, the *Only Method to make Reading easy*, the *New Year's Gift for Little Masters and Misses*, *Tommy Trip's History of Birds and Beasts*, and the like,—with sundry bill-heads, newspaper-heads, and advertisements,—these are all worthless, as engravings, whether the name of Bewick applied to them be wrong or right. The exact order of performance and cause of differences, haste, or cheapness, or what else, there is no knowing, nor use in knowing; and as in even later cuts we can by no examination or comparison ascertain what might be his and what by less skilful hands, of brother John or Bailby's other boy, we may at least refrain from fathering upon Thomas Bewick so discreditable a progeny. There is unfortunately, his life through, poor work enough, surely his (canny Tyneside refused no pennies), for any Devil's Advocate to bring up against him: beside what is duly noticed by Mr. Thomson, "the practice, of unscrupulous or ignorant booksellers, of selling nearly all volumes issued from 1770 to 1830 with cuts as containing the genuine works of Bewick." To 1830, he says. Even as I am writing this, appears a re-issue of the *Looking-Glass for the Mind*, "with the original cuts *by Bewick;*" no honest intimation appended to warn the unwary buyer that they are all by John.

Hodgson's *Curious Hieroglyphick Bible*, though the cuts are about as good as these by Bewick of the same date, can have but little of his doing, unless in a late edition, as the book was published in 1776, and he did not see London until the first of October in that year. The *Fables* of 1776 and 1779 (including thirteen cuts in the last which re-appear in 1784) display no remarkable ability, at best promise rather than performance. They are inferior, in design, in drawing, and engraving, to the Croxall *Fables* of 1722, a copy of which (the seventh edition, 1760, in the possession of Mr. Croal Thomson) was, as I have already said, in Bewick's hands, and to which he had continual reference. We find in all of these but signs of the growing, yet immature Bewick; nor is there anything by him important enough *as engraving* for either notice or preservation (however shocking so absolute a statement may be to a Bewick-Collector) until we arrive at that scarcely known book, the SELECT FABLES of 1784: a small octavo, very rare, containing a hundred and forty-one fable-headings, besides tail-pieces, both of various quality, an admixture probably of his own cutting and that of his brother John, his apprentice from 1777 to '82.

The Fables of 1784.

A copy of these SELECT FABLES is in the Library of the British Museum (12305. g. 16). The press-mark as well as the date is worth giving, for identification, that the seeker may not be misled by the same title having been used for the books of 1772 and '76; used also for a "reprint" by Charnley in 1820, and again by Pearson in more recent days. The history of the books brought out by these two worthies must not escape recording. It deserves a place among the Curiosities of Literature, and haply may serve as warning to some few collectors careful for what is admirable in art.

The Miller, his Son, and their Ass.

Spurious editions.

The *Select Fables* of 1784 were, like the *Fables* of 1772, '76, and '79, published by Saint, but it appears that Charnley, also of Newcastle, became afterwards possessed of all but about twenty of the blocks. So when Bewick brought out an altogether new series, the *Fables of Æsop*, in 1818, Charnley moved to oppose him; and in 1820 issued, as Vol. 1 of

Charnley's.

Bewick's Works, and of the same size as his *Quadrupeds* and *Birds*, a new edition of the *Select Fables* "with cuts designed and engraved by Thomas and John Bewick and others previous to the year 1784." The "others" was used to cover some wretched tail-pieces "by Isaac Nicholson, formerly a pupil of Mr. Bewick's," other additional cuts, good and bad; and to meet any question of re-engraving the blocks not in Charnley's hands. It is this volume which generally comes in the greedy collector's way, which has caused the neglect and forgetting of the original work, and of Bewick's own later book likewise.

Pearson's.

On this Charnley imposition Pearson based a new edition of "*Bewick's Select Fables*," put forth in 1871, and again in 1878: still offered to a confiding public. Pearson's sham is yet more impudent than the other. He does not scruple to advertise it as "a faithful reprint of the extremely rare and expensive edition published by Saint in 1784." It is not faithful. To begin with, the already worn cuts had been touched, not so improved, for Charnley; who also had cut away the various borders designed to suit different cuts. Pearson replaces the borders with badly engraved copies, a few only of them, repeatedly used, without a care or sense of appropriateness. Also some of the fable-headings are copies, unacknowledged: neither Bewick's work nor the same cuts that were printed by Charnley. A few good tail-pieces had been thrown in by him: Pearson's issue, without so much as these, is altogether worthless.

These two books, Charnley's *Select Fables* and Pearson's *Select Fables*, can be exactly characterised only as libels on Bewick, notable as most important of many such.

Returning to the original work. The Croxall series continues in requisition. From that, if not from his own cutting in metal, letters, seals, and the like, Bewick could not fail to learn the full value of the white line, closely studying as design after design was copied, sometimes wholly, though never servilely, sometimes altered to his other fancy,

The engraving is of the same imitative character. Mr. Dobson happily remarks that he used the Croxall cuts as "the basis of his designs." Nothing can be better said as a general statement; but I can not agree with the after Bewick-favouring comparison which Mr. Dobson draws. He specially takes note of two cuts as examples of the superiority of the later artist. Of the *Viper and File* he says, though Bewick "closely followed the earlier design, the advantage in execution, in black and white, and in the superior fidelity of accessories (*e.g.* the vice), is wholly on his side. So are the improvements in the relative proportions of the different objects : the viper of the old illustrator might be a youthful boa constrictor. In the *Young Man and the Swallow* the deviations are more apparent than the resemblances and little of similarity remains but in the attitude of the hero. The swallow, which in Croxall assumes the proportions of a barn-door fowl, Bewick reduces to reasonable dimensions. Croxall's spendthrift has literally denuded himself; he of Bewick's drawing, a civilized eighteenth-century rake, has only pawned his linen. Again, beyond the bare-boughed tree in Croxall there is no particular suggestion of winter; but in Bewick there is obvious ice and men sliding upon it, while he has given to the chief figure a look of nose-nipped and shivering dilapidation, which is wholly absent from its model. These specimens will show how Bewick dealt with Croxall." Mr. Dobson fairly presents his readers with reproductions of the two cuts from both books. Unfortunately they are very poor, yet still enough to show how little new thought is in the later drawings. For the first, it appears to me a mere copy, a little better in colour, not else, except for the correction of the viper's size. The second here before us for comparison with the Croxall cut (at p. 131) will show also what advance may be claimed for the engraving. The smaller size of the swallow is an improvement. But the landscape (a capital bit), despite the suggestive skaters, is not so wintry as the

The *Fables* of 1784.

The Old Man and Death.

The Young Man and the Swallow.

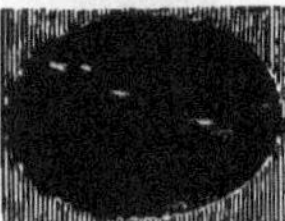

The Two Frogs

The Sheep and the Bramble

The *Fables* of 1784.

original, and we have lost the utter desolation of the ruin. The young man too is less the starved prodigal of the fable: his attitude indicating rather colic than cold. Going

THE CUR FOX

back again (to p. 131) for comparison of others, note how poor the drawing is, and how weak the cutting, of the *Old Man and Death* in its translation; and the *Two Frogs*, (like the *Swallow* cut) finer, not better, than Croxall's, is a close copy. On the other hand, the *Miller, his Son, and their Ass*, is a genuine Bewick; as also is the *Sheep and the Bramble*: both worthy of our admiration. In conclusion, I would say that in very many of the cuts his drawing is not so good as that of Croxall's artist, while his engraving is not often better. His average work is not beyond his forerunner's. But there are exceptions, in which he surpasses his teacher, the animals his own, the landscape peculiarly so, and the engraving more finished. In the course of the work (recollecting that the cuts of Part 3, the book being so divided, were in the *Fables* of 1779) we notice considerable improvement. He cuts a surer line and aims at more

THE SPANISH POINTER

expression. We can see that he feels his way, progressing on a path of originality.

The Quadrupeds, 1790.

Quitting this debatable ground we pass the threshold of assured fame. Whatever may have been borrowed or but creditably imitated till now, there is no question of the originality or the excellence of Bewick's QUADRUPEDS. Admiration here might be forgiven some excess. *The General History of Quadrupeds*, with three hundred cuts, animals and tail-pieces, begun in 1785, published first in 1790, is claimed by Bewick as altogether his own work. Although, as might be expected, all of the cuts

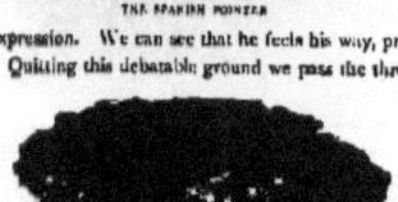

THE HEATH RAM

are not of equal excellence, few are without some good graver-work; and the best, very many, are powerfully and beautifully rendered, with a will-full mastery of line and touch not before seen in work on wood. I give three of the best and most characteristic cuts, the *Cur Fox*, the *Spanish Pointer*, and the *Heath Ram*, as specimens of truth to life, in form and in nice expression of varieties in texture. Bewick's line here is plainly seen to be intelligently drawn by the graver. It is the white line *par excellence*.

In the *History of British Birds*, we find increasing power and nicer finish, as we look through one hundred and seventeen figures and ninety-one tail-pieces of the LAND BIRDS, completed in 1797, and the one hundred and one birds and one hundred and thirty-nine tail-pieces of the WATER BIRDS, 1804. How perfect form and featheriness in the *Peacock*, and the distant peafowls! And in the *Night-Jar* what exactness of detail! As adequately represented (see page 142) is the downy softness

THE PEACOCK

of the *Common Gull*! Observe too the simplicity of line and daring use of black in the *Scaup Duck*! The *Tame Duck* is Bewick's masterpiece: it absolutely has colour. "The round, full form of the bird," writes Chatto, "is represented with the greatest fidelity; the plumage, in all its downy, smooth, and glossy variety,—on the sides, the rump, the back, the wings, and the head,—is singularly true to nature; while the legs, and toes, and even the webs between the toes, are engraved in a manner that proves the attention Bewick, when necessary, paid to minutest points of detail. The effect of the whole is excellent; and the background both in character and execution worthy of this master-piece of Bewick as a designer and engraver on wood."

Elsewhere he says: "Bewick's style

THE NIGHT-JAR

of engraving, displayed in the *Birds*, is exclusively his own. He adopts no conventional mode of representing texture or producing an effect; but skilfully avails himself of the most simple and effective means which his art affords." Certainly the most effective, as well as most simple: he has drawn with his graver (not meaning that he had no drawing on the wood, but that he chose his own lines to represent the drawing).

THE COMMON GULL

Triumphantly manifest is the worth of this white-line work. My concern here is chiefly with the engraving, not less to be admired if the figures are not always quite correct. The scientific naturalist may find fault for some nice points not seen by artists' eyes; but judged only as an artist, designer or engraver, Bewick's work is perfect, to a hair or a feather.

What qualification must be added to so broad a statement is this, that I must be understood to refer to his best work only, and especially of the figures which he had the opportunity of drawing from life. In the *Quadrupeds*, for lack of this advantage, are many failures. In them still, even in the poorest, we recognize the observant faculty, and in the most

THE SCAUP DUCK

tentative engraving the expression of a more intentional and more daring line than had been seen before. His backgrounds to the *Quadrupeds* are mostly but careless adjuncts, coarse, and the engraving not so good as the best of the 1784 *Fables;* but in the *Birds* we find abundant proof of advanced study and increase of skill. The mere backgrounds are pictures of themselves, appropriate to the birds, as carefully engraved as truthfully drawn. Choicest instance of such completeness is our *Tame Duck,* yet it is only one of the best of many. The same excellence

THE TAME DUCK

is observable in the backgrounds of the *Peacock* and *Night-Jar,* and in numerous bits of fitting and characteristic foreground such as the pebbly sand on which the *Gull* is lying.

In these cuts to the two volumes of the *Birds* we see the best of Bewick's graver-work. Among these tail-pieces also are the best of his designs. There he stands securely, first of all illustrators of English landscape and rustic life and bird-nature. The cuts here given are fair samples of the general quality of his work and of his power as an engraver and draftsman. All these,—the *Farm Yard*, the *Snow Man*, the *Dog with a Kettle at his tail*, the *Cows and Magpie*, and the *Old Man breaking stones*,—Chatto asserts to be engraved by Bewick's own hand; the first four from his own drawings upon the wood, the last from a drawing by his pupil Robert Johnson. Especially noteworthy is the truthfulness of his tree-work, lessons in which he could have found in the care for variety and distinction of growths in Milton's *Views in Ireland*, published at about 1773-7. This was however as probably the spontaneous outcome of that clear perception and constant observing of nature which so eminently characterised him. Except for this truth of foliage in tree or herb, and his perfect rendering of textures, either hair or feather, Bewick's engraving, looked at as engraving only, is not supremely good. His tints (so far as I am able to track his own doings) are raw and wanting gradation and tone; his line in sky or ground is generally weak and often without expression.

Nor is he successful in larger work. His famous *Chillingham Bull* does not satisfy me. Doubtless it is a faithful portrait, but I do not think it in any respect equal to the better cuts of the *Quadruped* series. The head and shoulders are well engraved; in the rest of the body and in the legs the drawing is undecided and the graver work is poor and feeble. Grass

and foliage also are formal, with neither freedom nor variety, and in execution very far below such cuts as the *Cur Fox* in the contemporary volume. Drawn and engraved in

1789, it is certainly not the best, though the most ambitious, of Bewick's works to that date. It has been much overvalued because the block was destroyed when a few impressions only had been taken, and partly perhaps because of its size,—seven inches and three quarters by five and five eighths, set in an ornamental border three quarters of an inch wide.

Some other large cuts of animals, two *Lions* (one in 1799, eight inches and a half by four), an *Elephant*, and a *Zebra*, done for show-bills, are poor coarse cuts: his own probably, yet of no worth. His "great work,"

of later time, 1828, the *Waiting for Death*, except as Bewick's last engraving, has little to interest me. I find it weak in line, weak yet harsh, unmodulated, indecisive, very ineffective, unsound, upon no account an admirable engraving. Even the horse is unsatisfactory. It is said that he did not cut the head. Something perhaps of the feebleness of age (of eye-sight or hand) may plead excuse; some inefficiency may be due to his intention of printing with it

a second block, to add to the effect; but the engraving has the appearance of a finished work, and it is hard to see what possibly could have been gained by help of another block printed under or over this. Better, it seems to me, is the little cut here below than this so ambitious attempt, the same story of *Waiting for death* as fully told in the smaller space. Better artistry, I think, is here; and certainly better than is shown in any of his larger works, whether this be by his hand or not, which is doubtful, many of the tail-pieces after 1797 having been cut by pupils, Clennell and others.

The same monotonous, characterless line which I notice in this largest and latest of Bewick's works is seen again in the larger of his engravings in copper; in the plates for Consett and Liddell's *Tour through Sweden*,

Lapland, Finland, and Denmark, 1789; in the *Whitley Ox* and *Kyloe Ox*, 1789, '90; and in thirty-six plates for a folio *Bible*" by Beilby and Bewick," published in 1806. We see in all these the same line, weak, scratchy, much-laboured, and unpleasant, though with good drawing in both the oxen and in the landscape backgrounds. It is in smaller cuts he excels. Some small work in silver by him, and bill-heads in copper, notably some horses—always good, are of very delicate and perfect workmanship; but his hand could not be accustomed to a bolder tooling. On wood with feather or fur, with small figures, human, or beasts and birds, and in certain favourite scenes, especially of winter, he never fails, and his best work there is unsurpassed; but his graver can not draw a wave. There is none of a painter's largeness in his touch; and, acknowledging his effectiveness, we are seldom attracted or charmed by any merely linear beauty. Putting aside all thoughts of subject, excellence of design, or satisfaction in the effect, judging of graver-work only, I would take the two cuts upon this page, from Parnell's *Hermit* and Somervile's *Chase*, as fairly presenting the quality of Bewick's own engraving.

These two cuts I suppose to be altogether his own cutting. Of *The Hermit and the Angel* the best part is the tree-work, which however is formal rather than free. All the rest (figures, water, bridge, and bank,) is poor, the line meaningless.

And of the other cut, admirable as the dogs are, the huntsman and rock are wretchedly engraved, and the sky might tempt one to think that Bewick was incapable of anything like sweetness of tone or certainty of gradation.

Goldsmith and Parnell.

In the *Poems of Goldsmith and Parnell*, 1795, four principal subjects are by him: one for the *Traveler*, one for the *Deserted Village* (which I think is but partly his), and two for the *Hermit*. They are all of much the same character. In them we should look for his best doing, the book intended to exhibit the highest accomplishment of the art, and having been begun by his brother John but a little before his death. But Bewick seems generally unsuccessful when not working from his own motives; and Chatto is right in the remark that "if his reputation as a wood-engraver rested on these cuts, it certainly would not stand very high." These are the cuts, Chatto tells us, which George III could not without inspection of the blocks believe to have been engraved on wood. The cuts

The Chase.

for *Somervile's Chase*, 1796, all but one engraved by Bewick, Chatto considers superior. I find little difference of quality. Nothing in either of these books will bear comparison with his tail-pieces, or with the backgrounds to the *Birds*.

Bewick's best

So far I have spoken of the Bewick books, producing certain cuts, with special intent to have his work understood, his own doing, where distinguishable from what might be done by pupils. It may not be superfluous, and it may help the student, to give farther comment, pointing out what I judge to be of greatest excellence in the *Quadrupeds* and the two series of *Birds*, making no question of engraver (except to notice ascriptions by Chatto), but calling attention to the cuts solely for themselves.

Best cuts in the Quadrupeds.

Of the QUADRUPEDS I would take as generally best the *Oxen*, *Sheep*, *Goats*, and *Dogs*, all fine in character and remarkable for nice distinction of textures. The *Lurcher* stands eminently among the Dogs, his rough coat contrasted with the sleekness of the *Pointer*; the *Greyhound Fox* and *Cur Fox* are worthy wood-companions. The *Common Boar* has suitably vigorous treatment; while the *Lesser Dormouse*, the *Little Beaver*, and the *Moles* are as fair examples of a finer cutting. The short wool of the *Cheviot Ram* claims attention; so also does the fitting background, the rugged boulder against which he stands and the distant fell with sheep upon it: few rough lines for all. The engraving of this and the *Heath Ram* is eight years later than the first edition of the book: the sheep are of improved breeds; and equal improvement is to be seen in the engravings up to date.

THE CHEVIOT RAM

Of the tail-pieces (always speaking of the engraving rather than the design) in the first edition there is little of much worth: the best are *Snow-folk with a Bear*, at page 256; a *Hunted Fox*, p. 265, grass and foliage rich and expressive and well drawn; a *Man eating*, his hungry dog watching him, p. 285; a *Wolf* falling into a trap, rich foliage also, p. 430; *Two Blind Fiddlers*, with a boy, p. 456.

In the second edition, 1791, we see one of the earliest of his remarkable winter scenes, the *Ewe and Lamb*, the starved sheep in the snow nibbling at a broom, p. 59; *Rain*, a Soldier crossing a moor, p. 127; "*Pulling the Colt's Tail*," p. 419. In the third edition, 1792, I note *Going to the mill*, p. 13; at p. 16 *Children* on an Ass, in panniers, finely rendered,—the sky with the heaviness of a snowy day; *Carrying Faggots*, p. 105,—ice very ice like; and a *Rain-storm*, p. 127.

In the Birds, where so many are good, choice is more difficult. Yet I may signalize, of Vol. I—Land Birds, edition of 1797, the *Sparrow-Hawk*; the *Tawny Owl* (all the Owls are excellent); the *Grosbeak*; the *Yellow Bunting*, where we know not which to admire more, the background or the bird (Bewick "considered this his best cut"); the *Mountain Sparrow*, and *Wood-Lark*; the *Red breast*,—with the snowy landscape against which the bird shows almost ruddily; the delicate *Blue Titmouse*; the *Ring-Dove*; the *Pheasant*

THE YELLOW BUNTING

and *Guinea Hen*; the *Grouse*, *Woodcock*, and *Partridges*. Of the tail-pieces, beside those I give at pages 143 144, I would choose (still referring to the edition of 1797, in which they are generally better printed) a *Dying Dog*, crows waiting, p. 70,—wind-blown reeds and sand and water, very cunningly rendered; *Night*, two horses, mist and rain, p. 97; *Poachers*, tracking a hare through snow, "glorious," says Ruskin, "in all intellectual and executive qualities," p. 147; another *Snow-scene*, p. 162; a *Hen and Chickens*, frightened by a dog, p. 226; a tiny cut of a *Nest*, p. 275; *Two Cocks*, fighting, p. 281,—daylight and nature, the effect grey and pearly, the black touches on the birds very brilliant in a fair impression; a dirty subject, but a marvel of engraving, at p. 285; and a *Sportsman with dogs*, p. 297,—reedy grass in front and stubble-field beyond treated with the naturalness in which Bewick delights. A *Feather* at the end of the book must not be left unnoticed.

Of Vol. 2, the WATER BIRDS, 1804, I may select the wonderfully delicate *Egret*; a dainty *Judcock*; the *Guillemot* and *Black Guillemot*, both engraved with rare simplicity of line;

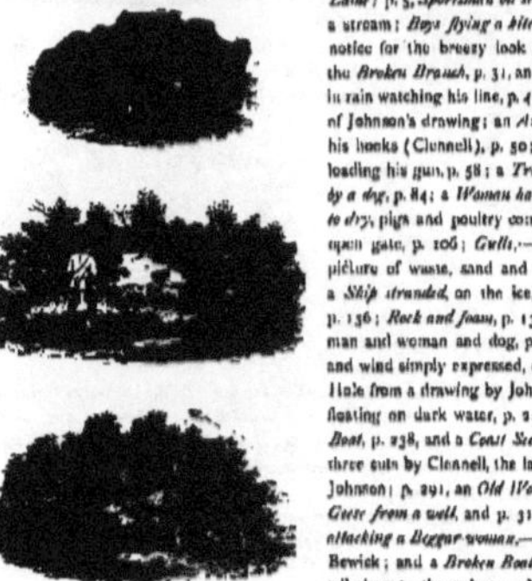

the *Goosander*, almost without line; the *Tame Swan, Grey Lag Goose*, and *Tame Goose*—as elaborate as the *Tame Duck* and equally well cut. I like these best, but many more are as worthy of praise. Of the tail-pieces (the edition of 1804) I would note particularly *Catching birds on Marsden Rocks*, after *Contents*, a very miniature; p. 3, a *Blind Man carrying a Lame*; p. 5, *Sportsman on stilts*, crossing a stream; *Boys flying a kite*, p. 9, worth notice for the breezy look throughout; the *Broken Branch*, p. 31, and an *Angler in rain watching his line*, p. 41,—two cuts of Johnson's drawing; an *Angler settling his hooks* (Clennell), p. 50; *Sportsman, loading his gun*, p. 58; a *Tramp attacked by a dog*, p. 84; a *Woman hanging clothes to dry*, pigs and poultry coming in at an open gate, p. 106; *Gulls*,—a wonderful picture of waste, sand and sea, p. 123; a *Ship stranded*, on the ice, (Clennell), p. 136; *Rock and foam*, p. 138; *Tramps, man and woman and dog*, p. 176,—rain and wind simply expressed, engraved by Hole from a drawing by Johnson; *Gulls floating on dark water*, p. 215, the *Pilot Boat*, p. 238, and a *Coast Scene*, p. 240,—three cuts by Clennell, the last drawn by Johnson; p. 291, an *Old Woman driving Geese from a well*, and p. 313, a *Gander attacking a Beggar-woman*,—both cut by Bewick; and a *Broken Boat*, ashore, the tail-piece to the volume. Many beside

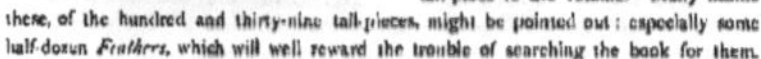

these, of the hundred and thirty-nine tail-pieces, might be pointed out: especially some half-dozen *Feathers*, which will well reward the trouble of searching the book for them.

Bewick himself claims both drawing and engraving of the cuts in the first edition of the *Quadrupeds*. In the first editions of the *Birds* (1797-1804) the bird-figures may also be considered his: though in backgrounds he was probably helped by Nesbit (with him from 1790 to 1797) and by Clennell (with him from 1797 to 1804); by Hole too in the latter period. Of the tail-pieces to these two volumes there is only partial, inconclusive evidence, external or internal, toward enabling us to attribute them. Chatto gives a list of forty-seven drawn by the pupils, chiefly Robert Johnson and Luke Clennell, many of them engraved by Clennell; but he does not say whether they were their own designs or sometimes only copies on the wood from designs by the master. Of cuts which Bewick gave in subsequent editions it were hardly worth while, if possible, to pursue the track.*

One great work remains for notice: THE FABLES OF Æsop AND OTHERS, "with designs on wood by Thomas Bewick:" one hundred and eighty-eight oval headings in roughest borders (the roughness enhancing the daintiness of the pictures) and many vignettes. Two editions were printed: in 1818 and 1823. The book is almost ignored by Chatto, and but slightingly alluded to by Thomson and Dobson. Chatto merely gives Dibdin's opinion of it, naming the pupils who did the work and crediting Bewick with three cuts. One is not quite sure that he had seen the book. "Refined and delicately manipulated designs, engraving executed in a manner foreign to that by which Bewick made his name and somewhat feelingless in character and feeble in workmanship:" this is the judgment of Mr. Thomson in his briefest notice of the book. And Mr. Dobson dismisses it with

---

* The following is from Chatto: only with different arrangement, for easier reading.

Cuts drawn and engraved by Bewick.

LAND BIRDS—edition of 1797:

The Farm Yard	heading to *Introduction*
Traveller drinking	tail-piece to *Contents*
Man "watering"	page 42
Drunkard asleep	64
Cows and Magpie	74
The Same Man	78
Night,—two horses, wind and rain	97
Poachers tracking a hare in snow	147
Man with a Midwife	157
Hanging a cat	194
Hen attacking a dog	216
Two Cocks fighting	281

WATER BIRDS—edition of 1804:—

Sportsman, on stilts, crossing a stream	3
Wooden-legged Beggar and Dog	17
Dog with a kettle at his tail	36
Crossing the ice	page 85
Monkey roasting a goose	163
Old Woman driving geese from a well	191
Gander attacking a Beggar-woman	313

Cuts engraved by Bewick, drawn by Johnson.

LAND BIRDS—edition of 1797:—

Sportsman and Shepherd	vi
Old Man breaking stones	16
Runaway Horse, with boys in a cart	81
Fox and Bird	139
Snow Scene,—the Goddard	163

WATER BIRDS—edition of 1804:—

Old Soldiers,—Honours of War	v
The Broken Breach	31
Angler in rain, watching his line	41
Coast Scene	161
Man and Cow	173
Skating	180
Coast Scene	145

The places of many are changed in later editions.

the conclusion that it "bears much the same relation to Bewick's earlier work that the performances of a man's decline generally do to the first sprightly runnings of his genius." Allowing for some exceptionally inferior cuts, I join issue with all the critics, who have, I think, been led by the poor printing of both editions to underrate the work.   For the

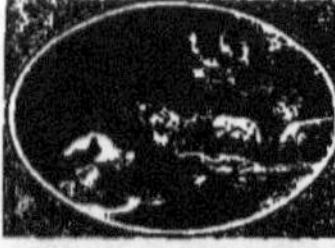

designs little needs saying.   Here, as in the *Fables* of 1784, the basis is Croxall.   What changes are made (not always improvement) may not warrant any imputation of decline. Many, I have no doubt, were drawn on the wood by Harvey; the greater number, says Chatto, designed by Robert Johnson.   We must find out those by Bewick before we can talk of decline.   It is not as fable illustrator that the peculiar genius of our artist reveals itself.   His artist-work, as distinct from his engraving, is in his birds, and beasts, in his landscape and homelier figure subjects; but comparing fables with fables, the best of his attempts in 1784 with the designs of 1818, I see nothing like decline.   The animals are as excellently drawn; and for the landscape setting of the figures, there is nothing better in respect of art throughout the *Quadrupeds* or *Birds*.   For the engraving Mr. Thomson must allow me an engraver's authority when I insist that the manner of it is not "foreign to that by which Bewick made his name." On the contrary, in the headings and in the best of the vignettes every line has Bewick's manner; it is the very best white-line work. More "refined and delicately manipulated," it is true, than any except a few earlier cuts, but refinement and delicacy are certainly not incompatible with strength, and the fine line, as the greatest of artists have taught us, may have more power than the coarse.   These cuts are not "feelingless," nor "feeble;" although some are poor, and the tail-pieces, a collection of odd cuts, generally unworthy of the book, many apparently not done for it.   But of the book itself, for the most of its principal subjects, beside admiring the designs, I have to say that I know no book, not

Fables of 1818

even the *Birds*, which contains more excellent examples of the Bewick school: speaking not as of scholars' work, but of such work as he had taught, graver-work which his own hand in his best days never surpassed and seldom equalled.

In the FABLES of 1818 (and 1823,—the printing uncertain in both editions, so bad at times that we can hardly discern what a cut really is), besides those here given, I would emphasize the excellence of a few others:—the *Ape and her Young*, good in composition and drawing, luminous in effect, the tooling of foliage rich and powerful; the *Master and Scholar*,—a willow here remarkable for truth and grace; the *Young Man and Swallow*, an admirable winter scene; the *Proud Frog and Ox*, a pastoral poem,—grasses and herbage finely distinguished, the solid black shadows of the frogs and the un-outlined houses and hills very notable; the *Stag looking at itself in the water*, with the distant huntsman and hounds simply white against the grey trees; the *Two Pots* in the river, beautifully drawn and as beautifully engraved: the *Goat, Kid, and Wolf*, with fine distinction of substance and texture; the *Sheep-Biter*, full of colour in the better 1823 impression; the *Woodman and Mercury* (evidently put on the wood by Harvey, most likely his engraving too); the *Swallow and other Birds*, minute and fine, yet rich; the *Wolves and sick Ass*, the *Dog in the manger*, and the *Ass and Jupiter*, all three more in the manner of Thurston than that of Bewick,—in the last a rolling cloud which Bewick had never attempted; the *Old Man and his Sons*, (not unlike to Clennell, but not his, more probably, I think, by Nesbit); the *Miser and his treasure*, very beautiful, a marvelous bit of wild wood and rock, well composed, well drawn, most minutely and sweetly engraved, very perfect,—but so badly printed that one must see both editions to appreciate its beauty, (I would give Nesbit the credit of this cut); the *Fox and Tiger*, another fine picture and beautiful cut lost through bad printing; the *Oak and Reed*, bold,

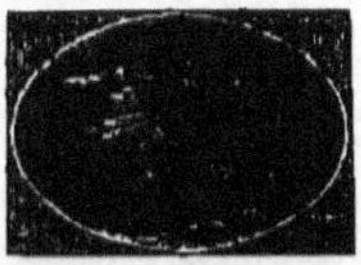

The Eagle, the Cat, and the Sow.

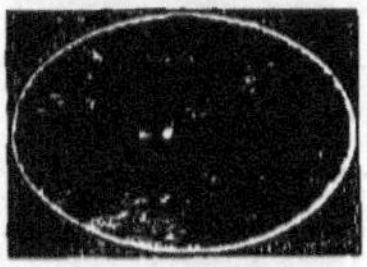

The Cat and the Fox.

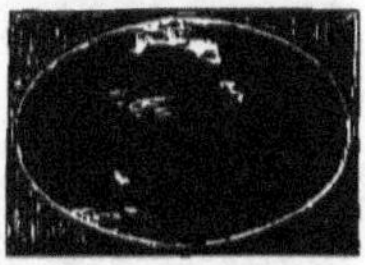

The Fox and the Bramble

and breezy in every graver-touch of the oak-boughs, the reeds, and the water; the *Bull and Goat*, full of air and sunlight, rich foliage, and rock-work; the *Fisherman*, everything drawn with the graver, the grey distance a picture of itself, the water excellent; the *Fox and Boar*, most rich and masterly; the *Old Hound*, another repeat of the old design for the figures, but adding a lovely view of distant country, wondrously delicate, and fine in its perspective,—much in little space, a characteristic of the series; the *Two Frogs*, the foliage large in treatment and rich as in Nesbit's *Rinaldo and Armida*; the *Magpie and Sheep*, sheep's wool, fern, distance (cottage, trees, mountains, and cloudy sky) capitally rendered; the *Fox and Goat*, vilely misrepresented by Jackson. Again I have had to pass by many as good as those I have selected. And unfortunately, from bad printing many are almost undiscernible,—lost except to the practised eyes of an expert.

It must be owned that the cuts are not all good. Many of them show a much inferior workmanship as well as marks of haste. The indoor subjects are generally the weakest, lacking sureness of line and regularity in tints; and the human figures are not engraved with the power of Clennell or Thompson. The drawing of the classical figures (where I think I recognise Harvey) is not so good as that of the Bewick rustics. But (these exceptions noted) for variety and veracity of landscape, for air and light, for truth and wealth of leafage and herbage, for the sense of form in every touch, for nice gradations of colour and distance obtained by a first simple cutting, no after toning needed, the line effective and always pleasant and free from affectation,—for the perfect engraving also of the animals, size considered,—this book is unequalled: the greatest yet produced as example of the art of wood-engraving in its especial sphere, the use of white-line.

Notwithstanding this, very many of the tail-pieces are quite unworthy of their place. These may be of Bewick's designing, but are without a hint of his graver in them. Not clever in design, they are in cutting poor even as boys' work; and some are black cross line, the opposite of all Bewick's teaching. It looks as if, with a chapman's economy, he crowded in everything he had by him, merely to add to number. One wonders more at their appearance, as some few others are equal to any of former time, equal to the best

in the *Birds*. Notably good of these are the following :—*Two Women*, standing by a precipice, driven back by the wind, p. 46; "*In memory of Sir Brook Boothby*," an inch-square picture, seen through an archway, of a mason's shed, the mason at his dinner, his dog watching, p. 52; a *Man on stilts* in snow, p. 54; *Catching a horse*, with corn in a sieve, p. 56; *Sow and Pigs* (here given); *Crossing deep water*, p. 132; *Sheep drinking*, p. 142; a *Peacock* at a park gate, p. 187; *Magpies and Cow*, p. 200; *Gulls* upon wet sand,

p. 136, admirably rendered.   These and others are worthy of Bewick's best days.   I have spoken of all these as engravings, giving an engraver's judgment of engravers' work.

Who drew and engraved these cuts we do not know: how much or little was by the master's hand.   The book was begun by Bewick on recovering from a severe sickness in 1812.   His own account of it is in the few words here following.   "As soon as I was so far recovered as to be able to sit at the window at home, I began to draw designs upon the wood of the fables and vignettes; and to me this was a delightful task.   In pushing forward impatiently to get to press with the publication, I availed myself of the help of my pupils, my son, William Harvey, and William Temple,—who were eager to do their utmost to forward me in the engraving business, and in my struggles to get the book ushered into the world.   Notwithstanding the pleasurable business of bringing out this publication, I felt it an arduous undertaking.   The execution of the fine work of the cuts during daylight was very trying to the eyes, and the compiling or writing the book by candlelight, in my evenings at home, together injured the optic nerve, and that put all the rest of the nerves 'out of tune;' so that I was obliged, for a short time, to leave off such intense application, until I somewhat recovered the proper tone of memory and of sight.   Indeed I found in this book more difficulties to conquer than I had experienced with either the *Quadrupeds* or the *Birds*.   The work was finished at press on the first of October, 1818.   It was not so well printed as I wished." (*Memoir*, by himself.)

This is all the information we get from Bewick regarding the doing of the cuts.   His words should lead us to infer that the designs were his, the drawing on the wood mainly so; that his pupils helped only with the engraving.   But Bewick was reticent, and little apt to give credit to others.   Even the acknowledged help "of my pupils" is not clear. Robert Bewick, when nearly completing his twenty-fourth year, had become his father's partner, on the first of January, 1812, before the book was begun.   Allowing the injury of the eyes to have lasted but "a short time," it seems unlikely that a man sixty years of age, who had only "somewhat recovered the proper tone of memory and sight," would devote himself to continuous work of a minuter character than that of his younger days. Chatto, a most conscientious writer, must have had authority for his confident assertion that "by far the greater number were designed by Robert Johnson, and engraved by W. W. Temple and William Harvey while yet in their apprenticeship," a service almost contemporaneous with the production of the book; that "in the whole volume there are not more than three of the largest cuts engraved by Bewick himself."   Though Johnson died in 1796, Bewick would hold a property in designs made for him during pupilage. *

---

* Johnson was apprenticed to Bewick in 1788.   He went to learn engraving in copper; but, showing no aptitude for that, was probably mainly employed in drawing.   In design and water-colour painting his work "was of the highest quality."   That Bewick kept possession of drawings made in hours of work is implied by Chatto's statement (*Treatise*, p. 517) that he brought suit for drawings done in overtime.

Mss of 1818.

Drawings which I believe to be by Johnson will be found placed among Bewick's in the daughters' collection; and, as already shown, tail-pieces by him were used in the *Birds*. The question of design lies mainly between him and Bewick, the greater probability on Johnson's side: Harvey's hand also evident in some, at least as copying the designs on *Harvey and Temple.* the wood. If Harvey engraved them, they are his best work. Had Temple much to do with them, a most capable engraver was lost when on termination of his apprenticeship he went into business as a draper. Some figures, however, of birds in the late editions, said to be by him, (the *Rough-legged Buzzard*, the *Pigmy Curlew*, the *Eared Grebe*, and the *Red Sandpiper*), give little indication of capacity. There is no chance of identifying his work on these *Fables*, or of finding out what may have been done by Robert Bewick. It is only guessing, with some unsure internal evidence to help the guesses: yet I think that, beside the drawing on the wood, most of the engraving would be done by Harvey, *Nesbit.* helped (to hazard one more conjecture) by Bewick's earlier pupil, Nesbit, returned to Tyneside in 1815. Looking at the best of the cuts, such cuts especially as the *Fox and Bramble*, judging only from the work, I should hardly hesitate to call them his.

Bewick's later work.

After 1818, to 1828 (the date of Bewick's death), we have nothing of any mark save in the *Supplements* to his *Land and Water Birds*, containing each twenty-one new figures of Birds and some forty tail-pieces; twenty-five more Birds in a sixth edition, in 1826; and yet fifteen more given as Addenda. They in no respect excel, and not often equal, the earlier work; nor do they show any of the delicacy and refinement of the *Fables*, by which we could be led to think the engraving there might be by the old man. Except some of these new Birds, I do not find in the cuts by him during the last ten years of his life anything worthy of his fame: certainly there is nothing in the many miscellaneous *His work appraised.* books floated on his name. All of worth of Thomas Bewick's doing, whether by his own hand or under his direction, is to be found in the books of *Fables*, 1784 and 1818; and in his *Quadrupeds* and *Birds*. Of little merit are the cuts of 1795-6, to Goldsmith, Parnell, and Somervile. And outside of these, hardly excepting the *Chillingham Bull* and (for our interest in his last work) the *Waiting for Death*, I am bound to say, duly regarding bibliographers and critics, all that collectors have raked together were better consigned to oblivion. The "interesting little books published in York, Alnwick and Newcastle," between 1805 and 1811, other such of later dates, and a "brilliant series" of book-plates in wood (examples of which are given in Thomson's *Life and Works*), if by him do but mark decline; and, his or not, may be flung aside as nought. A canny North-Country man, with a keen eye for the "main chance," having always apprentices,* taking orders

---

* I count sixteen :—his brother John, his son Robert, Willis, Nicholson, Harvey, Temple, Armstrong, White, Robert and John Johnson, Nesbit, Clennell, Hole, Anderson, Landells, and Jackson. These not all.

for anything, (however cheap or common, all was grist to the mill), from his workshop in Newcastle he sent out good and bad, much to which he had never put his hand; and dishonest printers and publishers discredited him with much besides. How much that he never saw has been picked out of the dust-bins of North-Country printing-offices by men eager to turn a penny through persuading some fond devotee that this or the other vile cut was by the Master; how many spurious editions have been foisted on the public by the Charnleys, the Pearsons, the Hoggs, the Walter Browns, and other as shameless speculators in the name of Bewick! The heaped rubbish has hidden the fairness of his monument. We may not read the inscription; but we see that the flawed and befouled figure on the pile is not BEWICK. To learn what he was we have to discard so much that has been falsely or foolishly ascribed to him. Chatto should have told us more. Quite independently of Jackson he could have learned far more than he gives us, from Nesbit, Harvey, or Robert Bewick: all three alive when he wrote his *Treatise*, Harvey certainly and Nesbit probably known personally to him. It is strangely sad how opportunities for knowledge have been allowed to pass unused. Robert Bewick, it would seem, made no collection of his father's works; and the daughters, through their ignorance of Art, have failed to render him fit honour. The indiscriminate gathering of nearly three thousand proofs, now in the British Museum, shows how unable they were to judge. Everything supposed to be "Father's" is there innocently stored, mixed with his best work much of the poorest character, without order and mostly undated, spoiled impressions sometimes, relics hoarded for love's sake, jewels with sherds and nail-parings. How shall they get sorted? Nothing but such judgment as only an engraver can be qualified for (and that uncertain) may help to determine how much of what is worthy of Bewick is by his own hand, how much only of his school, actually by Nesbit or Clennell or Hole or Harvey or Robert Bewick or lost William Temple. By these pupils, excepting the bird-figures in the first editions (certainly a magnificent exception), all the best of his engraving was done. In design also, and in drawing on the wood, we must take from him in justice to Johnson, to Clennell, and to Harvey. After all, the Master's fame suffers little. The Birds and what tail-pieces we know to be his are sufficient for his renown as a great and most original artist. He will not lose by being understood. The more we study his best work, the more we shall admire the originality of his genius, his clearness of perception and facility of execution, his fidelity to Nature, his humour and pathos. In his walk, not of " High Art," but of homely Truth, as a designer he has no superior; and if Clennell, Nesbit, Harvey, went beyond him in engraving, we have yet to recognize him as teacher and to allow how hard it so often is to distinguish his hand from theirs.

To fix the place of Bewick as a designer is not my business here: still I may exhibit two more cuts, sufficient of themselves to assert a lofty standing. Perfect as a picture (for pictorially we need not heed a touch of the coarseness into which Bewick's sense of humour too often dropped him) is a *Windy Day*, from the *Fables* of 1818. It is full of matter as a painting by Turner. Excellently drawn are the wind-blown trees, the steps and wall and water-trough, the distant houses, and horse and cart in the street, the old woman at her stall holding her bonnet on, a man trying to open his umbrella against the storm, and the important cow herself: all this in a wood-cut three inches by less than two. It is perhaps the finest picture and best piece of *finished* engraving ever in wood. In contrast with the fullness of this, I may take from the *Water Birds* the *Little Stint*, not so remarkable for the bird itself as for the simplicity of composition. It is only a little bird upon wet sand, with cloud and rain over a monotonous sea, but so much is so lightly and easily expressed. And the outer form is as elegant as if the later Harvey himself had vignetted it.

A Windy Day

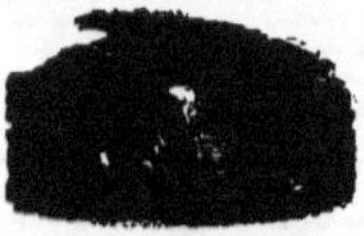

The Little Stint.

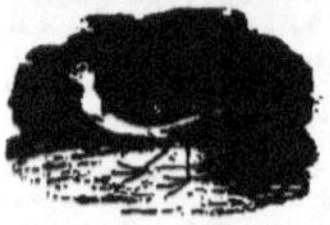

I have complained of the poor printing of Bewick's cuts. He himself speaks of his disappointment with the *Fables*. And yet, at times, especially in some of the *Birds*, I can only call the printing the most tasteful poor printing ever done. I enjoy the rich brown of the ink, pleasanter to the eye and fitter for the engraving than a French black. A respectful tenderness of impression, often seen in the *Birds*, is far better than forcing the effect and sacrificing tone to contrast. No less, points may be brought out with due emphasis and brilliance. In some there are fine lines which one could believe had been wiped before each printing. In the *Grosbeak* touches of black on the bird give value to the soft edges of the feathers, and to the grey foliage behind. Bewick cared to provide against the printers' lack of means and knowledge in his day. He lowers a solid black, and so obtains a grey; he scrapes a black with his graver's edge, taking out a light that looks as if laid on with a brush; he lowers a whole background, to insure more delicate printing. He prided himself on this lowering, as his own discovery,—though indeed it was not new, older than Papillon, who made much use of the same valuable procedure.

A word about printing.

Lowered work.

A few words more, of Bewick's original drawings, left by his daughters to the British Museum. Most are of the same size as the engravings, often not reversed on the wood. In many we see the mark of tracing; in some the shape of the block indenting the paper where the paper overlapped the edge. Generally we have only the Birds, more or less

The original drawings.

finished; but now and then a background is slightly indicated. Some of the tail-pieces, bolder in touch and less exact, I doubt to be Bewick's; and it is noticeable how few we find of the tail-pieces to the *Water Birds*. Is it because so many were by Johnson and Clennell? All the drawings are miniatures, the coloured ones (some are in Indian ink) prettily, I would rather say—daintily painted: as of the day when English water-colour was yet in its timid youth. Bewick's graver had more daring.

Not the restorer of a lost art, for his master, Beilby, practised it after a manner, and Hodgson, whose work is not to be altogether despised, with whom young Bewick found ready employment, was not the only wood-engraver in London,—not the discoverer of "white line," for that he could not fail to learn of the engraver of the 1722 *Fables*,—and not the most consummate of engravers, for Nesbit, Clennell, Branston, and Thompson, all outvie him: still Bewick will keep a sure place in our esteem, for his genius in design, and as the real founder of the new school of engraving in wood. If not all by his own hand, yet from his impulse and direction have proceeded the best examples of the art.

John Bewick's right of recognition rests mainly on his name. With some originality, he was a tolerably correct draftsman, and a graceful designer of the fashion of Stothard, his designs well suiting the subjects on which he was most engaged, moral Story Books for the little Masters and Misses of his time. As a wood-engraver he makes no mark.

A single cut (here given) from the well known and much over lauded *Looking Glass for the Mind* may be sufficient sample of his talent whether as draftsman or engraver. A larger and more ambitious cut, drawn and engraved by him, the *Water-Cress Gatherer*, for Goldsmith's *Deserted Village*, is hardly his best. He died in 1795, having just completed the drawings for Somervile's *Chase*, the drawings already spoken of at p. 146 as engraved by his brother. The engraver finds little to interest him in John.

Of Robert Elliot Bewick (born in 1788, the only son of his father) one would like to know more. In his father's radiance he has been lost to sight. All I can discover as likely to be his, except his not-to be-distinguished part (I think but small) in the *Fables* of 1818, is a series of eleven cuts for the *History of British Fishes*, left incomplete at his father's death and never afterwards continued. These cuts appeared for the first time in the *Memoir*, in 1862, as if the father's doing. Certainly, however, Robert drew them on the wood, and I think there can be no doubt that he also engraved them. They are advertised in 1824 as "engraved on wood by T. Bewick [of course for sake of his name] and Son;" and Dovaston, reporting of a visit to Bewick in August, 1825, writes,—"His Son engraves the Fishes for his new work, and Bewick says he does them admirably." (Bowman's Manuscript, quoted in Thomson's *Life and Works*, p. 267.) Even without this testimony, that Robert was capable of doing them is almost proved by an engraving of one in copper, known to have been done by him. He seems to have been continually out of health; and I doubt his working much with his own hands, though he carried on the business of an engraver, the unexpired lease of the "workshops offices and premises with the appurtenances situate in Saint Nicholas Churchyard in Newcastle upon Tyne" being bequeathed to him by his father's Will. He lived to 1849; but we know no more of his work, except seventy drawings of *Fishes*, which, says tradition, he was "afeard" to engrave. Perhaps a rumour of Yarrell's *Fishes*, four hundred cuts, some by Thompson, 1836, took the wind out of his sail. The drawings were included in the sisters' bequest to the British Museum. They are of microscopical minuteness and exceedingly delicate, as true to Nature as his father's *Birds*.

CHAPTER III

CLENNELL AND NESBIT

EARLIER as a beginner though Nesbit was, I give precedence here to Clennell. His works are more clearly identified in association with the Master's. And much of Nesbit's doing belongs to a later period when Clennell had long ceased to engrave.

LUKE CLENNELL, like Bewick, the son of a farmer, was born on the eighth of April, 1781, at Ulgham, a village near Morpeth, in Northumberland. At an early age—writes Chatto, "he was placed with a relation, a grocer of Morpeth, and continued with him until he was sixteen." Then, showing love and aptitude for art, his friends promoted him, to learn engraving in wood with Bewick, to whom, in April, 1797, he was bound apprentice for seven years. "He in a short time made great proficiency in engraving; and, as he drew with great correctness and power, Bewick employed him to copy on the block several of Robert Johnson's drawings and to engrave them as tail-pieces for the second volume of the *British Birds*. Clennell for a few months after the expiration of his apprenticeship continued to work for Bewick, who employed him in engraving some cuts for a *History of England*, published by Wallis and Scholey. Clennell, who was only paid two guineas a-piece for those cuts, having learned that Bewick received five, sent to the publishers a proof of one of them—*Alfred in the Danish Camp*, stating that it was of his own engraving. In the course of a few days he received an answer, inviting him to come to London and offering him employment until all the cuts intended for the work should be finished; he accepted the offer, and shortly afterward set out for London, where he arrived about the end of autumn, 1804." Chatto adds that between the expiration of his apprenticeship and his departure for London he engraved some "excellent cuts" for the *Hive of Ancient and Modern Literature*.

So far from Chatto, whose meagre account could when he was writing have so easily been amplified. What else we learn through him of Clennell's Newcastle time is found in the list of tail-pieces to the *Water Birds* (already referred to), "furnished by one of

Bewick's early pupils who saw most of Johnson's drawings and worked in the same room with Clennell when he was engraving those here ascribed to him."* The early pupil was probably Edward Willis, whose apprenticeship was contemporary with that of Clennell, and who lived in London when Chatto was writing the *Treatise*. Trusting to this list, I take as Clennell's the *Angler* here given, though except some graver touches on the water which I think are his I see nothing to tell me whether it is by the hand of Bewick or that of his clever pupil. For the *River Scene* I do not need inquiry: only Clennell could cut that water. The same freedom of hand distinguishes the three sea-pieces on the next page. The *Stranded Ship* was drawn and engraved by Clennell, says Chatto's informer; the *Coast Scene* next it engraved by him after Johnson. Wherever among these tail-pieces the water is so graver-drawn, or with crisp sharp lights as if done with a brush, as

in this cut and the one below it, we are sure of Clennell. A fourth cut, two dark ships and a third sunlit (*Water Birds*, p. 366), is of the same painter-like force and excellence.

---

* The following is Chatto's list of Clennell's cuts in the *Water Birds*: the edition of 1804.

Cuts from drawings by Robert Johnson:—

Creeping along a branch, to cross a stream . . page 3
Old Fisherman 25
Partridge-shooting 52
Coast Scene — moonlight 125
Men on a rock 132
Coast Scene 140
Boys riding on gravestones 304

Cuts of which the draftsman is not named:—

Men angling, his coat-shirts pinned up . . . 48
Angler setting his hooks 50
Man falling into water 94
Woman hanging out clothes 106
River Scene 107
Beggar and Mastiff 160

Sea-piece — moonlight . . . . page 194
Tired Sportsman 204
The Glutton 211
Sea-piece 215
Guns going home 271
Boys sailing a ship 281
Man smoking 337
Pumping water on a wreck log . . . 318
Three Sea-pieces 359 366 380

Cuts drawn by Clennell himself:—

Burying Ground 161
Stranded Ship—Icebergs 188
Eisquimaux and canoe 230
Sea-piece 238

This list, Chatto says, may be considerably enlarged. "The greater number [of tail-pieces] in the second volume were engraved by Clennell." (*Treatise*, 406)

The true wave-like character of these, in form and expression of motion, from quiet flow to the wild dash of seething foam, marks the work of Clennell, so well distinguished by Mr. Dobson as "the genius of the group" of Bewick's Scholars. Bewick had no vigour of line like this: the painter's larger mind informs the graver here.

Beside the tail-pieces Clennell no doubt helped with the headings of this volume, with the backgrounds, if not on the birds themselves. Chatto claims for him three: the *Brent Goose* (a good cut), the *Lesser Imber*, and the *Cormorant*. His cuts for the *Hive of Ancient and Modern Literature* were probably begun during apprenticeship. The first edition, 1799, has only three or four cuts, by Bewick; the third, 1806, is enriched with a number of "engravings on wood by T. Bewick and L. Clennell, both of Newcastle." Such a conjunction of names would imply that some of the cuts were done by him after he had left Newcastle. About twenty headings, some very bold and rich, I take to be his. They are however very unequal, some coarse and much hurried.

The small vignettes are Bewick's. Of an early time in London must have been his work for *Scripture Illustrated* from Craig's drawings; poor cuts, but not poorer than Craig, and likely to have been low-priced.

In the *History of England*, Hume's History in ten volumes and Smollett's Continuation in six, he came under the influence of John Thurston, a copper-engraver of considerable mark, employed by or with James Heath, but who had left engraving for designing.

Thenceforth we shall find that Clennell's work is altered in character. Thurston's drawings, I have been told (I have seen only one, shown to me by his friend John Thompson), were done line by line, with the precision of copper-plate engraving; with the result of some approach on the part of the engraver to the manner of copper. Still the drawings must sometimes have been partly with washes of colour. Chatto writes that Clennell was allowed by Thurston to "increase the lights and deepen the shadows, heightening the effect according to his own judgment;" which implies that he had not merely a drawing in lines of the Durer sort, to be followed closely and mechanically, but that he had room and opportunity for the free graver-line of his Newcastle practice. There will be little doubt of this when we come to the cuts for the *Hermit of Warkworth* and the *Religious Emblems*.

His *History of England* cuts are all in this Thurston vein: larger and far less finished than the tail-pieces to the *Water Birds*, and less his own. There are some forty odd in the Hume division, and thirty in the Smollett. Not all are Clennell's. In both series are cuts by Nesbit. Three of the poorest (the line rugged) have T. B. on them; they are probably Clennell's earliest, done at Newcastle. There is much improvement as the work proceeds. The second series, I think, is nearly all by Clennell; his name in full is on some, L. C. on others; but Thurston's drawing is so dominant that without a name it is hard to say certainly what may be Clennell's, what Nesbit's, or perhaps Branston's. In all I know to be by Clennell [and indeed the remark I have to make will apply to all these cuts, whoever the engraver] we shall find that, whatever the line he has to leave (to print as a black line) the line he cuts (the white line) is in his thought, and rules supreme throughout. Although in following Thurston he appears to imitate engraving in copper, his work never loses the essential characteristic of engraving in wood. This is most clearly manifest in four cuts for the *Hermit of Warkworth*. I have not seen the book; the reproductions on the opposite page are from proofs, the proofs unfortunately taken when the blocks were much worn.

The *Pilgrim's Progress* cuts, three of which in Mr. Thomson's *Life and Works* I have spoken of as wrongly attributed to Bewick, if by Clennell must have been of the first he did from Thurston's drawings. Published at Taunton in 1806, there is Bewick's name printed under one: fairly warranting Mr. Thomson in his ascription. But certainly there is nothing of Bewick in them. It is quite possible they were done by Hole, with Bewick at the same time as Clennell, though not so late: his name appearing to work in 1803. I can not say with any degree of assurance whether they are by Hole or Clennell. We shall find this similarity again in their other cuts after Thurston.

A *Vicar of Wakefield*, for which I have vainly sought among the multitude of editions, had four cuts by Thurston and Clennell: one, *Mr. Burchell in the hay-field reading to the two Primrose girls*, full of drawing and daylight, I note as perhaps the most perfect piece of white-line work ever done: not so mannered as Thurston, more of Clennell's own.

Religious Emblems, a set of twenty-one designs by Thurston,* published by Ackermann "to draw into one focus all the talent of the day," appeared in 1809. Of the engravings seven are by Clennell, seven by Nesbit, six by Branston; the remaining one is by Hole.

---

* Allegorical conceits, after the fashion of Quarles; the descriptions by the chaplain to the Earl of Cork, the Rev. J. Thomas, under whose name the book is to be found in the Library of the British Museum.

That Bewick's name, then in its zenith, should have been left out of "all the talent" may indicate his distaste for Thurston's drawing, or some consciousness of inability to stand among his fellows on that ground. The omission confirms me in my belief that there is nothing of Thurston's by his hand. It may be well to speak here of all the *Emblems* for

sake of comparison, though to be referred to again in relation to the engraver of each.

The work of the several masters is very equal; Thurston's decided drawing has kept them so close together. Clennell's are the boldest, but not else superior. The best of his, I think, are the *Soul encaged* and *Panting for the Living Waters*. The *Forest-Feller*

(Death), daringly bold, yet not to be called coarse,—the *Call to Vigilance*, more refined and bright,—and the *World made captive*, a brilliant cut, with not one useless line,—may rank next. His other two, *Flocks refreshed* and *Constancy*, are below those before-named and not so good as the cuts by Nesbit and Branston. Nesbit's work here is so like to Clennell's that it is only the name beneath which makes me sure. Something of this of course is due to the Thurston lines in all. *Hope departing, Joyful Retribution, Wounded in the mental eye*, and the *World well weighed*, all by Nesbit, might all be easily mistaken for Clennell's. So likewise might the figures of the *Daughters of Jerusalem*, the foliage however bespeaking Nesbit. *Sinners hiding in the grass*, except for Nesbit's name, might be by Clennell or Branston, so vignrous is it in line. *Awaiting the Dawn* is of the same character. Hole's one cut, *Seed sown*, is worthily associated with those of his compeers, yet not equal to the best. Branston's most successful is *Rescued from the floods*; but the *Destruction of Death and Sin*, a much larger cut, the largest in the book, is magnificently strong. Other four by Branston — *The Fate of Avarice, Self-sufficient Inquirers, Casting off Incumbrances*, and *Fertilizing Rills*, —are good too. All these cuts are governed and assimilated by Thurston's exact and somewhat conventional drawing; but through them all we can clearly perceive the use and the beauty of the always remembered white line.

And now I have to speak of Clennell's most important work, not of greater excellence than other, but important for its size (fourteen inches by more than ten) as well as for excellence: his heading to the *Diploma of the Highland Society*. This no doubt he took up immediately on the completion of the *Religious Emblems*, as it bears the same date of 1809. The design is by West; Thurston drew on the wood the allegorical group in the circular centre, and Clennell himself drew the Highland soldier and fisherman, who on

either side support the centre. Mr. Dobson well judges the engraving as characteristic of Clennell, "rather energetic than fine, and more spirited than minutely patient:" a far sounder criticism than that of Chatto, who considers "the lines in some places coarse, in others the execution careless," and who objects to the cross-lining as unnecessary and as done rather to display the engraver's ability: so contradicting his charge of carelessness. The cross-lining on the two large figures outside the circle (inside the circle is all white line) appears to me to be necessary to prevent any look of coarseness; and large as the treatment is (yet not coarse because large), there is not a sign of carelessness about it. Rich in line, whether the lines be simple or crossed, rich in colour, and everywhere well drawn, I look upon it as the greatest accomplishment of wood-engraving daring, on so large a scale, to compete with engraving in copper. Let us compare it with the best of Durer's obtaining—the *Ecce Homo*, or with Cranach's *St. Jerome in penitence*; and the difference will be seen at a glance. The most perfect knife-work looks poor beside the line of the artistic graver. Intelligently faithful mechanism is in the earlier cuts; in the later one is the richness and fullness of higher Art. Jerome of Nurnberg had not even Clennell's tools; Durer had to adapt his drawing to the only method of engraving then available: Clennell had no such lets and hindrances. I am speaking of engraving only, not touching so much as the hem of Durer's vesture. I am only comparing engravings when I call Clennell, as artist-engraver, our most consummate workman. There is no such command of the engraver's means, nor such engraving power, in Bewick. Of the Bewick school only Nesbit may fairly stand beside him, yet not he of so grand a build. Thompson, his equal as engraver in command of means, his superior as *engraver only* if one must be preferred, is far below him as an artist.

When, after the destruction of Clennell's block (at the burning of Bensley's printing-office), it had to be reëngraved, the work fell to Thompson. His engraving, of the same size as the original, and closely copied, seen by itself would be admired as a masterpiece: strong, and yet with all the finish the subject could require. But the two compared, the inferiority of our great engraver to his painter rival is but too plain. It is not the weakness of a copyist that we remark: Thompson's lines are as vigorous, as firm and determined as those of Clennell; but in all the subtleties of expression of form, though the original was before him, he fails,—fails, not wanting hand-power, but for lack of the artist's knowledge manifest in every cut by Clennell. 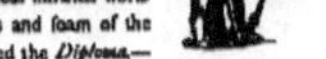

The artist is apparent in his smaller and more refined engravings as plainly as in this large and largely treated, yet not less finished work. From work so large we may turn again to the waves and foam of the *Water Birds*, or look forward to the cuts that followed the *Diploma*,— the thirty-four (one of them by Nesbit) lovely little pen-and-ink sketches by Stothard for Rogers' *Pleasures of Memory*, first printed by Bensley for Cadell and Davies in 1810. Hans Lutzelburger is come again! Saying that the engraver here also proves himself an artist, I do not imply that his individuality displaces the draftsman's. As Lutzelburger forgot himself yet did not lose his art in appreciative close fidelity to the lines of Holbein, so Clennell forsook his own manner to perfectly render these dainty lovelinesses of Stothard. We do not see an engraver's translation: we have pure Stothard.

The lesson here taught will be clearer when the reader compares these two cuts by Clennell with the one below. That, Nesbit's one cut (at p. 30 in the edition of 1810), being over heavy, was lightened by Thompson, who also engraved the additional drawings for succeeding editions. Refined as this is, it is tame beside Clennell's fac-similes, and the pen-and-ink touch of Stothard is altogether lost.

These were of Clennell's latest work: it were uselessly painful to notice some childish cuts that eased the tedium of long years of insanity. From 1810 he seems to have abandoned engraving for painting: exhibiting, at the Royal Academy in 1812, a picture of *Fox-Hunters regaling*, one of *Baggage Waggons in a thunder-storm*, in 1814, and other pictures in years following,—most notable of them *The Charge of the Guards at Waterloo*, in the British Institution, in 1816. His success in this brought him a commission from the Earl of Bridgewater to paint the *Banquet of the Allied Sovereigns in the Guildhall of London*. Anxiety regarding so great a work affected his mind, and broke him down; he never really recovered. The remnant of his life, more than twenty years, is a blank. He died in 1840. Here is not the place to judge him as a painter; only I may note that he was an admirable draftsman (which is the ground of his preeminence as an engraver), and a clever painter

in water-colour also, as may be seen at the South Kensington Museum in a fine picture of a *Saw-pit*, dated 1810. In the Art Library there too are some thirty spirited designs for a series of *British Novelists*. It is true, as observed by Mr. Dobson, that "they have not the grace of Stothard, but they have greater vigour." What little is known of him beyond his works (even those very insufficiently catalogued) is given with all requisite particularity in Mr. Dobson's *Bewick and his Pupils*.

For the sake of students it is well to state that Clennell too, like Bewick, has suffered from the jackals, the collector's providers: though the fact of his not being so much in vogue has made him a less coveted prey. I find his name unwarrantably made use of in the title-page of a wretched book thrust upon the public in 1875, a "*Parlour Menagerie*, with upwards of three hundred wood-engravings by Luke Clennell and others;" and the Introduction also asserts that "the wood-cuts which appear throughout the volume were chiefly drawn and engraved by Luke Clennell, who was trained by Bewick." There is not a single cut in the volume fairly attributable to Clennell. In another recent publication, *Our Feathered Families*, by H. G. Adams, I see the same mistaken or wilfully misleading ascription. *Caveat emptor!* Let collectors and connoisseurs beware!

CHARLTON NESBIT, another of our North-Country wood-men, apprenticed to Bewick in 1789, had completed his term of instruction before Clennell began, eight years later. Still less than is known of Clennell is to be learned of Nesbit. Only his works speak of him. He was born in 1775, the son of a keel-man, at Swalwell, near Gateshead, in the county of Durham. After serving his time with Bewick he, about 1799, left Newcastle for London, remaining there until 1815, when he returned to his native place, living in no great apparent activity until 1830. In that year he went back to London, where he died in 1838. There is nothing to be added to this brief memoir from Chatto's *Treatise* published in the year after Nesbit's death.

I have placed him beside Clennell but hardly at the same height. I may explain this by saying that I think he could not have engraved the *Diploma* cut, or those breezy sea pieces in the *Water Birds*. That said, allowing him to want the draftsman's facility, the painter's boldness, his general engraving is quite equal to that of Clennell.

Of early work however, done while with Bewick, I find nothing very notable. Chatto speaks of a few tail-pieces cut by him for the *Land Birds*, and there can be no doubt of his having been so employed; but there is nothing to distinguish him. The vignettes to Goldsmith's *Traveler* and Parnell's *Hermit*, 1795, toward the end of his apprenticeship, give little indication of any after excellence. The background to the *Departure* (in the *Traveler*) is better, but I only suppose it may be his from the likeness to his later work. His first really noteworthy doing is the engraving of *St. Nicholas' Church* at Newcastle, from a drawing by Robert Johnson, his fellow-pupil. Johnson's well-drawn little figures here are very nicely engraved, the tints are good, and the whole cut is carefully and well done; but it is chiefly remarkable for its size, not quite fifteen inches by twelve,—more remarkable then than now, the cut also being upon twelve pieces of box-wood, "firmly cramped together and mounted on a plate of cast iron to prevent their warping:" a very astonishing performance in those ante-illustrated-news days.

In London he did poor work from Craig's as poor drawings, for *Scripture Illustrated*; but must, as Mr. Dobson supposes, have soon found employment on the better drawings of Thurston, his name being to a frontispiece of an edition of Bloomfield's *Farmer's Boy*,

1802, the other cuts in which are probably also his. By 1805 we have the accomplished
engraver able to compete with the best. An edition of Thomson's *Seasons* of that date[*]
places him at once by the side of Clennell; and the cuts in Wallis and Scholey's *History*

of England are (as before said) only to be known from Clennell's latest and best by his
name or initials. The *Seasons* indeed are said to be by Bewick. His work they are not.
His name on the title-page will not persuade me to believe that his hand was employed
on them. When I first saw them I took them to be by Clennell; but I doubt his doing
such work between the completion of the *Water Birds* and his beginning for Wallis and
Scholey. They seem too good for Hole; and he had left Newcastle before this. Were
they undertaken by Bewick, his name therefore appearing to them, although he farmed
them out? There is no possibility of learning anything except from examination of the
cuts themselves; and when we would look at them the hand of Thurston binds our eyes.
Clennell's or Nesbit's: I may not say which; I think they are by Nesbit, but I am only
certain that they never were the handiwork of Bewick.

The same bewildering likeness, under the dominant influence of Thurston, is seen in
the *Religious Emblems*, 1809; though there we fortunately have the engravers' names to
set us right. I confess for these cuts likewise that, were no names given, despite what
judgment I may have as an engraver, I could not with any confidence assign the several
engravings to their engravers, either from manner or for merit. Certainly not so far as
Clennell and Nesbit are concerned. Of Nesbit's doing *Wounded in the mental eye, Hope*

---

[*] Printed again in 1809. These different editions,
not always dated, nor saying which is first, second,
third, etc., are very puzzling, and prevent anything
like assured correctness of chronological sequence.

departing, *Joyful Retribution*, *The World well weighed*, might be transferred to Clennell, and as many by Clennell assigned to Nesbit, without disturbing any critical perceptions of mine. After what I have written of Clennell, what need I add in praise of Nesbit? Other beautiful cuts by him may be found in Somerville's *Rural Sports*, 1813; and in Sir Egerton Brydges' reprints at the Lee Priory Press,—to be more readily seen collected in Quillinan's *Wood-cuts and Verses*, 1820, with "all the engravings used at this Press"

Between 1815 and the publication of Bewick's *Fables of Æsop* in 1818 Nesbit was at Swalwell and, it would seem, not busy for London publishers. I can not but think that he may have engraved some, perhaps many, of these fable cuts for his old master, while

Nesbit.
Fables of 1818.

Rinaldo and
Armida.

living so close to him. We know that Harvey drew and engraved some: the engraving yet not so like to his after-work as that in others is to Nesbit's. In the fable headings I have given (pp. 150 151), not selected with any thought of confirming my supposition, there is nothing that might not have been done by Nesbit then, and much of the same refined and finished character which marks his later work from Harvey's drawing.

In 1818 (Bewick's *Fables* then completed) Nesbit engraved the *Rinaldo and Armida*, one of four intended cuts for Savage's *Practical Hints on Decorative Printing*, published in 1822-3. Concerning which Savage in his Preface writes as follows. "I resolved to give four subjects by four different engravers, to show what the art is capable of at this present day in England. Of these four I have only been able to give two, . . one by Nesbit, the other by Branston, from designs by the late J. Thurston, Esq.

"Circumstances prevented my having one from Mr. Thompson, and I sincerely regret the loss of his abilities. The melancholy illness of Mr. Clennell is also a source of real regret to me, independently of the disappointment I experience in my not having, as a specimen of the powers of his burin, the subject which it was intended he should engrave from a drawing by T. Stothard, Esq., R.A. I was also anxious of including in my work one subject from the father of wood-engraving in England, Mr. Thomas Bewick, but his numerous engagements, among which was his edition of Æsop's Fables, prevented him acceding to my wishes." [*]

Bewick would hardly have succeeded with so large a work: still with the enterprising printer we may regret that he did not make the attempt, as fifth of the four. Yet more deeply must we regret the loss of opportunity for comparing Nesbit and Branston with Clennell and Thompson on so fair a tourney-ground. "The business of engraving on wood was brisk" at this time, writes Mr. Savage.

Criticised in the
Treatise.

The *Rinaldo and Armida* is Nesbit's greatest achievement. And here I have again to dissent from Chatto's (or perhaps I should say Jackson's) judgment. "The foliage, the trees, and the drapery," he says, "are admirably engraved; but the lines in the bodies of the figures are too much broken and 'chopped up.' The lines were originally continuous and distinct, but Mr. Thurston objecting to them as too dark, Nesbit went over his work again, . . . and gave them their present dotted appearance. As a specimen of the engraver's abilities, the first proof submitted to the designer was superior to the last." I have to contradict this. Designer and engraver knew well what they were about. In the first proof the flesh would be not only too dark, but coarse and harsh; and the cross white lines, whether suggested by Thurston or more probably chosen by Nesbit himself, not only reduced colour, but also enriched and softened the flesh and rendered it more

---

[*] But Bewick's *Fables* were finished by 1818; and Nesbit's cut was not done till then, the date cut on it by himself. It will be recollected too that Bewick was not employed on *Religious Emblems*, in 1809.

delicate and flesh-like. For the trees and foliage I am entirely in accord with Chatto; and I remark the resemblance to trees and foliage (those magnified) of the *Fables*.

To add a factitious value to the engravings in Savage's book, the faces of several blocks were sawn across. Nesbit's was repaired by Bonner, so skilfully that the mending can only be traced by a very slight want of close fitting in some of the inlaid wood. Proofs of the repaired block will be found quite equal to those in the book.

This and two cuts for Puckle's *Club*, in 1817, *Zany* (here given) and the *Quack*, are the last of the Thurston Nesbits. From this date I have found nothing of Nesbit's doing until after his return to London in 1830, except a few not remarkable cuts in the first series of *Northcote's Fables*, 1828. His work henceforth follows Harvey. He has two cuts in the *Blind Beggar of Bethnal-Green*, 1832, drawn by Harvey, and very excellently engraved. But the best of his later work is in a second series of *Northcote's Fables*, in 1833; and in the Rev. Gilbert White's *Natural History and Antiquities of Selborne.*—the edition of 1836. Thurston's vigour and richness have given place to the refinement and delicacy

of Harvey. Nothing can be more daintily sweet in line than the cuts in these two books. For the *Fables* he did nine headings and six tail pieces, worthy of his best days. If they want the freshness of the *Fables* of 1818, it is because Harvey is now mannered and not so close to Nature: no longer governed by the Johnson drawings of old Bewick days. We are already at the beginning of a decadent age, when fineness of line, tone, and "finish" (a misused word), will be preferred to the simple charm of truth. The engraving of these, good as it is, lacks the freedom of the Bewick cuts, with which the second Northcote series may most fairly bear

comparison. Could those cuts of 1818 have had the perfect printing of Whittingham, whose India-paper copy of 1833 is before me, there would have been no need to point out their transcendent beauty and artistic pre'mineuce. Still, for delicate manipulation the later work, in so far as the engraver Nesbit is concerned, is unsurpassed. The like quality will be seen in the *Selborne* cuts, in a delicious little landscape, *Hollow Lane Bridge*.

at p. 16, and a bit of rich copse undergrowth with a *Hen Partridge and young*, at p. 433. An *Eagle Owl* and a *Peregrine Falcon*, in the same volume, carry us back to the Bewick *Birds* and, for engraving, will stand the comparison. I have not attempted to name all of Nesbit's cuts; but one more must have notice,— *The River Jordan*, bold and rich, in Latrobe's *Scripture Illustrations*, published in 1838, the year of the engraver's death.

HENRY FULKE PLANTAGENET WOOLLCOMBE HOLE must be named here, if only as the fellow-pupil of Clennell, and with him credited by Chatto for work on the *Water Birds*, birds and tail pieces. The birds by Hole,—the *Whimbrell*, the *Tufted Duck*, the *Lesser Tern*, the *Velvet Duck*, the *Red-breasted Merganser*, and the *Crested Cormorant*,—are but poor; the *Velvet Duck* alone worth notice. Hole is best with the lines set by Thurston, in eight cuts for *The Press* published at Liverpool by John M'Creery in 1803, and in the *Seed sown* in *Religious Emblems*, 1809. He has also some fair cuts in *Poems* by Felicia Dorothea Browne (Mrs Hemans), 1808. There is nothing more to be said of him but that he was the son of a captain in the militia and succeeded to an estate. Whereupon he forsook wood-engraving, in which he might have made some mark.

JUDGING him only as an engraver, and taking into our account the number and the variety of his works, John Thompson is beyond question entitled to rank above all the men who have engraved in wood. Clennell as artist and Nesbit in landscape excel him; his master, Branston, perhaps equals him within certain limits. What these two, Branston and Thompson, were capable of I have now to show. Of their biography there is very little to record.

ROBERT ALLEN BRANSTON was born at Lynn in Norfolk, in 1778. His father appears to have been a copper-plate engraver, an heraldic painter also, and probably, like Beilby of Newcastle, undertook all sorts of engraving, including wood-cuts. Chatto therefore I take to be incorrect in writing that "Branston, like Bewick, acquired his knowledge of wood-engraving without the instruction of a master." Bewick himself says that Beilby engraved in wood, however poorly; and both he and the elder Branston as engravers in copper would be sufficiently qualified to teach all that needed to be taught of engraving in the other material. Redgrave, whose dates differ somewhat from Chatto's, says that Branston in his nineteenth year attempted to settle at Bath as painter and engraver, but not finding encouragement, after doing some cuts for a *Description of Bath*, removed to London in 1799 [about 1802, Chatto says, but must be wrong], and for a time supported himself by engraving music. It was an era of lotteries; and bills or prospectuses of the various schemes were embellished with wood-cuts to attract public attention. I recollect that twenty years later, when I was a lad, I had a collection of similar cuts: the rivalry between the several lottery-offices for the sale of tickets causing the issue of multitudes, liberally distributed in the streets to any passers by. On these bills, it is said Branston found early employment as a wood-engraver.

The earliest cuts I can identify as his are of Craig's drawing for *Scripture Illustrated*. They are not important: indeed Craig's drawings (some of them I have seen), poor and [illegible] careless, afforded little opportunity for the engraver's talent. Still, they are boldly cut. Far better was his work when he had the help of Thurston. I think he may have been employed with Nesbit and Clennell on the *History of England*: but there is no knowing. I do not find his initials. In 1809 he appears conspicuously in *Religious Emblems*. Of his work there I have already spoken. *Rescued from the floods* shows him at his best, yet

Religious Emblems.

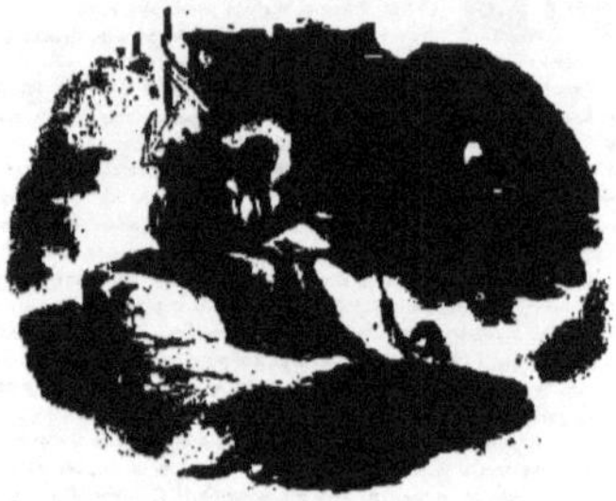

Rescued from the floods.

is hardly better than the larger cut, the *Destruction of Death and Sin*, which is vigorous as anything by Clennell himself. Of other four cuts by him in the *Emblems* I need only repeat the names, and that but for the sake of more conveniently counting them among his works: the *Fate of Avarice, Self-sufficient Inquirers, Fertilizing Rills*, and *Casting off Incumbrances*. All of them are good.

An edition of Bloomfield's *Wild Flowers*, dated 1806, and *Epistles in Verse* by George Marshall, 1812, both have cuts by him. In 1817 we see his hand in *The Club*, "a Gray Cap for a Green Head, a dialogue between a Father and a Son," by James Puckle, the reprint of a book published in 1711. This illustrated edition has twenty-four principal headings and as many small tail pieces, beside an engraved title page with the Club in full assembly. The Club is supposed to consist of twenty-four members, according with

Puckle's Club.

the letters of the alphabet : Antiquary, Buffoon, Critic, Detractor, Envioso, Flatterer, Gamester, Hypocrite, Impertinent, Knave, Lawyer, Moroso, Newsmonger, Opiniator,  Projector, Quack, Rake, Swearer, Traveler, Usurer, Wiseman, Xantippe, Youth, Zany · concerning whose conversation, conduct, and characters, the Son reports to his Father, the Father thereupon making his wise comment. The book is very notable for us on account of the designs by Thurston and for the excellent engravings, by Nesbit, Branston, Thompson, W. Hughes, White, and Mary Byfield. It is also a fine specimen of Whittingham's printing at the famous Chiswick Press. Three of the headings — *Critic, Envioso, Lawyer,*— two initial letters, and three slight tail-pieces, are by Branston. The *Lawyer* is the best. *Envioso* has too much of a look of imitation copper-plate : the line hard, and Thurston's richness lost

A year later is the *Title* to Chorley's *Metrical Index* ; and of that year also may be his most important work—yet not better engraved than works I have already noticed, the *Cave of Despair* (from Spenser's *Faerie Queene*), ordered by Savage in competition with Nesbit's *Rinaldo and Armida,* and like that drawn on the wood by Thurston. Chatto's criticism is sound. Between these two cuts, he writes, "it would be difficult to decide which is best. Both are good specimens of the style of their respective schools, and the subjects are well adapted to display the peculiar excellences of the engravers. Had they changed subjects, neither of the cuts would have been so well executed ; but there is little doubt that Nesbit would have engraved the figures and rocks in the *Cave of Despair* better than Branston would have engraved the trees and the foliage in the *Rinaldo and Armida.*" He has well hit the characteristics of the two men : Nesbit's richest work in foliage, though excellent in the figures ; Branston's comparative limitation to the figure. All I would notice in his criticism, not objecting 

but only qualifying, is the remark that they are good specimens of the respective schools. Different as the two styles — that of Bewick and that of Branston — distinctly are, that

Branston. The Cave of Despair. of Bewick (in his best work) having as little regard as possible to the conventional line of copper, while Branston's, based upon copper, closely adheres to it,—yet in these two cuts Thurston's influence is so pervading and so paramount that the apparent difference is more in the subject than the style or treatment. The difference of the styles is vital: but it is difficult to define it so as to be understood by any but an engraver. Two Schools. Bewick's line, as Branston's, is in fact the line of copper, an incised line, cut in the same manner as if he were working in copper, differing from copper only in effect, the printing causing that difference, as an impression from the surface of a relief cut gives white lines where an impression from the incised lines of copper-plate gives black. The Bewick principle is graver-drawing in white, with comparative disregard of lines to be left on the surface. This underlying principle is always kept in view by Bewick, and by Clennell and Nesbit. Branston, on the contrary, though he can not escape the necessity of white line in wood (that is when the lines of expression are left for his choice, when the drawing is not only in black lines to be kept fac-simile), seems to think of the black line of a copper-plate and, so motived, all his line has more or less an appearance of copper. So much we can perceive in our two cuts. Had they changed hands however, Nesbit's white lines would have little altered Branston's cut, whatever difference or loss had resulted from Branston in the place of Nesbit. No less Chatto is correct in speaking of the two schools: this Bewick white line and the Branston or—it is fairer to call it—the Thurston black line: two methods distinct in intention, although in practice necessarily running one into the other. In the three cuts here printed,—the *Philosophers' Mouse* (from Butler's *Remains*), *In the stocks* (*Hudibras*, edition of 1819), and the *Pike* (Walton's *Angler*, Major's edition, 1822),—it will be seen that Branston, using a free graver, also adopts the white line.

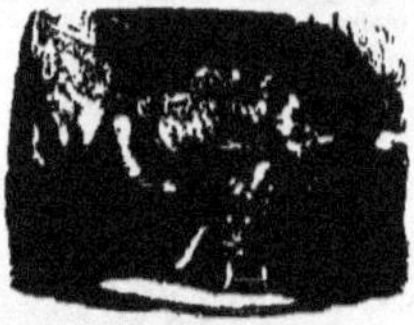

Philosophers and Mouse.

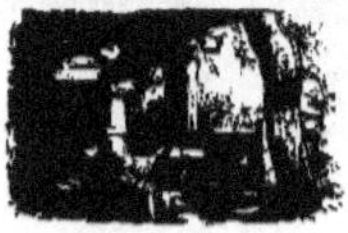

In the stocks.

With such opposite grounds for action, it can be understood how Branston would think himself capable of rivaling Bewick's *Fables* of 1818, and the *Birds* also: rather presumptuous imagining, and so proved. Chatto gives the only two *Fables* done; they sufficiently mark the difference between the two schools:

excellent engraving and artistic freedom. The *Bird*, also given by Chatto, is of course a failure: in Thurston *versus* Bewick the result could not be doubtful. Yet it has to be owned that, however formal, Branston is never weak. As engraver he is superior to Bewick. And his line, if conventional, is rich and expressive. Good work of his may be seen in the Lee Priory books (or with Nesbit's in Quillinan's *Wood-cuts and Verses*); good in figure and in landscape, in the last, however, not equal to Nesbit. Of his latest doing must be ten cuts with his name in the first series of Northcote's

Fables, published in 1828, a year after his death. They are not very successful: Harvey's drawing may not have pleased him; or some of them may be by one of his sons, Robert and Frederick, both fair engravers. Still, the *Fowler and Birds* is very well cut, and the *Mastiff and Goose* is not unworthy of him.

JOHN THOMPSON is the great exponent of the Thurston method. Whatever has been already said of Branston in comparing him with Bewick, I might also say of Thompson. In that imitative rivalry with copper-plate, learned of Branston and from long connection with Thurston, perhaps also deliberately preferred by him as better suited to his genius, he stands unequalled. He had not the original faculty of Bewick; but Bewick's graver work, meaning by that his handling of the graver, is weak as a child's untaught attempts beside the accomplishment of Thompson. Not Bewick surely, nor any other engraver, could have done the cut on our next page, the *Fight with the Soldan*, drawn by Corbould, the heading to the twentieth book of Tasso's *Jerusalem Delivered* (Wiffen's translation, published in 1826). The work there has all the delicacy of incised work, with nothing whatever (well printed) to distinguish it from that. In trees, foliage, and what else is part of landscape, he is inferior to the Bewick men. His landscape is seldom successful; he does not appear to have had any feeling for it: yet with Thurston to assist he could on occasion, as in the cut (on p. 179) of *Moroso*, from the Puckle *Club*, engrave as rich a bit of foliage as even Nesbit himself. His figure subjects, after Thurston, or Harvey, or Cruikshank, or Grandville, or Mulready, are supremely good. He had not a painter's knowledge, he had nothing of the painter-like quality, the brush-touch of Clennell; but he lacked only that to make him even Clennell's superior. He was mannered, because graver-work in copper is mannered, almost necessarily conventional; but it was with the best of copper-plate manner. I may not prefer the principle of his work; but certainly he carried it to perfection. And the perfection was constant. In all the multitude of his engravings that I have looked through I do not recollect a poor one. There was never a bad cut with *J. Thompson* signed beneath it, or bearing the famous monogram, as seen on the chair of *Moroso* (Thurston's mark on the opposite arm) and on the cut of *Youth*. Throughout his works we shall search in vain for an inefficient or useless line. Form is always expressed, drawing everywhere cared for; distances are well kept; there is none of the blurred confusion of an engraved photograph in all his doing. Everything is clear and distinct; and has a character of deliberate decision; the lines well-chosen, pleasant, and harmonious. This last quality he owed to Thurston, a master of harmonious line.

His daylight cuts have always the look of daylight. With full command of means, he never fails in effect. His cuts always print well: they print themselves.

Of Thompson's biography I have little to record. He was born at Manchester in 1785. "When but fourteen years of age," says the *London and Westminster Review* in 1838, "the interest he took in drawings and prints induced his father to make him a pupil of Branston, who was then what is called an engraver in general. The latter half of the term of his tuition was given solely to wood-engraving, and soon after its expiration he abandoned the manner of his teacher and formed a style of his own. He was supported by the advice of Thurston, then the principal draftsman for wood, and who, being a pupil of James Heath, had a general and profound knowledge of engraving." There is some incorrectness here. Branston may have been a general engraver in 1800, but was already working at wood-engraving; and would be employed, with Clennell and Nesbit, on Thurston's drawings before the end of Thompson's apprenticeship. It is most probable that while with Branston he made his beginning with Thurston; and it can not be said that he abandoned Branston's manner, which was Thurston's. The style of Thurston and Branston was also that of Thompson for many years and through all his best works.[*]

Leaving Branston, he must soon have been fully employed on Thurston's drawings. Dibdin's *London Theatre*, not completed until 1815, in twenty-six volumes, is full of his work: near upon a thousand small vignettes, some rather coarse, but all of them good,

---

[*] Thurston's period of drawing on wood was from the date of his beginning on the *History of England*, about 1804, to 1811, the year of his death. His reign was undisputed. Such work as Craig could do bears no comparison with his; and though Stothard, most prolific of designers, and Corbould and others, made a few occasional drawings on wood, they could not be considered as rivals. Nearly all of better book illustration on wood during all that period seems to have been intrusted to the able pencil of Thurston.

some remarkably so   Every play has a cut, an emblematical vignette or half or whole figure, for the title, and some scene as a heading for every act.   The illustrations only of Shakspere number two hundred and thirty.   Ample scope had Thompson for learning

his Thurston, although not engraving for Wallis and Scholey's *History of England*, which was only completed in 1810, nor for the *Religious Emblems of 1809*.*   In those days he perhaps was not so well advanced as to take a place by the side of the older engravers.   By 1817 he had put forth his full strength in the Puckle *Club*, and in a magnificent edition of *Jerusalem Delivered* (the old translation by Fairfax).

Thompson's cuts in the *Club* are the *Title-page*, with the Club in assembly, *Antiquary, Detractor, Flatterer, Hypocrite, Impertinent, Morose, Newsmonger, Opiniator, Swearer, Usurer, Wiseman, Xantippe, Youth*, beside

tail-pieces for *Envious, Projector, Traveler*, and *Knave*.   I give here *Morose* and *Youth* for the richness of one and the delicacy of the other; but *Wiseman* (with his family, in an arbour) shows the same Nesbit-like foliage, and there is the same richness in the figures here, and also in *Detractor* and *Xantippe*.   The other cuts are not less ably engraved, but the drawings are not so full. In the five cuts I have noticed we see the coöperation of Thompson with Thurston at its best.   But the whole book is good.

For Thompson only, his most charming work to my thinking is the Fairfax Tasso I give the full title (so rare a book should have distinction): "*Godfrey of Bulloigne or Jerusalem Delivered*, by Torquato Tasso: printed by Bensley and Son, Holt Court.

---

* Though Nagler credits him with work in it. The *Künstler-Lexikon* may not be trusted as regards our English draftsmen and engravers on wood. I may note one curious mistake: the statement, based on a distinction made by George Cruikshank between himself and his brother Robert, that George's name was really Simon Pure—("*denn eigentlicher Name Simon Pure ist*"). Redgrave also is not erroneous.

Fleet St., for R. Triphook, Old Bond St., and J. Major, Skinner St., 1817." There is a glorious copy on India paper in the Library of the British Museum (C. 43. d. 23). The engravings are all Thompson's. Each of the twenty books has a heading, and there are tail-pieces besides. My choice is the heading to the second book, *Sophronia and Olindo at the stake*, a delicious piece of engraving, characteristic of the style Thurston seems to have preferred, fac-simile, yet not fac-simile, every line preserved but at the same time freely rendered: so that the line has a peculiar richness, the richness of copper, with a beauty all its own. The heading to Book 4, *Hildraort and Armida*, is like the best of the Puckle cuts. A *Combat* in Book 5 is, if possible, yet richer. Book 6 is as perfect. *Erminia sitting at a tree-foot*, Book 7, is a lighter cut, grey and graceful, excellent in both drapery and foliage. *Rinaldo on the battle-field*, Book 8, is very fine in line. In *Rinaldo and Armida*, Book 20, the faces and the drawing everywhere are beautifully rendered; a quiver of arrows with a scarf thrown across it is a study for sweetness of line and perfect drawing. Again, though I point out the cuts I like best, I do not imply that the others are inferior; and of the tail-pieces also there are some as good. It is, I think, the best work of Thompson, who here loses himself in his engraving, so doing full justice to the designer. Also Thurston is lighter and more graceful, liker to Stothard than elsewhere, and freer from his usual mannerism. Looking at these cuts I almost forget the greater artistic worth of the pure white line of the *Fables* of 1818. It must however be allowed that the two methods draw very close together in their best expression. And Thurston knew how to happily marry them, with such workmen as Clennell, Nesbit, Branston, and Thompson, to carry out his intention. We shall see a change even in Thompson after Thurston's death. Dependence upon the draftsman weakens the hand of the engraver, who needs some originality to be even a satisfactory translator.

The *Title-page to Hudibras* is of the same character as the Puckle and the Tasso cuts. Other cuts by Thompson will be found in this 1819 edition. This one might have been drawn line for line on the block, like the one drawing I have seen of Thurston's; only, as already observed of other cuts, the lines not intended to be followed with close, hard exactness, but left to a free action of the graver. Taking the whole series of Thurston's drawings, by Nesbit, Clennell, Branston, and Thompson, [it is pleasant to repeat their names], and taking also Bewick's *Birds*, the *Tail-pieces*, and the *Fables* of 1818, we have to look upon the first quarter of this nineteenth century as remarkable for not only the morning but also the full noon-splendour of the art of engraving in wood. Nothing of work since done outshines the glory of that time. When that hour passes the worth of white line will be forgotten, though it may still be sometimes used merely as a quicker method; and we shall have Harvey instead of Thurston. The imitation of copper once accepted, even Thompson himself will be contented with fineness in place of the lovelier strength of his early days; while later men, wanting his power, will prefer the easy way

The Club;
or
A DIALOGUE
between
FATHER AND SON.
1817

of weakness. The decadence is sure, however slow; but we have still some noble work before us, for all of Thompson's work is noble, honest, straight forward, and complete.

In the *Portrait of Butler* (*Butler's Remains*, 1827) we notice the white cross line in the background. For the rest, head and dress have all the character of copper, the work scarcely recognisable as wood. As such it is a master-piece and, overcoming so much difficulty, has led other engravers to essay the same imitation of copper, unprofitably, with less happy result.

Very sweet and refined is the *Boudoir*, in the *Young Lady's Book*, 1829. All Harvey's gracefulness is there, refinement of line and niceness of tone; but we miss the healthier freshness of the old rendering of Johnson, under the eyes of Bewick; and we miss the strength of Thurston. *The Anniversary* for 1828-9 (one of the fashionable gift-books of the time) has two of Thompson's choicest cuts after Harvey; and about that date, as well as before, he appears continually employed by Whittingham on small title-page cuts from Harvey's drawings, beside others innumerable for the many publications printed at Chiswick, after Corbould, Stothard, Harvey, etc. He has capital engraving in the *Children in the Wood*, 1831; some lovely little cuts in *A Story without an end*, 1834; and work of his best will be seen in the *Natural History of Selborne*, 1836: these all drawn by Harvey. Specially to be noticed in the *Selborne* is a flying *Goat-sucker* (Bewick's Night jar), grand in colour, finer than Bewick, as an engraving. He has nothing in the first series of the Northcote *Fables*, 1828; but in the series of 1833 his name occurs frequently: to a few headings, but formal, liker Thompson than Harvey and not the best of either, and to many small vignette tail-pieces, few of which are likely to be his own. I recognize his hand in

Thompson

Butler's Remains.

Young Lady's Book.

Anniversary.

Chiswick.

Children in Wood.

Story without end.

History of Selborne.

The Beast.

Northcote Fables.

Thompson.

Northcote's
Fables.

Lion and
Lioness.

Milton

most of them only so far as needed to give effect after they had been cut, perhaps by his daughter or his sons, whose names appear in the Index. I would mark, as his own, the tail-piece to the Introduction, the *Fox and Bust*, the *Fox and Stork* the *Mischievous Dog*, *Griselda*, the *Wounded Deer*, and *Finis*: these excellently engraved. Admirable work by him will also be found in Harvey's *Milton*, 1843. Still, at best, the manliness of Thompson appears unequally mated with the fair-lady-like elegance of Harvey. Samson betrayed by Dalila were too hard a comparison; and he is not blinded by the Philistine. Yet one's thought turns back to that more characteristic and largest work of our chief engraver, the *Diploma of the Highland Society*.

Walton.

The Trout.

The *Trout*, from Major's magnificent edition of Walton and Cotton's *Angler*, 1822, Thompson's own drawing, is with other fishes there, *Chub*, *Skegger Trout*, *Salmon*, *Tench*, and *Perch*, worthy to be placed with the best of Bewick. In the *Lion and Lioness*, after Harvey, we have the very opposite of Bewick, and yet work to be praised without reserve. Bewick could neither have drawn nor have engraved this. In the Cruikshank, from *Mornings at Bow Street*, a gin-shop at the moment of closing, we see Thompson in simple fac-simile, as master of the mechanical. Of the same kind are six larger cuts for the *History of Napoleon Bonaparte*, 1829.

Mornings at
Bow Street.

History of
Napoleon.

Napoleon leaving the field (at Waterloo) and the *Bridge of Arcola* are brilliantly effective; and a *Charge of Mamelukes* is as sharp as an etching. It must however be noticed that it is only the keeping of a dry hard line (the drawing is Cruikshank's), a line without the variety of expression seen in the Stothard sketches for *Rogers*, or in Thurston's designs for *Tasso*. As already stated,

later editions of *Rogers* have additional cuts by Thompson. Beautifully engraved indeed are these, like that at p. 166, tasteful translations of Stothard, in the lines of Thompson.

A Dinner at Versailles may show his care for effect, clear definition and distinctness in everything, the due keeping of everything in its fit place. Unlike late engravings from photographs his background always keeps at a respectful distance; his crowds are not confused. Here too we see the real advantage of black, so valued by Mr. Hamerton. This cut may well exemplify the completeness of his work: always finished (that is, nothing left to do). That rarest quality of assured honesty is in everything that came from him, whether altogether the doing of his own hand or not: as a consequence his cuts are well printed. It is true he had the best of printers; but no printing could spoil a cut by Thompson. He did a vast amount of engraving for France, from drawings by Grandville and by other French artists.

I may not omit to speak of the much lauded engravings of Mulready's designs in the *Vicar of Wakefield*, 1843, by some thought to be his greatest achievement. Mulready is really weak, and Thompson appears to me as Thompson here solely because he can not but do all things well. Here, as in much of his later work, help may have been made use of. Though there is nothing unworthy of his highest repute, I still miss the old hand-power. Not to speak again of Dalila, shall I call it Heracles with Omphale? The strong one makes excellent play with his distaff, but the peculiar excellence of engraving in wood is not displayed in this easy refinement, in these so effeminately smooth outlines.

A complete catalogue of John Thompson's engravings would fill a volume. I can not here attempt so much as to give a list of the numerous books on which he was engaged.

I have only endeavoured to present fair and sufficient samples of his power and range; and perhaps I can not better conclude my exhibition than by here placing together an 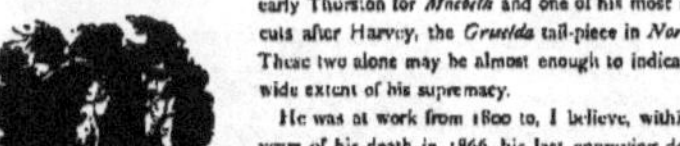 early Thurston for *Macbeth* and one of his most dainty cuts after Harvey, the *Gruelda* tail-piece in *Northcote*. These two alone may be almost enough to indicate the wide extent of his supremacy.

He was at work from 1800 to, I believe, within two years of his death in 1866, his last engraving done in his eightieth year. There are good cuts of his so late as 1857 in Moxon's illustrated *Tennyson*; and excellent exceedingly fine work of yet later date in Longman's *New Testament*, published in 1864, a book including nearly all the engravers of the period, in special rivalry and imitation of copper, therefore hardly to be counted among the master-pieces of wood-engraving.

In 1839 Thompson engraved on gun-metal, in relief, Mulready's design for a *Postage Envelope*. In 1852 he engraved on steel (relief also) the figure of *Britannia* to be seen on the notes of the Bank of England.

A large collection of his own proofs is preserved at South Kensington Museum.

FTER praise of the Greater with what words shall I extol the Less? Some next to the Best have merit, to which I would do justice by pointing out, with needful brevity, the excellence of each. There is good work done even in a time of decadence: for it is a time of decadence rather than aftergrowth of which I have now to give my account. Harvey is our one draftsman; Thompson stands alone. Some traditions of white line remain; but the imitation of copper prevails more and more. Thurston began it; Harvey will help it to its extreme.

WILLIAM HARVEY must yet stand among the *Dii Majores*. I may not underrate him as an engraver, however much I object to his influence as designer upon the engraver's art. Born at Newcastle in 1796, he was apprenticed to Bewick at the usual age; and if Chatto's statement is correct, that "in conjunction with his fellow pupil, W. W. Temple, he engraved most of the cuts in Bewick's *Fables*" of 1818, he had early shown his talent. Even if my surmise be right, attributing the best of the cuts to Nesbit, there would yet be enough left for proof of Harvey's young ability. Nor only of that, for indeed I value the simplicity of these cuts above all his later more ambitious elaboration. The *Fables* and his apprenticeship had completion at about the same time; and Harvey at the end of 1817 went to London and placed himself under the instruction of the painter Haydon. While studying with him he drew on the wood and engraved a copy of Haydon's picture -- the *Assassination of L. C. Dentatus*, publishing the same in 1821: "three years' work," the most daringly ambitious wood-engraving ever done. As an attempt to rival copper it was a mistake and is a failure; nevertheless it is a grand work, splendid in effect and engraved throughout with great richness and surprising mastery of line. Much of white line is seen in it, and yet more of black cross-line, as if the engraver were endeavouring to combine the two. The combination is forced and unhappy. In the flesh especially we see the impossibility of cutting fine and intricate black cross-lines in relief to equal the easily produced incised lines of copper. Flesh and drapery, though dexterously cut, are both spoiled by this imitation. Still the *heads* are good; and the landscape part of the picture is excellent in tone and colour. Nevertheless, in spite of this most important mistake in treatment, it is not merely a daring, but a really magnificent and unequalled work. Only a few impressions of it, I believe, were ever taken, as in consequence of the unfortunate sundering of the joined blocks every proof had to be gone over and touched by Harvey. The sundered and shrunken pieces, now in the Print Room of the British Museum, can not possibly be put together to become whole. The engraving measures nearly fifteen inches in height by a little over eleven in width.

This one engraving, even without the *Fables* of 1818, would entitle Harvey to rank, if not among, yet closely to our Greatest. Of after engraving by his hand I know only a portrait of the printer Johnson, in Johnson's *Typographia, or Printer's Instructor*, 1824; and, of the same date, eight vignette headings and tail-pieces, with twenty-four initials (two of these I give at pp. 159 183), all designed and drawn by himself, in Henderson's *History of Ancient and Modern Wines*. The *Portrait of Johnson* is a marvelous specimen of skilful manipulation, but of the same mistaken character as the *Dentatus*, with a like unfortunate confusion of white and black lines. The *Henderson Cuts* repeat the fault of over-elaborateness. They want the artistic freshness and richness of the better *Fables*, being rather florid than rich, their beauty but meretricious; with a look of incongruity

in the ill-considered combining of the two styles, copper and wood. Clever as a display of manual dexterity (not sufficient amends for the loss of simpler strength), they show, with all their faults, Harvey's great capacity as an engraver, and a grasp of his material

which might have made him (returning from this experimental work to the purer style of Clennell) the greatest of our engravers in wood, not excepting Thompson himself.

The drawings for the *Vines* placed him at once in the vacant seat of Thurston; and from this period he is only known as the able draftsman on wood,—not without faults, an exaggeration learned from Haydon and some mannerism of his own, but his drawing always well-studied and careful, graceful, and pleasant even to the shape of a vignette. His productions were multitudinous: of the most important Northcote's *Fables* (the two series); Knight's *Shakspere*, *Pictorial Bible*, and *Prayer-book*; the *Tower Menagerie*, and *Zoological Gardens* (he was great in animals); Lane's *Arabian Nights* (in that alone six hundred designs); *Paradise Lost*, and the *Pilgrim's Progress*. Like Thurston he had his twenty years of unchallenged supremacy on English ground, some contemporary artists in France his only rivals,—Cruikshank's fac-simile not competing. But he had honour during twice twenty years, until his death in 1866, the same year as that of Thompson.

WILLIAM HUGHES, of whom all I can learn is that he was born at Liverpool, in 1793, learned engraving of Hole, and died in 1825, was an excellent engraver. Some earliest work is in Gregson's *Fragment of Lancashire* and Rutter's *Delineations of Fonthill*. In the Puckle *Club* he has three headings, *Gamester*, *Knave*, and *Projector*, and five not important tail-pieces. In Butler's *Remains* (published in 1827, which throws a doubt on the date of his death) there are also capital cuts by him; and as good, after Cruikshank, in *Mornings at Bow Street*, 1824, and Washington Irving's *Knickerbocker's History of New York*, of about the same date. In Johnson's *Typographia*, 1824, he has several small cuts and one page subject: this last a kind of chapel-interior hung round with banners and shields of the Roxburgh Club,—an engraving which fairly bears a comparison with one of Thompson's best, in the same book. His manner, like that of Hole, shows the Thurston influence, not without occasional employment of the white line. All I find by him is good.

Of HUGH HUGHES (probably no relation to William) I have found no account at all. He is only known to us by the *Beauties of Cambria*, 1823, sixty views in North and South Wales; fifty-eight, as his preface tells us, "taken on the spot expressly for this work by the hand that engraved the whole of the cuts: the remaining two made previously, by Mr. J. Fenton." The preface bears date of June 1, 1823, at Meddiant, Glan Conway. The style of the cuts would indicate a self-taught artist; at the same time they are too

Margin notes:
Harvey.
His drawings.
W. Hughes
Puckle's Club. Gamester.
Butler's Remains.
Mornings at Bow Street.
Knickerbocker's New York.
Typographia.
H. Hughes. Beauties of Cambria.

determined in character and too equal in treatment to be the doing of a beginner. But how or where he learned his art, or if anything beside this book may have been done by him, there is apparently no means of ascertaining. The book, published by subscription at the price of one guinea (two guineas on India paper), was printed by Johnson, once manager of the Lee Priory Press, and the author of *Typographia*. The engraving below of the *Falls of Park Mawr* is a very fair sample of the average excellence of the series.

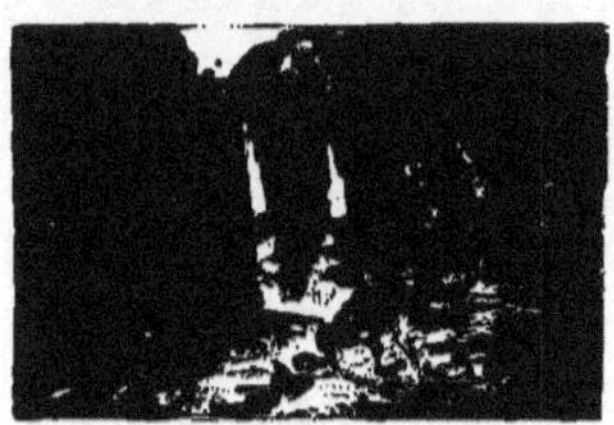

SAMUEL WILLIAMS, born at Colchester in 1788, "of poor but respectable parents," says Redgrave, was apprenticed to a house-painter, and taught himself engraving. He may also have taught himself to paint in oil and miniature, in both of which he showed some talent. He was a designer of much merit, frequently engraving his own drawing, ready with his pencil and clever as an engraver likewise. Chatto, although barely mentioning him, places him next in honour to Nesbit and Thompson. His manner is peculiarly his own, unborrowed, and distinct from all others. In his cuts he prefers a brilliant effect, the sharp accentuation of blacks with fine grey tints to enhance their brightness; but his line is always thin and meagre, without beauty or distinctive character, and he depends for effect too entirely on contrast; this especially in his own drawings. Redgrave says he was "skilled in rural scenery;" but in his engraving of landscape I find only the same sparkling black on grey which is found in his figure subjects. Always crisp and bright, he wants fullness, variety, and drawing; while his trees are little more than masses of monotonous *cribbl'* work, observable even in the *Arch of Titus*, engraved from a drawing by Harvey. Notwithstanding considerable ability, and some originality in both design and engraving, there is little in his work to be recommended as a good example for the engraver. His first work, I think, appears in 1810, a Natural History of no great merit, poorly Bewick-like. Another Natural History (Mrs. Trimmer's) with small clever cuts, drawing and engraving by him, appeared in 1823-4. Numerous spirited and brightly effective cuts, also of his own designing, embellished the numbers of the *Olio*, a weekly magazine, in the years 1828 to 1833. Very much of his doing will be found in Hone's *Year Book* and *Every-Day Book*, and in the *London Stage*. In the cuts to Lady Charlotte Guest's *Mabinogion*, 1838, and to Thomson's *Seasons and Castle of Indolence* (forty-eight of his own drawing), 1841, the engraver's manner is most conspicuous, and unpleasant, though the cuts are effective and delicately finished. *British Forest Trees*, 1842, fail for want of distinctive character, owing to this same prevalent manner. Less peculiar, and of his best, very excellent indeed, are his engravings after Corbould (Thompson's *Fight with the Soldan* in the same book) for Wiffen's translation of *Jerusalem Delivered*, 1823. Other admirable cuts, George Cruikshank's drawing, are the *Flight from Moscow*, in the *History of Napoleon Bonaparte*, 1829 (as good as Thompson's *Charge of Mamelukes*), and

S. Williams.

The Olio.

Thomson's Seasons.

Jerusalem Delivered

History of Napoleon.

Fogarty's State Cabin, in that budget of good stories and good designs, a few years later,

Three Courses and a Dessert. Of other cuts with S. Williams undersigned I may prefer those in Scott's *Bible*, 1833-4, (used again in Latrobe's *Scripture Illustrations*); in the *Solace of Song*, a most rare book, of which I can not find a copy in the British Museum, published by Seeley in 1836; and in Lane's *Arabian Nights.* In these works, however, (perhaps in others) he was largely assisted by a son, Joseph L. Williams, who has long since abandoned the art. *A High Priest on the Day of Atonement*, a large and excellent cut in *Scripture Illustrations*, I believe to be of the son's engraving, though it is very like the father's. The *Arch of Titus*, from the *Solace of Song*, with something still of the old manner, shown us (unless the son may be entitled to the credit here also) the best

of Samuel Williams. A large collection of work "by him," his own not distinguishable, is in the Print Room of the British Museum.

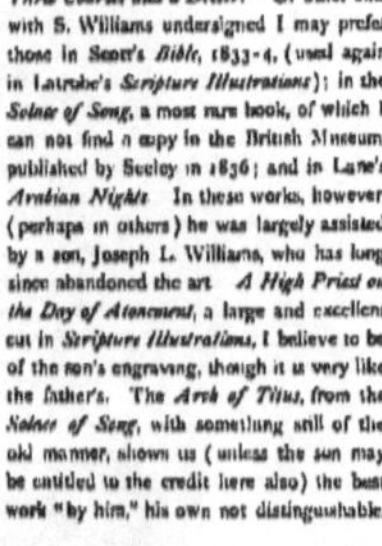

THOMAS WILLIAMS—a younger brother of Samuel—learned engraving from him. He had not his brother's faculty of design; but as an engraver he was nearly if not quite as good, with less of singularity, although his work betrays some effect of probable early training. I think the best of his scattered doings may be fairly represented by the two cuts herewith: *Habakkuk Bullswrinkle*, from *Three Courses and a Dessert*; and *Prudence and her Advisers*, from the 1833 Northcote, in which he has eight Fables and five small tail-pieces. The best of the Fables are the *Poet and Cobwebs*, the *Rat with a bell*, and the *Prudence*—which last might pass for work of either brother, for treatment of figures,

and for the fineness of tints and clearness therewithal cared for by both. A tail piece of

Puck, in Fable 22, is worthy of place beside our two vignettes (pp. 171 184) by Nesbit and Thompson from the same book. Of his other work I would notice good engraving in Martin and Westall's *Pictorial Illustrations to the Bible*, 1833; two capital Cruikshanks in *Sunday in London*, also 1833; and a number of cuts, the drawings by Johannot, Français, Huet, and Meissonier, in that most perfectly complete of illustrated books, Curmer's *Paul et Virginie*, Paris, 1838. Work by Samuel, and by a sister, Mary Ann, will also be seen in that, not in the usual Williams manner, but following the lead of the French artists. Except of his works I have no dates as to Thomas Williams, not even of birth or death.

GEORGE WILMOT BONNER, although a pupil of Branston, of whom he was a nephew, worked in white line; perhaps because, as a fair draftsman on wood and in water-colour, his artistic faculty abled him to use a graver in a more masterly fashion. For this alone he stands nearly with the Masters: his work being always intelligently graver-drawn, cut at once, as by the Newcastle men, with little attention given to, or wanted for, any after refinement. For which reason he appears to disadvantage in drawings by Harvey, where tone and delicacy were essentials. The general character of his work is seen in the best of fourteen cuts by him in the first series of Northcote's *Fables*: the *Oak and River*, the *Nursery-Man and the Plantation*, the *Wild and Tame Geese*, the *Goat and Fox*, and the *Trout and Fly*, all free graver line. The *Parrot*, here printed, compared with cuts of the second series on other pages, by Nesbit, Williams, Jackson, and Powis, may suffice to show the status of Bonner as an engraver. More careful, not better cuts, in the second series, are his *Young Fowler and Cupid*, the *Lion, Ape, and Dog*, and the *Pampered Owlet*. He has a notably excellent *Title-page* in Richard Thomson's *Chronicles of London Bridge*, 1827; another in the second volume of Johnson's *Typographia*; some bold well-engraved animals, such as the *Jaguar* (on our p. 191), in the *Tower Menagerie*, 1829, and the *Zoological Gardens*, 1835,—which two works passed under the names of (F.) Branston and Wright, though they employed the hands of nearly every capable engraver of the day. But the mass of his work, from poorer drawings, was of inferior quality, and much below his best power. He was born at Devizes, in 1796, and died, after a very brief sickness, in 1836.

JOHN JACKSON, born at Ovingham, in 1801, (dying in 1848), was at first the pupil of Armstrong, then for a year with Bewick, and afterwards under Harvey in London. He was largely employed on the *Penny Magazine*, the *Farmer's Series* and other publications of the "Society for the Diffusion of Useful Knowledge;" also for Knight, on *Shakspere*,

Pictorial Bible, and *Prayer-Book*, and Lane's *Arabian Nights*. Indeed, so vast an amount of work was under his direction that it is not easy to identify his own actual performance. That, perhaps, is better seen in Northcote's *Fables*, in both series of which his name very frequently appears. In that of 1828, beside good tail pieces, I note especially the *Village Quack*, *Æsop and the Poultry*, and the *Lobsters*, richer than his later time. The cuts of 1833 are harder, sharp and bright, and finished, but I find little of the artist, little of drawing or graver-mastery. The *Boastful Ass* and the *Beacon and Chandelier* are of his very best. The *Horse and Groom*, the *Sage and Linnet*, and the *Man, his Monkey, and Apollo*, also in

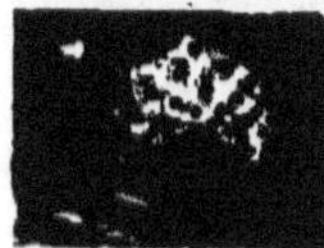

1833, are, I think, fair examples of him. In his work, so far as I know it to be his, what I have to commend is its excellent cleanness.

WILLIAM HENRY POWIS, a Londoner, though "one of the best wood-engravers of his time," is hardly known even to his fellow engravers. Redgrave says little save that he was "much esteemed in his art, making good progress," when he "ruined his health by his close and continuous labour," and died in 1836, aged 28. Date and age are in Chatto. The rest is not quite correct. Want of health had early unfitted him for any active occupation. He died, I believe, of consumption, not caused by overwork. He was a pupil of Bonner;

and after leaving Bonner did much work for Jackson, whose name consequently appears
to most of Powis' engraving. While with Bonner he engraved some of the copies from
Holbein's *Dance of Death*, for Pickering's edition. The *Old Man* and *Death's Armorial*

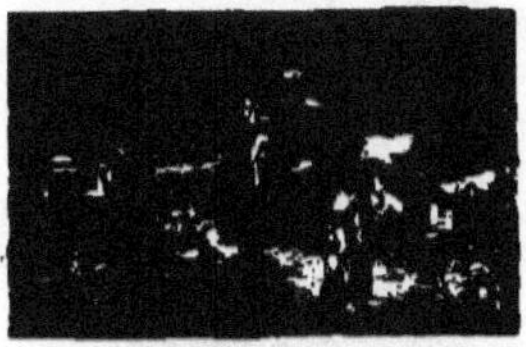

Bearings (added to the later edition of Chatto) I remember as his doing, I, his younger
fellow-pupil, sitting beside him at the time. They are of remarkable excellence, closest
of any copies I know. Four headings in the Northcote *Fables*, 1833,—the *Bee and Ant*,
the *Peacock and Owl* (p. 192), the *Delicate Heron*, and the *Elephant and Wolf*,—although
Jackson's name is to them as they were done for him, were engraved by Powis. With a
different capacity, they challenge
comparison with any of Jackson's
own or, excepting Nesbit's, with
any in the book. Some lameness
of line there is, from over-care or
mistrust of himself. His too are
the *House in Ocunlaska* and the
Rhinoceros; and a cut of *Harvest
Mice* in the *History of Selborne*, for
all the *Jackson sc.* engraved on it.
His likewise are a *Hawk Owl*, the
Palm Squirrel, and others, in the
Zoological Gardens; some best of

the *Cattle* in the *Farmers' Series* of the Useful Knowledge Society; and many other cuts
done for Jackson for the *Penny Magazine*. Of so much I speak positively, Powis' proofs
before me, having kept acquaintance with him during my apprenticeship, and working

with him for a year afterward. No unfairness, however, can be charged to Jackson for the non-appearance of Powis' name, custom warranting an employer in taking the credit (or discredit) of work done for him.

Powis' name will be found in the *Scripture Illustrations* of 1833-4; in the *Illustrations to the Bible* by Martin and Westall, of the same date; in the *Solace of Song*, and in an edition of Gray's *Elegy*, both of 1836. Some of my own work appears as his in *Scripture Illustrations*; but the *Tyre*, *Nineveh*, and a yet more excellent cut, the *Coast of the Red Sea*,

are entirely his, and perhaps the best landscapes for their size up to that time engraved in wood. I think he is unsuccessful in the Westall figure subjects. His figures are not equal to his landscapes: and these were weakly drawn. Martin's *Deluge*, steel-like, clear and pure in tint, is an admirable work. A fair impression of this will be found at p. 516 of the later edition of Chatto. Two small landscapes in Gray's *Elegy* are very charming renderings of Constable. Most noticeable in Powis' work is it that everything has been cut at once. In this he differed notably from Smith, who depended on after-toning.

JOHN ORRIN SMITH was born at Colchester in 1799; and had his first lessons in wood engraving from Samuel Williams. He was afterward for some time with an architect; but resumed engraving under Harvey, and with Jackson. He excelled in animals as is seen in the *Thibet Dog*, and in the *American Bison*, the *Four-horned Sheep*, and other cuts in the *Zoological Gardens*, admirably expressive of character and texture. In landscape he surpassed every one for tone and refinement: his best instances in the *Solace of Song*, for which he did seven of the eleven cuts (one below, the *Bay of Pozzuoli*). They mark the extreme of the imitation of copper, or steel, to which wood-engraving had long been tending. Allowing tone to be more important than expressiveness of line or the distinct assertion of form, these cuts may be considered perfect. I look on them as the best of

an essentially false style. Smith's excellence as well as his failure is here very apparent. His name will be frequently seen in Lane's *Arabian Nights*, in *Scripture Illustrations*, in Hall's *British Ballads*, and to drawings of Huet, Meissonier, and others in Wordsworth's *Greece*. He engraved very much from French drawings, and also for French publishers (little good work at that time done in France), notably for the superb *Paul et Virginie*, completed in 1838, his engraving for which was so much esteemed that his portrait was given in the book. In conjunction with his friend Kenny Meadows he brought out an edition of *Shakspere*, profusely illustrated with designs by Meadows. A series of clever *Heads of the People* by Meadows was also engraved under his supervision; and all of the drawings by Gilbert (of his earliest and best) to *Cowper*, 1841, with a large proportion of a *Milton* by Harvey, 1843. But except some animals, and cuts of the *Solace of Song*, it is difficult to say what is his own. In the Meadows and Gilbert cuts very much was done by the best of his pupils, Alfred Harral. My own work for him and in partnership with him dates from 1836 to the time of his death, in 1843.

Two American wood-engravers, Anderson and Adams, claim place beside the Masters of our art, and may not have their claims gainsaid.

ALEXANDER ANDERSON, born in 1775, probably in New York, was in his way a man as noteworthy as Bewick. When only a boy at school he got a silversmith to roll out some copper coin, made for himself a graver of the back-spring of a pocket-knife, ground to a point; and started as an amateur engraver in copper. Afterwards obtaining fitter tools, the lad did little cuts in relief for newspaper advertisements, ships, houses, horses, etc., not without pay, only one other person in New York being so engaged.

His father, a Scotch printer, holding no belief in engraving as a life-business, placed him with a physician to study medicine. During his five years' tutelage he continued in leisure hours his practice of engraving; and before the age of eighteen had employment by printers and publishers, not only in New York, but for Philadelphia, and Charleston. His cuts were of copper or type-metal, probably in both intaglio and relief. Some mere diagrams, geometric outlines, were his first work with wood; and in 1794, copying John Bewick's *Looking Glass for the Mind*, he abandoned type-metal, which had served him in the first part of the book, and engraved the remainder on the new material.

In 1795 he was licenced to practise medicine, in which he had already so good repute that he was in the same year appointed resident physician to the Bellevue Hospital, of New York. For three years he was at once physician, designer, and engraver in wood and copper. In 1798 the yellow fever, within the space of three months, carried off his wife and child, his father, mother, brother, and other relations. He gave up the active life of a physician, and sought for solace in the quiet pursuit of art.

Numerous cuts for New York publishers, generally reproductions of those in English books, occupied the time until 1802, when he undertook to copy Bewick's *Quadrupeds*: an undertaking very successfully accomplished. Anderson's engravings, not reversed on the block, are therefore as printed the reverse of Bewick; else they are close fac-simile, showing fine perception of Bewick's manner, to which Anderson ever remained faithful. Whether from absence of ambition or want of artist faculty, he never went beyond these copies. The mass of his work else is not very notable. The only exceptions I find are

a large cut, three feet in height, of the human *Skeleton*, drawn and engraved by him in 1796, a remarkable work for that time; and two engravings done in 1818,—*Water-Fowl* after Teniers and *Returning from a Boar-Hunt* by Ridinger, both in vigorous white line. These two cuts are of themselves enough to entitle him to a place, however humble, by

the side of those who cared to draw with the graver. Some honour also may be due to him as the first wood-engraver in America. He was at work, if only for his amusement, to within a few days of his death in 1870, in the ninety-fifth year of his age.

JOSEPH ALEXANDER ADAMS, an engraver more after the Branston pattern, takes place among the Masters for the quality of his work. He was born in 1803 at New German-town, New Jersey. Self-taught like Anderson, his first attempt at engraving was while he was apprentice to a printer. After some months' work, engraving on the blackened block without drawing, he was first shown by Dr. Anderson a drawing on the wood. In 1831 he spent some time in England, making acquaintance with English engravers and studying their works, soon to be fairly equalled by his own. A *Frontispiece* in 1834 for the *Treasury of Knowledge*, New York, for minuteness and delicacy may dare comparison with anything. On a small duodecimo page is a full-length portrait of Washington, in a square of two and a half by two inches, surrounded by small circles (about the size of a six-pence), with the arms of the thirteen States of the Union. A figure of Liberty is at the top. Two less minute, but as well finished engravings are *Jacob's Dream*, from Washington Allston's picture, and a *Massacre of the Innocents*, after Coignet. I know of nothing of their kind superior to these. The figures in the *Dream* are well drawn; the distant angels rendered more aerial by the scarcely perceptible white line lightening the first cutting; the clouds are pure in line and fine in tone; and the foreground is rich,—it might have been cut by Thompson. The *Massacre* is as good. A soldier coming down the steps is cross-lined so lightly that at first we do not see the lines. The intention is simply to reduce colour, to give air and distance; but with a true artist feeling, though the lines are not wanted to be apparent, he has been as careful with them as with those first cut, and they are as well disposed and in harmony with them. These two cuts were drawn on the wood by Adams himself.

Eight of the English *Scripture Illustrations* were reëngraved by Adams from transfers. His copy of Powis' *Coast of the Red Sea* is so close to the original, in both character and values, that it might easily be mistaken for it. I would also notice a *Landscape*, his own drawing, from a picture by Morse, first President of the National Academy of America, which in its clearness and purity of line reminds me again of Powis.

Another of his best cuts, drawn by Chapman, is *The Last Arrow*, engraved in 1837 for the *New York Mirror*. The subject is an Indian pursued by soldiers: he is standing on a rock in the foreground, aiming his last arrow at the nearest of his enemies; a woman with a child in her arms is at his feet. Larger than the *Dream* or the *Massacre*, it is so much bolder, but is equally good. As excellent also are many small cuts, some printed on a delicate grey ground, with high lights in white. I know all these cuts from proofs, proofs he gave me, now in the Boston Art Museum. The work by which he is generally known, his *Bible* (Harper, New York), does not fairly show him. Its sixteen hundred cuts, most of them very small, are nearly all by his pupils. The frontispieces and titles to the Old and New Testaments, the headings (with initial letters) to the first chapters of Genesis and Matthew, and some ornamental borders, are all that can be looked on as really his. And these, drawn by Chapman in a hard, dry, precise style, like most formal copper-plate, every line to be strictly followed, give nothing of the richness of Adams. They are firm, clear, honestly exact, but have more likeness to the work of Jackson than to the best of Adams himself. It is by this book that Adams is generally known, since the book was commercially a success; and gave him means for travel and a competence for life. He spent eight years in Europe, and after his return home devoted himself to scientific inventions (he had previously invented the Printing Press still known by his name), and a most capable man was lost to Art. He died in 1880.

CHAPTER VI

IN THE WINTER

("The winter of our discontent.")

N the very beginning of graver-work in wood were the premonitions of decadence and decay. A formal art, it had to be dogmatic and so in due time to become conventional and unmeaning.

The whole art of engraving consists in the expression, by black or white lines, of form, texture, and colour. For the line which is to represent *form* we perceive an absolute law, a law proclaimed in the flowing line of cloud or wave, convex or concave: its highest potentiality of beauty exemplified in the mountain curve, that continual departure from the finite circle (as told us by Ruskin),—the jagged precipices exposing the opposite extreme of angularity and roughness. I imagine that the law of line for an engraver, consciously or unconsciously, is based on this. Then there is the rendering of *texture*, showing the kind of substance, without apparent law, varying as different substances (metal or feathers, hair or flesh, stone or wood or paint, etc.) may dictate, seeming to depend entirely on observation of each individual object. In the rendering of texture as well as of form, however, certain characteristic lines seem to be absolute. For expression of *colour*, whether by contrast or tone, any lines whatever (so far as only *direction* of line is concerned—the *quality* of a line being a separate thing) may be of equal power. Setting aside the canon that in a work of beauty every constituent part must also be beautiful,—we may say that for the expression of colour (intending only the differences of degree between light and dark), no matter how heterogeneous, how discordant, how unsightly the lines, they can express that light or dark just as effectively as the most harmoniously pleasant. If my readers will bear in mind these distinctions, my judgments of different engravers and whatever arguments I may hold upon engraving will, I think, be more readily understood.

The first use of the graver for pictorial relief-work was in imitation of work incised. I refer to such engravings as those in the French books of *Hours*, which I suppose were done on metal because of the impossibility of preventing the warping of planks of wood (so rendered unfit for good printing) or because to men accustomed to goldsmiths' work, or the like, in metal, it was easier to use a graver than a knife. The best relief-work, so done and of that character, on wood or on metal, from that day to this, is generally but an inferior copy of incised work, some delicacy lost in printing from surface-lines, some freedom missed in the use of the graver, cutting up to lines to be left standing, instead of cutting the lines themselves. But so soon as the poorest ornament,—the first white scroll as background to an initial letter (such as the N at p. 73) was done, the worth of an incised line instead of a line left standing would be apparent. Strange that for two centuries engravers either did not appreciate the advantage of this incised white line or did not see the means of cutting it in wood. Our earliest examples beyond ornamental work are, as we have seen, the solitary *Kirkall Ticket* in 1707 and the Croxall *Fables* of 1722, metal work of Kirkall, Jackson, or another.

The white line of the wood-engraver (white instead of black in the print), reversing usual effect of incised metal-work, is still the line of the ordinary engraver in copper. In all his figure-work, and in mere tints, Bewick never departs from this. So far we find that the line used by him in wood is precisely that used by him in copper: conventional in both, poor, without a touch of originality. Only in foliage and grasses, and textures as of hair or feathers, he invented lines, drawing with his graver, unable else to produce an effect corresponding with or equivalent to the black line of copper. He found, as we can well see, that his white line was not only equivalent but even more effective. Nesbit and Clennell (and Harvey if he engraved those *Fables* of 1818), educated in this white line manner, carried it to perfection: Nesbit rich in all of tree-work; Clennell with free artist hand drawing everything, not as one untaught who had never seen a copper-plate, but with too much originality to merely copy a conventional manner,—his line not less free when under the influence of Thurston, who, however formal in his arrangement of line, was a master in his method, always true to the law of beauty and fitness underlying an engraver's treatment of form. Nesbit and Clennell (leaving Bewick in his high place of artist-naturalist) have done the best of all work done in wood: Nesbit with the aid of Thurston and Harvey, Clennell with or without aid. I know not what artistic capacity may have been in Nesbit behind his manifest talent as an engraver; but Clennell stands proved, accomplished artist. What might not he have done had he kept to engraving! I imagine a larger sea-piece like his *Pilot Boat*, of his own drawing; or a landscape after Turner or Constable, of whatever size, fairly competing with, and in atmospheric effect and in painter-like touch and feeling excelling, the best engravings of Milton or of Pye. I imagine a figure-subject such as Harvey's *Dentatus*, but of greater excellence, treated with more simplicity, with all the largeness proper to a noble theme. Of all our other wood-engravers I think I gauge the power, but of Clennell's I do not perceive the limit.

Our best, and yet promise-full, it is to him that I would direct the student ambitiously wishful to learn of the yet unreached possibilities of engraving in wood; unreached, for the Spring-time of our Art was very brief. One rich crop, some aftermath; since then the Winter. Will there be another Spring?

Even with Thurston and most accomplished Thompson I think the decadence began. Bewick and Clennell and Harvey drew for their own engraving. With the separation of draftsman and engraver began the decline of engraving as an art. I do not mean that an engraver should engrave only his own drawings. Excellent is the farther education of variety. Clennell learned from Thurston, and would have learned from Leitch and Duncan and others of our painters in water-colour, our later draftsmen on wood. I do not imply that Branston and Thompson could not draw. But with Thurston began the system of special employment; and having to depend on draftsmen, engravers ceased to draw, ceased to rely upon themselves. Wanting the wider power, the inevitable course was only in following years through mediocrity to mechanism. Let me mark that which has taken place, without as yet adverting to what is the condition now.

Thurston was a copper-engraver. His drawings were of that character: a black line the pervading intention. Branston, at first a copper-engraver, had his style fixed in like manner. Thompson traveled on the same track. Clennell and Nesbit could not but be somewhat influenced. Bonner, and Mosses (who did some good work), and Sears, had enough of graver-power to use white line,—Sears vigorously but, little of an artist, with no taste. There the pure white line had its end. Thompson, strong as he was, looked to attaining the effect of copper. Samuel Williams cared chiefly for colour, disregarding variety of line. And Harvey, after his *Dentatus*, that unsuccessful attempt to imitate the intricate elaborations of copper, never troubled himself about line at all. Fineness, tone and delicacy, fulfilled the purpose of his drawings; the refinement of copper sought for, without the beauty of the copper line in which Thurston was preëminent. One taught us to value a pretentious likeness to copper more than the proper appearance of wood; the other led to neglect of a most important constituent of line engraving. So nothing was left except colour, the fine gradation of meaningless lines: only colour for expression of form, material, or distance. Wonderfully fine tints and clean firm lines of surprising thinness Samuel Williams and Jackson give us, Jackson's most sharp and delicate; but I find little expression in the courses of their lines, no art in the arrangement. Williams, cutting from his own drawing, is answerable for his own work; Jackson's monotony was the dictation of Harvey. Smith surpasses all men in refinement of tone; but his line is weak. The very painful touching and retouching, the entering and reëntering of lines to graduate and refine them, and produce the required softness of imperceptible change, necessarily takes away, with strength, whatever of beauty may be in the original cutting. The highest beauty has also strength: as the manly form (apart from any feeling of sex) is even more beautiful than the womanly. Powis alone of these imitators of copper had the virtue of engraving finely gradated colour without depending upon after-refinement. While Smith's *Pozzuoli* was laboriously toned after the first cutting, Powis' *Nineveh* (to use the technical term for sweetening or correcting) was scarcely *touched* at all. Powis was not in any degree an artist as our master Bonner was; I doubt he could have drawn even copies of Hughes' Cambrian views; his engraving showed nothing of the painter's faculty: but as only engraving it was well considered,—his lines were cut with intention and certainty of result.

Here I may own to being conscious that I am open to the charge of neglecting to give due presentment or even a passing notice of many estimable engravers whose names and works are commemorated by Bohn in his additional chapter, of *Artists and Engravers on wood of the present day*, in the 1861 edition of Chatto's *Treatise*. But I am bound by the purpose of my book: the recognition of only the Best. Though I could point out good cuts, better in many instances than those chosen by Bohn [scarcely chosen, so many from his own publications], I find few above the unartistic monotony of book-illustration after the first edition of the *Treatise* in 1839, nothing entitling the doers to rank as Masters, Teachers of our Art.

I speak of English work. Hereto, concerning graver-work, I have treated, with but two American exceptions, only of English engravers: because indeed, as the birth-place of knife-work is Germany, so the birth-place of graver-work in wood is England. And Anderson and Adams were English in their work. As before said, the graver was not used in France until Charles Thompson went to Paris in 1816. Thereafter, albeit for a quarter of a century later a large amount of French drawing was engraved in England, chiefly by John Thompson and Orrin Smith, there arose a host of French engravers, of considerable talent; but with no novelty of style or manner to call for special criticism. Work by Breviere, Bertrand, Rouget, Huyot, and others, may be classed, like the mass of contemporary English production, as fac-simile or from washed drawing (sometimes of course a mixture), but in either class had no remarkable difference except what was absolutely due to the subject or the draftsman. I find nothing of which I can say—This as engraving tells me something which I had not learned from English teaching. I am not depreciating the work in saying this.

The drawings of Grandville, Jacque, Meissonier, Johannot, Huet, and others, gave ample occasion for excellence, and French publications, notably *La Magasin Pittoresque*, abundantly display the advance of French engraving; but so wide a field requires quite separate consideration to do anything like justice to individual desert. All that I must care for here, all indeed that I can do, is to recognise the fact of French accomplishment, that I may not be accused of careless neglect. In France during what I have called our Winter engraving was much better than in England: again remarking that there is not

anything new or beyond the doing of our own Masters. In the best cuts I find little of drawing with the graver, the white line; only fair tints, not difficult, and commendable fidelity to lines drawn. Lavaignac's delicate rendering of Meissonier's minute drawings for Chevigné's *Contes Rémois*, 1861, might pass for etching.

German fac-simile is most admirable: good, whether we look to bold cuts by Gaber, Obermann, Steinbrecher, Zscheckel, and others of equal merit (I can not give all their names), in Schnorr's Bible Pictures (*Bibel in Bildern*), Leipsic, 1854; to Kretzschmar's exactest following of Menzel's *Heroes of War and Peace* ("In King Frederic's Time"), Berlin, 1855; or the minutely beautiful work of Reusche in Choulant's Bibliography of Anatomical Teaching (*Geschichte und Bibliographie der Anatomischen Abbildung*), Leipsic, 1852. Later work of similar character, by Allgaier and Siegle from Knullach's designs for *Reynard the Fox*, 1863,—in the *Imitation of Christ*, 1873, by Oertel,—and very much in the *German Illustrated News,*—is of the same degree of excellence. But German tint work is harsh; and again, of white line I have found little calling for any special remark. There is no lack of cleverness, nor of daring: but neither is equivalent to mastership.

If now I dare to write of my own work, it is not gracelessly to thrust myself among the Masters, but because new opportunities, not offered to them, that came especially in my way need to be recorded, and what I have done, if only in part successful, may also help to explain the views I have been endeavouring to set forth.

Apprenticed to Bonner from 1828 to 1834, I afterward worked for a year with Powis, and then during a year or more for Thompson. After that I had much employment for Smith, on the *Heads of the People, Shakspere,* and *Cowper,* and on landscape foregrounds, until our partnership in 1842; soon after which we began work for the *Illustrated London News.* The size and number of the cuts for that called for new talent in drawing, giving occasion for new endeavours in engraving. Harvey hitherto had stood alone. Now we obtained drawings from some of our best painters-in-water-colour, W. Leighton Leitch, Duncan, Dodgson, and others, whose work upon wood marks an era in wood-engraving. Most of these drawings were done for and passed through the work-rooms of Smith and Linton. Not all the credit ours: we had able assistants,—the brothers Harral (Alfred and Horace), Henry Linton, C. Mins, Cheltnam, E. K. Johnson, G. Pearson, and more. What we did can be seen in the *History and Art of Wood-Engraving,* Chatto's writing for the *Illustrated London News* in 1844, and also published separately in 1848. *Choosing the Wedding-Gown,* after Mulready, drawn on the wood by Archer, is the only cut entirely by my own hand; all the rest are composite, with more or less of my engraving in each. *
However unsuccessful, I yet may claim the distinction of ordering the whole toward the revival of white line, the intelligent graver-work of the Bewick school. These various engravings by many draftsmen, copies sometimes of prints, sometimes of pictures put on the wood by the painters themselves, afforded an excellent field of practice, such as had not previously been available. Boldly treated, as was necessary for the rapid production of a newspaper, they were a healthy change from the then prevailing tameness.

Smith's death left too heavy a burden on me. The newspaper-proprietors undertook their own engraving. Manufacture was everywhere displacing Art. I had simply made a protest against the barrenness of the time. Barren indeed, for outside of my attempt, with the exception of Thompson's always masterly engraving, there was in England only combed smoothness of tints, formless and void of expression, or an imbecile niggling at fac-simile, mere rat-like gnawing between the lines of Leech and Gilbert: as Thompson himself said to me, "not engraving at all."

John Leech's style was motived by his incapacity for determinate drawing. What an Academician would call drawing he had not. I admire his facility in catching character and see improvement from long practice; but he was not an artist. With easy-scribbled

---

* Later works, also for the *News,* entirely my own, are the *Portrait at Home* and *Dead Birds,* drawn by Archer after a picture by Lance, and the *Old Mill* and *Landscape* on the wood by Duncan and Dodgson.

lines instead of drawing he covered the less important parts of his subject; and, as they had not the firm intention of the manipulation of Durer or Thurston, there was no real need for exact adherence to them. It was work for boys, profitable to the manufacturer. Gilbert was a trained artist, an able draftsman; and his early work, such as the *Cooper*, was careful and finished. Marvelously rapid in execution, with much feeling for beauty of line, his drawing became more and more linear and like to etching. It was not a fault in the draftsman; but it did not help to advance the art of engraving. Drawings such as those of Gilbert and Leech and Cruikshank, and Seymour of earlier time, misled the engraver back to mechanism. That such drawing well suited the hasty sketches needed in Hone's *Political Tracts* and *Punch*, that as sketches they satisfied the special occasion, that there is a charm in this loose free handling, that they were quickly drawn and easily —only too easily engraved, that they were satisfactorily cheap to publishers,—is true; yet no less were they detrimental to the *art* of engraving. In the factories of Swain and Dalziel [I speak not unkindlily nor disrespectfully of men who as men of business—the brothers Dalziel were clever as artists too—looked to profit of their work] the engraver was degraded, retrograded to the old *Helgen* time, and became again a mere mechanic. Capital mechanism was after long practice obtained in the factories. Quite satisfactory after a time was the cutting of Tenniel's clear Durer-like penciling by Swain's assistants; excellent is the fac-simile in some later Dalziel work, though to me it seems an unhappy waste of pains to treat a sky in dry cross-line, with never the grace or the freedom of an etching; very perfect, as imitation-etchings, are Kretzschmar's twelve magnificent cuts after Menzel (already mentioned), most ambitious and laborious of fac-similes in wood. This last work indeed recalls the Maximilian days of Master Jerome of Nurnberg much praised for fac-simile knife-work. Ay! but how much because it was knife-work? The graver is misused when it does no more. The best of this fac-simile, by knife or graver, is mechanical: only escaping that reproach in the engraving of Jerome or Lutzelburger after Beham or Holbein; or when, three centuries later, the graver of Clennell repeats that exceptional artistry. Even Bertrand's delicate tracery in our cut of *La Vie Humaine* (*Magasin Pittoresque*, 1851), which for its sweetness and purity might be metal, like the old *Hours*, beautiful as it is, is but the perfection of mechanism. Fac-simile in wood has indeed its right of place for certain needs, and sometimes, as in the examples of Holbein and Stothard, and Cruikshank and others also, and in the French and modern German work already noted, is valuable of itself; but only the engraving of a pictorially finished drawing will entitle the engraver in wood to his full rank as Artist. Wood-engraving, with the graver, is a distinctive art, needs not and ought not to be confined to imitating what it can but seldom equal. The graver has a power and a faculty beyond the knife. With a plough moved by the artist's hand, shall not the furrow be as his hand is moved by a directing thought? Why should a ploughed line intended to be white in the print have less of meaning than a ploughed line which is to be printed black? This leads me to the consideration of two very different kinds of work: the French work of the *atelier* of Pannemaker and the latest "development" of wood-engraving in America.

I speak of the *atelier* of Pannemaker (a Belgian, I believe), taking him as exponent of a large class of French work: but the name of the engraver of the crude extravagances of Doré (the works I would especially notice) is Legion. And I choose Doré's works' because in them, from variety of subjects, and from their size and treatment (generally washed drawings), there was room and an excellent opportunity for showing what could be done by wood-engraving. As in all French art, there is no lack of daring, or power; but seldom in the lines used is there any display of taste or sense of beauty or of fitness. The bolder work is harsh, and coarse (which the boldest work need not be), lines often grinning and offensive, and very metallic. Black line or white, the motive is imitation of copper, though certainly with sufficient recognition of the value of solid black for glaring contrast. Doré's theatrical effects are well maintained; colour is kept; tints are firmly engraved; there is delicacy in some of the work of Ligny and Trichon, and in a few cuts signed Pannemaker-Doms. But with the vast mass of the Doré illustrations (his *Bible* alone has two hundred and thirty-two page-subjects) I can only express dissatisfaction. I find little which I would care to look at twice. From his *Paradise Lost* (cuts like those of the *Bible*) I select one better cut by Ligny, *Satan resting*, worthy of particular notice. Here the sky is admirable, full of form and gradation, the clouds well rounded. Colour and tone are excellent; and the line has meaning, is simple, bold and sweet, cut at once without need of after-toning. It is like the work of a more able Powis. But the figure of Satan has only colour; the lines are ugly in their opposition to each other, and there is nothing drawn. The figure mars what were else a masterly work.

French engraving has always the merit of artistic dash, and generally of an intelligent though it may sometimes be an unpleasant use of the graver. Jonnard's work here is of the best. I must speak with less of qualifying reserve of "the new American School," so plainly speaking because most unfortunately extolled by Mr. Hamerton, whose opinions assume too much authority to be disregarded.

"There can be no question," he says, "that the Americans have far surpassed all other nations in delicacy of execution. The manual skill they display in their wood-cuts is a continual marvel, and it is accompanied by so much intelligence—I mean by so much critical understanding of different graphic arts—that a portfolio of their best wood-cuts is most interesting. . They understand engraving thoroughly. . The two superiorities in American wood-engraving are in tone and texture." (*The Graphic Arts*, 1882.)

I join issue with Mr. Hamerton, as to his correctness, on all these points: delicacy of execution, tone, texture, and intelligence. On what comparisons is his judgment based? Does American work surpass in delicacy work of which I have here given examples,—

Nesbit's *Redbreast and Sparrow*, Thompson's *Boudoir* or *Youth*, or Jackson's *Bacon and Chandelier?* In manual skill I think the work of France or Germany not yet surpassed by American, even accompanied by so much intelligence: of which intelligence there is yet something to be said. In tone are late American cuts superior to Powis' *Nineveh* or Smith's *Possnett?* In texture do they approach that of Bewick? But Mr. Hamerton may explain himself (*The Graphic Arts*), as here follows.

The two superiorities of American wood-engraving, he says, are in tone and texture. "Tone in wood-cutting depends entirely on the management of greys. In etching there are half a dozen different qualities of black,—all black, but yet producing quite different effects upon the eye; in wood-cut there is only one black. In painting there are many different whites, all of them equally called white, yet bearing little relation to each other; in wood-cut is only a single white, and it is always got in the same way by excavating the wood. This being so, white and black are settled for the wood-engraver, and he has not to think about them; but it is not so with intermediate shades; and I can not but heartily admire the almost unlimited ingenuity with which the Americans vary not only the tone but the very quality of these intermediates, getting not one gamut only, but several, with the faculty of going from one to another on occasion, as if changing the stops of an organ. Some of their greys are pure and clear, others cloudy; others 'like veils of thinnest lawn;' others again are semi-transparent, like a very light wash of body colour; and, whatever their quality, it is always surprising how steadily a delicate tone is maintained in them. As for texture, these engravers seem able to imitate anything that is set before them. It would be an exaggeration to say that they get the exact textures of an oil-painting, but they come near enough to recall them vividly to our minds."

It may seem perhaps only a change of phrase, but it is more exact, instead of talking of "different qualities of black in etching," to say that there is no absolute black, and for "many different whites in painting" to say that there is only one pure white; also that in wood-engraving there is the solid black of uncut surface-wood, and pure white (if the print be on white paper) at every excavation. So we come at the wood-engraver having to think only of intermediate shades. I allow in this matter of *tone* that some additions to the number of shades may be obtained from the one remarkable American ingenuity (novel only in its excessive employment) of this "cutting up the lines to nothing," as we irreverently called it in my 'prentice days, when we had occasion to get rid of awkwardly obtrusive lines or any unsatisfactory bits of work. Remedially the process was of service. It rendered bad lines less unsightly and, instead of an ugly distinctness, gave (if I may borrow the expression) surprising delicacy of tone. All that I now find surprising is the extravagant use, or abuse, of our old annihilating process in the semi-transparent veils of thinnest lawn too flimsy to have meaning, merely supplying the admired delicacy, a false delicacy like that of consumption, the delicacy of disappearance. Doubtless, where the unlearned engraver knows not what lines to use, ignorant of any power of expression or beauty in lines, cutting them to nothing may be a wise proceeding. The expressionless engraving can then be admired for its one quality — *tone*, the transparent faculty of going from one gamut to another, which Mr. Hamerton deems so important.

In *texture* I deny that the new school is either eminent or able. These engravers do not get the texture of an oil-painting,—unless the texture of an oil-painting is shown in brush-marks and plasterings of the palette-knife. They succeed in representing these. They are partially successful in imitations of charcoal drawing and lithography. Of any textures of *substances represented in their cuts* they are absolutely innocent. I have taken note of much applauded gift-books; I have looked through the magazines, *Harper's* and the *Century* (formerly *Scribner's*); I recall but a single cut remarkable for truthfulness of texture, a cut of *Lobsters* by F. S. King. Indeed one striking characteristic of the new school is the confusion of substances, the want of distinction of texture.*

For tone and texture the school is praised by Mr. Hamerton. Manual skill certainly is evident in tone. But "accompanied by so much intelligence"? I miss the intelligence. Versatility, also apparent to Mr. Hamerton, I do not see. The work of the new school, for all its gamuts of intelligence, is most monotonously inexpressive. And conceding an attention to tone, is nothing to be said of inattention to form and perspective, to which both tone and texture surely should be subordinate? Has our eloquent art-critic not a word for beauty of line; † or does he share Dr. Seymour Haden's contempt for the art of line-engraving? This art finds no advancement in the new American school, which advances only on the downward slope of preferring a mere pretty fineness to the nobler requisitions of Art, forgetting the higher appointments of the Law while browsing upon wayside mint and anise. The main difference between the elder engravers (of Europe or America) of our Winter Days and the heralds of this delusive Spring consists in this:

---

* I do not forget the texture-work of Henry Marsh, the marvelously close representation of beetles and butterflies and moths in Harris' *Insects Injurious to vegetation*, Boston, U.S.A., 1862: work as good as Bewick's feather-work, but which unhappily turned the artist into a specialist, spoiling him for all other engraving. His work precedes the "development," and also has no relation to it.

† I may be pardoned for repeating here some few words of former utterance, in explanation of what I mean by beauty and finesse under a law of line.

—"If you were drawing waves with a pencil, you would naturally follow in some measure their flow and form; that is, had you perceived so much. If you were drawing in line a hand or face, you would find yourself soon imitating the roundness of a part projecting, or a hollow, with corresponding curved lines. Your mere thought of the form on your first attempt at outlining it dictates the after course, and the law that governs such almost instinctive action is at the base of all good lining for engraving. The man who is unable to see the beauty and propriety of this harmonious identification of treatment with its subject, who sees no beauty in line, ay! even in mere regularity and the pleasant accordance of lines one with another, is not an artist (or, with allowance for too general onesidedness of practitioners, lacks something of the artist's completeness); can never become a first-rate engraver, and is as unfitted to give an opinion on engraving as a man colour-blind to judge of painting." (From *Some Practical Hints on Wood-Engraving*, Boston, U.S.A., 1879.)

the first used, and may still use, lines meaningless but otherwise inoffensive; while the last disgust us with lines not only meaningless, but also obtrusively ugly. To point out how much of this may have been occasioned by careless and insufficient drawing (called impressionist), or how much by the over-use of photography (in the place of drawing), which last has hindered more than it has forwarded the engraver, would require a longer argument than might fairly come within the scope of my present writing. Of these two adverse influences I have said enough elsewhere. Some, if not all, of the "consummate workmen" (of the new school) whom Mr. Hamerton names, and other good workmen unnamed, would, I am confident, acknowledge the justice of my criticism. I know that some who follow the passing fashion do so against their own judgment and better taste. They do what is ordered. They will do better when they have opportunity.

Kruell, a German, whom I may hardly count with the new school, and Juengling and others, of the school, have shown themselves capable of good and artistic work. But in this unhealthy eccentricity they can neither earn enduring praise nor advance the art of engraving in wood. Any real advance must come, not from the present fashion, but as a reaction against it through a conviction of the insufficiency of merely tone and colour. Such a head as that of *Richter*, lately engraved by Klinkicht (another German), so good in line, so powerfully graver-drawn, nor lacking tone, promises a possible return to the wholesomeness of art. With relation to it I would ask attention to a head, a portrait of the French painter *Delacroix*, engraved by Serinkoff, a Russian, now dead. The coat is nought; but the head is excellent,—both in modeling and in colour, though I object to the black cross-lines on the cheek, chin, and eyebrows, as a waste of labour and as out of harmony with other white line. These two heads, largely and minutely done, show the range of wood-engraving in portrait. The figure of *Narcissus*, in which I have followed Nesbit's treatment of his *Rinaldo and Armida*, may serve to farther indicate the value of pure white line for flesh. Water, it hardly need be said, could not be rendered tolerably in wood except with the white line. And in every thing except imitation-etching (that, I repeat, an unequal imitation at best) a line drawn by the graver is the true procedure. What of my own engravings are here given, all but the *Don Cæsar de Bazan*, in which as a foil to the *Infant Bacchus* nearly all the figure is in close fac-simile, I venture to bring forward only in exemplification of the worth and advantage of the white line.

I look back lovingly and regretfully to the drawings of the Painters in Water-Colour, which ought to have revived the method of Bewick and Clennell and reëstablished wood engraving as an art. The drawings on the block by William Leighton Leitch, in Indian ink or sepia with so much pencilling as might be sometimes needed for clearer definition, were as well studied, as carefully drawn, as his exhibited pictures. So were the drawings by Duncan, Dodgson, Topham, Archer, and others, which passed through my hands. To have to study with what fittest lines to adequately render such drawings, so as fully to represent every beauty of form, to express substance where required, to care for the perspective of distances, to give light and atmosphere, to mind also the characteristics of the draftsman, so that the artist's picture might be recognised as really and truly his, though but a translation, the engraver's art and judgment chiefly there apparent,—this was an education for an engraver; this, and only such a course as this, is calculated to make him an artist. More than once Duncan's drawing on the block has been in colour, he trusting me to translate it into black and white. That I may not have done justice to such drawings, nor taken full advantage of opportunities, speaks only against myself. I have still to assert the value of such an education. All that is required for perfection of a great painter, except invention and the handling of colours, seems to me necessary to qualify the engraver. What a man can draw, that only can he engrave,—using the word in an artistic sense. I confess the secret of my own failures.

Can the Art of Engraving in Wood renew its life? Only when engravers are artists, as artists recognising what can be and therefore should be done in so facile a material. If they fail to perceive the worth of expressiveness in line and of beauty with expression, contented with mechanical excellence or caring farther only for tone, eccentricity, and a vain "finish," then, despite all publishers' approval, critic-congratulations, and popularity, the days of wood-engraving are numbered. The wise employer will take new processes able to compete with mere manual skill, nay! in all but what is strictly artistic, to excel it, and at less cost. I would fain hope for the happier course: for Engraving in Wood, as an art, has its own especial beauty, not surpassed, in some things (painter-like touch and atmosphere) not equalled, by copper. But again and again it must be repeated that its dignity, and the sole reason for its continued existence is *as an Art*. The highest art is the presentment of beauty, in strong and complete expression.

BOOTH AS DON CÆSAR DE BAZAN (W. J. Linton)

CHIAROSCURO

IF CHIAROSCURO we have two kinds: the first drawn with a pen in outlines and cross-hatchings (lines crossed for shading) with high lights in white on a tint, done in two printings; the second without lines, altogether done with a brush, in three or four or more shades of the one colour,—the first of these shades or tints furnishing the contours and strongest shadows, the last supplying the lightest tint with the whites, or high lights. A drawing in lines may sometimes underlie a number of tints; but the above distinction sufficiently defines the two kinds. Of the first kind is the *Adam and Eve*, after Baldung Grun, opposite our next page; the second is shown in the initial letter to this chapter. The mere process of the engraving is precisely the same in both kinds.

Chiaroscuros (engravings in such manner) are not necessarily nor always wood-cuts, nor is there anything in their execution entitling them to be considered as master-pieces of engraving. Most easily engraved, their effectiveness is due to the designer and the printer. What we generally mean by engraving, with knife or graver, is the production of pictorial effect by lines; and it will be seen at once that the difficulty and the merit of such works as the *Birds* of Bewick, Nesbit's *Rinaldo and Armida*, Powis' *Nineveh*, or the cuts by Lutzelburger of Holbein's simpler drawing, find no occasion in a few white lines cut as lights, or in the mere clearing out of larger masses when only masses of the wood surface are to be left from which to print the darker portions. There is no difficulty nor opportunity for distinction in cutting the broad work of chiaroscuro.

Moreover, of chiaroscuros usually classed as wood-engravings many are not in wood. In some the engraving (so distinguishing what is done in lines) is cut in metal, either with incised lines or in relief; and, if the work is in relief for surface-printing, it is very difficult to determine whether it is in metal or wood. This difficulty is so much greater when we have only the brush-drawing, without lines, that in some cases I should think nothing conclusive except a sight of the very metal plate or the block or plank of wood. Some slight graver-touch might show it to be metal, some little mark of a knife show it to be wood. Looking through a collection of chiaroscuros, although size of subject or other consideration may influence me, I confess to being often unable to form a decided opinion. Here I think to confine myself to subjects which I suppose to be in wood.

In chiaroscuro, I repeat, the line-engraving (wood or metal) as engraving is of little worth. Speaking now of early German and Italian works, I can not account anything I have seen as masterly. The best is only good mechanical work; and in many excellent chiaroscuros the lines are no better than any *Helyen* cutting. Considered as engraving, therefore, chiaroscuro hardly has place in my book. Nevertheless, were it only for its association, it must not be altogether left out.

The earliest dated chiaroscuro is German, a *Venus and Cupid*, by the elder Cranach, done with two printings, its date 1506; the next, another Cranach, a *Repose in Egypt*, is dated 1509. Following these we have *Witches going to their Sabbath*, in three printings, 1510, and *Adam and Eve*, 1511, in two,—both by Hans Baldung Grun. Dr. Willshire praises this last as "the finest of the old German chiaroscuros." Design and drawing are spirited; but I can only say of the knife-work that it is clean, by no means difficult with a bold drawing measuring ten inches by fourteen and a half. A *Flying Woman*, by Jobst Dienecker, 1510, and two portraits, of Pope Julius, 1511, and Baumgartner, 1512, after Burgkmair, engraved by Dienecker, perhaps by him drawn on the wood, are of a like character; and establish the priority of German over Italian cuts of the kind. All these here named I consider to be in wood.

It is not until 1518 that we get the first dated Italian work, the *Death of Ananias*, after Raffaele, by Ugo da Carpi, who, petitioning the Venetian Senate for protection of his "invention," describes himself as an engraver in wood. Vasari gives a *Sybil reading* as an earlier essay. *David and Goliath*, the *Miraculous Draught of Fishes*, the *Descent from the Cross*, the *Resurrection*, *Æneas carrying Anchises*, all from Raffaele, and a *Diogenes*, after Parmigiano (which Vasari thinks his finest), are of his principal works. Generally he dispensed with outlines and line-shadings, drawing his contours with a brush: which may be taken broadly as the Italian method. Admirable chiaroscuros, like the German cuts, they are of little account as knife-work.

Of other workers in chiaroscuro (designers, if not the actual engravers) the chief are —in Germany, Hans Wechtelin (miscalled Pilgrim, says Passavant); later in Holland, Hendrik Goltz or Goltzius (designs cut by Christoph Van Sichem); in Italy, Antonio da Trento, Niccolo Boldrini Vicentino, Andrea Andreani, and Bartolomeo Coriolano.

Andrea Andreani, born at Mantua, about 1555-60, dying in 1623, devoted himself to the production of chiaroscuros. His works are many, even if he must not be credited

with everything bearing his mark, sometimes affixed by him (it is said) to other men's doings, merely touched or repaired (*rétablis*) by him. So Bartsch; but it is hard to say what *rétablis* means. It might be that he rearranged or added tints, so making the work his own. His *Triumph of Julius Cæsar*, 1598, in ten sheets, each about thirteen inches square, after Mantegna, Bernard Malpizzi's name on it as draftsman, is Andreani's most important work, and capitally engraved in parts; but, notwithstanding its size, I can not rid myself of a suspicion of metal. Others of his doing are *Abraham's Sacrifice*, copied from Beccafumi's pavement in the Siena cathedral, six feet by two and a half, and *Moses breaking the Tables of the Law*, from the same, six feet by four, on jointed wood (*douze pièces jointes ensemble, qui forment un grand morceau*, says Bartsch). These two, already named at page 110, are there spoken of lightly, as of little worth as engravings. They may be differently estimated as chiaroscuros. The mere cutting of the lines of drawing, except in some parts of the *Triumph of Cæsar*, has no distinction; and I see no certain ground on which to attribute all the works of Andreani to his own hand. I doubt not their having been done under his direction. Although not the *Triumph*, he may have drawn others on the wood, and probably arranged and drew also the shadow-forms, the chiaroscuro; he perhaps cut the lines giving the high lights and outlined with the knife the several tints. This would sufficiently warrant him in calling himself *Intagliatore*, and the credit of the chiaroscuro would be fairly his. For this, not for mere knife cutting, he may claim a place among the Masters of Wood-Engraving.

Bartolomeo Coriolano is called by Bartsch the last of the good chiaroscuro engravers. He worked at Bologna between 1630 and 1647. Very notable among his doings is the *Overthrow of the Titans*, boldly executed after Guido, in four parts, the whole measuring nearly three feet in height by two in width.

Very numerous were these chiaroscuros during the sixteenth century and in the first half of the seventeenth; copies of Raffaele, Parmigiano, Titian, Giulio Romano, Guido, and other of the great painters. Bartsch specifies of the Old and New Testaments 38, Virgins 28, Saints (male and female) 36, Mythology 29, beside Pious Subjects, Subjects from Profane History, Allegory, Portraits, and Inventions. I do not need to critically distinguish the degrees of excellence (and many of them are very excellent) since that is so little due to the actual wood-cutter.

After Coriolano the practice appears to have fallen into disuse until the next century, to be then revived by Count Antonio Maria Zanetti, an enthusiastic amateur, of whose works Bartsch enumerates seventy-one, most of them Virgins or Saints, in size varying from two inches to ten, in two, three, and four printings. The Zanetti collection, dating from 1721, was published at Venice in 1749. He burned the blocks, that poorer prints might not go forth; aware how much depended on careful printing, not only to keep the cuts in exact register, but to preserve the gradations of colour ordered by the designer.

Nicolas le Sueur, born in 1691, dying in 1764, appears according to Chatto as engraver of wood blocks from which the sepia tints were printed, over outlines etched by Caylus. Chatto also speaks of chiaroscuros by him wholly in wood, executed with great boldness and spirit: a criticism not applicable to the cutting, but only to the drawing, which he does not state to be Le Sueur's. Papillon, printing two specimens, speaks of him as an able draftsman, without invention, praising his chiaroscuros, after Raffaele, Parmigiano, and others, as perfect for their precision and correctness of register. Something more may be said for him. His *Venus and Cupid* after Parmigiano, 1731, six inches and three eighths by seven and five eighths, delicately printed, outline and three tints in yellowish brown, is not only well drawn but is beautifully engraved. So also is a subject twice the size, after Faranati, two draped figures in a chariot drawn by four horses careering over and through the clouds. These two chiaroscuros are of the most perfect I have seen, though neither the strongest nor the most ambitious.

Arthur Pond, an Englishman, is mentioned by Papillon as engraver in chiaroscuro of nine landscapes after Claude. I have not seen them.

The chiaroscuros, 1712-4, of Kirkall (supposed engraver of the Croxall *Æsop*) are a combination of etching and mezzotint with wood. Seventeen views of shipping, copies of Van der Velde, are only engravings printed in a greenish blue ink.

John Baptist Jackson, writes Chatto, engraved in 1738 a chiaroscuro of *Christ taken from the Cross*, after Rembrandt; and between 1738 and 1742, at Venice, twenty-seven large chiaroscuros, after pictures by Titian, G. Bassano, Tintoretto and Paul Veronese, published in 1742: "unequal in merit, some harsh and crude, others flat and spiritless, when compared with similar productions of the old Italian wood-engravers." But Chatto underrates him. I find his works very excellent and effective. The *Finding of Moses* (two feet high by sixteen inches wide), the *Virgin climbing the steps of the Temple* (after Veronese), and others, are admirable in every respect, though there be little of difficulty in the mere engraving. Six large landscapes (twenty-four inches by eighteen), printed "in all their original colours," may be considered as the first attempts at the imitation of oil-paintings. After returning to England, Jackson sought to apply his "invention" to paper-hangings for rooms; and, in an essay published by him in 1754, to show forth the advantages of his method, gives specimens, not very successful, of both colour-printing and chiaroscuro, claiming to have "invented ten positive tints in chiaroscuro, whereas Hugo di Carpi knew but four."

After Jackson our next chiaroscurist is another Englishman, an amateur artist, John Skippe, who between 1771 and 1809 executed in wood a number of copies of the works of the Old Masters. Nagler names twenty-eight. Chatto and Redgrave (perhaps only quoting Chatto) find them much superior to Jackson's. What I have seen appear to me of inferior quality. I speak of them as chiaroscuros; the engraving is of small account.

In *Practical Hints on Decorative Printing*, printed and published, 1819-22, by William Savage, printer (Redgrave calls him painter and engraver), we see considerable advance in the printing of chiaroscuro, and also some ambitious attempts in colours, not always successful. Considerable credit may here be given to the engravers. All the subjects are graver-work in wood: with employment of from two to nine blocks for chiaroscuro, and from two to twenty-nine in colours. My business is with the chiaroscuros, of which there are eleven examples, beside some unimportant page-headings. *A Street Sweeper*, one of the most simple, engraved by Branston, from drawings by W. M. Craig, is given by Savage not only as a chiaroscuro, but also in its several parts, to show the process of printing. Much more elaborate are a *Bas-relief* by Branston and the Phidian *Theseus* by William Hughes, from drawings by William Hunt, in three and five blocks; *Ruins of Kirkstal Abbey*, with seven blocks, by Craig, engraved by J. Lee; and *Passage Boats*, by R. Branston junior, with seven blocks, in imitation of a drawing by Callcott, an outline with sky and water in wash. These are the finest, the most finished chiaroscuros from wood that I know: admirable copies of the original drawings, tints efficiently arranged and most carefully printed, the engraver's part well done. How far this completeness is due to the draftsmen, how much to Savage's printing, there are no means of finding out. But there is nothing which could not be done in metal, nothing to reflect distinction on the Art of Wood-Engraving, except as showing farther most valuable applicability in a direction independent of the accustomed employment of lines.

The worth of chiaroscuro engraving consists in the arrangement of broad masses of shade and gradation of tints so as to give a perfect representation of a washed drawing. In all this the engraver is but secondary. He may have nothing to do with the design, it may not be for him to separate and arrange the composing shades; and, when he has cut the several blocks, from combination of which the complete work will be produced, the keeping of right tone and colour is the charge of the printer. Occasions there may be, as in the *Theseus* engraved by Hughes for Savage, when the engraver's artist-faculty has scope; but the poorest workman may suffice for an excellent chiaroscuro.

I do not depreciate the artistic value as chiaroscuros of the various prints here noted nor underestimate the difficulty of production; but my business has been solely with the not difficult knife-cutting and graver-cutting of the same.

INDEX TO NAMES

ARTISTS AND ENGRAVERS

ADAMS, 196, 197, 198, 202
ALLGAIER, 203
ALLSTON, 197
ALTDORFER, 109, 111, 113, 123
AMMAN, 15, 16, 114, 116, 117, 121, 126
ANDERSON, 196, 193, 201
ANDREA (JEROME), 79, 90 to 94, 107, 109, 111, 121, 123, 124, 165, 205
ANDREANI, 110, 117, 273
ARCHER, 104, 109
ARMSTRONG, 154, 192
AUSTIN, 134

BALDUNG GRUN, 111, 117
BARBARJ (WALLON), 80, 109, 111
BARLOW, 131
BASSANO, 114
BEGCAFUMI, 110, 113
BEHAM, 41, 94, 112, 113, 114, 123, 205
BEILBY, 128, 135, 137, 143
BELLINI, 71
BERTRAND, 202, 205
BEWICK, 106, 128, 130 to 173, 175, 176, 177, 181, 182, 185, 189, 191, 196, 200, 201, 204, 207, 209, 211
BEWICK (J.), 131, 133, 134, 137, 138, 146, 154, 157, 196

BEWICK (R.), 153, 154, 155, 157, 158
BLAKE, 41
BOLDRINI, 116, 211
BOHN, 90
BOWYER, 99, 134, 171, 191, 192, 193, 201, 202, 204
BOTTICELLI, 71
BRANSTON, 153, 162, 164, 170, 173 to 178, 180, 191, 197, 201, 215
BRANSTON (F.), 172, 191
BRANSTON (R.), 177, 215
BARTRAM, 202
DUROGMAIS, 87, 89, 91, 92, 95, 211
BYFIELD (J.), 99
BYFIELD (MARY), 175

CACCIA, 118
CALLCOTT, 115
CAMBIANO, 177
CARPI (UGO DA), 211
CATLIN, 214
CHAPMAN, 197, 198
CHEETHAM, 204
CLAUDE, 114
CLENNELL, 134, 144, 148, 149, 151, 154, 156, 155, 157, 159 to 171, 174, 176, 177, 178, 180, 187, 200, 201, 205, 209
COIGNET, 197

CONSTABLE, 194, 200
CORFOULD, 177, 178, 181, 189
CORIOLANO, 212, 213
CRANE, 161, 167, 173, 178, 215
CRANACH, 94, 165, 212
CRUIKSHANK, 177, 179, 181, 187, 189, 195, 205

DALZIEL, 205
DEACON, 181
DIETRICHER, 90, 91, 92, 95, 96, 98, 117, 212
DODGSON, 104, 109
DORÉ, 106
DUNCAN, 202, 204, 209, 210
DÜRER, 7, 35, 61, 70, 71, 79 to 87, 89, 90, 92, 93, 94, 107, 108, 111, 112, 114, 115, 122, 123, 124, 165, 205

EYCK (VAN), 29, 41, 63

FARAMATY, 214
FEYERABEND, 117
FRANÇAIS, 191
FRANK (HANS), 90, 91, 92, 95
FRID, 117

GABER, 203
GILBERT, 195, 196, 204, 205
GOLTZIUS, 212
GRANDVILLE, 177, 183, 202
GREENE (D. DALLE), 109, 111
GREEN, 134
GRINGONNEUR, 22, 24
GRUN (BALDUNG), 111, 112
GUIDO, 89, 113
GULDENMUND, 90

HARRAL (A.), 196, 204
HARRAL (H.), 204
HARVEY, 150 to 156, 170, 171, 177, 180, 181, 182, 184, 185, 186, 188, 191, 194, 196, 200, 201, 204
HAYTER, 195
HEATH, 161, 178
HODGSON, 131, 134, 137

HOGARTH, 112
HOLBEIN, 7, 95 to 108, 112, 113, 114, 119, 122, 123, 124, 166, 193, 203, 205, 221
HOLE, 154, 155, 162, 164, 168, 178, 187
HUET, 191, 195, 209
HUGHES (H.), 187, 202
HUGHES (W.), 175, 187, 215
HUNT, 215
HUYOT, 202

JACKSON (J.), 99, 113, 152, 154, 191, 192, 193, 194, 197, 198, 202, 207
JACKSON (J. B.), 127, 129, 130, 191, 200, 214
JACQUE, 202
JEGHER, 119
JOHANNOT, 191, 202
JOHNSON (E. K.), 204
JOHNSON (J.), 134
JOHNSON (R.), 143, 148, 149, 150, 152, 153, 154, 155, 157, 159, 160, 167, 171, 181
JOLLAT, 77
JONNARD, 206

KAULBACH, 203
KING, 208
KIRKALL, 127, 128, 129, 130, 200, 214
KLINKICHT, 109
KLUBER, 103
KRAFT, 80
KRETZSCHMAR, 103, 105
KRUELL, 209

LANDSEER, 154
LANCE, 204
LAVAIGNAC, 203
LE CLERC, 130, 131
LEE, 131, 134, 215
LEECH, 204, 205
LEITCH, 201, 204, 209
LE SUEUR, 110, 214
LEYDEN (VAN), 119
LEPÈRE, 90, 91, 117, 120

LIGHT, 206
LINDERAFT, 80
LINDT, 90
LINTON, 204, 209
LINTON (H.), 204
LUTZELBURGER, 90, 91, 95 to 108, 112, 113, 114, 121, 122, 123, 124, 166, 205, 212

MALPIEL, 113
MANTEGNA, 71, 113
MARAM, 208
MARTIN, 192, 194
MEADOWS, 185, 195, 196
MEISSONIER, 191, 195, 202, 203
MENZEL, 203, 205
MILL, 121
MILTON, 143, 200
MINE, 204
MORSE, 197
MOSSES, 201
MULREADY, 177, 183, 184, 204

NEWBY, 131, 149, 151, 152, 154, 155, 157, 159, 162, 164 to 180, 185, 188, 191, 192, 200, 201, 202, 205, 217
NICHOLSON, 138, 154

OBERMANN, 203
OERTEL, 203

PAGE, 185
PANNEMAKER, 206
PAPILLON, 18, 34, 38, 72, 109, 111, 112, 120 to 129, 156, 214
PARMIGIANO, 112, 113, 114
PEARSON, 194
PECKHAM, 134
PLAYDENWURFF, 70
POND, 214
POWLE, 99, 191 to 194, 197, 202, 204, 206, 207, 211
POVEY, 19
PYE, 200

RAFFAELLE, 211, 213, 214

REMBRANDT, 197, 214
REACH (RÖSCH), 79, 90, 93
REUMERS, 203
RIMMOER, 196
ROMANO (C.), 113
ROBERT, 207
RUBENS, 119
RUFF, 90, 91

SALOMON, 113, 114, 115, 116
SCHAUFFELIN, 82, 90, 91
SCHNORR, 203
SEARS, 201
SEEMAN, 90
SAMAKOFF, 209
SEYMOUR, 105
SICHEM (VAN), 117, 119, 212
SIEGLE, 203
SKIPPE, 214
SMITH, 134, 194, 195, 202, 204, 205, 207
SOLIS (V.), 114, 116
STEINABECHER, 203
STIMMER, 114, 116, 117, 121
STIMMER (C.), 117
STOTHARD, 165, 166, 180, 181, 182, 183, 205
STOLL, 80
SWAIN, 205
SWITZER, 119

TABERITH, 90
TEMPLE, 153, 154, 155, 185
TENIERS, 196
TERNIEL, 203
THOMPSON, 156, 157, 158, 161, 162, 164, 173, 175, 177 to 185, 187, 189, 191, 197, 201, 202, 204, 207
THOMPSON (C.), 122, 202
THURSTON, 161, 162, 163, 164, 167, 168, 170, 171, 174 to 181, 184, 185, 187, 200, 201, 203
TINTORETTO, 214
TITIAN, 109, 110, 111, 119, 213, 214
TOPHAM, 209
TRENTO (A. DA), 212

INDEX TO SUBJECTS

AARON'S CROWN (Exodus, xxxix, 30),—page 3.

ACHILLES' SHIELD,— 3.

ANAUS,— 197.

ALPHABET of 1464,—61; Holbein's Alphabets, 108.

ALTDORFER,—Minute work by him, the Fall and Redemption of Man his engraving, 111.

AMERICAN ENGRAVING :—Anderson, 196; Adams, 197; Hamerton's praises of later work, 206, 207; his judgment disputed, 207, 208; of tone and of texture, 207 to 209.

AMMAN,—His numerous works, 116; the supposed engravers, 117.

ANDERSON,—196.

ANDREÆ (Jerome of Nurnberg) :—His right name, 79; of Nurnberg and Durer, 80 to 90; Jerome's work on the Maximilian Triumph, the Arch, Car, and Procession, 92, 93; his contention with King Ferdinand, 93; character, 93; official document, 94; probable portrait of his wife by Holbein, 94; inscription on his tomb, 94; the likelihood of his engraving Beham's Apocalypse, 111.

ANNUNCIATION (Salutation of the Virgin) :— where found and how printed, 32, 33; description, 34; certain lines omitted and Krimmer's reason, 35.

APOCALYPSE :— Beham's, 111; Durer's, 80 to 82.

APOCALYPSE :—The earliest known of Block Books, 39; description, place of production and designer, 40, 41.

APOCRYPHAL GOSPELS, 85, 86.

ARS MORIENDI:— Description of the book, 53, 54; and of the several designs, 54 to 58.

BABYLONIAN,— Bricks, 2; clay tablets, 3; cylinders found by Layard, 8.

BEGINNINGS OF ENGRAVING,—1 to 16; in Babylon, and Egypt, 2, 3; in China, 3; engraving told of in Exodus, by Homer, Æschylus, and Herodotus, 3; Etruscan work, 3; known in India, 4; by the ancient Greeks and Romans, 4; in the South Sea Islands, 5; opinions of D'Ankerville, of Wiltshire, and De Vinne, 5 to 9; supposed borrowing from China, 17; Papillon's tale of the Cunio twins, 18; playing-cards, 20 to 27; the Helyre, 17, 20, 27 to 38; the Block-Books, 39.

BEHAM :—Beautiful cuts in his Apocalypse, whose engraving, most likely the work of Andreæ, 112; his larger designs and other smaller series, 113.

BERLIN (The Virgin of),— 76.

BEWICK :— Ignorant worship, 133; poor specimens of his genius, 134; his early life and work, 134 to 138; Select Fables, of 1784, editions by Charnley and Pearson, 138; copies from the Croxall Æsop, 138 to 140; the Quadrupeds and Birds, described and criticised, 140 to 143, 146 to 149; his larger cuts, the Chillingham Bull, Lions, Elephant, and Zebra, "Waiting for death," 143, 144; his work in metal, 144, 145; Somerville's Chase and Parnell's Hermit, 145, 146; Chatto's list of the Tail-pieces drawn by Bewick and of those by Johnson, 149; the Fables of 1818, 149 to 154; by whom drawn and engraved, 143, 154; supplementary cuts, 154; spurious posthumous editions, 155; Chatto might have told us much more of the work of his pupils —Clennell, Nesbit, Harvey, and others, 155; his rank as artist, 155, 156; examples in proof, 156;

the printing of his cuts, 151, 152, 156; his drawings, 156, 157; JOHN BEWICK, 157; ROBERT BEWICK, 153, 155, 157, 158.

BIBLIA PAUPERUM:—Not the Bible for Poor Folk, 44; description of the designs, 45 to 47; Chatto on Heinecken's editions, 47, 48, 49; Sotheby, his opinions at variance with the views of Heinecken, 49; comparison of editions in the British Museum and Bodleian Libraries, 50 to 52; added designs in later editions, 52, 53.

BLOCK:—The term misused for Plank, 39.

BLOCK-BOOKS:—Picture and text cut in wood, the wood sawn lengthway, the word block so wrongly used, 39; the Apocalypsis, 40, 41; the Canticum Canticorum, 41, 42, 43, 44; the Biblia Pauperum, 44 to 53; Chatto on Heinecken's editions, 47, 48; Sotheby here does not agree with Heinecken, 49; Sotheby would prove difference of effect between vertical and hand pressure on the surface of lines in relief, 49; comparison of editions of the Biblia Pauperum in the British Museum and Bodleian Libraries, 50 to 52; the Ars Moriendi, 53 to 58; the books compared, 58; later Block-Books, 59.

BONNER:—191, 192.

BOOKS:—Roman books, 8, 9; books of the Middle Ages,—work in the monasteries and in the public schools, the *scriptorium*, independent artists, 18; the Renaissance, 19; illuminator and miniaturist, 19; Poyet's book of Hours for Anne of Brittany, Froissart's Chronicles, the Romance of the Rose, 19; the Hours, 76, 78. (See WOOD-ENGRAVING.)

BRANSTON:—173 to 177.

BREYDENBACH'S TRAVELS, 69.

BRICKS:—Babylonish, 2, 8.

BRUSSELS VIRGIN:—Account of its discovery, 17, 18; description, 18; discussion as to authenticity of the date of 1418, 19, 20; judgment against, 20.

BURGKMAIR:—His part in the Maximilian Triumph (the Procession), 87 to 89; lists of the engravers by Bartsch, Von Perger, and Schestag, 90; names of engravers and the word *Maler* on the backs of cuts, 91; letter of Dienecker to Maximilian, 91; Burgkmair's Saints and White King, 91.

CANTICUM CANTICORUM, 41; Inappropriateness of the usual title, 42; designs described, 42 to 44.

CARDS:—Singer on Playing-Cards, 20; Passavant, 20, 21; Becker, Chatto, Von Murr, 21; supposed borrowing from Arabia or India, 21; earliest use in Europe, 21, 22; the modes of production, 22; Old Cards in the British Museum mistaken to be stencil-work by Chatto, 23; the first mention of a card-maker, 24; confusion of the different terms *kartenmacher* and *formschneider*, 24; importation of foreign cards forbidden at Venice, 27.

CAXTON:—His books, 69.

CHARNLEY:—His edition of Bewick's Select Fables, the inexact edition of 1820, 138.

CHIAROSCURO:—Nature and method, 111 to 115. [Workers and works noted:—
Andreani,—Abraham's Sacrifice, Moses breaking the Tables, 112, 113; Triumphs of Cæsar, 113.
Baldung Grun,—Adam and Eve, Witches going to their Sabbath, 112.
Baldrini (Vicentino),—Venus and Cupid, 111.
Branston,—Bas-relief and Street Sweeper, 114.
Branston (R.),—Passage Boats, 115.
Carpi (Ugo da),—Æneas and Anchises, David and Goliath, Death of Ananias, Descent from the Cross, Diogenes, Draught of Fishes, Sybil reading, 112.
Coriolano,—Overthrow of the Titans, 113.
Cranach,—Repose in Egypt, Venus and Cupid, 112.
Dienecker,—Flying Woman, Portrait, 92.
Hughes (W.),—Theseus, 115.
Jackson (J. B.),—Christ taken from the Cross, the Finding of Moses, the Virgin climbing the steps of the Temple, 114.
Lee,—Kirkstall Abbey, 115.
Le Sueur,—Venus and Cupid, 114.
Zanetti,—Virgins and Saints, 113.

CHINA:—Wood-Engraving there, 3, 17.

CIPHERS,—11, 12.

CLENNELL:—His early work, 159; his Tail-pieces to Bewick's Water Birds, 160; Chatto's list, 169; later book-work, 161 to 164, 166; the Diploma of the Highland Society, 164, 165; the reengraving of this by Thompson, 165; Clennell as a painter and draftsman, 166; cuts falsely called his, 167.

COINS,—in early times, 11, 12.

COLOURER (*Briefmaler*),—14, 15.

COLOUR-PRINTING, by J. B. Jackson, 117, 114.

COLOURS of the *Helyas*, 37; coloured prints, 111.

COSTER,—His discovery of printing, 63.

CRANMER'S CATECHISM:—Two designs by Holbein the rest by Bernard Salomon, suspicion of metal, poor copies in Chatto and Jackson's Treatise, 113

CHILD WORK:—Dotted white work in the French books of Hours, not wood but metal, 76; reasons for so judging beside Dupré's statement of some done on copper, 77; none of the better sort done on wood, 78; advantages of the process, 78; the Hours sometimes coloured to imitate illuminated manuscripts, 78.

CROSS-HATCHING,—69, 70, 223.

CROXALL,—his edition of Æsop's Fables, Chatto's criticism, 130, 131; examination of the work, 131, 132; the designs copied from Barlow and copied by Bewick, 131, 132, 138 to 140; Austin Dobson's remarks, 139, 140. (See METAL-ENGRAVINGS.)

CUNIO, brother and sister,—Papillon's story of their engravings in wood, 18.

CYLINDERS found by Layard at Babylon, 8.

DANCE OF DEATH:—Forty cuts printed at Basle, at about 1527, not in book-form till printed at Lyons in 1538, 96, 97; a probable reason for delay, 97; suspicious character of preface, 97, 104; contents of the book, 97, 98; several editions, additional cuts, and copies, 98, 99; subjects of the cuts, 99 to 103; it is properly the Masque of Death, 105; meaning of the words *Macabre* and *Machabé*, 105; the popularity of the subject, 105, 106; the cuts are depreciated by Hamerton, 106; his remarks objected to, 106, 107.

DE VINNE, on Babylonish bricks, and the cylinders found by Layard, 8; on the brass Lar, 8; and on the *frottee*, 33, 34; on black and brown inks and the use of metal instead of wood, 62, 63.

DIENECKER (Joss de Negher):—His work for the Burgkmair Procession (the Maximilian Triumph), 90, 91; his letter to the Emperor, 91; work upon Schaufelin's Sir Theurdank, and on Burgkmair's Saints and White King, 91; his cuts not excelling those of his fellows, 91; his Dance of Death, 98.

DIFFERENCE between ancient and modern engraving stated by Willshire, 5, 6; objections, 7, 8.

DISTINCTION of wood-engraving as an art, 105.

DRAWING ON THE WOOD:—Use of glued paper, 35; drawing on wood by Wohlgemuth, 71; Dürer, 83, 84; Burgkmair and Schaufelin, 91, 92; Holbein, 96, 106, 107, 108, 113; Barberj, Dalle Greche and Andreani, 109, 110, 111; Altdorfer, 111; Beham, 111; Salomon, 113, 115; Solis, 114, 115; Amman and Stimmer, 116; Papillon, 120; Bewick, 138 to 156; Robert Johnson, 143 to 160; Clennell, 159, 160, 164; Thurston, 161 to 167; Harvey, 149 to 167; Chapman, 198; Leech, 204, 203; Gilbert, 205; Doré, 206; English Water-colour Painters, Archer, Dodgson, Duncan, Leitch, 209, 210; the Chiaroscurists, 211 to 215.

DÜRER:—State of Nuremberg and of Germany in his days, 79, 80, 81; Dürer's drawings on wood, 79; the Apocalypse, 81, 82; not engraved by Dürer, 83; the nature and the extent of his influence on wood-engraving, 84, 85; the Life of the Virgin, the Greater Passion, and the Lesser Passion, 85 to 87; the Triumph of Maximilian, 87; the Arch, 87, 88; the Triumphal Car, and Car of Victory, 89; the Engravers, 90, 91; Dienecker, 90 to 91; Jerome Andreæ, 92 to 94; some single engravings of Dürer's drawing, 94.

EGYPTIAN STAMP, cut in wood, 2; engraved metal plates in mummy-cases, 3.

ENGLISH KNIFE-WORK:—Early work of no worth, 118; Hogarth's Progress of Cruelty, Rogers' Prints in imitation of drawings, 122; wood-cut pictures as decorations on walls, 122, 134.

ENGRAVERS IN WOOD:—Adam, Enoch, Noah, 1; in Babylon and Egypt, 2; in China, 3; the Cunio prints, 18; Card engravers, 20 to 24; the Monks, 29, 36, 38; the eleven engravers of Maximilian's Triumph,—Jerome Andreæ, 92, Dienecker, Jean de Bom, Hans Frank, Linck, Rupp, William and Cornelius Liefrink, Taberith, Resch, and Seeman, 92; Lutzelburger, 95; Vien and Altdorfer, 111; Van Sichem, Frig, Feyerabendt, C. Stimmer, 117; Jeghar, and a second Van Sichem, 119; Swizer, 119; Le Sueur, Papillon, 120; two Ungers, 121; Unselmann, 121; Wang and Deacon, 122.

J. B. Jackson, 119; Hodgson, and Lee, 131; Bewick, 134; Clennell, 159; Nesbit, 167; Hole, 177; Branston, 173; Thompson, 177; Harvey, 185; W. and H. Hughes, 187; S. Williams, 188; T. Williams, 190; Bonner, 191, J. Jackson, 191; Fewin, 191; Smith, 194; Anderson, 196; Adams, 197. Other and later engravers, English, French, German and Russian, 201, 202, 203, 204, 205, 206, 208, 209; engravers in chiaroscuro, 211 to 215.

ENGRAVERS' TOOLS (for engraving in wood),—the knife, 38, 73; gouge and mallet, 143; the scrive, 143; the graver, 25, 115, 116.

ENGRAVING,—the same process to-day as in oldest usage, 7; engraving the beginning of sculpture, 13; of form, texture, and colour, 190; the Law of Line in engraving, 193, 208; Hamerton's view of tone and texture in late American work, 207.

ETRUSCAN PATERA,—carved and engraved, 3.

EXODUS,—Engraving there spoken of, 3.

FABLES:—Virgil Solis, 114, 115; the Croxall Æsop, 130 to 131; Ogilby, Barlow, and Le Clerc, 131; Bewick's Select Fables, 137 to 140; Charnley's edition, and Pearson's, 138; the Fables of 1818, 149 to 154; Northcote's Fables, first and second series, 1818 and 1833, 171, 177, 181, 184, 185, 186, 187, 188.

FAC-SIMILE WORK,—Most of it but mechanism, 123.

FYVRAARNUT,—probably the engraver of some of Salomon's designs, 117.

FRENCH ENGRAVING:—The Hours, 76, 78; works of Bernard Salomon, 115; French knife-work of little importance, 118; modern graver-work, 201, 203, 205, 206.

FROTTON,—Its supposed employment for printing early wood-cuts, 33, 34.

GERMAN WOOD-ENGRAVING:—Earlier knife-work, 117, 118; modern knife-work, the two Ungers and Unzelmann, 101, 102; more recent graver-work, 203, 205, 209.

GILBERT,—His influence on wood-engraving, 205.

GRAVER:—Not used on the side of the wood—the plank, Chatto's mistranslation of Hans Sachs, 15; first late use on wood in France, 122; Papillon's incredulity as to its use on the end (a section) of the wood, 115 to 117.

GRAVER-WORK.—Metal for relief cuts (See METAL WORK and METAL ENGRAVINGS); only to be done in wood on the end, butt or section, of the wood, 115; Papillon on the impossibility of so using a graver, and on what is proper in wood-engraving, 115 to 117; his "fordgoer," 117; Jackson's work and Kirkall's, 117 to 130; Lee and Hodgson, 132; Bewick and the English School, from 133 to 210; modern French work, 201 to 206; German, 203 to 209; American, 196, 197, 206 to 209; Russian, 209; fac-simile,—Leech and Gilbert, Swain and Dalziel, 204, 205; Kretzschmar, Bertrand, 206; artistic merit belonging to work in white line, only that displaying the full power of the graver, 205.

HAMERTON:—His depreciation of the engraving in Holbein's Dance of Death, 106; his praise of late American engraving, 206, 207.

HARVEY:—His early work for Bewick, on the Fables of 1818, 149, 150 to 154; the Annunciation of J. C. Dentatus, 185, Henderson's Wines, 186; other designs, 171, 172, 177, 181, 184; Northcote's two series of Fables, 171 to 193; Harvey's excellence as an engraver, 185; his popularity as a designer, 187; his influence on wood-engraving, 201.

HEINECKEN:—His order of the several editions of the Biblia Pauperum, 47 to 49.

HELGEN (Pictures of Saints):—single-leaf outlines on paper, for colouring, the earliest of Prints, 17; wood-engraving for their production suggested by its use for stamps, 20; these Helgen earlier than Playing-Cards, 26, 27; the earliest-dated claimed to be of 1418, a Virgin with Saints, in the Royal Library at Brussels, 28; description of this, and an examination of the claim, 28 to 30; judgment against it, 30; the Saint Christopher of 1423, the first with assured date, 30; Chatto's remarks, 31; description, 31, 32; some other Helgen, the Annunciation, St. Bridget, the Virgin "of Berlin," 32 to 36; Ottley on inks used and the modes of printing, 33, 34; the "frotton," 33, 34; Krämer's test of early engraving, 35; whose work were the Helgen, 35 to 37; and what their purpose, 36; the colours employed on them and fancied differences in the engraving, 37.

HOLBEIN:—His Dance (or Masque) of Death, 97 to 107; his Bible, 107, Alphabets, 108. (See DANCE OF DEATH and LÜTZELBURGER.)

HOLL,—149, 155, 162, 164, 168, 172, 187.

HOURS (books of devotion so called), 76, 78.

HUGHES (H.), 187; HUGHES (W.), 187.

HUGO,—The Bewick-Collector, 133, 134.

HYPNEROTOMACHIA POLIPHILI, 71, 72. (See METAL ENGRAVINGS.)

ILLUMINATED BOOKS,—18 to 20, 78.

ILLUSTRATED LONDON NEWS:—Engravings there, by Smith and Linton, 204.

INDIA:—Early engraving, 4; Indian seal described by Landseer, 4.

INTAGLIO:—Wood-cuts as well as metal-work both in intaglio and relief, 73.

INVENTERS OF WOOD-ENGRAVING, 1, 2.

ITALIAN ENGRAVING:—The Hypnerotomachia, 71, 72; a Dante of 1491, 75; Vico's Charles V, 110; Baldrini's Venus and Cupid, 111; a Decameron, a Dante, 118; Caccia's St. Elizabeth giving alms, 118; Andreani, 110, 113; Carpi, 112; Coriolano, 113; Zanetti, 113. (See CHIAROSCURO.)

JACKSON (J.)—The cuts in the Treatise on Wood Engraving, 113; work for him by Powis, and his own work as engraver, 192.

JACKSON (J. B.)—Was he the first engraver on the end of the wood, 127; the engraver of Croxall's Æsop, 129, 130; his work, 129; in chiaroscuro, and colour-printing, 214.

JEROME OF NUREMBERG, 79.   (See ANISSER.)

JOHNSON (R.)—His drawings under Bewick, 143, 147, 150, 160.

KIRKALL (E.)—Engravings in copper, 127; cuts attributed to him by Chatto, 127, 128; doubts of his having engraved them, 128; the Kirkall Ticket, 129, 200.

KNIFE (of the old engravers), 38, 67, 73.

KNIFE-WORK:—Egyptian stamp, 7; no variation in technique, Wiltshire and Conway unwarranted in their findings, 37; the process described, 37, 38; an engraver's knife, 38, 67; the one tool available on wood sawn plank-wise, 73; the great difficulty in distinguishing works in wood from relief-work in metal, 73; both French and English knife-cuts poor, Italian is inferior to German, 118; modern German work, 122, 127; what is only difficult and what of worth in knife-work, its limitation, 124; the graver useless on the plank, 125; knife-work and graver-work compared, the work for Dürer with the work of Clennell, 164.

LAW OF LINE: in engraving, absolute in representing form, 199; lines to represent texture and colour, 199; law of fitness and beauty, endeavour at explanation, 208.

LEECH (JOHN)—Nature of his talent, and its influence on engraving, 204, 205.

LUTZELBURGER:—Little known of him personally, 95; Woltmann and His concerning him, 95, 96; the first work with his name, 96; some cuts done at Basle beside those for the Dance of Death, 96; the Hence cuts probably done between 1523 and 1526, 96; proofs of forty cuts taken at Basle by 1527, the book with forty-one printed at Lyons in 1538, 97; reason for the delay in publication, 97; copies, 98, 99; seventeen cuts added in the later editions, 98, 103; list of the cuts, 99 to 103; were these later cuts also by Lutzelburger, 103, 105; inconclusive testimony of his death, 104; Ottley's conjectural history, 104; Hamerton depreciating the cuts, 106; his criticism challenged, 106, 107; Holbein's Bible cuts, Lutzelburger's work there, and on the Holbein Alphabet, 107, 108.

MANUFACTURE:—Mechanism displacing Art, 204.

MARTIAL'S EPIGRAMS, 9.

MAXIMILIAN'S TRIUMPH:—The Arch, 87, 88; the Car, 89; the Procession, 90; the Engravers, 90.

MEDITATIONS of John of Turrecremata, 68, 69, 75.

MERCHANTS' MARKS, 11, 12.

METAL-ENGRAVINGS (surely or sculpti?):—
 Baldini's Venus and Cupid, 111.
 Books of Hours, 76, 100.
 Caxton's Chess, Mirrour of the World, Golden Legend, Æsop, and Canterbury Tales, 69.
 Cranmer's Catechism, 113.
 Croxall's Æsop, 130, 200.
 Dante of 1491, 75.
 Decameron of 1548, 118.
 Dryden's Plays, 198.
 Fust and Schoeffer's Psalter, 60.
 Holbein's Little Dance of Death Alphabet, 108.
 Hollinshed's Chronicles, 118.
 Howell's Medulla Historiæ Anglicanæ, 117.
 Hypnerotomachia Poliphili, 71, 72, 75.
 Jackson's (J. B.) Frontispiece to Suetonius, 119.
 Kirkall Ticket, 129.
 Maittaire's Sallust, 128.
 Meditations of John of Turrecremata, 68, 69, 75.
 Salomon's Ovid and Bible Quatrains, 115.
 St. Bernardin of Sienna, 77.
 St. Elizabeth giving alms, 118.
 Thompson's Britannia and Postage-envelope, 184.

METAL-WORK:—In relief, and in intaglio, Egyptian, Greek, Etruscan, Roman, and Indian, 3 to 5; the brass Lar, 7, 8; monograms, ciphers, coins, seals, monumental brasses, 10 to 14; the initial letters in Fust and Schoeffer's Psalter, 60; doubts as to wood or metal, 68; cuts in metal of the sixteenth century, for surface-printing, found at Basle, 68; jewels in use in the twelfth century, 68; many of presumed wood-cuts are metal, 68; Meditations of John of Turrecremata certainly metal, 69; cuts in Caxton doubtful, 69; of the Hypnerotomachia probably metal, 74; metal early in use for textile fabrics, book-covers, etc., cut both in intaglio and relief by the graver, 73; means for distinguishing metal-cuts from wood, 73; Wiltshire's indications insufficient, 74; surer indications, 75; metals in use, 75; the Books of Hours nearly all in metal, 76, 77; criblé work metal, 76; Bernard Salomon's work metal, 115; other metal-work, 115, 116, 117; (See METAL-ENGRAVING.)

MONUMENTAL BRASSES, 16.

NESBIT:—St. Nicholas' Church and early cuts, 167; later cuts after Thurston, not easily distinguished from Clennell's, 168; Rinaldo and Armida, 170; work after Harvey, 171, 172; Bewick's Fables of 1818, 151 to 154.

NORTHCOTE'S FABLES, 171, 177, 179, 181, 184, 189, 190 to 193.

NUREMBERG,—Its condition in Dürer's time, 79.

NUREMBERG CHRONICLE,—the cuts not engraved by Wohlgemuth, 70.

OVID,—Metamorphoses by Virgil Solis, 114, and by Bernard Salomon, 115.

PAINTERS (as engravers):—Engraving in wood is wrongly attributed to Wohlgemuth, 70; to Durer, 83, 84; and to others, 111; Vico and Altdorfer wood-engravers, and perhaps Boldrini, 111; the painters in water-colour, 209, 210.

PARKEMAKER:—French engravings with his name, from Dürer's drawings, 206.

PAPER,—The first of fit quality for printing, 15.

PAPILLON:—His account of the Curio twins, 19; directions for printing with a hand-roller, 34; his ability as an engraver, 110; as an artist, 111; his Treatise of the history and practice of Engraving in Wood, 101; of engraving with a graver on the end or butt of the wood, 125 to 127.

PEARSON,—His edition of Bewick's Fables, 138.

PLANK,—Instead of "Block," for knife-work, 39.

POWIS:—His engraving in wood, 193, 194.

PRINTING:—An impression is a print, 8; printing coeval with engraving in relief, 14; printing upon cloth and other fabrics, 9, 15, 16; typography had to wait for fit paper, 15; vellum not liked by the printer, 15; linen paper and moveable types, 14, 15; the new occasion for printing, 15; available presses preceding the printing-press, 16; stamped initial letters used in illuminated manuscripts, 19; cards, 22, 23; foreign prints prohibited at Venice, *stampido* means printed, 27; of inks used in early days, 30; time of engraving not proved by time or manner of a print, 33; reason of light-coloured inks, 33; the *fruston*, 33, 34; roller-printing, 34; press-work with moveable types, 59; Gutenberg's Bible, 59; Fust and Schoeffer's Psalter, 59, 60; De Vinne on black and brown inks in early work, 61; his reason for use of metal instead of wood, 62, 63; Coster's "discovery," 63; Weigel's means of deciding between wood and metal through the effect of inks, 54, 55; printing of Bewick's works, 151, 152, 156; Whittingham's printing, 181, 183; chiaroscuro, 211 to 215; J. B. Jackson and printing in colours, 114; Savage's Decorative Printing, 215.

PRINTS mistaken Engravings, 6.

PUCKLE'S CLUB,—171, 174, 179, 187.

QUATRAINS HISTORIQUES (Bible Quatrains), 115.

QUINTILIAN,—His plan for teaching writing by the aid of stencil plates, 9.

RELIEF-WORK:—In metal as well as in wood, as also in intaglio, 73.

RELIGIOUS EMBLEMS,—162 to 164, 168, 172, 174.

REPAIRING damage to wood-cuts, 48.

REPRODUCTION of old cuts:—The Dance of Death, by Schlotthauer, by Humphreys, and the Holbein Society, 98; Becker's *Auriras Molitris*, and the works of Holtrop, Ames, and Dibdin, 114.

ROMAN BOOKS,—8, 9.

RUBENS,—His designs not causing any advance in wood-engraving, 119.

RUSSIAN ENGRAVING, 209.

SALOMON (Bernard):—Bible Quatrains and Ovid's Metamorphoses, both in metal, 115.

SALUTATION of the Virgin (See ANNUNCIATION).

SANDWICH ISLANDERS,—Engraving and printing by them, 3.

SCRIBES, 9; the Scriptorium, 18.

SCRIVE,—122; how fashioned and employed, 123.

SCULPTURE,—originating in engraving,—a growth from the first attempt in relief, 13.

SEALS, 12; Indian seal described by Landseer, 4.

SIR THEUERDANK (Teurdannckh), 91.

SMITH,—His engraving and its character, 194, 195, 196; Smith and Linton, 204.

SOLIS (Virgil):—Bible Figures, Æsop's Fables, and Ovid's Metamorphoses, 114.

SOTHEBY, on the effects of friction, 49.

SPECULUM HUMANÆ SALVATIONIS:—Not a block book, 61; how printed, 62, 63; time, character, and place of the designs, 63; Veldener's reprints, 63; speculations as to its first printer, 63; origin of the work, 64; list of the subjects, 64, 65; their resemblance to the Biblia Pauperum, 66; Ottley's supposition of the same engraver for both, 66, 67.

STAMPS:—Used for bricks, in Babylon and Egypt, 3; an Indian seal, 4; brands for slaves, captives, criminals, and cattle, stamps for clay vessels, for marking cloth, with coloured inks, and among the Sandwich Islanders, 4, 5; a brass Roman stamp, the word Lar, in the British Museum, 7; stamped cylinders found by Layard at Babylon, 8; stamps of Theodoric and Charlemagne, stamps used from the ninth to the thirteenth century, 10; Spanish monograms, Runic ciphers, marks of notaries and traders, coins and seals, 11, 12; gem-engraving, 12; prints on various fabrics, examples shown by Weigel, 13, 16; stamps used for inked letters in illuminated manuscripts, 19; *stampide*—stamped means printed, 23.

St. Bridget, 33.

St. Christopher:—Where found, 17; before 1844 the undisputed earliest dated print, 17; the date of 1423 to be trusted, 30; Chatto's criticism, 30, 31; description of design, intended for colouring, 31, 32; method of production, 32.

Stencils:—Known in the time of Quintilian and Pliny, 9; what a stencil is, 9; Chatto's mistakes as to stencils, 10, 20, 23, 24, 26, 32; stencil used in illuminated works, 19; stencilling cards, 21 to 24; a stencil-cutter (*tiripagus*), 25; the stencil colours, 25, 26; prints "wholly by stencil," 26; difficulty of distinguishing stencil-colouring, 26; the St. Christopher of 1423, the Annunciation, St. Bridget, 30 to 34.

Stimmer:—His designs, 106; by whom engraved, speculation as to Feyerabends, 113.

Stone Stamps (Roman), found in France, 3.

Stothard:—Designs to Rogers' Poems, 165, 166.

Temple (Bewick's pupil), 153, 155.

Thompson:—The exponent of the Thurston black line method, 177; his apprenticeship to Branston, 178; his many works after Thurston, 178 to 180; after: Harvey, Cruikshank, Stothard, Grandville, Mulready, and others, 180 to 184; his Diploma of the Highland Society, 165, 180; metal cuts, 184.

Thurston:—Designs engraved by Clennell, 161 to 164; Nesbit, 167 to 170; Hole, 170; Branston, 174 to 176; White and Byfield, 175; Thompson, 175 to 180; W. Hughes, 187.

Tiripagus, a stencil cutter, 25.

Tone and Texture,—199; Hamerton's praise of American work, 206 to 209.

Triumph of Maximilian, 87. (See Maximilian.)

Turrecremata (John of),—Meditations, 68, 69.

Unger,—Johann Georg and J. Friedrich Gottlieb, father and son, German engravers, 121, 122.

Valturius,—De Re Militari, the first Italian book with wood-cuts, 67, 69.

Varro,—His invention, spoken of by Pliny, 9.

Vellum,—preferred by illuminators, but not good for printing, 13.

Virgin of Berlin, 36. (See Berlin.)

Virgin of Brussels, 17. (See Brussels.)

Water-colour:—Drawings on wood by painters in water-colour, J. W. Archer, Dalziel, Duncan, W. L. Leitch, Topham, 209, 210.

White King, 91.

White-line:—By the graver and the scrive, 125; the Kirkall Ticket and Croxall's Æsop, 129, 130; drawing with the graver, 131; Bewick, Clennell, and Nesbit, as exponents of white-line work, 153 to 172; the white line of Bewick and the black line of Thurston, 175; Bonner and Sears worked also in white line, 201; white line further treated of, 200, 203 to 210.

Williams (S.), 188 to 190; Williams (T.), 190, 191.

Wohlgemuth:—The Nuremberg Chronicle cuts not engraved by him, 70; he was not the founder of a new school of wood-engraving, 71.

Wood used for engraving, 37, 73, 113.

Wood-Engravings (*either in heads or series*):

    Knife-work—

Alphabet of 1464, 61.

Aldegrever's Fall and Redemption of Man, 109.

Amman, Beasts of Chase, Bible Figures, Costume, Josephus, Ranks and Trades, Roman History, Title-page to Livy, 116.

Beham's Apocalypse, 112; Das Bohemun, Bible, and New Testament, 113.

Block-Books:—Apocalypsis, 40;

        Ars Moriendi, 53;

        Biblia Pauperum, 44;

        Canticum Canticorum, 41.

Breydenbach's Travels, 69.

Burgkmair's Procession (Maximilian's Triumph), 88; White King, 91.

Cuningham's Cosmographical Glasse, 118.

WOOD-ENGRAVINGS (*Knife-work continued*):—

Dürer's Apocalypse, 80, 81; Life of the Virgin, 85, 86; the Greater Passion, 86, 87; the Lesser Passion, 86; the Green Passion, 86.

Fox's Acts and Monuments, 118.

Holbein's Dance of Death, 97; Bible, 107.

Nurnberg Chronicle, 70.

Papillon's Treatise of Wood-Engraving, *Le Petit Almanach de Paris, Recueil des Papillon*, 120.
Parkinson's Paradisus Terrestris, 119.
Pfister's Fables, and Four Histories, 60.

Rogers' Prints in imitation of Drawings, 147.

Schäufelin's Sir Theurdank, 91.
Solis' Ovid, and Æsop, 114.
Speculum Humanæ Salvationis, 61.
Speed's History of Britain, 119.
Stimmer's Bible Figures, 117.

Topsel's Four-footed Beasts and Serpents, 116.

Valturius, De Re Militari, 67, 69.

Zainer's Legends of the Saints, 67.

Single Prints.—

Beham's Fountain of Youth, and Procession, 113.
Cranach's St. Jerome in penitence, 94.
Christ taken from the Cross, 111.
Doge with Officers of State, 110.
Dürer's Arch of Maximilian, 88; Triumphal Car, 89; Trinity, Mass of St. Gregory, 94.
Entry of Charles V into Bologna, 110.
Genealogical Tree, 110.
Hogarth's Progress of Cruelty, 129.
Jegher's Repose in Egypt, Boys with Lamb, 119.
Pharaoh's Host in the Red Sea, 109.
St. Christopher, 27, 30.
Vico's Charles V, 111.
View of Venice, by Barbari, 109.
(See CHIAROSCURO, METAL ENGRAVINGS.)

GRAVER-WORK (*in books or series*):—

Anniversary for 1828-9, 181.

Beauties of Cambria, 187.
Bewick's Fables [1771, 1776, 1779], 137.
Fables of 1784, 138.
History of Quadrupeds, 140, 146, 196.
Land and Water Birds, 141, 147, 156.
Fables of 1818, 149, 167, 185.
Blind Beggar of Bethnal-Green, 171.
Bloomfield, Farmer's Boy, 167, Wild-flowers, 174.
British Ballads, 195.
British Forest Trees, 189.
Butler's Hudibras, 176, 180; Remains, 176, 181.

WOOD-ENGRAVINGS (*Graver-work continued*):—

Century Magazine, 208.
Children in the Wood, 181.
Choulant's Bibliography of Anatomical Teaching,
Chronicles of London Bridge, 191.   [203.
Contes Rémois, 203.
Craig's Scripture Illustrated, 167, 173.

Dibdin's London Theatre, 178.
Doré's Bible, and Paradise Lost, 206.

Fairfax's Tasso (Jerusalem Delivered), 179, 181.
Farmers' Series, 191, 193.
Fonthill (Delineations of), 187.
Frederic the Great (Works of), 149.

German Illustrated News, 203.
Gilbert's Cowper, 193, 194, 205.
Goldsmith's Traveler and Deserted Village, 149.
Gray's Elegy, 194.   [187.
Gregson's Fragment of Lancashire, 187.
Guest's Mabinogion, 189.

Harper's Bible, 198; Harper's Magazine, 208.
Harris' Insects injurious to vegetation, 208.
Harvey's Milton, 180, 187, 196.
Heads of the People, 195, 204.
Henderson's Ancient and Modern Wines, 186.
Hermit of Warkworth, 161.
Hieroglyphick Bible, 137.
History of England, 160, 168, 174, 179.
Hive of Ancient and Modern Literature, 159.
Hone's Year Book and Every Day Book, 189; Political Tracts, 203.

Illustrated London News, 204.
Imitation of Christ, 203.

Johnson's Typographia, 166, 187, 192.

Kaulbach's Reynard the Fox, 203.
Knickerbocker's History of New York, 187.
Knight's Shakspere, Pictorial Bible, and Prayer Book, 187, 192.

Lane's Arabian Nights, 187, 190, 192, 195.
Latrobe's Scripture Illustrations, 190, 194, 195.
London Songs, 189.   [197.
Longman's New Testament, 184.
Looking Glass for the Mind, 153, 196.

Magasin Pittoresque, 202, 205.
Marshall's Epistles in Verse, 174.
Martin and Westall's Bible, 191, 194.
Meadows' Shakspere, 193, 204.
Menzel's Heroes of War and Peace, 203.
Mornings at Bow Street, 181, 187.
Moxon's Tennyson, 184.

Napoleon Bonaparte (History of), 171, 189

WOOD-ENGRAVINGS (*Government continued*) :—

New York Mirror, Treasury of Knowledge, 197.
Northcote's Fables, 1818, 172, 177, 187, 191, 197.
Northcote's Fables, 1833, 171, 181, 184, 185, 186, 190 to 193.

Olio, 189.

Parnell's Hermit, 146, 167.
Paul et Virginie, 191, 193.
Penny Magazine, 191, 193.
Pilgrim's Progress, 160, 181.
Puckle's Club, 171, 174, 177, 187.
Punch, 205.

Quillinan's Wood-cuts and Verses, 169, 177.

Religious Emblems, 160, 168, 169, 172, 174, 179.
Rogers' Pleasures of Memory, 166, 181.
Rogers' Prints in Imitation of Drawings, 211.

Savage's Hints on Decorative Printing, 170, 174.

Selborne (Natural History of), 171, 181.
Solace of Song, 190, 194.
Somerville's Chase, 146; Rural Sports, 169.
Story without an end, 181.
Sunday in London, 191.

Thomson's Seasons, 168, 189.
Three Courses and a Dessert, 190.
Tower Menagerie, 187, 191.

Vicar of Wakefield, 161, 183.

Walton's Angler, 176, 180.
Wiffen's Tasso (Jerusalem Delivered), 177, 184.
Wordsworth's Greece, 195.

Yarrell's Fishes, 158.
Young Lady's Book, 181.

Zoological Gardens, 187, 191, 195.

For *Single Prints* see LIST OF ILLUSTRATIONS.